COUNTING UP, COUNTING DOWN

COUNTING UP, COUNTING DOWN

HARRY TURTLEDOVE

BALLANTINE BOOKS • NEW YORK

A Del Rey® Book
Published by The Random House Publishing Group

Copyright © 2002 by Harry Turtledove
Excerpt from *Homeward Bound* copyright © 2005 by Harry Turtledove

The stories in this work were originally published in the following publications: "Forty, Counting Down"—ASIMOV'S, December 1999; "Must and Shall"—ASIMOV'S, November 1995; "Ready for the Fatherland"—WHAT MIGHT HAVE BEEN 3, edited by Gregory Benford and Martin H. Greenberg, 1991; "The Phantom Tolbukhin"—ALTERNATE GENERALS, edited by Harry Turtledove, 1998; "Deconstruction Gang"—AMAZING, September 1992; "The Green Buffalo"—THE ULTIMATE DINOSAUR, edited by Robert Silverberg, 1991; "The Maltese Elephant"—ANALOG, August 1995; "Vermin"—THE MAGAZINE OF FANTASY AND SCIENCE FICTION, March 1993; "Ils ne passeront pas"—ARMAGEDDON, edited by David Drake and Billie Sue Mosiman, 1998; "In This Season"—A CHRISTMAS BESTIARY, edited by Martin H. Greenberg, 1992; "Honeymouth"—PULPHOUSE 9, Winter 1990; "Myth Manners' Guide to Greek Missology #1: Andromeda and Perseus"—CHICKS 'N CHAINED MALES, edited by Esther Friesner, 1999; "Goddess for a Day"—CHICKS IN CHAINMAIL, edited by Esther Friesner, 1996; "After the Last Elf Is Dead"—WEIRD TALES, Summer 1988; "The Decoy Duck"—AFTER THE KING: STORIES IN HONOR OF J. R. R. TOLKIEN, edited by Martin H. Greenberg, 1992; "The Seventh Chapter"—THE MAGAZINE OF FANTASY AND SCIENCE FICTION, September 1997; "Twenty-one, Counting Up"—ANALOG, December 1999

This book contains an excerpt from the forthcoming book *Homeward Bound* by Harry Turtledove. This excerpt has been set for this edition only and may not reflect the final content of the forthcoming edition.

www.delreybooks.com

ISBN 0-345-47798-7

Manufactured in the United States of America

First Edition: February 2002
First Mass Market Edition: March 2005

OPM 9 8 7 6 5 4 3 2 1

Contents

Forty, Counting Down

This story is a mirror-image twin of "Twenty-one, Counting Up," the last piece in this book. If you read one, you'll see one thing. If you read the other, you'll see something else. If you read them both, I hope they prove more than the sum of their parts. I don't recommend that you read them back to back—I think they should have a little time between them. But if you choose not to listen to me, who's going to know?

"Hey, Justin!" Sean Peters' voice floated over the top of the Superstrings, Ltd., cubicle wall. "It's twenty after six—quitting time and then some. Want a drink or two with me and Garth?"

"Hang on," Justin Kloster answered. "Let me save what I'm working on first." He told his computer to save his work as it stood, generate a backup, and shut itself off. Having grown up in the days when voice-recognition software was imperfectly reliable, he waited to make sure the machine followed orders. It did, of course. Making that software idiotproof had put Superstrings on the map a few years after the turn of the century.

Justin got up, stretched, and looked around. Not much to see: the grayish-tan fuzzy walls of the cubicle and an astringently neat desktop that held the computer, a wedding photo of Megan and him, and a phone/fax. His lips narrowed. The marriage had lasted four years—four and a half, actually. He hadn't come close to finding anybody else since.

Footsteps announced Peters' arrival. He looked like a high-

1

school linebacker who'd let most of his muscle go to flab since. Garth O'Connell was right behind him. He was from the same mold, except getting thin on top instead of going gray. "How's the Iron Curtain sound?" Peters asked.

"Sure," Justin said. "It's close, and you can hear yourself think—most of the time, anyhow."

They went out into the parking lot together, bitching when they stepped from air conditioning to San Fernando Valley August heat. Justin's eyes started watering, too; L.A. smog wasn't so bad as it had been when he was young, but it hadn't disappeared.

An Oasis song was playing when the three software engineers walked into the Iron Curtain, and into air conditioning chillier than the office's. The music took Justin back to the days when he'd been getting together with Megan, though he'd liked Blur better. "Look out," Sean Peters said. "They've got a new fellow behind the bar." He and Garth chuckled. They knew what was going to happen. Justin sighed. So did he.

Peters ordered a gin and tonic, O'Connell a scotch on the rocks. Justin asked for a Bud. Sure as hell, the bartender said, "I'll be right with you two gents"—he nodded to Justin's coworkers—"but for you, sir, I'll need some ID."

With another sigh, Justin produced his driver's license. "Here."

The bartender looked at him, looked at his picture on the license, and looked at his birthdate. He scowled. "You were born in 1978? No way."

"His real name's Dorian Gray," Garth said helpfully.

"Oh, shut up," Justin muttered, and then, louder, to the bartender, "Yeah, I really turned forty this past spring." He was slightly pudgy, but he'd been slightly pudgy since he was a toddler. And he'd been very blond since the day he was born. If he had any silver mixed with the gold, it didn't show. He also stayed out of the sun as much as he could, because he burned to a crisp when he didn't. That left him with a lot fewer lines and wrinkles than his buddies, who were both a couple of years younger than he.

Shaking his head, the bartender slid Justin a beer. "You

coulda fooled me," he said. "You go around picking up high-school girls?" His hands shaped an hourglass in the air.

"No." Justin stared down at the reflections of the ceiling lights on the polished bar.

"Middle school," Garth suggested. He'd already made his scotch disappear. Justin gave him a dirty look. It was such a dirty look, it got through to Sean Peters. He tapped Garth on the arm. For a wonder, Garth eased off.

Justin finished the Bud, threw a twenty on the bar, and got up to leave. "Not going to have another one?" Peters asked, surprised.

"Nope." Justin shook his head. "Got some things to do. See you in the morning." Out he went, walking fast so his friends couldn't stop him.

As soon as the microchip inside Justin's dead-bolt lock shook hands with the one in his key, his apartment came to life. Lamps came on. The stereo started playing the Pulp CD he'd left in there this morning. The broiler heated up to do the steak the computer knew was in the refrigerator. From the bedroom, the computer called, "Now or later?"

"Later," Justin said, so the screen stayed dark.

He went into the kitchen and tossed a couple of pieces of spam snailmail into the blue wastebasket for recycling. The steak went under the broiler; frozen mixed vegetables went into the microwave. Eight minutes later, dinner.

After he finished, he rinsed the dishes and silverware and put them in the dishwasher. When he closed the door, the light in it came on; the machine judged it was full enough to run a cycle in the middle of the night.

Like the kitchen, his front room was almost as antiseptically tidy as his cubicle at Superstrings. But for a picture of Megan and him on their honeymoon, the coffee table was bare. All his books and DVDs and audio CDs were arranged alphabetically by author, title, or group. None stood even an eighth of an inch out of place. It was as if none of them dared move without his permission.

He went into the bedroom. "Now," he said, and the computer monitor came to life.

A picture of Megan and him stood on the dresser, another on the nightstand. Her high-school graduation picture smiled at him whenever he sat down at the desk. Even after all these years, he smiled back most of the time. He couldn't help it. He'd always been happy around Megan.

But she hadn't been happy around him, not at the end. Not for a while before the end, either. He'd been a long, long time realizing that. "Stupid," he said. He wasn't smiling now, even with Megan's young, glowing face looking right at him out of the picture frame. "I was stupid. I didn't know enough. I didn't know how to take care of her."

No wonder he hadn't clicked with any other woman. He didn't want any other woman. He wanted Megan—and couldn't have her any more.

"E-mail," he told the computer, and gave his password. He went through it, answering what needed answering and deleting the rest. Then he said, "Banking." The computer had paid the monthly Weblink bill, and the cable bill, too. "All good," he told it.

The CD in the stereo fell silent. "Repeat?" the computer asked.

"No." Justin went out to the front room. He took the Pulp CD out of the player, put it in its jewel box, and put the jewel box exactly where it belonged on the shelf. Then he stood there in a rare moment of indecision, wondering what to pull out next. When he chose a new CD, he chuckled. He doubted Sean or Garth would have heard of the Trash Can Sinatras, let alone heard any of their music. His work buddies had listened to grunge rock back before the turn of the century, not British pop.

As soon as *Cake* started, he went back into the bedroom and sat down at the computer again. This time, he did smile at Megan's picture. She'd been crazy for the Trash Can Sinatras, too.

The music made him especially eager to get back to work. "Superstrings," he said, and gave a password, and "Virtual reality" and another password, and "Not so virtual" and one more. Then he had to wait. He would have killed for a Mac a quarter this powerful back in 1999, but it wasn't a patch on the one he used at the office. The company could afford the very best. He couldn't, not quite.

He went to the keyboard for this work: for numbers, it was more precise than dictating. And he had to wait again and again, while the computer did the crunching. One wait was long enough for him to go take a shower. When he got back, hair still damp, the machine hadn't finished muttering to itself. Justin sighed. But the faster Macs at the office couldn't leap these numbers at a single bound. What he was asking of his home computer was right on the edge of what it could do.

Or maybe it would turn out to be over the edge. In that case, he'd spend even more lunch hours in his cubicle in the days ahead than he had for the past six months. He was caught up on everything the people above him wanted. They thought he worked his long hours to stay that way.

"What they don't know won't hurt them," Justin murmured. "And it may do me some good."

He didn't think anyone else had combined superstring physics, chaos theory, and virtual reality this way. If anyone had, he was keeping quiet about it—nothing in the journals, not a whisper on the Web. Justin would have known; he had virbots out prowling all the time. They'd never found anything close. He had this all to himself . . . if he hadn't been wasting his time.

Up came the field parameters, at long, long last. Justin studied them. As the computer had, he took his time. He didn't want to let enthusiasm run away with him before he was sure. He'd done that half a lifetime ago, and what had it got him? A divorce that blighted his life ever since. He wouldn't jump too soon. Not again. Not ever again. But things looked good.

"Yes!" he said softly. He'd been saying it that particular way since he was a teenager. He couldn't have named the disgraced sportscaster from whom he'd borrowed it if he'd gone on the rack.

He saved the parameters, quit his application, and had the computer back up everything he'd done. The backup disk went into his briefcase. And then, yawning, he hit the sack.

* * *

Three days later, Garth O'Connell was the first to gape when Justin came into the office. "Buzz cut!" he exclaimed, and ran a hand over his own thinning hair. Then he laughed and started talking as if the past twenty years hadn't happened: "Yo, dude. Where's the combat boots?"

In my closet, Justin thought. He didn't say that. What he did say was, "I felt like doing something different, that's all."

"Like what?" Garth asked. "Globalsearching for high-school quail, like the barkeep said? The competition doesn't wear short hair any more, you know."

"Will you melt it down?" Justin snapped.

"Okay. Okay." Garth spread his hands. "But you better get used to it, 'cause everybody else is gonna say the same kind of stuff."

Odds were he was right, Justin realized gloomily. He grabbed a cup of coffee at the office machine, then ducked into his cubicle and got to work. That slowed the stream of comments, but didn't stop them. People would go by the cubicle, see the side view, do a double take, and start exclaiming.

Inside half an hour, Justin's division head came by to view the prodigy. She rubbed her chin. "Well, I don't *suppose* it looks unbusinesslike," she said dubiously.

"Thanks, Ms. Chen," Justin said. "I just wanted to—"

"Start your midlife crisis early." As it had a few evenings before, Sean Peters' voice drifted over the walls of the cubicle.

"And thank *you*, Sean." Justin put on his biggest grin. Ms. Chen smiled, which meant he'd passed the test. She gave his hair another look, nodded more happily than she'd spoken, and went off to do whatever managers did when they weren't worrying about haircuts.

Sean kept his mouth shut till lunchtime, when he stuck his head into Justin's cubicle and said, "Feel like going over to Omino's? I've got a yen for Japanese food." He laughed. Justin groaned. That made Peters laugh harder than ever.

Justin shook his head. Pointing toward his monitor, he said, "I'm brown-bagging it today. Got a ton of stuff that needs doing."

"Okay." Peters shrugged. "Anybody'd think you worked here or something. I'll see you later, then."

Between noon and half past one, Superstrings was nearly deserted. Munching on a salami sandwich and an orange, Justin worked on his own project, his private project. The office machine was better than his home computer for deciding whether possible meant practical.

"Yes!" he said again, a few minutes later, and then, "Time to go shopping."

Being the sort of fellow he was, he shopped with a list. Vintage clothes came from Aaardvark's Odd Ark, undoubtedly the funkiest secondhand store in town, if not in the world. As with his haircut, he did his best to match the way he'd looked just before the turn of the century.

Old money was easier; he had to pay only a small premium for old-fashioned smallhead bills at the several coin-and-stamp shops he visited. "Why do you want 'em, if you don't care about condition?" one dealer asked.

"Maybe I think the new bills are ugly," he answered. The dealer shrugged, tagging him for a nut but a harmless one. When he got to $150,000, he checked *money* off the list.

He got to the office very early the next morning. The security guard chuckled as he unlocked the door. "Old clothes and everything. Looks like you're moving in, pal."

"Seems like that sometimes, too, Bill." Justin set down his suitcases for a moment. "But I'm going out of town this afternoon. I'd rather have this stuff indoors than sitting in the trunk of my car."

"Oh, yeah." Bill nodded. He had to be seventy, but his hair wasn't any lighter than iron gray. "I know that song." He knew lots of songs, many dating back to before Justin was born. He'd fought in Vietnam, and been a cop, and now he was doing this because his pension hadn't come close to keeping up with skyrocketing prices. Justin wondered if his own would, come the day.

But he had different worries now. "Thanks," he said when the guard held the door for him.

He staggered up the stairs; thanks to the stash of cash (a new compact car here, nothing more, even with the premium he'd had to pay, but a young fortune before the turn of the century), some period clothes scrounged—like the Dilbert T-shirt and baggy jeans he had on—from secondhand stores, and the boots, those suitcases weren't light, and he'd never been in better shape than he could help. The backpack in which he carried his PowerBook and VR mask did nothing to make him more graceful, either.

Once he got up to the second floor, he paused and listened hard. "Yes!" he said when he heard nothing. Except for Bill down below, he was the only person here.

He went into the men's room, piled one suitcase on the other, and sat down on them. Then he took the laptop out of its case. He plugged the VR mask into its jack, then turned on the computer. As soon as it came up, he put on the mask. The world went black, then neutral gray, then neutral . . . neutral: no color at all, just virtual reality waiting to be made real.

It all took too long. He wished he could do this back at his desk, with an industrial-strength machine. But he didn't dare take the chance. This building had been here nineteen years ago. This men's room had been here nineteen years ago. He'd done his homework as well as he could. But his homework hadn't been able to tell him where the goddamn cubicle partitions were back before the turn of the century.

And so . . . the john. He took a deep breath. "Run program superstrings–slash–virtual reality–slash–not so virtual," he said.

The PowerBook quivered, ever so slightly, on his lap. His heart thudded. Talk about your moments of truth. Either he was as smart as he thought he was, or Garth or Sean or somebody would breeze in and ask, "Justin, what the *hell* are you doing?"

A string in space-time connected this place now to its earlier self, itself in 1999. As far as Justin knew, nobody but him had thought of accessing that string, of sliding along it, with VR technology. When the simulation was good enough, it became the reality—for a while, anyhow. That was what the math said. He thought he'd done a good enough job here.

And if he had . . . oh, if he had! He knew a hell of a lot more now, at forty, than he had when he was twenty-one. If he-now could be back with Megan for a while instead of his younger self, he could make things right. He could make things last. He knew it. He had to, if he ever wanted to be happy again.

I'll fix it, he thought. *I'll fix everything. And when I slide back to here-and-now, I won't have this emptiness in my past. Everything will be the way it could have been, the way it should have been.*

An image began to emerge from the VR blankness. It was the same image he'd seen before slipping on the mask: blue tile walls with white grouting, acoustic ceiling, sinks with a mirror above them, urinals off to the left, toilet stalls behind him.

"Dammit," he muttered under his breath. Sure as hell, the men's room hadn't changed at all.

"Program superstrings–slash–virtual reality–slash–not so virtual reality is done," the PowerBook told him.

He took off the mask. Here he sat, on his suitcases, in the men's room of his office building. 2018? 1999? He couldn't tell, not staying in here. If everything had worked out the way he'd calculated, it would be before business hours back when he'd arrived, too. All he had to do was walk out that front door and hope the security guard wasn't right there.

No. What he really had to hope was that the security guard wasn't Bill.

He put the computer in his backpack again. He picked up the suitcases and walked to the men's-room door. He set down a case so he could open the door. His heart pounded harder than ever. Yes? Or no?

Justin took two steps down the hall toward the stairs before he whispered, "Yes!" Instead of the gray-green carpet he'd walked in on, this stuff was an ugly mustard yellow. He had no proof he was in 1999, not yet. But he wasn't in Kansas any more.

The place had the quiet-before-the-storm feeling offices get waiting for people to show up for work. That fit Justin's calculations. The air conditioner was noisier, wheezier, than the system that had been—would be—in his time. But it kept the corridor noticeably cooler than it had been when he lugged his stuff into the men's room. The '90s had ridden an oil glut. They burned lavishly to beat summer heat. His time couldn't.

There was the doorway that led to the stairs. Down he went. The walls were different: industrial yellow, not battleship gray. When he got to the little lobby, he didn't recognize the furniture. What was there seemed no better or worse than what he was used to, but it was different.

If there was a guard, he was off making his rounds. Justin didn't wait for him. He opened the door. He wondered if that would touch off the alarm, but it didn't. He stepped out into the cool, fresh early morning air of . . . when?

He walked through the empty lot to the sidewalk, then looked around. Across the street, a woman out power-walking glanced his way, but didn't stop. She wore a cap, a T-shirt, and baggy shorts, which proved nothing. But then he looked at the parked cars, and began to grin a crazy grin. Most of them had smooth jelly-bean lines, which, to his eyes, was two style changes out of date. If this wasn't 1999, it was damn close.

With a clanking rumble of iron, a MetroLink train pulled into the little station behind his office. A couple of people got off; a handful got on. In his day, with gas ever scarcer, ever costlier, that commuter train would have far more passengers.

Standing on the sidewalk, unnoticed by the world around him, he pumped a fist in the air. "I did it!" he said. "I really did it!"

Having done it, he couldn't do anything else, not for a little while. Not much was open at half past five. But there was a Denny's up the street. Suitcases in hand, he trudged toward it. The young, bored-looking Hispanic waitress who seated him gave him a fishy stare. "You coulda left your stuff in the car," she said pointedly.

His answer was automatic: "I don't have a car." Her eyebrows flew upward. If you didn't have a car in L.A., you were nobody. If you didn't have a car and did have suitcases, you were liable to be a dangerously weird nobody. He had to say something. In-spiration struck: "I just got off the train. Somebody should've picked me up, but he blew it. Toast and coffee, please?"

She relaxed. "Okay—coming up. White, rye, or whole wheat?"

"Wheat." Justin looked around. He was the only customer in the place. "Can you keep an eye on the cases for a second? I want to buy a *Times*." He'd seen the machine out front, but hadn't wanted to stop till he got inside. When the waitress nodded, he got a paper. It was only a quarter. That boggled him; he paid two bucks weekdays, five Sundays.

But the date boggled him more. *June 22, 1999.* Right on the money. He went back inside. The coffee waited for him, steaming gently. The toast came up a moment later. As he spread grape jam over it, he glanced at the *Times* and wondered what his younger self was doing now.

Sleeping, you dummy. He'd liked to sleep late when he was twenty-one, and finals at Cal State Northridge would have just ended. He'd have the CompUSA job to go to, but the place didn't open till ten.

Megan would be sleeping, too. He thought of her lying in a T-shirt and sweats at her parents' house, wiggling around the way she did in bed. Maybe she was dreaming of him and smiling. She would be smiling now. A few years from now . . . Well, he'd come to fix that.

He killed forty-five minutes. By then, the restaurant was filling up. The waitress started to look ticked. Justin ordered bacon and eggs and hash browns. They bought him the table for another hour. He tried not to think about what the food was doing to his coronary arteries. His younger self wouldn't have cared. His younger self loved Denny's. *My younger self was a fool,* he thought.

He paid, again marveling at how little things cost. Of course, people didn't make much, either; you could live well on $100,000 a year. He tried to imagine living on $100,000 in 2018, and shook his head. You couldn't do it, not if you felt like eating, too.

When he went out to the parking lot, he stood there for forty minutes, looking back toward the train station. By then, it was getting close to eight o'clock. Up a side street from the Denny's was a block of apartment buildings with names like the Tivoli, the Gardens, and the Yachtsman. Up the block he trudged. The Yachtsman had a vacancy sign.

The manager looked grumpy at getting buzzed so early, but the sight of greenbacks cheered him up in a hurry. He rented

Justin a one-bedroom furnished apartment at a ridiculously low rate. "I'm here on business," Justin said, which was true . . . in a way. "I'll pay three months in advance if you fix me up with a TV and a stereo. They don't have to be great. They just have to work."

"I'd have to root around," the manager said. "It'd be kind of a pain." He waited. Justin passed him two fifties. He nodded. So did Justin. This was business, too. The manager eyed his suitcases. "You'll want to move in right away, won't you?"

Justin nodded again. "And I'll want to use your phone to set up my phone service."

"Okay," the manager said with a sigh. "Come into my place here. I'll get things set up." His fish-faced wife watched Justin with wide, pale, unblinking eyes while he called the phone company and made arrangements. The manager headed off with a vacuum cleaner. In due course, he came back. "You're ready. TV and stereo are in there."

"Thanks." Justin went upstairs to the apartment. It was small and bare, with furniture that had seen better decades. The TV wasn't new. The stereo was so old, it didn't play CDs, only records and cassettes. Well, his computer could manage CDs. He accepted a key to the apartment and another for the security gates, then unpacked. He couldn't do everything he wanted till he got a phone, but he was here.

He used a pay phone to call a cab, and rode over to a used-car lot. He couldn't do everything he wanted without wheels, either. He had no trouble proving he was himself; he'd done some computer forgery before he left to make his driver's license expire in 2003, as it really did. His number hadn't changed. Security holograms that would have given a home machine trouble here-and-now were a piece of cake to graphics programs from 2018. His younger self didn't know he'd just bought a new old car: a gray early-'90s Toyota much like the one he was already driving.

"Insurance is mandatory," the salesman said. "I can sell you a policy . . ." Justin let him do it, to his barely concealed delight. It was, no doubt, highway robbery, especially since Justin was nominally only twenty-one. He'd dressed for the age he affected, in T-shirt and jeans. To him, though, no 1999 prices seemed expensive. He paid cash and took the car.

Getting a bank account wasn't hard, either. He chose a bank his younger self didn't use. Research paid off: he deposited only $9,000. Ten grand or more in cash and the bank would have reported the transaction to the government. He didn't want that kind of notice. He wanted no notice at all. The assistant manager handed him a book of temporary checks. "Good to have your business, Mr. Kloster. The personalized ones will be ready in about a week."

"Okay." Justin went off to buy groceries. He wasn't a great cook, but he was a lot better than his younger self. He'd had to learn, and had.

Once the groceries were stowed in the pantry and the refrigerator, he left again, this time to a bookstore. He went to the computer section first, to remind himself of the state of the art. After a couple of minutes, he was smiling and shaking his head. Had he done serious work with this junk? He supposed he had, but he was damned if he saw how. Before he was born, people had used slide rules because there weren't any computers yet, or even calculators. He was damned if he saw how they'd done any work, either.

But the books didn't have exactly what he wanted. He went to the magazine rack. There was a *MacAddict* in a clear plastic envelope. The CD-ROM that came with the magazine would let him start an account on a couple of online services. Once he had one, he could e-mail his younger self, and then he'd be in business.

If I—or I-then—don't flip out altogether, he thought. Things might get pretty crazy. Now that he was here and on the point of getting started, he felt in his belly how crazy they might get. And he knew both sides of things. His younger self didn't.

Would Justin-then even listen to him? He had to hope so. Looking back, he'd been pretty stupid when he was twenty-one. No matter how stupid he'd been, though, he'd have to pay attention when he got his nose rubbed in the facts. Wouldn't he?

Justin bought the *MacAddict* and took it back to his apartment. As soon as he got online, he'd be ready to roll.

He chose AOL, not Earthlink. His younger self was on Earthlink, and looked down his nose at AOL. And AOL let him pay by debiting his checking account. He didn't have any credit cards that worked in 1999. He supposed he could get one, but it would take time. He'd taken too much time already. He thought he had about three months before the space-time string he'd manipulated would snap him back to 2018. With luck, with skill, with what he knew then that he hadn't known now, he'd be happier there. But he had no time to waste.

His computer, throttled down to 56K access to the outside world, might have thought the same. But AOL's local access lines wouldn't support anything faster. "Welcome," the electronic voice said as he logged on. He ignored it, and went straight to e-mail. He was pretty sure he remembered his old e-mail address. *If I don't,* he thought, chuckling a little as he typed, *whoever is using this address right now will get awfully confused.*

He'd pondered what he would say to get his younger self's attention, and settled on the most provocative message he could think of. He wrote, *Who but you would know that the first time you jacked off, you were looking at Miss March 1993, a little before your fifteenth birthday? Nobody, right? Gorgeous blonde, wasn't she? The only way I know is that I am you, more or less. Let me hear from you.* He signed it, *Justin Kloster, age 40,* and sent it.

Then he had to pause. His younger self would be working now, but he'd check his e-mail as soon as he got home. Justin remembered religiously doing that every day. He didn't remember getting e-mail like the message he'd just sent, of course, but that was the point of this exercise.

Waiting till half past five wasn't easy. He wished he could use his time-travel algorithm to fast-forward to late afternoon, but he didn't dare. Too many superstrings might tangle, and even the office machine up in 2018 hadn't been able to work out the ramifications of that. In another ten years, it would probably be child's play for a computer, but he wouldn't be able to pretend he was twenty-one when he was fifty. Even a baby face and pale gold hair wouldn't stretch that far. He hoped they'd stretch far enough now.

At 5:31, he logged on to AOL again. "Welcome!" the voice told him, and then, "You've got mail!"

"You've got spam," he muttered under his breath. And one of the messages in his mailbox *was* spam. He deleted it without a qualm. The other one, though, was from his younger self @earthlink.net.

Heart pounding, he opened the e-mail. *What kind of stupid joke is this?* his younger self wrote. *Whatever it is, it's not funny.*

Justin sighed. He supposed he shouldn't have expected himself-at-twenty-one to be convinced right away. This business was hard to believe, even for him. But he had more shots in his gun than one. *No joke,* he wrote back. *Who else but you would know you lost your first baby tooth in a pear at school when you were in the first grade? Who else would know your dad fed you Rollos when he took you to work with him that day when you were eight or nine? Who else would know you spent most of the time while you were losing your cherry staring at the mole on the side of Lindsey Fletcher's neck? Me, that's who: you at 40.* He typed his name and sent the message.

His stomach growled, but he didn't go off and make supper. He sat by the computer, waiting. His younger self would still be online. He'd have to answer . . . wouldn't he? Justin hadn't figured out what he'd do if himself-at-twenty-one wanted nothing to do with him. The prospect had never crossed his mind. Maybe it should have.

"Don't be stupid, kid," he said softly. "Don't complicate things for me. Don't complicate things for yourself, either."

He sat. He waited. He worried. After what seemed forever but was less than ten minutes, the AOL program announced, "You've got mail!"

He read it. *I don't watch* X-Files *much,* his younger self wrote, *but maybe I ought to. How could you know all that about me? I never told* anybody *about Lindsey Fletcher's neck.*

So far as Justin could recall, he hadn't told anyone about her neck by 2018, either. That didn't mean he'd forgotten. He wouldn't forget till they shoveled dirt over him.

How do I know? he wrote. *I've told you twice now—I know because I am you, you in 2018. It's not* X-Files *stuff—it's good programming.* The show still ran in endless syndication, but he hadn't watched it for years. He went on, *Believe me, I'm back here for a good reason,* and sent the e-mail.

Again, he waited. Again, the reply came back fast. He imagined his younger self eyeing the screen of his computer, eyeing it and scratching his head. His younger self must have been scratching hard, for what came back was, *But that's impossible.*

Okay, he typed. *It's impossible. But if it is impossible, how do I know all this stuff about you?*

More waiting. *The hell with it,* he thought. He'd intended to broil lamb chops, but he would have had to pay attention to keep from cremating them. He took a dinner out of the freezer and threw it into the tiny microwave built in above the stove. He could punch a button and get it more or less right. Back to the computer.

"You've got mail!" it said once more, and he did. *I don't know,* his younger self had written. *How* do *you know all this stuff about me?*

Because it's stuff about me, too, he answered. *You don't seem to be taking that seriously yet.*

The microwave beeped. Justin started to go off to eat, but the PowerBook told him he had more mail. He called it up. *If you're supposed to be me,* himself-at-twenty-one wrote, *then you'll look like me, right?*

Justin laughed. His younger self wouldn't believe that. He'd probably think it would make this pretender shut up and go away. But Justin wasn't a pretender, and didn't need to shut up— he could put up instead. *Right,* he replied. *Meet me in front of the B. Dalton's in the Northridge mall tomorrow night at 6:30 and I'll buy you dinner. You'll see for yourself.* He sent the message, then did walk away from the computer.

Eating frozen food reminded him why he'd learned to cook.

He chucked the tray in the trash, then returned to the bedroom to see what his younger self had answered. Three words: *See you there*.

The mall surprised Justin. In his time, it had seen better years. In 1999, just a little after being rebuilt because of the '94 earthquake, it still seemed shiny and sparkly and new. Justin got there early. With his hair short, with the Cow Pi T-shirt and jeans and big black boots he was wearing, he fit in with the kids who shopped and strutted and just hung out.

He found out how well he fit when he eyed an attractive brunette of thirty or so who was wearing business clothes. She caught him doing it, looked horrified for a second, and then stared through him as if he didn't exist. At first, he thought her reaction was over the top. Then he realized it wasn't. *You may think she's cute, but she doesn't think you are. She thinks you're wet behind the ears.*

Instead of leaving him insulted, the woman's reaction cheered him. *Maybe I can bring this off.*

He leaned against the brushed-aluminum railing in front of the second-level B. Dalton's as if he had nothing better to do. A gray-haired man in maroon polyester pants muttered something about punk kids as he walked by. Justin grinned, which made the old fart mutter more.

But then the grin slipped from Justin's face. What replaced it was probably astonishment. Here came his younger self, heading up from the Sears end of the mall.

He could tell the moment when his younger self saw him. Himself-at-twenty-one stopped, gaped, and turned pale. He looked as if he wanted to turn around and run away. Instead, after gulping, he kept on.

Justin's heart pounded. He hadn't realized just how strange seeing himself would feel. And he'd been expecting this. For his younger self, it was a bolt from the blue. That meant he had to be the one in control. He stuck out his hand. "Hi," he said. "Thanks for coming."

His younger self shook hands with him. They both looked down. The two right hands fit perfectly. *Well, they would, wouldn't they?* Justin thought. His younger self, still staring, said, "Maybe I'm not crazy. Maybe you're not crazy, either. You look just like me."

"Funny how that works," Justin said. Seeing his younger self wasn't like looking in a mirror. It wasn't because himself-at-twenty-one looked that much younger—he didn't. It wasn't even because his younger self wasn't doing the same things he did. After a moment, he figured out what it was: his younger self's image wasn't reversed, the way it would have been in a mirror. That made him look different.

His younger self put hands on hips. "Prove you're from the future," he said.

Justin had expected that. He took a little plastic coin purse, the kind that can hook onto a key chain, out of his pocket and squeezed it open. "Here," he said. "This is for you." He handed himself-at-twenty-one a quarter.

It looked like any quarter—till you noticed the date. "It's from 2012," his younger self whispered. His eyes got big and round again. "Jesus. You weren't kidding."

"I told you I wasn't," Justin said patiently. "Come on. What's the name of that Korean barbecue place on . . . Reseda?" He thought that was right. It had closed a few years after the turn of the century.

His younger self didn't notice the hesitation. "The Pine Tree?"

"Yeah." Justin knew the name when he heard it. "Let's go over there. I'll buy you dinner, like I said in e-mail, and we can talk about things."

"Like what you're doing here," his younger self said.

He nodded. "Yeah. Like what I'm doing here."

None of the waitresses at the Pine Tree spoke much English. That was one reason Justin had chosen the place: he didn't want anybody eavesdropping. But he liked garlic, he liked the odd vegetables, and he enjoyed grilling beef or pork or chicken or fish on the gas barbecue set into the tabletop.

He ordered for both of them. The waitress scribbled on her pad in the odd characters of *hangul*, then looked from one of them to the other. "Twins," she said, pulling out a word she did know.

"Yeah," Justin said. *Sort of,* he thought. The waitress went away.

His younger self pointed at him. "Tell me one thing," he said.

"What?" Justin asked. He expected anything from *What are you doing here?* to *What is the meaning of life?*

But his younger self surprised him: "That the Rolling Stones aren't still touring by the time you're—I'm—forty."

"Well, no," Justin said. That was a pretty scary thought, when you got down to it. He and his younger self both laughed. They sounded just alike. *We would,* he thought.

The waitress came back with a couple of tall bottles of OB beer. She hadn't asked either one of them for an ID, for which Justin was duly grateful. His younger self kept quiet while she was around. After she'd gone away, himself-at-twenty-one said, "Okay, I believe you. I didn't think I would, but I do. You know too much—and you couldn't have pulled that quarter out of your ear from nowhere." He sipped at the Korean beer. He looked as if he would sooner have gone out and got drunk.

"That's right," Justin agreed. *Stay in control. The more you sound like you know what you're doing, the more he'll think you know what you're doing. And he has to think that, or this won't fly.*

His younger self drank beer faster than he did, and waved for a second tall one as soon as the first was empty. Justin frowned. He remembered drinking more in his twenties than he did at forty, but didn't care to have his nose rubbed in it. He wouldn't have wanted to drive after two big OBs, but his younger self didn't worry about it.

With his younger self's new beer, the waitress brought the meat to be grilled and the plates of vegetables. She used aluminum tongs to put some pork and some marinated beef over the fire. Looking at the strips of meat curling and shrinking, himself-at-twenty-one exclaimed, "Oh my God! They killed Kenny!"

"Huh?" Justin said, and then, "Oh." He managed a feeble

chuckle. He hadn't thought about *South Park* in a long time.

His younger self eyed him. "If you'd said that to me, I'd have laughed a lot harder. But the show's not hot for you any more, is it?" He answered his own question before Justin could: "No, it wouldn't be. 2018? Jesus." He took another big sip of beer.

Justin grabbed some beef with the tongs. He used chopsticks to eat, ignoring the fork. So did his younger self. He was better at it than himself-at-twenty-one; he'd had more practice. The food was good. He remembered it had been.

After a while, his younger self said, "Well, *will* you tell me what this is all about?"

"What's the most important thing in your life right now?" Justin asked in return.

"You mean, besides trying to figure out why I'd travel back in time to see me?" his younger self returned. He nodded, carefully not smiling. He'd been looser, sillier, at twenty-one than he was now. Of course, he'd had fewer things go wrong then, too. And his younger self went on, "What else could it be but Megan?"

"Okay, we're on the same page," Justin said. "That's why I'm here, to set things right with Megan."

"Things with Megan don't need setting right." Himself-at-twenty-one sounded disgustingly complacent. "Things with Megan are great. I mean, I'm taking my time and all, but they're great. And they'll stay great, too. How many kids do we have now?"

"None." Justin's voice went flat and harsh. A muscle at the corner of his jaw jumped. He touched it to try to calm it down.

"None?" His younger self wasn't quick on the uptake. He needed his nose rubbed in things. He looked at Justin's left hand. "You're not wearing a wedding ring," he said. He'd just noticed. Justin's answering nod was grim. His younger self asked, "Does that mean we don't get married?"

Say it ain't so. Justin did: "We get married, all right. And then we get divorced."

His younger self went as pale as he had when he first saw Justin.

Even at twenty-one, he knew too much about divorce. Here-and-now, his father was living with a woman not much older than he was. His mother was living with a woman not much older than he was, too. That was why he had his own apartment: paying his rent was easier for his mom and dad than paying him any real attention.

But, however much himself-at-twenty-one knew about divorce, he didn't know enough. He'd just been a fairly innocent bystander. He hadn't gone through one from the inside. He didn't understand the pain and the emptiness and the endless might-have-beens that kept going through your mind afterwards.

Justin had had those might-have-beens inside his head since he and Megan fell apart. But he was in a unique position, sitting here in the Pine Tree eating *kimchi*. He could do something about them.

He could. If his younger self let him. Said younger self blurted, "That can't happen."

"It can. It did. It will," Justin said. The muscle started twitching again.

"But—how?" Himself-at-twenty-one sounded somewhere between bewildered and shocked. "We aren't like Mom and Dad—we don't fight all the time, and we don't look for something on the side wherever we can find it." Even at twenty-one, he spoke of his parents with casual contempt. Justin thought no better of them in 2018.

He said, "You can fight about sex, you can fight about money, you can fight about in-laws. We ended up doing all three, and so ..." He set down his chopsticks and spread his hands wide. "We broke up—will break up—if we don't change things. That's why I figured out how to come back: to change things, I mean."

His younger self finished the second OB. "You must have wanted to do that a lot," he remarked.

"You might say so." Justin's voice came harsh and ragged. "Yeah, you just might say so. Since we fell apart, I've never come close to finding anybody who makes me feel the way Megan did. If it's not her, it's nobody. That's how it looks from here, anyhow. I want to make things right for the two of us."

"Things *were* going to be right." But his younger self lacked conviction. Justin sat and waited. He was better at that than he had been half a lifetime earlier. Finally, himself-at-twenty-one asked, "What will you do?"

He didn't ask, *What do you want to do?* He spoke as if Justin were a force of nature. Maybe that was his youth showing. Maybe it was just the beer. Whatever it was, Justin encouraged it by telling his younger self what he *would* do, not what he'd like to do: "I'm going to take over your life for the next couple of months. I'm going to be you. I'm going to take Megan out, I'm going to make sure things are solid—and then the superstring I've ridden to get me here will break down. You'll live happily ever after: I'll brief you to make sure you don't screw up what I've built. And when I get back to 2018, I *will have lived* happily ever after. How does that sound?"

"I don't know," his younger self said. "You'll be taking Megan out?"

Justin nodded. "That's right."

"You'll be . . . taking Megan back to the apartment?"

"Yeah," Justin said. "But she'll think it's you, remember, and pretty soon it'll be you, and it'll keep right on being you till you turn into me, if you know what I mean."

"I know what you mean," his younger self said. "Still . . ." He grimaced. "I don't know. I don't like it."

"You have a better idea?" Justin folded his arms across his chest and waited, doing his best to be the picture of inevitability. Inside, his stomach tied itself in knots. He'd always been better at the tech side of things than at sales.

"It's not fair," himself-at-twenty-one said. "You *know* all this shit, and I've gotta guess."

Justin shrugged. "If you think I did all this to come back and tell you lies, go ahead. That's fine." It was anything but fine. But he couldn't let his younger self see that. "You'll see what happens, and we'll both be sorry."

"I don't know." His younger self shook his head, again and again. His eyes had a trapped-animal look. "I just don't know. Everything sounds like it hangs together, but you could be bullshitting, too, just as easy."

"Yeah, right." Justin couldn't remember the last time he'd said that, but it fit here.

Then his younger self got up. "I won't say yes and I won't say no, not now I won't. I've got your e-mail address. I'll use it." Out he went, not quite steady on his feet.

Justin stared after him. He paid for both dinners—it seemed like peanuts to him—and went home himself. His younger self needed time to think things through. He saw that. Seeing it and liking it were two different things. And every minute himself-at-twenty-one dithered was a minute he couldn't get back. He stewed. He fumed. He waited. What other choice did he have?

You could whack him and take over for him. But he rejected the thought with a shudder. He was no murderer. All he wanted was some happiness. Was that too much to ask? He didn't think so, not after all he'd missed since Megan made him move out. He checked his e-mail every hour on the hour.

Two and a half mortal days. Justin thought he'd go nuts. He'd never dreamt his younger self would make him wait so long. At last, the computer told him, "You've got mail!"

All right, dammit, himself-at-twenty-one wrote. *I still don't know about this, but I don't think I have any choice. If me and Megan are going to break up, that* can't *happen. You better make sure it doesn't.*

"Oh, thank God," Justin breathed. He wrote back, *You won't be sorry.*

Whatever, his younger self replied. *Half of me is sorry already. More than half.*

Don't be, Justin told him. *Everything will be fine.*

It had better be, his younger self wrote darkly. *How do you want to make the switch?*

Meet me in front of the B. Dalton's again, Justin answered. *Park by the Sears. I will, too. Bring whatever you want in your car. You can move it to the one I'm driving. I'll do the same here. See you in two hours?*

Whatever, his younger self repeated. Justin remembered saying that a lot. He hoped it meant *yes* here. The only things he didn't want his younger self getting his hands on here were his laptop (though it would distract himself-at-twenty-one from worrying about Megan if anything would) and some of his cash. He left behind the TV and the stereo and the period clothes—and, below the underwear and socks, the cash he wasn't taking along. His younger self could eat and have some fun, too, provided he did it at places where Megan wouldn't run into him.

This time, his younger self got to the mall before him. Thoroughly grim, himself-at-twenty-one said, "Let's get this over with."

"Come on. It's not a root canal," Justin said. Now his younger self looked blank—he didn't know about root canals. Justin wished *he* didn't; that was a bit of the future less pleasant to contemplate than life with Megan. He went on, "Let's go do it. We'll need to swap keys, you know."

"Yeah." Himself-at-twenty-one nodded. "I had spares made. How about you?"

"Me, too." Justin's grin twisted up one corner of his mouth. "We think alike. Amazing, huh?"

"Amazing. Right." His younger self started back toward Sears. "This better work."

"It will," Justin said. *It has to, goddammit.*

They'd parked only a couple of rows apart. His younger self had a couple of good-sized bundles. He put them in Justin's car while Justin moved his stuff to the machine himself-at-twenty-one had been driving. "You know where I live," his younger self said after they'd swapped keys. "What's my new address?"

"Oh." Justin told him. "The car's insured, and you'll find plenty of money in the underwear drawer." He put a hand on his younger self's shoulder. "It'll be fine. Honest. You're on vacation for a couple of months, that's all."

"On vacation from my *life*." Himself-at-twenty-one looked grim again. At twenty-one, everything was urgent. "Don't fuck up, that's all."

"It's my life, too, remember." Justin got into the car his

younger self had driven to the mall. He fumbled a little, finding the right key. When he fired up the engine, the radio started playing KROQ. He laughed. Green Day was the bomb now, even if not quite to his taste. It wasn't music for people approaching middle age and regretting it. He cranked the radio and drove back to his younger self's apartment.

The Acapulco. He nodded as he drove up to it. It looked familiar. That made him laugh again. It hadn't changed. He had.

After he drove through the security gate, he found his old parking space more by letting his hands and eyes guide his brain than the other way round. He couldn't remember his apartment number at all, and had to go to the lobby to see which box had KLOSTER Dymo-taped onto it. He walked around the pool and past the rec room hardly anybody used, and there it was—his old place. But it wasn't old now. This was where his younger self had lived and would live, and where he was living now.

As soon as he opened the door, he winced. He hadn't remembered the bile-colored carpet, either, but it came back in a hurry. He looked around. Here it was—all his old stuff, a lot of it things he hadn't seen in half a lifetime. Paperbacks, CDs, that tiny statuette of a buglike humanoid standing on its hind legs and giving a speech . . . During which move had that disappeared? He shrugged. He'd been through a lot of them. He fondly touched an antenna as he went past the bookcase, along a narrow hall, and into the bedroom.

"My old iMac!" he exclaimed. But it wasn't old; the model had been out for less than a year. Bondi blue and ice case—to a taste formed in 2018, it looked not just outmoded but tacky as hell, but he'd thought it was great when it came out.

His younger self had left a note by the keyboard. *In case you don't remember, here's Megan's phone number and e-mail. Don't screw it up, that's all I've got to tell you.*

He had remembered her e-mail address, but not her phone number. "Thanks, kid," he said to himself-at-twenty-one. There by the phone on the nightstand lay his younger self's address book, but having things out in the open made it easier.

Instead of calling her, he walked into the bathroom. His hand shook as he flipped on the light. He stared at the mirror. *Can I do this?* He ran a palm over his cheek. *Yeah, I look young. Do I look that young? What will Megan think when I come to the door? What will her folks think? I'm only a couple of years younger than they are, for Christ's sake.*

If I come to the door wearing his—my—clothes, though, and talking like me, and knowing things only I could know, who else would I be but Justin Kloster? She'll think I'm me, because I can't possibly be anybody else. And I'm not anybody else— except I am.

He was still frowning and looking for incipient wrinkles when the telephone rang. As he hurried back to the bedroom, he hoped it would be a telemarketer. *I'm not ready, I'm not ready, I'm not . . .* "Hello?"

"Hiya! How the hell are you?" It was Megan, all right. He hadn't heard her in more than ten years, but he knew her voice. He hadn't heard her sound bouncy and bubbly and glad to be talking to *him* in a lot more than ten years. Before he could get a word in, she went on, "You mad at me? You haven't called in two days."

By the way she said it, it might have been two years. "I'm not mad," Justin answered automatically. "Just—busy."

"Too busy for *me*?" Now she sounded as if she couldn't imagine such a thing. Justin's younger self must have been too caught up in everything else to have time for her. At least he hadn't blabbed about Justin's return to 1999. "What were you doing? Who were you doing it with—or to?"

She giggled. Justin remembered her asking him questions like that later on, in an altogether different tone of voice. Not now. She didn't know she would do that. If he changed things here, she wouldn't. "Nothing," he said. "Nobody. Things have been hairy at work, that's all."

"A likely story." But Megan was still laughing. He remembered her doing things like that. He remembered her stopping, too. She said, "Well, you're not working now, right? Suppose I come over?"

"Okay," he said, thinking about baptism by total immersion. Either this would work, or it would blow up in his face. *What do I do if it blows up? Run back to 2018 with my tail between my legs, that's what.*

But Megan didn't even give him time to panic. "Okay?" she said, mock-fierce. "Okay? I'll okay you, mister, you see if I don't. Ten minutes." She hung up.

Justin ran around like a madman, to remind himself where things were and to clean up a little. He hadn't remembered his younger self as such a slob. He checked the refrigerator. Frozen dinners, beer, Cokes—about what he'd expected.

He waited for the buzz that would mean Megan was at the security door. But he'd forgotten he'd given her a key. The first he knew she was there was the knock on the door. He opened it. "Hi," he said, his voice breaking as if he really were twenty-one, or maybe sixteen.

"Hiya." Megan clicked her tongue between her teeth. "You do look tired. Poor baby."

He was looking at her, too, looking and trying not to tremble. She looked just like all the photos he'd kept: a swarthy brunette with flashing dark eyes, a little skinny maybe, but with some meat on her bones even so. She always smiled as if she knew a secret. He'd remembered. Remembering and seeing it in the flesh when it was fresh and new and a long way from curdling were very different things. He hadn't imagined how different.

"How tired *are* you?" she said. "Not *too* tired, I hope." She stepped forward, put her arms around him, and tilted her face up.

Automatically, his arms went around her. Automatically, he brought his mouth down to hers. She made a tiny noise, deep in her throat, as their lips met.

Justin's heart pounded so hard, he was amazed Megan couldn't hear it. He wanted to burst into tears. Here he was, holding the only woman he'd ever truly loved, the woman who'd so emphatically stopped loving him—only now she did again. If that wasn't a miracle, he didn't know what was.

She felt soft and smooth and warm and firm. Very firm, he noticed—a lot firmer than the women he'd been seeing, no matter how obsessively they went to the gym. And that brought the second realization, almost as blinding as realizing he, Justin, was alone with her, Megan: he, a forty-year-old guy, was alone with her, a twenty-year-old girl.

What had the bartender asked? *You go around picking up high-school girls?* But it wasn't like that, dammit. Megan didn't know he was forty. She thought he was his going-into-senior-year self. He had to think that way, too.

Except he couldn't, or not very well. He'd lived half a lifetime too long. He tried not to remember, but he couldn't help it. "Wow!" he gasped when the kiss finally ended.

"Yeah." Megan took such heat for granted. She was twenty. Doubt never entered her mind. "Not bad for starters." Without waiting for an answer, she headed for the bedroom.

Heart pounding harder than ever, Justin followed. Here-and-now, they hadn't been lovers very long, and neither had had a whole lot of experience beforehand. That was part of what had gone wrong; Justin was sure of it. They'd gone stale, without knowing how to fix things. Justin knew a lot more now than he had at twenty-one. And here he was, getting a chance to use it when it mattered.

He almost forgot everything the next instant, because Megan was getting out of her clothes and lying down on the bed and laughing at him for being so slow. He didn't stay slow very long. As he lay down beside her, he thanked God and Superstrings, Ltd., not necessarily in that order.

His hands roamed her. She sighed and leaned toward him for another kiss. *Don't hurry,* he thought. *Don't rush.* In a way, that was easy. He wanted to touch her, caress her, taste her, forever. In another way . . . He wanted to do more, too.

He made himself go slow. It was worth it. "Oh, Justin," Megan said. Some time later, she said, "Ohhh, Justin." He didn't think he'd ever heard her sound like that the first time around. What she said a few minutes after that had no words, but was a long way from disappointed.

Then it was his turn. He kept having the nagging thought that he was taking advantage of a girl half his age who didn't know exactly who he was. But then, as she clasped him with arms and legs, all the nagging thoughts went away. And it was just as good as he'd hoped it would be, which said a great deal.

Afterwards, they lay side by side, sweaty and smiling foolishly. Justin kept stroking her. She purred. She stroked him, too, expectantly. When what she was expecting didn't happen, she gave him a sympathetic look. "You *must* be tired," she said.

Did she think he'd be ready again right then? They'd just finished! But memory, now that he accessed it, told him she did. He clicked his tongue between his teeth. He might look about the same at forty as he had at twenty-one, but he couldn't perform the same. Who could?

Had he thought of this beforehand, he would have brought some Viagra back with him. In his time, it was over-the-counter. He wasn't even sure it existed in 1999. He hadn't had to worry about keeping it up, not at twenty-one.

But Megan had given him an excuse, at least this time. "Yeah, day from hell," he said. "Doesn't mean I can't keep you happy." He proceeded to do just that, and took his time about it, teasing her along as much as he could.

Once the teasing stopped, she stared at him, eyes enormous. "Oh, sweetie, why didn't you ever do anything like that before?" she asked. All by itself, the question made him sure he'd done the right thing, coming back. It also made him sure he needed to give his younger self a good talking-to before he slid up the superstring to 2018. But Megan found another question: "Where did you *learn* that?"

Did she think he had another girlfriend? Did she wonder if that was why he could only do it once with her? Or was she joking? He hoped she was. How would his younger self have answered? With pride. "I," he declared, "have a naturally dirty mind."

Megan giggled. "Good."

And it was good. A little later, in the lazy man's position, he managed a second round. That was very good. Megan thought so, too. He couldn't stop yawning afterwards, but he'd already said he was tired. "See?" he told her. "You wear me out." He wasn't kidding. Megan didn't know how much he wasn't kidding.

She proved that, saying, "I was thinking we'd go to a club tonight, but I'd better put you to bed. We can go tomorrow." She went into the bathroom, then came back and started getting dressed. "We can do all sorts of things tomorrow." The smile she gave him wasn't just eager; it was downright lecherous.

Christ, he thought, *she'll expect me to be just as horny as I was tonight.* His younger self would have been. To him, the prospect seemed more nearly exhausting than exciting. *Sleep. I need sleep.*

Megan bent down and kissed him on the end of the nose. "Pick me up about seven? We'll go to the Probe, and then who knows what?"

"Okay," he said around another yawn. "Whatever." Megan laughed and left. Justin thought he heard her close the door, but he wasn't sure.

He couldn't even sleep late. He had to go do his younger self's job at CompUSA, and himself-at-twenty-one didn't keep coffee in the apartment. He drank Cokes instead, but they didn't pack the jolt of French roast.

Work was hell. All the computers were obsolete junk to him. Over half a lifetime, he'd forgotten their specs. Why remember when they were obsolete? And his boss, from the height of his late twenties, treated Justin like a kid. He wished he'd told his younger self to keep coming in. But Megan stopped by every so often, and so did other people he knew. He wanted himself-at-twenty-one out of sight, out of mind.

His younger self probably *was* going out of his mind right now. He wondered what the kid was doing, what he was thinking. Worrying, he supposed, and dismissed himself-at-twenty-one as casually as his boss had dismissed him, believing him to be his younger self.

His shift ended at five-fifteen. He drove home, nuked some

supper, showered, and dressed in his younger self's club-hopping clothes: black pants and boots, black jacket, white shirt. The outfit struck him as stark. You needed to be skinny to look good in it, and he'd never been skinny. He shrugged. It was what you wore to go clubbing.

Knocking on the door to Megan's parents' house meant more strangeness. He made himself forget all the things they'd say after he and Megan went belly-up. And, when Megan's mother opened the door, he got another jolt: she looked pretty damn good. He'd always thought of her as old. "H-Hello, Mrs. Tricoupis," he managed at last.

"Hello, Justin." She stepped aside. No, nothing old about her—somewhere close to his own age, sure enough. "Megan says you've been working hard."

"That's right." Justin nodded briskly.

"I believe it," Mrs. Tricoupis said. "You look tired." Megan had said the same thing. It was as close as they could come to *You look forty.* But her mother eyed him curiously. He needed a minute to figure out why: he'd spoken to her as an equal, not as his girlfriend's mother. *Gotta watch that,* he thought. It wouldn't be easy; he saw as much. Even if nobody else did, he knew how old he was.

Before he could say anything else to raise eyebrows, Megan came out. She fluttered her fingers at Mrs. Tricoupis. "See you later, Mom."

"All right," her mother said. "Drive safely, Justin."

"Yeah," he said. Nobody'd told him that in a long time. He grinned at Megan. "The Probe."

He'd had to look up how to get there in the Thomas Brothers himself-at-twenty-one kept in the car; he'd long since forgotten. It was off Melrose, the center of youth and style in the '90s—and as outmoded in 2018 as the corner of Haight and Ashbury in 1999.

On the way down, Megan said, "I hear there's going to be another rave at that place we went to a couple weeks ago. Want to see?"

"Suppose." Justin hoped he sounded interested, not alarmed. After-hours illicit bashes didn't hold the attraction for him they once had. And he had no idea where they'd gone then. His younger self would know. He didn't.

He had as much trouble not grinning at the fashion statements the kids going into the club were making as Boomers did with tie-dye and suede jackets with fringe. Tattoos, pierced body parts . . . Those fads had faded. Except for a stud in his left ear, he'd never had more holes than he'd been born with.

Somebody waved to Megan and him as they went in. He waved back. His younger self would have known who it was. He'd long since forgotten. He got away with it. And he got carded when he bought a beer. That made him laugh. Then he came back and bought another one for Megan, who wasn't legal yet.

She pointed toward the little booth with the spotlight on it. "Look. Helen's deejaying tonight. She's good!"

"Yeah." Justin grinned. Megan sounded so excited. Had he cared so passionately about who was spinning the music? He probably had. He wondered why. The mix hadn't been that much different from one deejay to another.

When the music started, he thought the top of his head would blow off. Coming home with ears ringing had been a sign of a good time—and a sign of nerve damage, but who cared at twenty-one? He cared now.

"What's the matter?" Megan asked. "Don't you want to dance?" He thought that was what she said, anyhow; he read her lips, because he couldn't hear a word.

"Uh, sure." He hadn't been a great dancer at twenty-one, and hadn't been on the floor in a lot of years since. But Megan didn't criticize. She'd always liked getting out there and letting the music take over. The Probe didn't have a mosh pit, for which Justin was duly grateful. Looking back, pogoing in a pit reminded him more of line play at the Super Bowl than of dancing.

He hadn't been in great shape when he was twenty-one, either. Half a lifetime riding a desk hadn't improved things. By the time the first break came, he was blowing like a whale. Megan's face was sweaty, too, but she loved every minute of it. She wasn't even breathing hard. "This is *so* cool!" she said.

She was right. Justin had long since stopped worrying about

whether he was cool. You could stay at the edge till you were thirty—thirty-five if you really pushed it. After that, you were either a fogy or a grotesque. He'd taken fogydom for granted for years. Now he had to ride the crest of the wave again. He wondered if it was worth it.

Helen started spinning more singles. Justin danced till one. At least he had the next day off. Even so, he wished he were home in bed—not with Megan but alone, blissfully unconscious. No such luck. Somebody with enough rings in his ears to set off airport metal detectors passed out Xeroxed directions to the rave. That told Justin where it was. He didn't want to go, but Megan did. "You wearing out on me?" she asked. They went.

He wondered who owned the warehouse—a big Lego block of a building—and if whoever it was had any idea what was going on inside. He doubted it. It was a dreadful place for a big party—concrete floor, wires and metal scaffolding overhead, acoustics worse than lousy. But Megan's eyes glowed. The thrill of the not quite legal. The cops might show up and throw everybody out.

He knew they wouldn't, not tonight, because they hadn't. And, at forty, the thrill of the not quite legal had worn off for him. Some smiling soul came by with little plastic bottles full of greenish liquid. "Instant Love!" he said. "Five bucks a pop."

Megan grabbed two. Justin knew he had to grab his wallet. "What's in it?" he asked warily.

"Try it. You'll like it," the guy said. "A hundred percent natural."

Megan had already gulped hers down. She waited expectantly for Justin. He remembered taking a lot of strange things at raves, but that had been a long time ago—except it wasn't. Nothing had killed him, so he didn't suppose this would.

And it didn't, but not from lack of trying. The taste was nasty plus sugar. The effect . . . when the shit kicked in, Justin stopped wishing for coffee. He felt as if he'd just had seventeen cups of the strongest joe ever perked. His heart pounded four hundred beats a minute. His hands shook. He could feel the veins in his eyeballs sticking out every time he blinked.

"Isn't it *great*?" Megan's eyes were bugging out of her head.

"Whatever." When Justin was twenty-one, he'd thought this kind of rush was great, too. Now he wondered if he'd have a coronary on the spot. He did dance a lot more energetically.

And, when he took Megan back to his place, he managed something else, too. With his heart thudding the way it was, remembering anything related to foreplay wasn't easy, but he did. Had he been twenty-one, it surely would have been wham-bam-thank-you-ma'am. Megan seemed suitably appreciative; maybe that Instant Love handle wasn't altogether hype.

But his real age told. Despite the drug, whatever it was, and despite the company, he couldn't have gone a second round if he'd had a crane to get it up. If that bothered Megan, she didn't let on.

Despite his failure, he didn't roll over and go to sleep, the way he had the first night. He wondered if he'd sleep for the next week. It was past four in the morning. "Shall I take you home?" he asked. "Your folks gonna be worried?"

Megan sat up naked on the bed and shook her head. Everything moved when she did that; it was marvelous to watch. "No problem," she said. "They aren't on me twentyfour-seven like some parents. You don't want to throw me out, I'd just as soon stay a while." She opened her eyes very wide to show she wasn't sleepy, either.

"Okay. Better than okay." Justin reached out and brushed the tip of her left breast with the backs of his fingers. "I like having you around, you know?" She had no idea how much he wanted to have her around. With luck, she'd never find out.

"I like being around." She cocked her head to one side. "You've been kind of funny the last couple days, you know?"

To cover his unease—hell, his fear—Justin made a stupid face. "Is that funny enough for you?" he asked.

"Not funny like that," Megan said. He made a different, even more stupid, face. It got a giggle from her, but she persisted: "Not funny like that, I told you. Funny a different sort of way."

"Like how?" he asked, though he knew.

Megan didn't, but groped toward it: "Lots of little things. The way you touch me, for instance. You didn't used to touch me like that." She looked down at the wet spot on the sheets. "I like what you're doing, believe me I do, but it's not what you were doing last week. How did you . . . find this out, just all of a sudden? It's great, like I say, but . . ." She shrugged. "I shouldn't complain. I'm *not* complaining. But . . ." Her voice trailed off again.

If I'd known then what I know now—everybody sang that song. But he didn't just sing it. He'd done something about it. This was the thanks he got? At least she hadn't come right out and asked him if he had another girlfriend.

He tried to make light of it: "Here I spent all night laying awake, trying to think of things you'd like, and—"

"I do," Megan said quickly. She wasn't lying, not unless she was the best actress in the world. But she went on, "You looked bored in the Probe tonight. You never looked bored in a club before."

Damn. He hadn't known it showed. What was hot at twenty-one wasn't at forty. *Been there, done that.* That was what people said in the '90s. One more thing he couldn't admit. "Tired," he said again.

Megan nailed him for it. "You never said that, either, not till yesterday—day before yesterday now." Remorselessly precise.

"Sorry," Justin answered. "I'm just me. Who else would I be?" Again, he was conscious of knowing what she didn't and keeping it from her. It felt unkosher, as if he were the only one in class who took a test with the book open. But what else could he do?

Megan started getting into her clothes. "Maybe you'd better take me home." But then, as if she thought that too harsh, she added some teasing: "I don't want to eat what you'd fix for breakfast."

He could have made her a damn fine breakfast. He started to say so. But his younger self couldn't have, not to save his life. He shut up and got dressed, too. Showing her more differences was the last thing he wanted.

Dawn was turning the eastern sky gray and pink when he pulled up in front of her parents' house. Before she could take off her seat belt, he put his arm around her and said, "I love you, you know?"

His younger self wouldn't say those words for another year. *Taking my time,* the socially backwards dummy called it. For Justin at forty, the words weren't just a truth, but a truth that defined his life—for better and, later on, for worse. He had no trouble bringing them out.

Megan stared at him. Maybe she hadn't expected him to say that for quite a while yet. After a heartbeat, she nodded. She leaned over and kissed him, half on the cheek, half on the mouth. Then she got out and walked to her folks' front door. She turned and waved. Justin waved back. He drove off while she was working the dead bolt.

He finally fell asleep about noon. The Instant Love kept him up and bouncing till then. At two-thirty, the phone rang. By the way he jerked and thrashed, a bomb might have gone off by his head. He grabbed the handset, feeling like death. "Hello?" he croaked.

"Hi. How are things?"

Not Megan. A man's voice. For a second, all that meant was that it didn't matter, that he could hang up on it. Then he recognized it: the voice on his own answering machine. But it wasn't a recording. It was live, which seemed more than he could say right now. His younger self.

He had to talk, dammit. "Things are fine," he said. "Or they were till you called. I was asleep."

"Now?" The way himself-at-twenty-one sounded, it might have been some horrible perversion. "I called now 'cause I figured you wouldn't be."

"Never mind," Justin said. The cobwebs receded. He knew they'd be back pretty soon. "Yeah, things are okay. We went to the Probe last night, and—"

"Did you?" His younger self sounded—no, *suspicious* wasn't right. *Jealous.* That was it. "What else did you do?"

"That after-hours place. Some guy came through with flyers, so I knew how to get there."

"Lucky you. And what *else* did you do?" Yeah. Jealous. A-number-one jealous.

Justin wondered how big a problem that would be. "About what you'd expect," he answered tightly. "I'm you, remember. What would you have done?"

The sigh on the other end of the line said his younger self knew exactly what he would have done, and wished he'd been doing it. *But I did it better, you little geek.*

Before his younger self could do anything but sigh, Justin added, "And when I took her home, I told her I loved her."

"Jesus!" himself-at-twenty-one exclaimed. "What did you go and do that for?"

"It's true, isn't it?"

"That doesn't mean you've got to *say* it, for Christ's sake," his younger self told him. "What am I supposed to do when you go away?"

"Marry her, doofus," Justin said. "Live happily ever after, so I get to live happily ever after, too. Why the hell do you think I came back here?"

"For your good time, man, not mine. I'm sure not having a good time, I'll tell you."

Was I really that stupid? Justin wondered. But it wasn't quite the right question. *Was my event horizon that short?* Holding on to patience with both hands, he said, "Look, chill for a while, okay? I'm doing fine."

"Sure you are." His younger self sounded hot. "You're doing fucking great. What about me?"

Nope, no event horizon at all. Justin said, "You're fine. Chill. You're on vacation. Go ahead. Relax. Spend my money. That's what it's there for."

That distracted his younger self. "Where'd you get so much? What did you do, rob a bank?"

"It's worth a lot more now than it will be then," Justin answered. "Inflation. Have some fun. Just be discreet, okay?"

"You mean, keep out of your hair." His younger self didn't stay distracted long.

"In a word, yes."

"While you're in Megan's hair." Himself-at-twenty-one let out a long, angry breath. "I don't know, dude."

"It's for you." Justin realized he was pleading. "It's for her and you."

Another angry exhalation. "Yeah." His younger self hung up.

Everything went fine till he took Megan to the much bally-hooed summer blockbuster two weekends later. She'd been caught up in the hype. And she thought the leading man was cute, though he looked like a boy to Justin. On the other hand, Justin looked like a boy himself, or he couldn't have got away with this.

But that wasn't the worst problem. Unlike her, he'd seen the movie before. He remembered liking it, though he'd thought the plot a little thin. Seen through forty-year-old eyes, it had no plot at all. He had a lot less tolerance for loud soundtracks and things blowing up every eight and a half minutes than his younger self would have. And even the most special special effects seemed routine to somebody who'd been through another twenty years of computer-generated miracles.

As the credits finally rolled, he thought, *No wonder I don't go to the movies much any more.*

When Megan turned to him, though, her eyes were shining. "Wasn't that great?" she said as they headed for the exit.

"Yeah," he said. "Great."

A different tone would have saved him. He realized that as soon as the words were out of his mouth. Too late. The one he'd used couldn't have been anything but sarcastic. And Megan noticed. She was good at catching things like that—better than he'd ever been, certainly. "What's the matter?" she demanded. "Why didn't you like it?"

The challenge in her voice reminded Justin of how she'd sounded during the quarrels before their breakup. She couldn't know that. His younger self wouldn't have known, either—he hadn't been through it. But Justin had, and reacted with a challenge of his own: "Why? Because it was really dumb."

It was a nice summer night, clear, cooling down from the hot day, a few stars in the sky—with the lights of the San Fernando

Valley, you never saw more than a few. None of that mattered to Megan. She stopped halfway to the car. "How can you say that?"

Justin saw the special-effects stardust in her eyes, and the effect of a great many closeups of the boyishly handsome—pretty, to his newly jaundiced eye—leading man. He should have shut up. But he reacted viscerally to that edge in her voice. Instead of letting things blow over, he told her exactly why the movie was dumb.

He finished just as they got to the Toyota. He hadn't let her get in word one. When he ran down, she stared at him. "Why are you so mean? You never sounded so mean before."

"You asked. I told you," he said, still seething. But when he saw her fighting back tears as she fastened her seat belt, he realized he'd hit back too hard. It wasn't quite like kicking a puppy, but it was close, too close. He had a grown man's armor, and weapons to pierce a grown woman's—all the nastier products of experience—and he'd used them on a kid. Too late, he felt like an asshole. "I'm sorry," he mumbled.

"Whatever." Megan looked out the window toward the theater complex, not at him. "Maybe you'd better take me home."

Alarm tore through him. "Honey, I said I was sorry. I meant it."

"I heard you." Megan still wouldn't look at him. "You'd better take me home anyhow."

Sometimes, the more you argued, the bigger the mess you made. This looked like one of those times. Justin recognized that now. A couple of minutes sooner would have been better. "Okay," he said, and started the car.

The ride back to her folks' house was almost entirely silent. When he pulled up, Megan opened the door before the car stopped rolling. "Goodnight," she said. She started for the front door at something nearly a run.

"Wait!" he called. If that wasn't raw panic in his voice, it would do. She heard it, too, and stopped, looking back warily, like a frightened animal that *would* bolt at any wrong move. He said, "I won't do that again. Promise." To show how much he meant it, he crossed his heart. He hadn't done that since about the third grade.

Megan's nod was jerky. "All right," she said. "But don't call me for a while anyway. We'll both chill a little. How does that sound?"

Terrible. Justin hated the idea of losing any precious time here. But he saw he couldn't argue. He wished he'd seen that sooner. He made himself nod, made himself smile, made himself say, "Okay."

The porch light showed relief on Megan's face. Relief she wouldn't be talking to him for a while. He had to live with that all the way home.

He wished he could have walked away from his younger self's job at CompUSA, but it would have looked bad. He'd needed a few days to have the details of late-1990s machines come back to him. Once they did, he rapidly got a reputation as a maven. His manager bumped him a buck an hour—and piled more hours on him. He resisted as best he could, but he couldn't always.

Three days after the fight with Megan, his phone rang as he got into his—well, his younger self's—apartment. He got to it just before the answering machine could. "Hello?" He was panting. If it was himself-at-twenty-one, he was ready to contemplate murder—or would it be suicide?

But it was Megan. "Hiya," she said. "Didn't I ask you not to call for a little bit? I know I did."

"Yeah, you did. And I—" Justin broke off. *He* hadn't called her. What about his younger self? *Maybe I ought to rub him out, if he's going to mess things up.* But that thought vanished. He couldn't deny a conversation she'd surely had. "I just like talking to you, that's all."

Megan's laughter was rainbows to his ears. "You were *so* funny," she said. "It was like we hadn't fought at all. I couldn't stay pissed. Believe me, I tried."

"I'm glad you didn't," Justin said. *And I* do *need to have a talk with my younger self.* "You want to go out this weekend?"

"Sure," Megan answered. "But let's stay away from the movies. What do you think?"

"Whatever," he said. "Okay with me."

"Good." More relief. "Plenty of other things we can do. Maybe I should just come straight to your place."

His younger self would have slavered at that. He liked the idea pretty well himself. But, being forty and not twenty-one, he heard what Megan didn't say, too. What she meant, or some of what she meant, was, *You're fine in bed. Whenever we're not in bed, whenever we go somewhere, you get weird.*

"Sure," he said, and then, to prove he wasn't only interested in her body, he went on, "Let's go to Sierra's and stuff ourselves full of tacos and enchiladas. How's that?"

"Fine," Megan said.

Justin thought it sounded fine, too. Sierra's was a Valley institution. It had been there since twenty years before he was born, and would still be going strong in 2018. He didn't go there often then; he had too many memories of coming there with Megan. Now those memories would turn from painful to happy. That was why he was here. Smiling, he said, "See you Saturday, then."

"Yeah," Megan said. Justin's smile got bigger.

Ring. Ring. Ring. "Hello?" his younger self said.

"Oh, good," Justin said coldly. "You're home."

"Oh. It's you." Himself-at-twenty-one didn't sound delighted to hear from him, either. "No, *you're* home. I'm stuck here."

"Didn't I tell you to lay low till I was done here?" Justin demanded. "God damn it, you'd better listen to me. I just had to pretend I knew what Megan was talking about when she said I'd been on the phone with her."

"She's my girl, too," his younger self said. "She was my girl first, you know. I've got a *right* to talk with her."

"Not if you want her to keep being your girl, you don't," Justin said. "You're the one who's going to screw it up, remember?"

"That's what you keep telling me," his younger self answered. "But you know what? I'm not so sure I believe you any more. When I called her, Megan sounded like she was really torqued at me—at you, I mean. So it doesn't sound like you've got all the answers."

"*Nobody* has *all* the answers," Justin said with such patience as he could muster. He didn't think he'd believed that at twenty-one; at forty, he was convinced it was true. He was convinced something else was true, too: "If you think you've got more of them than I do, you're full of shit."

"You want to be careful how you talk to me," himself-at-twenty-one said. "Half the time, I still think your whole setup is bogus. If I decide to, I can wreck it. You know damn well I can."

Justin knew only too well. It scared the crap out of him. But he didn't dare show his younger self he was afraid. As sarcastically as he could, he said, "Yeah, go ahead. Screw up your life for good. Keep going like this and you will."

"You sound pretty screwed up now," his younger self said. "What have I got to lose?"

"I had something good, and I let it slip through my fingers," Justin said. "That's enough to mess anybody up. You wreck what I'm doing now, you'll go through life without knowing what a good thing was. You want that? Just keep sticking your nose in where it doesn't belong. You want to end up with Megan or not?"

Where nothing else had, that hit home. "All right," his younger self said sullenly. "I'll back off—for now." He hung up. Justin stared at the phone, cursed, and put it back in its cradle.

Megan stared at her empty plate as if she couldn't imagine how it had got that way. Then she looked at Justin. "Did I really eat all that?" she said. "Tell me I didn't really eat all that."

"Can't do it," he said solemnly.

"Oh, my God!" Megan said: not Valley-girl nasal but sincerely astonished. "All those refried beans! They'll go straight to my thighs."

"No, they won't." Justin spoke with great certainty. For as long as he'd known—would know—Megan, her weight hadn't varied by more than five pounds. He'd never heard that she'd turned into a blimp after they broke up, either. He lowered his voice. "I like your thighs."

She raised a dark eyebrow, as if to say, *You're a guy. If I let you get between them, of course you like them.* But the eyebrow came down. "You talk nice like that, maybe you'll get a chance to prove it. Maybe."

"Okay." Justin's plate was as empty as hers. Loading up on heavy Mexican food hadn't slowed him down when he was twenty-one. Now it felt like a bowling ball in his stomach. But he figured he'd manage. Figuring that, he left a bigger tip than he would have otherwise.

The waiter scooped it up. *"Gracias, señor."* He sounded unusually sincere.

Driving north up Canoga Avenue toward his place, Justin used a sentence that had the phrase "after we're married" in it.

Megan had been looking at the used-car lot across the street. Her head whipped around. "After we're what?" she said. "Not so fast, there."

For the very first time, Justin thought to wonder whether his younger self knew what he was doing when he took another year to get around to telling Megan he loved her. He-now had the advantage of hindsight; he knew he and Megan would walk down the aisle. But Megan didn't know it. Right this minute, she didn't sound delighted with the idea.

Worse, Justin couldn't explain that he knew, or how he knew. "I just thought—" he began.

Megan shook her head. Her dark hair flipped back and forth. She said, "No. You didn't think. You're starting your senior year this fall. I'm starting my junior year. We aren't ready to think about getting married yet, even if . . ." She shook her head again. "We aren't ready. What would we live on?"

"We'd manage." Justin didn't want to think about that *even if.* It had to be the start of something like, *even if I decide I want to marry you.* But Megan hadn't said all of it. Justin clung to that. He had nothing else to cling to.

"We'd manage?" Megan said. "Yeah, right. We'd go into debt

so deep, we'd never get out. I don't want to do that, not when I'm just starting. I didn't think you did, either."

He kept driving for a little while. Clichés had women eager for commitment and men fleeing from it as if from a skunk at a picnic. He'd gone and offered to commit, and Megan reacted as if he ought to be committed. What did that say about clichés? Probably not to pay much attention to them.

"Hey." Megan touched his arm. "I'm not mad, not for that. But I'm not ready, either. Don't push me, okay?"

"Okay." But Justin had to push. He knew it too damn well. He couldn't stay in 1999 very long. Things between Megan and him had to be solid before he left the scene and his younger self took over again. His younger self, he was convinced, could fuck up a wet dream, and damn well had fucked up what should have been a perfect, lifelong relationship.

He opened the window and clicked the security key into the lock. The heavy iron gate slid open. He drove in and parked the car. They both got out. Neither said much as they walked to his apartment.

Not too much later, in the dark quiet of the bedroom, Megan clutched the back of his head with both hands and cried out, "Ohhh, Justin!" loud enough to make him embarrassed to show his face to the neighbors—or make him a minor hero among them, depending. She lay back on the bed and said, "You drive me crazy when you do that."

"We aim to please." Did he sound smug? If he did, hadn't he earned the right?

Megan laughed. "Bull's-eye!" Her voice still sounded shaky.

He slid up to lie beside her, running his hands along her body as he did. *Strike while the iron is hot,* he thought. He felt pretty hot himself. He said, "And you don't want to talk about getting married yet?"

"I don't want to talk about anything right now," Megan said. "What I want to do is . . ." She did it. If Justin hadn't been a consenting adult, it would have amounted to criminal assault. As things were, he couldn't think of any stretch of time he'd enjoyed more.

"Jesus, I love you," he said when he was capable of coherent speech.

Megan kept straddling him—not that he wanted to escape. Her face was only a couple of inches above his. Now she leaned down and kissed him on the end of the nose. "I love this," she said, which wasn't the same thing at all.

He ran a hand along the smooth, sweat-slick curves of her back. "Well, then," he said, as if the two things were the same.

She laughed and shook her head. Her hair brushed back and forth across his face, full of the scent of her. Even though she kissed him again, she said, "But we can't do this all the time." At that precise moment, he softened and flopped out of her. She nodded, as if he'd proved her point. "See what I mean?"

Justin wished for his younger self's body. Had himself-at-twenty-one been there, he would have been hard at it again instead of wilting at the worst possible time. But he had to play the hand he'd been dealt. He said, "I know it's not the only reason to get married, but isn't it a nice one?" To show how nice it was, he slid his hand between her legs.

Megan let it stay there for a couple of seconds, but then twisted away. "I asked you not to push me about that, Justin," she said, all the good humor gone from her voice.

"Well, yeah, but—" he began.

"You didn't listen," she said. "People who get married have to, like, listen to each other, too, you know? You can't just screw all the time. You really can't. Look at my parents, for crying out loud."

"*My* parents are screwing all the time," Justin said.

"Yeah, but not with each other." Megan hesitated, then said, "I'm sorry."

"Why? It's true." Justin's younger self had been horrified at his parents' antics. If anything, that horror had got worse since. Up in 2018, he hadn't seen or even spoken to either one of them for years, and he didn't miss them, either.

Then he thought, *So Dad chases bimbos and Mom decided she wasn't straight after all. What you're doing here is a lot weirder than any of that.* But was it? All he wanted was a happy marriage, one like Megan's folks had, one that probably looked boring from the outside but not when you were in it.

Was that too much to ask? The way things were going, it was liable to be.

Megan said, "Don't get me wrong, Justin. I like you a lot. I wouldn't go to bed with you if I didn't. Maybe I even love you, if you want me to say that. But I don't know if I want to try and spend my whole life with you. And if you keep riding me twentyfour-seven about it, I'll decide I don't. Does that make any sense to you?"

Justin shook his head. All he heard was a clock ticking on his hopes. "If we've got a good thing going, we ought to take it as far as we can," he said. "Where will we find anything better?" He'd spent the rest of his life looking not for something better but for something close to as good. He hadn't found it.

"Goddammit, it's not a good thing if you won't listen to me. You don't want to notice that." Megan got up and went into the bathroom. When she came back, she started dressing. "Take me home, please."

"Shouldn't we talk some more?" Justin heard the panic in his own voice.

"No. Take me home." Megan sounded very sure. "Every time we talk lately, you dig the hole deeper for yourself. Like I said, Justin, I like you, but I don't think we'd better talk for a while. It's like you don't even hear me, like you don't even have to hear me. Like you're the grownup and I'm just a kid to you, and I don't like that a bit."

How seriously did a forty-year-old need to take a twenty-year-old? Unconsciously, Justin must have decided, *not very*. That looked to be wrong. "Honey, please wait," he said.

"It'll just get worse if I do," she answered. "Will you drive me, or shall I call my dad?"

He was in Dutch with her. He didn't want to get in Dutch with her folks, too. "I'll drive you," he said dully.

Even more than the drive back from the movie theater had, this one passed in tense silence. At last, as Justin turned onto her street, Megan broke it: "We've got our whole lives ahead of us, you know? The way you've been going lately, it's like you want everything nailed down tomorrow. That's not gonna happen. It can't happen. Neither one of us is ready for it."

"I am," Justin said.

"Well, I'm not," Megan told him as he stopped the car in front of her house. "And if you keep picking at it and picking at it, I'm never going to be. In fact . . ."

"In fact, what?"

"Never mind," she said. "Whatever." Before he could ask her again, she got out and hurried up the walk toward the house. He waved to her. He blew her a kiss. She didn't look back to see the wave or the kiss. She just opened the door and went inside. Justin sat for a couple of minutes, staring at the house. Then, biting his lip, he drove home.

Over the next three days, he called Megan a dozen times. Every time, he got the answering machine or one of her parents. They kept telling him she wasn't home. At last, fed up, he burst out, "She doesn't want to talk to me!"

Her father would have failed as White House press secretary. All he said was, "Well, if she doesn't, you can't make her, you know"—hardly a ringing denial.

But that's what I came back for! Justin wanted to scream it. That wouldn't have done any good. He knew as much. He still wanted to scream it. He'd come back to make things better, and what had he done? Made them worse.

On the fourth evening, the telephone rang as he walked in the door from his shift at CompUSA. His heart sank as he hurried into the bedroom. His younger self would be flipping out if he'd tried to call Megan and discovered she wouldn't talk to him. He'd told his younger self not to do that, but how reliable was himself-at-twenty-one? Not very. "Hello?"

"Hello, Justin." It wasn't his younger self. It was Megan.

"Hi!" He didn't know whether to be exulted or terrified. Not knowing, he ended up both at once. "How are you?"

"I'm okay." She paused. Terror swamped exultation. When she went on, she said, "I've been talking with my folks the last few days."

That didn't sound good. Trying to pretend he didn't know how bad it sounded, he asked, "And?" The word hung in the air.

Megan paused again. At last, she said, "We—I've—decided I'd better not see you any more. I'm sorry, Justin, but that's how things are."

"They're making you say that!" If Justin blamed Megan's parents, he wouldn't have to blame anyone else: himself, for instance.

But she said, "No, they aren't. My mom, especially, thought I ought to give you another chance. But I've given you a couple chances already, and you don't know what to do with them. Things got way too intense way too fast, and I'm not ready for that. I don't want to deal with it, and I don't have to deal with it, and I'm not going to deal with it, and that's that. Like I said, I'm sorry and everything, but I can't."

"I don't believe this," he muttered. Refusing to believe it remained easier than blaming himself. "What about the sex?"

"It was great," Megan said at once. "I won't tell you any lies. If you make other girls feel the way you make—*made*—me feel, you won't have any trouble finding somebody else. I hope you do."

Christ, Justin thought. *She's letting me down easy. She's trying to, anyhow, but she's only twenty and she's not very good at it.* He didn't want to be let down easy, or at all. He said, "What about you?"

"I'll keep looking. If you can do it for me, probably other fellows can, too," Megan answered with devastating pragmatism. Half to herself, she added, "Maybe I need to date older guys, or something, if I can find some who aren't too bossy."

That would have been funny, if only it were funny. Justin whispered, "But I love you. I've always loved you." He'd loved her for about as long as she'd been alive here in 1999. What did he have to show for it? Getting shot down in flames not once but twice.

"Don't make this harder than it has to be. Please?" Megan said. "And don't call here any more, okay? You're not going to change my mind. If I decide I was wrong, I'll call your place, all right? Goodbye, Justin." She hung up without giving him a chance to answer.

Don't call us. We'll call you. Everybody knew what that meant. It meant what she'd been telling him anyhow: so long. He didn't want to hang up. Finally, after more than a minute of dial tone, he did.

"What do I do now?" he asked himself, or possibly God. God might have known. Justin had no clue.

He thought about calling his younger self and letting him know things had gone wrong: he thought about it for maybe three seconds, then dropped the idea like a live grenade. Himself-at-twenty-one would want to slaughter him. He metaphorically felt like dying, but not for real.

Why not? he wondered. *What will it be like when you head back to your own time? You wanted to change the past. Well, you've done that. You've screwed it up bigtime. What kind of memories will you have when you come back to that men's room in 2018? Not memories of being married to Megan for a while and then having things go sour, that's for sure. You don't even get those. It'll be nineteen years of nothing—a long, lonely, empty stretch.*

He lay down on the bed and wept. He hadn't done that since Megan told him she was leaving him. *Since the last time Megan told me she was leaving me,* he thought. Hardly noticing he'd done it, he fell asleep.

When the phone rang a couple of hours later, Justin had trouble remembering when he was and how old he was supposed to be. The old-fashioned computer on the desk told him everything he needed to know. Grimacing, he picked up the telephone. "Hello?"

"You son of a bitch." His younger self didn't bellow the words. Instead, they were deadly cold. "You goddamn stupid, stinking, know-it-all son of a bitch."

Since Justin was calling himself the same things, he had trouble getting angry when his younger self cursed him. "I'm sorry," he said. "I tried to—"

He might as well have kept quiet. His younger self rode over him, saying, "I just tried calling Megan. She said she didn't want to talk to me. She said she never wanted to talk to me again. She said she'd told me she never wanted to talk to me again, so what was I doing on the phone right after she told me that? Then she hung up on me."

"I'm sorry," Justin repeated. "I—"

"Sorry?" This time, his younger self did bellow. "You think you're sorry now? You don't know what sorry is, but you will. I'm gonna beat the living shit out of you, dude. Fuck up my life, will you? You think you can get away with that, you're full of—" He slammed down the phone.

Justin had never been much for fisticuffs, not at twenty-one and not at forty, either. But his younger self was so furious now, who could guess what he'd do? What with rage and what had to be a severe case of testosterone poisoning, he was liable to mean what he'd said. Justin knew to the day how many years he was giving away.

He also knew his younger self had keys to this apartment. If himself-at-twenty-one showed up here in fifteen minutes, did he want to meet him?

That led to a different question: did he want to be here in 1999 at all any more? All he'd done was the opposite of what he'd wanted. Why hang around, then? Instead of waiting to slide back along the superstring into 2018 in a few more weeks, wasn't it better to cut the string and go back to his own time, to try to pick up the pieces of whatever life would be left to him after he'd botched things here?

Justin booted up the PowerBook from his own time. The suitcases he'd brought to 1999 were at the other apartment. So was a lot of the cash. His mouth twisted. He didn't think he could ask his younger self to return it.

As he slipped the VR mask onto his head, he hoped he'd done his homework right, and that he would return to the men's room from which he'd left 2018. That was what his calculations showed, but how good were they? Only real experience would tell. If this building still stood then and he materialized in somebody's bedroom, he'd have more explaining to do than he really wanted.

He also wondered what memories he'd have when he got back to his former point on the time line. The old ones, as if he hadn't made the trip? The old ones, plus his memories of seeing 1999 while forty? New ones, stemming from the changes he'd made back here? Some of each? He'd find out.

From its initial perfect blankness, the VR mask view shifted to show the room in which he now sat, PowerBook on his lap. "Run program superstrings–slash–virtual reality–slash–not so virtual–slash–reverse," he said. The view began to shift. Part of that was good old-fashioned morphing software, so what he saw in the helmet looked less and less like this bedroom and more and more like the restroom that was his destination. And part was the superstring program, pulling him from one point on the string to the other. He hoped part of it was the superstring software, anyhow. If the program didn't run backwards, he'd have to deal with his angry younger self, and he wasn't up to that physically or mentally.

On the VR screen, the men's room at the Superstrings building had completely replaced the bedroom of his younger self's apartment. "Program superstrings–slash–virtual reality–slash–not so virtual reality–slash–reverse is done," the PowerBook said. Justin kept waiting. If he took off the helmet and found himself still in that bedroom . . .

When he nerved himself to shed the mask, he let out a long, loud sigh of relief: what he saw without it matched what he'd seen with it. His next worry—his mind coughed them up in carload lots—was that he'd gone to the right building, but in 1999, not 2018.

His first step out of the men's room reassured him. The carpeting was its old familiar color, not the jarring one from 1999. He looked at the VR mask and PowerBook he was carrying. He wouldn't need them any more today, and he didn't feel like explaining to Sean and Garth and everybody else why he'd brought them. He headed downstairs again, to stow them in the trunk of his car.

As he walked through the lobby toward the front door, the security guard opened it for him. "Forget something, sir?" the aging Boomer asked.

"Just want to put this stuff back, Bill." Justin held up the laptop and mask. Nodding, the guard stepped aside.

Justin was halfway across the lot before he realized the car toward which he'd aimed himself wasn't the one he'd parked there before going back to 1999. It was in the same space, but it wasn't the same car. He'd driven here in an aging Ford, not a top-of-the-line Volvo.

He looked around the lot. No Ford. No cars but the Volvo and Bill's ancient, wheezing Hyundai. If he hadn't got here in the Volvo, how had he come? Of itself, his hand slipped into his trouser pocket and came out with a key ring. The old iron ring and the worn leather fob on it were familiar; he'd had that key ring a long time. The keys . . .

One was a Volvo key. He tried it in the trunk. It turned in the lock. Smoothly, almost silently, the lid opened. Justin put the computer and the VR mask in the trunk, closed it, and slid the keys back into his pants pocket.

They weren't the pants he'd worn when he left his apartment that morning: instead of 1990s-style baggy jeans, they were slacks, a lightweight wool blend. His shoes had changed, too, and he was wearing a nice polo shirt, not a Dilbert T-shirt.

He ran his left hand over the top of his head. His hair was longer, the buzz cut gone. He started to wonder if he was really himself. His memories of what he'd been before he went back and changed his own past warred with the ones that had sprung from the change. He shook his head; his brain felt overcrowded.

He started back toward the Superstrings building, but wasn't ready to go in there again quite yet. He needed to sit down somewhere quiet for a while and straighten things out inside his own mind.

When he looked down the street, he grinned. There was the

Denny's where he'd had breakfast right after going back to 1999. It hadn't changed much in the years since. He sauntered over. He was still on his own time.

"Toast and coffee," he told the middle-aged, bored-looking Hispanic waitress.

"White, rye, or whole wheat?"

"Wheat," he answered.

"Yes, sir," she said. She brought them back with amazing speed. He smeared the toast with grape jelly, let her refill his cup two or three times, and then, still bemused but caffeinated, headed back to Superstrings, Ltd.

More cars in the lot now, and still more pulling in as he walked up. There was Garth O'Connell's garish green Chevy. Justin waved. "Morning, Garth. How you doing?"

O'Connell smiled. "Not too bad. How are you, Mr. Kloster?"

"Could be worse," Justin allowed. Part of him remembered Garth being on a first-name basis with him. The other part, the increasingly dominant part, insisted that had never happened.

They went inside and upstairs together, talking business. Garth headed off into the maze of cubicles that made up most of the second floor. Justin started to follow him, but his feet didn't want to go that way. He let them take him where they would. They had a better idea of where exactly he worked than his conscious mind did right now.

His secretary was already busy at the computer in the anteroom of his office. She nodded. "Good morning, Mr. Kloster."

"Good morning, Brittany," he said. Had he ever seen her in all his life? If he hadn't, how did he know her name? How did he know she'd worked for him the past three years?

He went into the office—*his* office—and closed the door. Again, he had that momentary disorientation, as if he'd never been here before. But of course he had. If the founder and president of Superstrings, Ltd., didn't deserve the fanciest office in the building, who did?

The part of him that had traveled back through time still felt confused. Not the rest, the part that had been influenced by his trip back to 1999. Knowing such things were possible—and having the seed money his time-traveling self left behind—wouldn't he naturally have started getting involved in this area as soon as he could? Sure he would have—he damn well had. On the wall of the office, framed, hung, not the first dollar he'd ever made, but a quarter dated 2012. He'd had it for nineteen years.

He sat down at his desk. The view out the window wasn't much, but it beat the fuzzy, grayish-tan wall of a cubicle. On the desk stood a framed picture of a smiling blond woman and two boys he'd never seen before—his sons, Saul and Lije. When he stopped and thought, it all came back to him, just as if he'd really lived it. As a matter of fact, he had. *He'd* never got over Megan. His younger self, who'd never married her, was a different story—from the way things looked, a better story.

Why, he even knew how the image had been ever so slightly edited. She could be vain about the silliest things. His phone buzzed. He picked it up. "Yes, Brittany?"

"Your wife's on the line, Mr. Kloster," his secretary said. "Something she wants you to get on the way home."

"Sure, put her through." Justin was still chuckling when his wife came on the line. "Okay, what do you need at the store, Lindsey?"

Must and Shall

Most alternate-history stories about the Civil War have to do with a Confederate victory. I've done some of that sort myself—*The Guns of the South* and *How Few Remain* look at two different ways the South might have won, and create two very different worlds. What's less immediately obvious is that the North also had different ways of winning the war, ways that would have produced different aftermaths. "Must and Shall" looks at one of the less pleasant of these.

12 July 1864—Fort Stevens, North of Washington, D.C.

General Horatio Wright stood up on the earthen parapet to watch the men of the Sixth Corps, hastily recalled from Petersburg, drive Jubal Early's Confederates away from the capital of the United States. Down below the parapet, a tall, thin man in black frock coat and stovepipe hat asked, "How do we fare, General?"

"Splendidly." Wright's voice was full of relief. Had Early chosen to attack the line of forts around Washington the day before, he'd have faced only militiamen and clerks with muskets, and might well have broken through to the city. But Early had been late, and now the veterans from the Sixth Corps were pushing his troopers back. Washington City was surely saved. Perhaps because he was so relieved, Wright said, "Would you care to come up with me and see how we drive them?"

"I should like that very much, thank you," Abraham Lincoln said, and climbed the ladder to stand beside him.

Never in his wildest nightmares had Wright imagined the President accepting. Lincoln had peered over the parapet several times already, and drawn fire from the Confederates. They were surely too far from Fort Stevens to recognize him, but with his height and the hat he made a fine target.

Not far away, a man was wounded and fell back with a cry. General Wright interposed his body between President Lincoln and the Confederates. Lincoln spoiled that by stepping away from him. "Mr. President, I really must insist that you retire to a position of safety," Wright said. "This is no place for you; you must step down at once!"

Lincoln took no notice of him, but continued to watch the fighting north of the fort. A captain behind the parapet, perhaps not recognizing his commander-in-chief, shouted, "Get down, you damn fool, before you get shot!"

When Lincoln did not move, Wright said, "If you do not get down, sir, I shall summon a body of soldiers to remove you by force." He gulped at his own temerity in threatening the President of the United States.

Lincoln seemed more amused than anything else. He started to turn away, to walk back toward the ladder. Instead, after half a step, he crumpled bonelessly. Wright had thought of nightmares before. Now one came to life in front of his horrified eyes. Careless of his own safety, he crouched by the President, whose blood poured from a massive head wound into the muddy dirt atop the parapet. Lincoln's face wore an expression of mild surprise. His chest hitched a couple of times, then was still.

The captain who'd shouted at Lincoln to get down mounted to the parapet. His eyes widened. "Dear God," he groaned. "It is the President."

Wright thought he recognized him. "You're Holmes, aren't you?" he said. Somehow it was comforting to know the man you were addressing when the world seemed to crumble around you.

"Yes, sir, Oliver W. Holmes, 20th Massachusetts," the young captain answered.

"Well, Captain Holmes, fetch a physician here at once,"

Wright said. Holmes nodded and hurried away. Wright wondered at his industry—surely he could see Lincoln was dead. Who, then, was the more foolish, himself for sending Holmes away, or the captain for going?

21 July 1864—Washington, D.C.

From the hastily erected wooden rostrum on the East Portico of the Capitol, Hannibal Hamlin stared out at the crowd waiting for him to deliver his inaugural address. The rostrum was draped with black, as was the Capitol, as had been the route his carriage took to reach it. Many of the faces in the crowd were still stunned, disbelieving. The United States had never lost a President to a bullet, not in the eighty-eight years since the nation freed itself from British rule.

In the front row of dignitaries, Senator Andrew Johnson of Tennessee glared up at Hamlin. He had displaced the man from Maine on Lincoln's reelection ticket; had this dreadful event taken place a year later (assuming Lincoln's triumph), he now would be President. But no time for might-have-beens.

Hamlin had been polishing his speech since the telegram announcing Lincoln's death reached him up in Bangor, where, feeling useless and rejected, he had withdrawn after failing of renomination for the Vice Presidency. Now, though, his country needed him once more. He squared his broad shoulders, ready to bear up under the great burden so suddenly thrust upon him.

"Stand fast!" he cried. "That has ever been my watchword, and at no time in all the history of our great and glorious republic has our heeding it been more urgent. Abraham Lincoln's body may lie in the grave, but we shall go marching on—to victory!"

Applause rose from the crowd at the allusion to "John Brown's Body"—and not just from the crowd, but also from the soldiers posted on the roof of the Capitol and at intervals around the building to keep the accursed rebels from murdering two Presidents, not just one. Hamlin went on, "The responsibility for this great war, in which our leader gave his last full measure of devotion, lies solely at the feet of the Southern slaveocrats who conspired to take their states out of our grand Union for their own evil ends. I promise you, my friends—Abraham Lincoln shall be avenged, and those who caused his death punished in full."

More applause, not least from the Republican Senators who proudly called themselves Radical: from Thaddeus Stevens of Pennsylvania, Benjamin Wade of Ohio, Zachariah Chandler of Michigan, and bespectacled John Andrew of Massachusetts. Hamlin had been counted among their number when he sat in the Senate before assuming the duties, such as they were, of the Vice President.

"Henceforward," Hamlin declared, "I say this: let us use every means recognized by the Laws of War which God has put in our hands to crush out the wickedest rebellion the world has ever witnessed. This conflict is become a radical revolution—yes, gentlemen, I openly employ the word, and, what is more, I revel in it—involving the desolation of the South as well as the emancipation of the bondsmen it vilely keeps in chains."

The cheers grew louder still. Lincoln had been more conciliatory, but what had conciliation got him? Only a coffin and a funeral and a grieving nation ready, no eager, for harsher measures.

"They have sowed the wind; let them reap the whirlwind. We are in earnest now, and have awakened to the stern duty upon us. Let that duty be disregarded or haltingly or halfway performed, and God only in His wisdom can know what will be the end. This lawless monster of a Political Slave Power shall forevermore be shorn of its power to ruin a government it no longer has the strength to rule.

"The rebels proudly proclaim they have left the Union. Very well: we shall take them at their word and, once having gained the victory Providence will surely grant us, we shall treat their lands as they deserve—not as the states they no longer desire to be, but as conquered provinces, won by our sword. I say we shall hang Jefferson Davis, and hang Robert E. Lee, and hang Joe Johnston, yes, hang them higher than Haman, and the other *rebel generals and colonels and governors and members of their false Congress. The living God is merciful, true, but He is also just and vengeful, and we, the people of the United States, we shall be His instrument in advancing the right."*

Now great waves of cheering, led by grim Thaddeus Stevens himself, washed over Hamlin. The fierce sound reminded him of wolves baying in the backwoods of Maine. He stood tall atop the rostrum. He would lead these wolves, and with them pull the rebel Confederacy down in ruin.

11 August 1942—New Orleans, Louisiana

Air brakes chuffing, the Illinois Central train pulled to a stop at Union Station on Rampart Street. "New Orleans!" the conductor bawled unnecessarily. "All out for New Orleans!"

Along with the rest of the people in the car, Neil Michaels filed toward the exit. He was a middle-sized man in his late thirties, most of his dark blond hair covered by a snap-brim fedora. The round, thick, gold-framed spectacles he wore helped give him the mild appearance of an accountant.

As soon as he stepped from the air-conditioned comfort of the railroad car out into the steamy heat of a New Orleans summer, those glasses steamed up. Shaking his head in bemusement, Michaels drew a handkerchief from his trouser pocket and wiped away the moisture.

He got his bags and headed for the cab stand, passing on the way a horde of men and boys hawking newspapers and rank upon rank of shoeshine stands. A fat Negro man sat on one of those, gold watch chain running from one pocket of his vest to the other. At his feet, an Irish-looking fellow plied the rag until his customer's black oxfords gleamed.

"There y'are, sir," the shoeshine man said, his half-Brooklyn, half-Southern accent testifying he was a New Orleans native. The Negro looked down at his shoes, nodded, and, with an air of great magnanimity, flipped the shoeshine man a dime. "Oh, thank you very much, sir," the fellow exclaimed. The insincere servility in his voice grated on Michaels' ears.

More paperboys cried their trade outside the station. Michaels bought a *Times-Picayune* to read while he waited in line for a taxi. The war news wasn't good. The Germans were still pushing east in Russia and sinking ship after ship off the American coast. In the South Pacific, Americans and Japanese were slugging away at each other, and God only knew how that would turn out.

Across the street from Union Station, somebody had painted a message: YANKS OUT! Michaels sighed. He'd seen that slogan painted on barns and bridges and embankments ever since his train crossed into Tennessee—and, now that he thought about it, in Kentucky as well, though Kentucky had stayed with the Union during the Great Rebellion.

When he got to the front of the line at the cab stand, a hack man heaved his bags into the trunk of an Oldsmobile and said, "Where to, sir?"

"The New Orleans Hotel, on Canal Street," Michaels answered.

The cabbie touched the brim of his cap. "Yes, sir," he said, his voice suddenly empty. He opened the back door for Michaels, slammed it shut after him, then climbed into the cab himself. It took off with a grinding of gears that said the transmission had seen better days.

On the short ride to the hotel, Michaels counted five more scrawls of YANKS OUT, along with a couple of patches of white-wash that probably masked others. Servicemen on the street walked along in groups of at least four; several corners sported squads of soldiers in full combat gear, including, in one case, a machine-gun nest built of sandbags. "Nice quiet little town," Michaels remarked.

"Isn't it?" the cabbie answered, deadpan. He hesitated, his jaw working as if he were chewing his cud. After a moment, he decided to go on: "Mister, with an accent like yours, you want to be careful where you let people hear it. For a damnyankee, you don't seem like a bad fellow, an' I wouldn't want nothin' to happen to you."

"Thanks. I'll bear that in mind," Michaels said. He wished the Bureau had sent somebody who could put on a convincing drawl. Of course the last man the FBS had sent ended up floating in the Mississippi, so evidently his drawl hadn't been convincing enough.

The cab wheezed to a stop in front of the New Orleans Hotel. "That'll be forty cents, sir," the driver said.

Michaels reached into his trouser pocket, pulled out a half-dollar. "Here you go. I don't need any change."

"That's right kind of you, sir, but—you wouldn't happen to have two quarters instead?" the cabbie said. He handed the big silver coin back to his passenger.

"What's wrong with it?" Michaels demanded, though he thought he knew the answer. "It's legal tender of the United States of America."

"Yes, sir, reckon it is, but there's no place hereabouts I'd care to try and spend it, even so," the driver answered, "not with *his* picture on it." The obverse of the fifty-cent piece bore an image of the martyred Lincoln, the reverse a Negro with his manacles broken and the legend SIC SEMPER TYRANNIS. Michaels had known it was an unpopular coin with white men in the South, but he hadn't realized how unpopular it was.

He got out of the cab, rummaged in his pocket, and came up with a quarter and a couple of dimes. The cabbie didn't object to Washington's profile, or to that of the god Mercury. He also didn't object to seeing his tip cut in half. That told Michaels all he needed to know about how much the half-dollar was hated.

Lazily spinning ceiling fans inside the hotel lobby stirred the air without doing much to cool it. The colored clerk behind the front desk smiled to hear Michaels' accent. "Yes, sir, we do have your reservation," she said after shuffling through papers. By the way she talked, she'd been educated up in the Loyal States herself. She handed him a brass key. "That's room 429, sir. Three dollars and twenty-five cents a night."

"Very good," Michaels said. The clerk clanged the bell on the front desk. A white bellboy in a pillbox hat and uniform that made him look like a Philip Morris advertisement picked up Michaels' bags and carried them to the elevator.

When they got to room 429, Michaels opened the door. The bellboy put down the bags inside the room and stood waiting for his tip. By way of experiment, Michaels gave him the fifty-cent piece the cabbie had rejected. The bellboy took the coin and put it in his pocket. His lips shaped a silent word. Michaels thought it was *damnyankee*, but he wasn't quite sure. The bellboy left in a hurry.

A couple of hours later, Michaels went downstairs to supper. Something shiny was lying on the carpet in the hall. He looked down at the half-dollar he'd given the bellboy. It had lain here in plain sight while people walked back and forth; he'd heard them. Nobody had taken it. Thoughtfully, he picked it up and stuck it in his pocket.

A walk through the French Quarter made fears about New Orleans seem foolish. Jazz blasted out of every other doorway. Neon signs pulsed above gin mills. Spasm bands, some white, some Negro, played on streetcorners. No one paid attention to blackout regulations—that held true North and South. Clog-dancers shuffled, overturned caps beside them inviting coins. Streetwalkers in tawdry finery swung their hips and flashed knowing smiles.

Neil Michaels moved through the crowds of soldiers and sailors and gawking civilians like a halfback evading tacklers and heading downfield. He glanced at his watch, partly to check the time and partly to make sure nobody had stolen it. Half past eleven. Didn't this place ever slow down? Maybe not.

He turned right off Royal Street onto St. Peter and walked southeast toward the Mississippi and Jackson Square. The din of the Vieux Carré faded behind him. He strode past the Cabildo, the old Spanish building of stuccoed brick that now housed the Louisiana State Museum, including a fine collection of artifacts and documents on the career of the first military governor of New Orleans, Benjamin Butler. Johnny Rebs kept threatening to dynamite the Cabildo, but it hadn't happened yet.

Two great bronze statues dominated Jackson Square. One showed the square's namesake on horseback. The other, even taller, faced that equestrian statue. Michaels thought Ben Butler's bald head and rotund, sagging physique less than ideal for being immortalized in bronze, but no one had asked his opinion.

He strolled down the paved lane in the formal garden toward the statue of Jackson. Lights were dimmer here in the square, but not too dim to keep Michaels from reading the words Butler had had carved into the pedestal of the statue: THE UNION MUST AND SHALL BE PRESERVED, an adaptation of Jackson's famous toast, "Our Federal Union, it must be preserved."

Michaels' mouth stretched out in a thin hard line that was not a smile. By force and fear, with cannon and noose, bayonet and prison term, the United States Army had preserved the Union. And now, more than three-quarters of a century after the collapse of the Great Rebellion, U.S. forces still occupied the states of the rebel Confederacy, still skirmished in hills and forests and sometimes city streets against men who put on gray shirts and yowled like catamounts when they fought. Hatred bred hatred, reprisal bred reprisal, and so it went on and on. He sometimes wondered if the Union wouldn't have done better to let the Johnny Rebs get the hell out, if that was what they'd wanted so badly.

He'd never spoken that thought aloud; it wasn't one he could share. Too late to worry about such things anyhow, generations too late. He had to deal with the consequences of what vengeful Hamlin and his like-minded successors had done.

The man he was supposed to meet would be waiting behind Butler's statue. Michaels was slightly surprised the statue had no guards around it; the Johnny Rebs had blown it up in the 1880s and again in the 1920s. If New Orleans today was reconciled to rule from Washington, it concealed the fact very well.

Michaels ducked around into the darkness behind the statue. "Four score and seven," he whispered, the recognition signal he'd been given.

Someone should have answered, "New birth of freedom." No one said anything. As his eyes adapted to the darkness, he made out a body sprawled in the narrow space between the base of the statue and the shrubbery that bordered Jackson Square. He stooped beside it. If this was the man he was supposed to meet, the fellow would never give him a recognition signal, not till Judgment Day. His throat had been cut.

Running feet on the walkways of the square, flashlight beams probing like spears. One of them found Michaels. He threw up an arm against the blinding glare. A hard Northern voice shouted, "Come out of there right now, you damned murdering Reb, or you'll never get a second chance!"

Michaels raised his hands high in surrender and came out.

Outside Antoine's, the rain came down in buckets. Inside, with oysters Rockefeller and a whiskey and soda in front of him and the prospect of an excellent lunch ahead, Neil Michaels was willing to forgive the weather.

He was less inclined to forgive the soldiers from the night before. Stubbing out his Camel, he said in a low but furious voice, "Those great thundering galoots couldn't have done a better job of blowing my cover if they'd rehearsed for six weeks, God damn them."

His companion, a dark, lanky man named Morrie Harris, sipped his own drink and said, "It may even work out for the best. Anybody the MPs arrest is going to look good to the Johnny Rebs around here." His New York accent seemed less out of place in New Orleans than Michaels' flat, Midwestern tones.

Michaels started to answer, then shut up as the waiter came over and asked, "You gentlemen are ready to order?"

"Let me have the *pompano en papillote*," Harris said. "You can't get it any better than here."

The waiter wrote down the order, looked a question at Michaels. He said, "I'll take the *poulet chanteclair*." The waiter nodded, scribbled, and went away.

Glancing around to make sure no one else was paying undue attention to him or his conversation, Michaels resumed: "Yeah, that may be true now. But Ducange is dead now. What if those stupid dogfaces had busted in on us while we were dickering? That would have queered the deal for sure, and it might have got me shot." As it hadn't the night before, his smile did not reach his eyes. "I'm fond of my neck. It's the only one I've got."

"Even without Ducange, we've still got to get a line on the underground," Harris said. "Those weapons are somewhere. We'd better find 'em before the whole city goes up." He rolled his eyes. "The whole city, hell! If what we've been hearing is true, the Nazis have shipped enough guns and God knows what all else into New Orleans to touch off four or five states. And wouldn't that do wonders for the war effort?" He slapped on irony with a heavy trowel.

"God damn the Germans," Michaels said, still quietly but with savage venom. "They played this game during the last war, too. But you're right. If what we've heard is the straight goods, the blowup they have in mind will make the Thanksgiving Revolt look like a kiss on the cheek."

"It shouldn't be this way," Harris said, scowling. "We've got more GIs and swabbies in New Orleans than you can shake a stick at, and none of 'em worth a damn when it comes to tracking this crap down. Nope, for that they need the FBS, no matter how understaffed we are."

The waiter came then. Michaels dug into the chicken marinated in red wine. It was as good as it was supposed to be. Morrie Harris made ecstatic noises about the sauce on his pompano.

After a while, Michaels said, "The longer we try, the harder it gets for us to keep things under control down here. One of these days—"

"It'll all go up," Harris said matter-of-factly. "Yeah, but not now. Now is what we gotta worry about. We're fighting a civil war here, we ain't gonna have much luck with the Germans and the Japs. That's what Hitler has in mind."

"Maybe Hamlin and Stevens should have done something different—God knows what—back then. It might have kept us out of—this," Michaels said. He knew that was heresy for an FBS man, but everything that had happened to him since he got to New Orleans left him depressed with the state of things as they were.

"What were they supposed to do?" Harris snapped.

"I already said I didn't know," Michaels answered, wishing he'd kept his mouth shut. What did the posters say?—LOOSE LIPS SINK SHIPS. His loose lips were liable to sink him.

Sure enough, Morrie Harris went on as if he hadn't spoken: "The Johnnies rebelled, killed a few hundred thousand American boys, and shot a President dead. What should we do, give 'em a nice pat on the back? We beat 'em and we made 'em pay. Far as I can see, they deserved it."

"Yeah, and they've been making us pay ever since." Michaels raised a weary hand. "The hell with it. Like you said, now is what we've got to worry about. But with Ducange dead, what sort of channels do we have into the Rebel underground?"

Morrie Harris' mouth twisted, as if he'd bitten down on something rotten. "No good ones that I know of. We've relied too much on the Negroes down here over the years. It's made the whites trust us even less than they would have otherwise. Maybe, though, just maybe, Ducange talked to somebody before he got killed, and that somebody will try to get hold of you."

"So what do you want me to do, then? Hang around my hotel room hoping the phone rings, like a girl waiting to see if a boy will call? Hell of a way to spend my time in romantic New Orleans."

"Listen, the kind of romance you can get here, you'll flunk a shortarm inspection three days later," Harris answered, chasing the last bits of pompano around his plate. "They'll take a damnyankee's money, but they'll skin you every chance they get. They must be laughing their asses off at the fortune they're making off our boys in uniform."

"Sometimes they won't even take your money." Michaels told of the trouble he'd had unloading the Lincoln half-dollar.

"Yeah, I've seen that," Harris said. "If they want to cut off their nose to spite their face, by me it's all right." He set a five and a couple of singles on the table. "This one's on me. Whatever else you say about this damn town, the food is hellacious, no two ways about it."

"No arguments." Michaels got up with Harris. They went out of Antoine's separately, a couple of minutes apart. As he walked back to the New Orleans Hotel, Michaels kept checking to make sure nobody was following him. He didn't spot anyone, but he didn't know how much that proved. If anybody wanted to put multiple tails on him, he wouldn't twig, not in crowded streets like these.

The crowds got worse when a funeral procession tied up traffic on Rampart Street. Two black horses pulled the hearse; their driver was a skinny, sleepy-looking white man who looked grotesquely out of place in top hat and tails. More coaches and buggies followed, and a couple of cars as well. "All right, let's get it moving!" an MP shouted when the procession finally passed.

"They keep us here any longer, we all go in the ovens from old age," a local said, and several other people laughed as they crossed the street. Michaels wanted to ask what the ovens were, but kept quiet since he exposed himself as one of the hated occupiers every time he opened his mouth.

When he got back to the hotel, he stopped at the front desk to ask if he had any messages. The clerk there today was a Negro man in a sharp suit and tie, with a brass name badge on his right lapel that read THADDEUS JENKINS. He checked and came back shaking his head. "Rest assured, sir, we shall make sure you receive any that do come in," he said—a Northern accent bothered him not in the least.

"Thank you very much, Mr. Jenkins," Michaels said.

"Our pleasure to serve you, sir," the clerk replied. "Anything we can do to make your stay more pleasant, you have but to ask."

"You're very kind," Michaels said. Jenkins had reason to be kind to Northerners. The power of the federal government maintained Negroes at the top of the heap in the old Confederacy. With the Sixteenth Amendment disenfranchising most Rebel soldiers and their descendants, blacks had a comfortable majority among those eligible to vote—and used it, unsurprisingly, in their own interest.

Michaels mused on that as he walked to the elevator. The operator, a white man, tipped his cap with more of the insincere obsequiousness Michaels had already noted. He wondered how the fellow liked taking orders from a man whose ancestors his great-grandfather might have owned. Actually, he didn't need to wonder. The voting South was as reliably Republican as could be, for the blacks had no illusions about how long their power would last if the Sixteenth were ever to be discarded.

Suddenly curious, he asked the elevator man, "Why don't I see 'Repeal the Sixteenth' written on walls along with 'Yanks Out'?"

The man measured him with his eyes—measured him for a coffin, if his expression meant anything. At last, as if speaking to a moron, he answered, "You don't see that on account of askin' you to repeal it'd mean you damnyankees got some kind o' business bein' down here and lordin' it over us in the first place. And you *ain't*."

So there, Michaels thought. The rest of the ride passed in silence.

With a soft whir, the ceiling fan stirred the air in his room. That improved things, but only slightly. He looked out the window. Ferns had sprouted from the mortar between bricks of the building across the street. Even without the rain—which had now let up—it was plenty humid enough for the plants to flourish.

Sitting around waiting for the phone to ring gave Michaels plenty of time to watch the ferns. As Morrie Harris had instructed, he spent most of his time in his room. He sallied forth mostly to eat. Not even the resolute hostility of most of white New Orleans put a damper on the food.

He ate boiled beef at Maylié's, crab meat *au gratin* at Galatoire's, crayfish bisque at La Louisiane, *langouste* Sarah Bernhardt at Arnaud's, and, for variety, pig knuckles and sauerkraut at Kolb's. When he didn't feel like traveling, he ate at the hotel's own excellent restaurant. He began to fancy his trousers and collars were getting tighter than they had been before he came South.

One night, he woke to the sound of rifle fire not far away. Panic shot through him, panic and shame. Had the uprising he'd come here to check broken out? How would that look on his

FBS personnel record? Then he realized that if the uprising had broken out, any damnyankee the Johnnies caught was likely to end up too dead to worry about what his personnel record looked like.

After about fifteen minutes, the gunfire petered out. Michaels took a couple of hours falling asleep again, though. He went from one radio station to another the next morning, and checked the afternoon newspapers, too. No one said a word about the firefight. Had anybody tried, prosecutors armed with the Sedition Act would have landed on him like a ton of bricks.

Back in the Loyal States, they smugly said the Sedition Act kept the lid on things down South. Michaels had believed it, too. Now he was getting a feeling for how much pressure pushed against that lid. When it blew, if it blew . . .

A little past eleven the next night, the phone rang. He jumped, then ran to it. "Hello?" he said sharply.

The voice on the other end was so muffled, he wasn't sure whether it belonged to a man or a woman. It said, "Be at the Original Absinthe House for the three a.m. show." The line went dead.

Michaels let out a martyred sigh. "The three a.m. show," he muttered, wondering why conspirators couldn't keep civilized hours like anyone else. He went down to the restaurant and had a couple of cups of strong coffee laced with brandy. Thus fortified, he headed out into the steaming night.

He soon concluded New Orleans' idea of civilized hours had nothing to do with those kept by the rest of the world, or possibly that New Orleans defined civilization as unending revelry. The French Quarter was as packed as it had been when he went through it toward Jackson Square, though that had been in the relatively early evening, close to civilized even by Midwestern standards.

The Original Absinthe House, a shabby two-story building with an iron railing around the balcony to the second floor, stood on the corner of Bourbon and Bienville. Each of the four doors leading in had a semicircular window above it. Alongside one of the doors, someone had scrawled, *Absinthe makes the heart grow fonder*. Michaels thought that a distinct improvement on *Yanks Out!* You weren't supposed to be able to get real absinthe any more, but in the Vieux Carré nothing would have surprised him.

He didn't want absinthe, anyway. He didn't particularly want the whiskey and soda he ordered, either, but you couldn't go into a place like this without doing some drinking. The booze was over-priced and not very good. The mysterious voice on the telephone hadn't told him there was a five-buck charge to go up to the sec-ond story and watch the floor show. Assuming he got out of here alive, he'd have a devil of a time justifying that on his expense ac-count. And if the call had been a Johnny Reb setup, were they try-ing to kill him or just to bilk him out of money for the cause?

Michaels felt he was treading in history's footsteps as he went up the stairs. If the plaque on the wall didn't lie for the benefit of tourists, that stairway had been there since the Original Absinthe House was built in the early nineteenth century. Andrew Jackson and Jean Lafitte had gone up it to plan the defense of New Or-leans against the British in 1814, and Ben Butler for carefully undescribed purposes half a century later. It was made with wooden pegs: not a nail anywhere. If the stairs weren't as old as the plaque said, they sure as hell were a long way from new.

A jazz band blared away in the big upstairs room. Michaels went in, found a chair, ordered a drink from a waitress whose cos-tume would have been too skimpy for a burly queen most places up North, and leaned back to enjoy the music. The band was about half black, half white. Jazz was one of the few things the two races shared in the South. Not all Negroes had made it to the top of the heap after the North crushed the Great Rebellion; many still lived in the shadow of the fear and degradation of the days of slavery and keenly felt the resentment of the white majority. That came out in the way they played. And the whites, as conquered people will, found liberation in their music that they could not have in life.

Michaels looked at his watch. It was a quarter to three. The jazz men were just keeping loose between shows, then. As he sipped his whiskey, the room began filling up in spite of the five-dollar cover charge. He didn't know what the show would be, but he figured it had to be pretty hot to pack 'em in at those prices.

The lights went out. For a moment, only a few glowing cigarette coals showed in the blackness. The band didn't miss a beat. From right behind Michaels' head, a spotlight came on, bathing the stage in harsh white light.

Saxophone and trumpets wailed lasciviously. When the girls paraded onto the stage, Michaels felt his jaw drop. A vice cop in Cleveland, say, might have put the cuffs on his waitress because she wasn't wearing enough. The girls up there had on high-heeled shoes, headdresses with dyed ostrich plumes and glittering rhinestones, and nothing between the one and the other but big, wide smiles.

He wondered how they got themselves case-hardened enough to go on display like that night after night, show after show. They were all young and pretty and built, no doubt about that. Was it enough? His sister was young and pretty and built, too. He wouldn't have wanted her up there, flaunting it for horny soldiers on leave.

He wondered how much the owners had to pay to keep the local vice squad off their backs. Then he wondered if New Orleans bothered with a vice squad. He hadn't seen any signs of one.

He also wondered who the devil had called him over here and how that person would make contact. Sitting around gaping at naked women was not something he could put in his report unless it had some sort of connection with the business for which he'd come down here.

Soldiers and sailors whooped at the girls, whose skins soon grew slick and shiny with sweat. Waitresses moved back and forth, getting in the way as little as possible while they took drink orders. To fit in, Michaels ordered another whiskey-and-soda, and discovered it cost more than twice as much here as it had downstairs. He didn't figure the Original Absinthe House would go out of business any time soon.

The music got even hotter than it had been. The dancers

stepped off the edge of the stage and started prancing among the tables. Michaels' jaw dropped all over again. This wasn't just a floor show. This was a— He didn't quite know what it was, and found himself too flustered to grope for *le mot juste*.

Then a very pretty naked brunette sat down in his lap and twined her arms around his neck.

"Is that a gun in your pocket, dearie, or are you just glad to see me?" she said loudly. Men at the nearest table guffawed. Since it was a gun in his pocket, Michaels kept his mouth shut. The girl smelled of sweat and whiskey and makeup. What her clammy hide was doing to his shirt and trousers did not bear thinking about. He wanted to drop her on the floor and get the hell out of there.

She was holding him too tight for that, though. She lowered her head to nuzzle his neck; the plumes from her headdress got in his eyes and tickled his nose. But under the cover of that frantic scene, her voice went low and urgent: "You got to talk with Colquit the hearse driver, mister. Tell him Lucy says Pierre says he can talk, an' maybe he will."

Before he could ask her any questions, she kissed him on the lips. The kiss wasn't faked; her tongue slid into his mouth. He'd had enough whiskey and enough shocks by then that he didn't care what he did. His hand closed over her breast—and she sprang to her feet and twisted away, all in perfect time to the music. A moment later, she was in somebody else's lap.

Michaels discovered he'd spilled most of his overpriced drink. He downed what was left with one big swig. When he wiped his mouth with a napkin, it came away red from the girl's—Lucy's—lipstick.

Some of the naked dancers had more trouble than Lucy disentangling themselves from the men they'd chosen. Some of them didn't even try to disentangle. Michaels found himself staring, bug-eyed. You couldn't do *that* in public . . . could you? Hell and breakfast, it was illegal in private, most places.

Eventually, all the girls were back on stage. They gave it all they had for the finale. Then they trooped off and the lights came back up. Only after they were gone did Michaels understand the

knowing look most of them had had all through the perform-
ance: they knew more about men than men, most often, cared to
know about themselves.

In the palm of his hand, he could still feel the memory of the
soft, firm flesh of Lucy's breast. Unlike the others in the room,
he'd had to be here. He hadn't had to grab her, though. Sometimes, facetiously, you called a place like this educational. He'd
learned something, all right, and rather wished he hadn't.

Morrie Harris pursed his lips. "Lucy says Pierre says Colquit
can talk? That's not much to go on. For all we know, it could be
a trap."

"Yeah, it could be," Michaels said. He and the other FBS man
walked along in front of the St. Louis Cathedral, across the
street from Jackson Square. They might have been businessmen,
they might have been sightseers—though neither businessmen
nor sightseers were particularly common in the states that had
tried to throw off the Union's yoke. Michaels went on, "I don't
think it's a trap, though. Ducange's first name is—was—Pierre,
and we've found out he did go to the Original Absinthe House.
He could have gotten to know Lucy there."

He could have done anything with Lucy there. The feel of her
would not leave Michaels' mind. He knew going back to the upstairs room would be dangerous, for him and for her, but the
temptation lingered like a bit of food between the teeth that
keeps tempting back the tongue.

Harris said, "Maybe we ought to just haul her in and grill her
till she cracks."

"We risk alerting the Rebs if we do that," Michaels said.

"Yeah, I know." Harris slammed his fist into his palm. "I hate
sitting around doing nothing, though. If they get everything they
need before we find out where they're squirreling it away, they
start their damn uprising and the war effort goes straight out the
window." He scowled, a man in deep and knowing it. "And
Colquit the hearse driver? You don't know his last name? You
don't know which mortuary he works for? Naked little Lucy
didn't whisper those into your pink and shell-like ear?"

"I told you what she told me." Michaels stared down at the pavement in dull embarrassment. He could feel his dubiously shell-like ears turning red, not pink.

"All right, all right." Harris threw his hands in the air. Most FBS men made a point of not showing what they were thinking—Gary Cooper might have been the Bureau's ideal. Not Morrie Harris. He wore his feelings on his sleeve. *New York City,* Michaels thought, with scorn he nearly didn't notice himself. Harris went on, "We try and find him, that's all. How many guys are there named Colquit, even in New Orleans? And yeah, you don't have to tell me we got to be careful. If he knows anything, we don't want him riding in a hearse instead of driving one."

A bit of investigation—if checking the phone book and getting somebody with the proper accent to call the Chamber of Commerce could be dignified as such—soon proved funerals were big business in New Orleans, bigger than most other places, maybe. There were mortuaries and cemeteries for Jews, for Negroes, for French-speakers, for Protestants, for this group, for that one, and for the other. Because New Orleans was mostly below sea level (Michaels heartily wished the town were underwater, too), burying people was more complicated than digging a hole and putting a coffin down in it. Some intrepid sightseers made special pilgrimages just to see the funeral vaults, which struck Michaels as downright macabre.

Once they had a complete list of funeral establishments, Morrie Harris started calling them one by one. His New York accent was close enough to the local one for him to ask, "Is Colquit there?" without giving himself away as a damnyankee. Time after time, people denied ever hearing of Colquit. At one establishment, though, the receptionist asked whether he meant Colquit the embalmer or Colquit the bookkeeper. He hung up in a hurry.

Repeated failure left Michaels frustrated. He was about to suggest knocking off for the day when Harris suddenly jerked in his chair as if he'd sat on a tack. He put his hand over the receiver and mouthed, "Said he just got back from a funeral.

She's going out to get him." He handed the telephone to Michaels.

After just over a minute, a man's voice said, "Hello? Who's this?"

"Colquit?" Michaels asked.

"Yeah," the hearse driver said.

Maybe it was Michaels' imagination, but he thought he heard suspicion even in one slurred word. Sounding like someone from the Loyal States got you nowhere around here (of course, a Johnny Reb who managed to get permission to travel to Wisconsin also raised eyebrows up there, but Michaels wasn't in Wisconsin now). He spoke quickly: "Lucy told me Pierre told her that I should tell you it was okay for you to talk with me."

He waited for Colquit to ask what the hell he was talking about, or else to hang up. It would figure if the only steer he'd got was a bum one. But the hearse driver, after a long pause, said, "Yeah?" again.

Michaels waited for more, but there wasn't any more. It was up to him, then. "You do know what I'm talking about?" he asked, rather desperately.

"Yeah," Colquit repeated: a man of few words.

"You can't talk where you are?"

"Nope," Colquit said—variety.

"Will you meet me for supper outside Galatoire's tonight at seven, then?" Michaels said. With a good meal and some booze in him, Colquit was more likely to spill his guts.

"Make it tomorrow," Colquit said.

"All right, tomorrow," Michaels said unhappily. More delay was the last thing he wanted. No, not quite: he didn't want to spook Colquit, either. He started to say something more, but the hearse driver did hang up on him then.

"What does he know?" Morrie Harris demanded after Michaels hung up, too.

"I'll find out tomorrow," Michaels answered. "The way things have gone since I got down here, that's progress." Harris nodded solemnly.

*   *   *

The wail of police sirens woke Neil Michaels from a sound sleep. The portable alarm clock he'd brought with him was ticking away on the table by his bed. Its radium dial announced the hour: five past three. He groaned and sat up.

Along with the sirens came the clanging bells and roaring motors of fire engines. Michaels bounced out of bed, ice running down his back. Had the Rebs started their revolt? In that kind of chaos, the pistol he'd brought down from the North felt very small and useless.

He cocked his head. He didn't hear any gunfire. If the Southern men were using whatever the Nazis had shipped them, that would be the biggest part of the racket outside. Okay, it wasn't the big revolt. That meant walking to the window and looking out was likely to be safe. What the devil *was* going on?

Michaels pushed aside the thick curtain shielding the inside of his room from the neon glare that was New Orleans by night. Even as he watched, a couple of fire engines tore down Canal Street toward the Vieux Carré. Their flashing red lights warned the few cars and many pedestrians to get the hell out of the way.

Raising his head, Michaels spotted the fire. Whatever was burning was burning to beat the band. Flames leaped into the night sky, seeming to dance as they flung themselves high above the building that fueled them. A column of thick black smoke marked that building's funeral pyre.

"Might as well find out what it is," Michaels said out loud. He turned on the lamp by the bed and then the radio. The little light behind the dial came on. He waited impatiently for the tubes to get warm enough to bring in a signal.

The first station he got was playing one of Benny Goodman's records. Michaels wondered if playing a damnyankee's music was enough to get you in trouble with some of the fire-eating Johnny Rebs. But he didn't want to hear jazz, not now. He spun the dial.

"—terrible fire on Bourbon Street," an announcer was saying. That had to be the blaze Michaels had seen. The fellow went on, "One of New Orleans' long-standing landmarks, the Original

Absinthe House, is going up in flames even as I speak. The Absinthe House presents shows all through the night, and many are feared dead inside. The building was erected well over a hundred years ago, and has seen—"

Michaels turned off the radio, almost hard enough to break the knob. He didn't believe in coincidence, not even a little bit. Somewhere in the wreckage of the Original Absinthe House would lie whatever mortal fragments remained of Lucy the dancer, and that was just how someone wanted it to be.

He shivered like a man with the grippe. He'd thought about asking Colquit to meet him there instead of at Galatoire's, so Lucy could help persuade the hearse driver to tell whatever he knew—and so he could get another look at her. But going to a place twice running was a mistake. That let the opposition get a line on you. Training had saved his life and, he hoped, Colquit's. It hadn't done poor Lucy one damn bit of good.

He called down to room service and asked for a bottle of whiskey. If the man to whom he gave the order found anything unusual about such a request at twenty past three, he didn't show it. The booze arrived in short order. After three or four good belts, Michaels was able to get back to sleep.

Colquit didn't show up for dinner at Galatoire's that night.

When Morrie Harris phoned the mortuary the next day, the receptionist said Colquit had called in sick. "That's a relief," Michaels said when Harris reported the news. "I was afraid he'd call in dead."

"Yeah." Harris ran a hand through his curly hair. "I didn't want to try and get a phone number and address out of the gal. I didn't even like making the phone call. The less attention we draw to the guy, the better."

"You said it." Michaels took off his glasses, blew a speck from the left lens, set them back on his nose. "Now we know where he works. We can find out where he lives. Just a matter of digging through the papers."

"A lot of papers to dig through," Harris said with a grimace, "but yeah, that ought to do the job. Shall we head on over to the Hall of Records?"

Machine-gun nests surrounded the big marble building on Thalia Street. If the Johnny Rebs ever got their revolt off the ground, it would be one of the first places to burn. The Federal army and bureaucrats who controlled the conquered provinces of the old Confederacy ruled not only by force but also by keeping tabs on their resentful, rebellious subjects. Every white man who worked had to fill out a card each year listing his place of employment. Every firm had to list its employees. Most of the clerks who checked one set of forms against the other were Negroes. They had a vested interest in making sure nobody put one over on the government.

Tough, unsmiling guards meticulously examined Harris' and Michaels' identification papers, comparing photographs to faces and making them give samples of their signatures, before admitting them to the hall. They feared sabotage as well as out-and-out assault. The records stored here helped hold down all of Louisiana.

Hannibal Dupuy was a large, round black man with some of the thickest glasses Michaels had ever seen. "Mortuary establishments," he said, holding up one finger as he thought. "Yes, those would be in the Wade Room, in the cases against the east wall." Michaels got the feeling that, had they asked him about anything from taverns to taxidermists, he would have known exactly where the files were hidden. Such men were indispensable in navigating the sea of papers before them.

Going through the papers stored in the cases against the east wall of the Wade Room took a couple of hours. Michaels finally found the requisite record. "Colquit D. Reynolds, hearse driver—yeah, he works for LeBlanc and Peters," he said. "Okay, here's an address and phone number and a notation that they've been verified as correct. People are on the ball here, no two ways about it."

"People have to be on the ball here," Morrie Harris answered. "How'd you like to be a Negro in the South if the whites you've been sitting on for years grab hold of the reins? Especially if they grab hold of the reins with help from the Nazis? The first

thing they'd do after they threw us damnyankees out is to start
hanging Negroes from lampposts."

"You're right. Let's go track down Mr. Reynolds, so we don't
have to find out just how right you are."

Colquit Reynolds' documents said he lived on Carondelet, out
past St. Joseph: west and south of the French Quarter. Harris had
a car, a wheezy Blasingame that delivered him and Michaels to
the requisite address. Michaels knocked on the door of the
house, which, like the rest of the neighborhood, was only a
small step up from the shotgun shack level.

No one answered. Michaels glanced over at Morrie Harris.
FBS men didn't need a warrant, not to search a house in Johnny
Reb country. That wasn't the issue. Both of them, though, feared
they'd find nothing but a corpse when they got inside.

Just as Michaels was about to break down the front door, an
old woman stuck her head out a side window of the house next
door and said, "If you lookin' for Colquit, gents, you ain't gonna
find him in there."

Morrie Harris swept off his hat and gave a nod that was almost a bow. "Where's he at, then, ma'm?" he asked, doing his
best to sound like a local and speaking to the old woman as if
she were the military governor's wife.

She cackled like a laying hen; she must have liked that. "Same
place you always find him when he wants to drink 'stead of
workin': the Old Days Saloon round the co'ner." She jerked a
gnarled thumb to show which way.

The Old Days Saloon was painted in gaudy stripes of red, white,
and blue. Those were the national colors, and so unexceptionable,
but, when taken with the name of the place, were probably meant
to suggest the days of the Great Rebellion and the traitors who had
used them on a different flag. Michaels would have bet a good
deal that the owner of the place had a thick FBS dossier.

He and Harris walked in. The place was dim and quiet. Ceiling fans created the illusion of coolness. The bruiser behind the
bar gave the newcomers the dubious stare he obviously hauled
out for any stranger: certainly the four or five men in the place

had the look of longtime regulars. Asking which one was
Colquit was liable to be asking for trouble.

One of the regulars, though, looked somehow familiar. After a
moment, Michaels realized why: that old man soaking up a beer
off in a corner had driven the horse-drawn hearse that had
slowed him up on his way back to the hotel a few days before.
He nudged Morrie Harris, nodded toward the old fellow. Together, they went over to him. "How you doin' today, Colquit?"
Harris asked in friendly tones. The bartender relaxed.

Colquit looked up at them with eyes that didn't quite focus.
"Don't think I know you folks," he said, "but I could be wrong."

"Sure you do," Harris said, expansive still. "We're friends of
Pierre and Lucy."

"Oh, Lord help me." Colquit started to get up. Michaels didn't
want a scene. Anything at all could make New Orleans go off—
hauling a man out of a bar very much included. But Colquit
Reynolds slumped back onto his chair, as if his legs didn't want
to hold him. "Wish I never told Pierre about none o' that stuff,"
he muttered, and finished his beer with a convulsive gulp.

Michaels raised a forefinger and called out to the bartender:
"Three more High Lifes here." He tried to slur his words into a
Southern pattern. Maybe he succeeded, or maybe the dollar bill
he tossed down on the table was enough to take the edge off
suspicions. The Rebs had revered George Washington even
during the Great Rebellion, misguided though they were in
other ways.

Colquit Reynolds took a long pull at the new beer. Michaels
and Harris drank more moderately. If they were going to get anything out of the hearse driver, they needed to be able to remember
it once they had it. Besides, Michaels didn't much like beer. Quietly, so the bartender and the other locals wouldn't hear, he
asked, "What do you wish you hadn't told Pierre, Mr. Reynolds?"

Reynolds looked up at the ceiling, as if the answer were written there. Michaels wondered if he was able to remember; he'd
been drinking for a while. Finally, he said, "Wish I hadn't told
him 'bout this here coffin I took for layin' to rest."

"Oh? Why's that?" Michaels asked casually. He lit a Camel,

offered the pack to Colquit Reynolds. When Reynolds took one, he used his Zippo to give the hearse driver a light.

Reynolds sucked in smoke. He held it longer than Michaels thought humanly possible, then exhaled a foggy cloud. After he knocked the coal into an ashtray, he drained his Miller High Life and looked expectantly at the FBS men. Michaels ordered him another one. Only after he'd drunk part of that did he answer, "On account of they needed a block and tackle to get it onto my hearse an' another one to get it off again. Ain't no six men in the world could have lifted that there coffin, not if they was Samson an' five o' his brothers. An' it *clanked*, too."

"Weapons," Morrie Harris whispered, "or maybe ammunition." He looked joyous, transfigured, likely even more so than he would have if a naked dancing girl had plopped herself down in his lap. *Poor Lucy,* Michaels thought.

He said, "Even in a coffin, even greased, I wouldn't want to bury anything in this ground—not for long, that's for damn sure. Water's liable to seep in and ruin things."

Colquit Reynolds sent him a withering, scornful look. "Damnyankees," he muttered under his breath—and he was helping Michaels. "Lot of the times here, you don't bury your dead, you put 'em in a tomb up above ground, just so as coffins don't get flooded out o' the ground come the big rains."

"Jesus," Morrie Harris said hoarsely, wiping his forehead with a sleeve, and then again: "Jesus." Now he was the one to drain his beer and signal for another. Once the bartender had come and gone, he went on, "All the above-ground tombs New Orleans has, you could hide enough guns and ammo to fight a big war. Goddamn sneaky Rebs." He made himself stop. "What cemetery was this at, Mr. Reynolds?"

"Old Girod, out on South Liberty Street," Colquit Reynolds replied. "Don't know how much is there, but one coffinload, anyways."

"Thank God some Southern men don't want to see the Great Rebellion start up again," Michaels said.

"Yeah." Harris drank from his second High Life. "But a hell of a lot of 'em *do*."

*   *   *

Girod Cemetery was hidden away in the railroad yards. A plaque on the stone fence surrounding it proclaimed it to be the oldest Protestant cemetery in New Orleans. Neil Michaels was willing to believe that. The place didn't seem to have received much in the way of legitimate business in recent years, and had a haunted look to it. It was overgrown with vines and shrubs. Gray-barked fig trees pushed up through the sides of some of the old tombs. Moss was everywhere, on trees and tombs alike. Maiden-hair ferns sprouted from the sides of the above-ground vaults; as Michaels had seen, anything would grow anywhere around here.

That included conspiracies. If Colquit Reynolds was right, the ghost of the Great Rebellion haunted this cemetery, too, and the Johnnies were trying to bring it back to unwholesome life.

"He'd better be right," Michaels muttered as the jeep he was riding pulled to a stop before the front entrance to the cemetery.

Morrie Harris understood him without trouble. "Who, that damn hearse driver? You bet he'd better be right. We bring all this stuff here"—he waved behind him—"and start tearin' up a graveyard, then don't find anything . . . hell, that could touch off a revolt all by itself."

Michaels shivered, though the day was hot and muggy. "Couldn't it just?" Had Reynolds been leading them down the path, setting them up to create an incident that would make the South rise up in righteous fury? They'd have to respond to a story like the one he'd told; for the sake of the Union, they didn't dare not respond.

They'd find out. Behind the jeep, Harris' *all this stuff* rattled and clanked: not just bulldozers, but also light M3 Stoneman tanks and heavy M3 Grants with a small gun in a rotating turret and a big one in a sponson at the right front of the hull. Soldiers—all of them men from the Loyal States—scrambled down from Chevy trucks and set up a perimeter around the wall. If anybody was going to try to interfere with this operation, he'd regret it.

Against the assembled might of the Federal Union (*it must and shall be preserved,* Michaels thought), Girod Cemetery mustered a stout metal gate and one elderly watchman. "Who the devil are y'all, and what d'you want?" he demanded, though the *who* part, at least, should have been pretty obvious.

Michaels displayed his FBS badge. "We are on the business of the federal government of the United States of America," he said. "Open the gate and let us in." Again, no talk of warrants, not in Reb country, not on FBS business.

"Fuck the federal government of the United States of America, and the horse it rode in on," the watchman said. "You ain't got no call to come to no cemetery with tanks."

Michaels didn't waste time arguing with him. He tapped the jeep driver on the shoulder. The fellow backed the jeep out of the way. Michaels waved to the driver of the nearest Grant tank. The tank man had his head out of the hatch. He grinned and nodded. The tank clattered forward, chewing up the pavement and spewing noxious exhaust into the air. The wrought-iron gate was sturdy, but not sturdy enough to withstand thirty-one tons of insistent armor. It flew open with a scream of metal; one side ripped loose from the stone to which it was fixed. The Grant ran over it, and would have run over the watchman, too, had he not skipped aside with a shouted curse.

Outside the cemetery, people began gathering. Most of the people were white men of military age or a bit younger. To Michaels, they had the look of men who'd paint slogans on walls or shoot at a truck or from behind a fence under cover of darkness. He was glad he'd brought overwhelming force. Against bayonets, guns, and armor, the crowd couldn't do much but stare sullenly.

If the cemetery was empty of contraband, what this crowd did wouldn't matter. There'd be similar angry crowds all over the South, and at one of them. . . .

The watchman let out an anguished howl as tanks and bulldozers clanked toward the walls of above-ground vaults that ran the length of the cemetery. "You can't go smashin' up the ovens!" he screamed.

"Last warning, Johnny Reb," Michaels said coldly: "don't you try telling officers of the United States what we can and can't do. We have places to put people whose mouths get out in front of their brains."

"Yeah, I just bet you do," the watchman muttered, but after that he kept his mouth shut.

A dozer blade bit into the side of one of the mortuary vaults—an oven, the old man had called it. Concrete and stone flew. So did chunks of a wooden coffin and the bones it had held. The watchman shot Michaels a look of unadulterated hatred and scorn. He didn't say a word, but he might as well have screamed, *See? I told you so.* A lot of times, that look alone would have been plenty to get him on the inside of a prison camp, but Michaels had bigger things to worry about today.

He and Harris hadn't ordered enough bulldozers to take on all the rows of ovens at once. The tanks joined in the job, too, knocking them down as the first big snorting Grant had wrecked the gate into Girod. Their treads ground more coffins and bones into dust.

"That goddamn hearse driver better not have been lying to us," Morrie Harris said, his voice clogged with worry. "If he was, he'll never see a camp or a jail. We'll give the son of a bitch a blindfold; I wouldn't waste a cigarette on him."

Then, from somewhere near the center of Girod Cemetery, a tank crew let out a shout of triumph. Michaels had never heard sweeter music, not from Benny Goodman or Tommy Dorsey. He sprinted toward the Grant. Sweat poured off him, but it wasn't the sweat of fear, not any more.

The tank driver pointed to wooden boxes inside a funeral vault he'd just broken into. They weren't coffins. Each had *1 Maschinengewehr 34* stenciled on its side in neat black-letter script, with the Nazi eagle-and-swastika emblem right next to the legend.

Michaels stared at the machine-gun crates as if one of them held the Holy Grail. "He wasn't lying," he breathed. "Thank you, God."

"Omayn," Morrie Harris agreed. "Now let's find out how much truth he was telling."

The final haul, by the time the last oven was cracked the next day, astonished even Michaels and Harris. Michaels read from the list he'd been keeping: "Machine guns, submachine guns, mortars, rifles—including antitank rifles—ammo for all of them, grenades . . . Jesus, what a close call."

"I talked with one of the radio men," Harris said. "He's sent out a call for more trucks to haul all this stuff away." He wiped his forehead with the back of his hand, a gesture that had little to do with heat or humidity. "If they'd managed to smuggle all of this out of New Orleans, spread it around through the South . . . well, hell, I don't have to draw you a picture."

"You sure don't. We'd have been so busy down here, the Germans and the Japs would have had a field day over the rest of the world." Michaels let out a heartfelt sigh of relief, then went on, "Next thing we've got to do is try and find out who was caching weapons. If we can do that, then maybe, just maybe, we can keep the Rebs leaderless for a generation or so and get ahead of the game."

"Maybe." But Harris didn't sound convinced. "We can't afford to think in terms of a generation from now, anyhow. It's what we were talking about when you first got into town: as long as we can hold the lid on the South till we've won the damn war, that'll do the trick. If we catch the guys running guns with the Nazis, great. If we don't, I don't give a damn about them sneaking around painting YANKS OUT on every blank wall they find. We can deal with that. We've been dealing with it since 1865. As long as they don't have the toys they need to really hurt us, we'll get by."

"Yeah, that's true—if no other subs drop off loads of goodies someplace else." Michaels sighed again. "No rest for the weary. If that happens, we'll just have to try and track 'em down."

A growing rumble of diesel engines made Morrie Harris grin. "Here come the trucks," he said, and trotted out toward the ruined entryway to Girod Cemetery. Michaels followed him. Harris pointed. "Ah, good, they're smart enough to have jeeps riding shotgun for 'em. We don't want any trouble around here till we get the weapons away safe."

There were still a lot of people outside the cemetery walls. They booed and hissed the newly arrived vehicles, but didn't try anything more than booing and hissing. They might hate the damnyankees—they *did* hate the damnyankees—but it was the damnyankees who had the firepower here. Close to eighty years of bitter experience had taught that they weren't shy about using it, either.

Captured German weapons and ammunition filled all the new trucks to overflowing. Some of the ones that had brought in troops also got loaded with lethal hardware. The displaced soldiers either piled into jeeps or clambered up on top of tanks for the ride back to barracks, where the captured arms would be as safe as they could be anywhere in the endlessly rebellious South.

Michaels and Harris had led the convoy to the cemetery; now they'd lead it away. When their jeep driver started up the engine, a few young Rebs bolder than the rest made as if to block the road.

The corporal in charge of the pintle-mounted .50-caliber machine gun in the jeep turned to Michaels and asked, "Shall I mow 'em down, sir?" He sounded quiveringly eager to do just that.

"We'll give 'em one chance first," Michaels said, feeling generous. He stood up in the jeep and shouted to the Johnnies obstructing his path: "You are interfering with the lawful business of the Federal Bureau of Suppression. Disperse at once or you will be shot. First, last, and only warning, people." He sat back down, telling the driver, "Put it in gear, but go slow. If they don't move—" He made hand-washing gestures.

Sullenly, the young men gave way as the jeep moved forward. The gunner swung the muzzle of his weapon back and forth, back and forth, encouraging them to fall back farther. The expression on his face, which frightened even Michaels, might have been an even stronger persuader.

The convoy rattled away from the cemetery. The Johnnies hooted and jeered, but did no more than that, not here, not now. Had they got Nazi guns in their hands . . . but they hadn't.

"We won this one," Morrie Harris said.

"We sure did," Michaels agreed. "Now we can get on with the business of getting rid of tyrants around the world." He spoke altogether without irony.

Ready for the Fatherland

We win. The Nazis win. Does that cover the waterfront for World War II? Not quite. There's one other possibility—a military stalemate, followed by a peace of exhaustion. That's the world of "Ready for the Fatherland." This story was written before Yugoslavia self-destructed, but I take no great credit for prophecy—anyone who'd watched the Balkans a bit could see that that was in the cards. Much of the local color comes courtesy of my wife, who's been to Rijeka.

19 February 1943—Zaporozhye, German-Occupied USSR

Field Marshal Erich von Manstein looked up from the map table. Was that the distant rumble of Soviet artillery? No, he decided after a moment. The Russians were in Sinelnikovo today, yes, but Sinelnikovo was still fifty-five kilometers north of his headquarters. Of course, there were no German troops to speak of between there and here, but that would not matter—if he could make Hitler listen to him.

Hitler, however, was not listening. He was talking. He always talked more than he listened—if he'd listened just once, Manstein thought, Sixth Army might have gotten out of Stalingrad, in which case the Russians would not be anywhere near Sinelnikovo. *They'd come more than six hundred kilometers since November.*

"No, not one more step back!" Hitler shouted. The Führer *had shouted that when the Russians broke through around Stalin-*

grad, too. *Couldn't he remember from one month to the next what worked and what didn't? Behind him, Generals Jodl and Keitel nodded like the brainless puppets they were.*

Manstein glanced over at Field Marshal von Kleist. *Kleist was a real soldier, surely he would tell the* Führer *what had to be said. But Kleist just stood there. Against the Russians, he was fearless. Hitler, though, Hitler made him afraid.*

On my shoulders, *Manstein thought.* Why, ever since Stalingrad, has everything—everything save gratitude—landed on my shoulders? *Had it not been for him, the whole German southern front in Russia would have come crashing down. Without false modesty, he knew that. Sometimes—not nearly often enough—Hitler glimpsed it, too.*

One more try at talking sense into the Führer, then. *Manstein bent over the map, pointed.* "We need to let the Soviets advance, sir. Soon, soon they will overextend themselves. Then we strike."

"No, damn it, damn you! Move on Kharkov now, I tell you!"

SS Panzer Division Totenkopf, *the force with which he wanted Kharkov recaptured, was stuck in the mud outside Poltava, a hundred fifty kilometers away. Manstein said as much. He'd been saying it, over and over, for the past forty-eight hours. Calmly, rationally, he tried once more:* "I am sorry, my Führer, but we simply lack the resources to carry out the attack as you desire. A little more patience, a little more caution, and we may yet achieve satisfactory results. Move too soon and we run the risk of—"

"I did not fly to this godforsaken Russian excuse for a factory town to listen to the whining of your cowardly Jewish heart, Field Marshal." *Hitler invested the proud title with withering scorn.* "And from now on you will keep your gross, disgusting Jewish nose out of strategic planning and simply obey. Do you understand me?"

*Manstein's right hand went to the organ Hitler had mentioned. It was indeed of impressive proportions and impressively hooked. But to bring it up, to insult it, in what should have been a serious council of war was—*insane *was the word Manstein found. As insane as most of the decisions Hitler had made, most*

*of the orders he had given, ever since he'd taken all power into
his own hands at the end of 1941, and especially since things
began to go wrong at Stalingrad.*

*Insane . . . Of itself, Manstein's hand slid down from his nose
to the holster that held his Walther P-38 pistol. Of itself, it un-
snapped the holster flap. And of itself, it raised the pistol and
fired three shots into Adolf Hitler's chest. Wearing a look of horrified disbelief, the* Führer *crumpled to the floor.*

*Generals Jodl and Keitel looked almost as appalled as Hitler
had. So did Field Marshal von Kleist, but he recovered faster. He
snatched out his own pistol, covered Hitler's toadies.*

*Manstein still felt as if he were moving in a dream, but even in
a dream he was a General Staff–taught officer, trained to deduce
what needed doing. "Excellent, Paul," he said. "First we must
dispose of the carrion there, then devise a story to account for it
in suitably heroic style."*

Kleist nodded. "Very good. And then—"

*"And then—" Manstein cocked his head. Yes, by God, he did
hear Russian artillery. "This campaign has been botched beyond
belief. Given the present state of affairs, I see no reasonable hope
of our winning the war against the Russians. Do you agree?"*

Kleist nodded again.

*"Very good," Manstein said. "In that case, let us make certain
we do not lose it. . . ."*

27 July 1979—Rijeka, Independent State of Croatia

The little fishing boat put-putted its way toward the harbor.
The man who called himself Giorgio Ferrero already wore a
black wool fisherman's cap. He used his hand to shield his eyes
further. Seen through the clear Adriatic air, the rugged Croatian
coastline seemed almost unnaturally sharp, as if he were wearing a new pair of spectacles that were a little too strong.

"Pretty country," Ferrero said. He spoke Italian with the accent of Ancona.

So did Pietro Bevacqua, to whom he'd addressed the remark: "That it is." Bevacqua and Ferrero were both medium-
sized, medium-dark men who would not have seemed out of

place anywhere in the Mediterranean. Around a big pipe full of vile Italian tobacco, Bevacqua added, "No matter how pretty, though, me, I wish I were back home." He took both hands off the boat's wheel to show by gesture just how much he wished that.

Ferrero chuckled. He went up to the bow. Bevacqua guided the boat to a pier. Ferrero sprang up onto the dock, rope in hand. He tied the boat fast. Before he could finish, a pair of Croatian customs men were heading his way.

Their neatly creased khaki uniforms, high-crowned caps, gleaming jackboots, and businesslike assault rifles all bespoke their nation's German alliance. The faces under those caps, long, lined, dark, with the deep-set eyes of icons, were older than anything Germany dreamed of. "Show me your papers," one of them said.

"Here you are, sir." Ferrero's Croatian was halting, accented, but understandable. He dug the documents out of the back pocket of his baggy wool pants.

The customs man studied them, passed them to his comrade. "You are from the Social Republic, eh?" the second man said. He grinned nastily. "Not from Sicily?"

Ferrero crossed himself. "Mother of God, no!" he exclaimed in Italian. Sicily was a British puppet regime; admitting one came from there was as good as admitting one was a spy. One did not want to admit to spying, not in Croatia. The *Ustashi* had a reputation for savagery that even the *Gestapo* envied. Ferrero went on, in Croatian again, "From Ancona, like you see. Got a load of eels on ice to sell here, my partner and I."

"Ah." Both customs men looked interested. The one with the nasty grin said, "Maybe our wives will buy some for pies, if they get to market."

"Take some now," Ferrero urged. If he hadn't urged it, the eels would not have got to market. He knew that. The pair of fifty-dinar notes folded in with his papers had disappeared now, too. The Croatian fascists were only cheap imitations of their German prototypes, who would have cost much more to bribe.

Once they had the eels in a couple of sacks, the customs men gave only a cursory glance at Bevacqua's papers (though they did not fail to pocket his pair of fifty-dinar notes, either) and at the rest of the ship's cargo. They plied rubber stamps with vigor and then strode back down the dock, obviously well pleased with themselves.

The fishermen followed them. The fish market was, sensibly, close to the wharves. Another uniformed official demanded papers before he let Ferrero and Bevacqua by. The sight of the customs men's stamps impressed him enough that he didn't even have to be paid off.

"Eels!" Ferrero shouted in his bad but loud Croatian. "Eels from Italian waters! Eels!" A crowd soon formed around him. Eels went one way, dinars another. While Ferrero cried the wares and took money, Bevacqua kept trotting back and forth between market and boat, always bringing more eels.

A beefy man pushed his way to the front of the crowd. He bought three hundred dinars' worth of eels, shoving a fat wad of bills into Ferraro's hand. "For my restaurant," he explained. "You wouldn't happen to have any squid, would you?"

Ferrero shook his head. "We sell those at home. Not many like them here."

"Too bad. I serve calamari when I can." The beefy man slung his sack of eels over his shoulder, elbowed himself away from Ferrero as rudely as he'd approached. Ferrero rubbed his chin and stuck the three hundred dinars in a pocket different from the one he used for the rest of the money he was making.

The eels went fast. Anything new for sale went fast in Rijeka; Croatia had never been a fortunate country. By the time all the fish were gone from the hold of the little boat, Ferrero and Bevacqua had made three times as much as they would have by selling them in Ancona.

"We'll have to make many more trips here," Bevacqua said enthusiastically, back in the fishing boat's cramped cabin. "We'll get rich."

"Sounds good to me," Ferrero said. He took out the wad of bills the fellow from the restaurant had given him. Stern and unsmiling, the face of Ante Pavelic, the first Croatian *Poglavnik*, glared at him from every twenty-dinar note he peeled off. Pavelic hadn't invented fascism, but he'd done even more unpleasant things with it than the Germans, and his successors weren't any nicer than he had been.

In the middle of the notes was a scrap of paper. On it was scrawled a note, in English: *The Church of Our Lady of Lourdes. Tomorrow 1700.* George Smith passed it to Peter Drinkwater, who read it, nodded, and tore it into very small pieces.

Still speaking Italian, Drinkwater said, "We ought to give thanks to Our Lady for blessing us with such a fine catch. Maybe she will reward us with another one."

"She has a fine church here, I've heard," Smith answered in the same tongue. The odds the customs men had planted ears aboard the boat were small, but neither of them believed in taking chances. The Germans made the best and most compact ears in the world, and shared them freely with their allies.

"May Our Lady let us catch the fish we seek," Drinkwater said piously. He crossed himself. Smith automatically followed suit, as any real fisherman would have. If he ever wanted to see Sicily—or England—again, he had to *be* a real fisherman, not just act like one.

Of course, Smith thought, if he'd really wanted to work toward living to a ripe old age, he would have been a carpenter like his father instead of going into Military Intelligence. But even a carpenter's career would have been no guarantee of collecting a pension, not with Fascist Germany, the Soviet Union, the USA, and Britain all ready to throw sunbombs about like cricket balls. He sighed. No one was safe in today's world—his own danger was merely a little more obvious than most.

Not counting Serbian slave laborers (and one oughtn't to have counted them, as they seldom lasted long), Rijeka held about 150,000 people. The older part of the city was a mixture of medieval and Austro-Hungarian architecture; the city hall, a masterpiece of gingerbread, would not have looked out of place in old Vienna. The newer buildings, as was true from the Atlantic to the fascist half of the Ukraine, were in the style critics in free countries sneered at as Albert Speer Gothic: huge colonnades and great vertical masses, all intended to show the individual what an ant he was when set against the immense power of the State.

And in case the individual was too dense to note such symbolism, less subtle clues were available: an *Ustashi* roadblock, where the secret police hauled drivers out of their Volkswagens and Fiats to check their papers; three or four German *Luftwaffe* troops, probably from the antiaircraft missile base in the hills above town, strolling along as if they owned the pavement. By the way the Croats scrambled out of their path, the locals were not inclined to argue possession of it.

Smith watched the *Luftwaffe* men out of the corner of his eye till they rounded a corner and disappeared. "Doesn't seem fair, somehow," he murmured in Italian to Drinkwater. Out in the open like this, he could be reasonably sure no one was listening to him.

"What's that?" Drinkwater murmured back in the same language. Neither of them would risk the distinctive sound patterns of English, not here.

"If this poor, bloody world held any justice at all, the last war would have knocked out either the Nazis or the bloody Reds," Smith answered. "Dealing with one set of devils would be bad enough; dealing with both sets, the way we have the last thirty-odd years, and it's a miracle we haven't all gone up in flames."

"We still have the chance," Drinkwater reminded him. "Remember Tokyo and Vladivostok." A freighter from Russian-occupied Hokkaido had blown up in American-occupied Tokyo harbor in the early 1950s, and killed a couple of hundred thousand people. Three days later, courtesy of the U.S. Air Force, the Russian port also suddenly ceased to be.

"Funny how it was Manstein who mediated," Smith admitted. "Of course, Stalin's dying when he did helped a bit, too, eh?"

"Just a bit," Drinkwater said with a small chuckle. "Manstein would sooner have thrown bombs at the Russians himself, I expect, if he could have arranged for them not to throw any back."

Both Englishmen shut up as they entered the square in front of the Cathedral of Our Lady. Like the Spanish fascists, the

Croatians were ostentatiously pious, invoking God's dominion over their citizens as well as that of the equally holy State. Any of the men and women heading for the Gothic cathedral ahead might have belonged to the *Ustashi*; it approached mathematical certainty that some of them did.

The exterior of the church reminded Smith of a layer cake, with courses of red brick alternating with snowy marble. A frieze of angels and a statue of the Virgin surmounted the door to the upper church. As Smith climbed the ornate stairway toward that door, he took off his cap. Beside him, Drinkwater followed suit. Above the door, golden letters spelled out ZA DOM SPREMNI—Ready for the Fatherland—the slogan of fascist Croatia.

Though Our Lady of Lourdes was of course a Catholic church, the angels on the ceiling overhead were long and thin, as if they sprang from the imagination of a Serbian Orthodox icon-painter. Smith tried to wipe that thought from his mind as he walked down the long hall toward the altar: even thinking of Serbs was dangerous here. The Croats dominated Serbia these days as ruthlessly as the Germans held Poland.

The pews of dark, polished wood, the brilliant stained glass, and the statue of the Virgin behind the altar were familiarly Catholic, and helped Smith forget what he needed to forget and remember what he needed to remember: that he was nothing but a fisherman, thanking the Lord for his fine catch. He took out a cheap plastic rosary and began telling the beads.

The large church was far from crowded. A few pews away from Smith and Drinkwater, a couple of Croatian soldiers in khaki prayed. An old man knelt in front of them; off to one side, a *Luftwaffe* lieutenant, more interested in architecture than spirituality, photographed a column's acanthus capital. And an old woman with a broom and dustpan moved with arthritic slowness down each empty length of pew, sweeping up dust and scraps of paper.

The sweeper came up on Smith and Drinkwater. Obviously a creature of routine, she would have gone right through them had they not moved aside to let her by. "Thank you, thank you," she wheezed, not caring whether she broke the flow of their devotions. A few minutes later, she bothered the pair of soldiers.

Smith looked down to the floor. At first he thought the sweeper simply incompetent, to go right past a fair-sized piece of paper. Then he realized that piece hadn't been there before the old woman went by. Working his beads harder, he slid down into a genuflection. When he went back up into the pew, the paper was in his pocket.

He and Drinkwater prayed for another hour or so, then went back to their fishing boat. On the way, Drinkwater said, "Nothing's simple, is it?"

"Did you expect it to be? This is Croatia, after all," Smith answered. "The fellow who bought our eels likely hasn't the slightest idea where the real meeting will be. It's the God's truth he's better off not knowing, that's for certain."

"Too right there," Drinkwater agreed. "And besides, if we were under suspicion, the *Ustashi* likely would have come down on us in church. This way we run another set of risks for—" He broke off. Some names one did not say, not in Rijeka, not even if no one was close by to hear, not even in the middle of a sentence spoken in Italian.

Back at the boat, the two Englishmen went on volubly—and still in Italian—about how lovely the church of Our Lady of Lourdes had been: no telling who might be listening. As they talked, Smith pulled the paper from the church out of his pocket. The message was short and to the point: *Trsat Castle, the mausoleum, night after tomorrow, 2200.*

The mausoleum? *Bloody melodrama,* Smith thought. He passed the note to Drinkwater. His companion's eyebrows rose as he read it. Then he nodded and ripped the paper to bits.

Both men went out on deck. Trsat Castle, or what was left of it after long years of neglect, loomed over Rijeka from the hills outside of town. By its looks, it was likelier to shelter vampires than the Serbian agent they were supposed to meet there. It was also unpleasantly close to the *Luftwaffe* base whose missiles protected the local factory district.

But the Serb had made his way across Croatia—no easy trick,

that, not in a country where *Show me your papers* was as common a greeting as *How are you today?*—to contact British military intelligence. "Wouldn't do to let the side down," Smith said softly.

"No, I suppose not," Drinkwater agreed, understanding him without difficulty. Then, of themselves, his eyes went back to Trsat Castle. His face was not one to show much of what he was feeling, but he seemed less than delighted at the turn the mission had taken. A moment later, his words confirmed that: "But this once, don't you wish we could?"

Smith contrived to look carefree as he and Drinkwater hauled a wicker basket through the streets of Rijeka. The necks of several bottles of wine protruded from the basket. When he came up to a checkpoint, Smith took out a bottle and thrust it in a policeman's face. "Here, you enjoy," he said in his Italian-flavored Croatian.

"I am working," the policeman answered, genuine regret in his voice. The men at the previous checkpoint hadn't let that stop them. But this fellow, like them, gave the fishermen's papers only a cursory glance and inspected their basket not at all. That was as well, for a Sten gun lurked in the straw under the bottles of wine.

Two more checkpoints and Smith and Drinkwater were up into the hills. The road became a dirt path. The Englishmen went off into a narrow meadow by the side of that path, took out a bottle, and passed it back and forth. Another bottle replaced it, and then a third. No distant watcher, assuming any such were about, could have noticed very little wine actually got drunk. After a while, the Englishmen lay down on the grass as if asleep.

Maybe Peter Drinkwater really did doze. Smith never asked him afterwards. He stayed awake the whole time himself. Through his eyelashes, he watched the meadow fade from green to gray to black. Day birds stopped singing. In a tree not far away, an owl hooted quietly, as if surprised to find itself awake. Smith would not have been surprised to hear the howl of a wolf—or, considering where he was, a werewolf.

Still moving as if asleep, Smith shifted to where he could see the glowing dial of his wristwatch. 2030, he saw. It was full dark. He sat up, dug in the basket, took out the tin tommy gun and clicked in a magazine. "Time to get moving," he said, relishing the feel of English on his tongue.

"Right you are." Drinkwater also sat, then rose and stretched. "Well, let's be off." Up ahead—and the operative word was *up*—Trsat Castle loomed, a deeper blackness against the dark, moonless sky. It was less than two kilometers ahead, but two kilometers in rough country in the dark was nothing to sneeze at. Sweating and bruised and covered with brambles, Smith and Drinkwater got to the ruins just at the appointed hour.

Smith looked up and up at the gray stone towers. "In England, or any civilized country, come to that, a place like this would draw tourists by the bloody busload, you know?"

"But here it doesn't serve the State, so they don't bother keeping it up," Drinkwater said, following his thought. He ran a sleeve over his forehead. "Well, no law to say we can't take advantage of their stupidity."

The way into the castle courtyard was open. Whatever gates had once let visitors in and out were gone, victims of some long-ago cannon. Inside . . . inside, George Smith stopped in his tracks and started laughing. Imagining the sort of mausoleum that would belong to a ruined Balkan castle, he had visualized something somber and Byzantine, with tiled domes and icons and the ghosts of monks.

What he found was very different: a neoclassical Doric temple, with marble columns and entablature gleaming whitely in the starlight. He climbed a few low, broad steps, stood and waited. Drinkwater came up beside him. In the judicious tones of an amateur archaeologist, he said, "I am of the opinion that this is not part of the original architectural plan."

"Doesn't seem so, does it?" Smith agreed. "It—"

In the inky shadows behind the colonnade, something stirred. Smith raised the muzzle of the Sten gun. A thin laugh came from the darkness. A voice followed: "I have had a bead on you since you came inside. But you must be my Englishmen, both because you are here at the time I set and because you chatter over the building. To the *Ustashi*, this would never occur."

Smith jumped at the scratch of a match. The brief flare of

light that followed showed him a heavyset man of about fifty, with a deeply lined face, bushy eyebrows, and a pirate's mustache. "I am Bogdan," the man said in Croatian, though no doubt he thought of his tongue as Serbian. He took a deep drag on his cigarette; its red glow dimly showed his features once more. "I am the man you have come to see."

"If you are Bogdan, you will want to buy our eels," Drinkwater said in Italian.

"Eels make me sick to my stomach," Bogdan answered in the same language. He laughed that thin laugh again, the laugh of a man who found few things really funny. "Now that the passwords are out of the way, to business. I can use this tongue, or German, or Russian, or even my own. My English, I fear, is poor, for which I apologize. I have had little time for formal education."

That Smith believed. Like Poland, like the German Ukraine, Serbia remained a military occupation zone, with its people given hardly more consideration than cattle: perhaps less than cattle, for cattle were not hunted for the sport of it. Along with his Italian, Smith spoke fluent German and passable Russian, but he said, "This will do well enough. Tell us how it is with you, Bogdan."

The partisan leader drew on his cigarette again, making his face briefly reappear. Then he shifted the smoke to the side of his mouth and spat between two columns. "That is how it goes for me, Englishman. That is how it goes for all Serbia. How are we to keep up the fight for freedom if we have no weapons?"

"You are having trouble getting supplies from the Soviets?" Drinkwater asked, his voice bland. Like most of the Balkans antifascists, Bogdan and his crew looked to Moscow for help before London or Washington. That he was here now—that the partisans had requested this meeting—was a measure of his distress.

He made a noise, deep in his throat. "Moscow has betrayed us again. It is their habit; it has been their habit since '43."

"Stalin betrayed us then, too," Smith answered. "If the Russians hadn't made their separate peace with Germany that summer, the invasion of Italy wouldn't have been driven back into the sea, and Rommel wouldn't have had the men to crush the Anglo-American lodgement in France." Smith shook his head—so much treachery since then, on all sides. He went on, "Tell us how it is in Serbia these days."

"You have what I need?" Bogdan demanded.

"Back at the boat," Drinkwater said. "Grenades, cordite, blasting caps . . ."

Bogdan's deep voice took on a purring note it had not held before. "Then we shall give the Germans and the Croat pigs who are their lackeys something new to think on when next they seek to play their games with us in our valleys. Let one of their columns come onto a bridge—and then let the bridge come down! I do not believe in hell, but I shall watch them burn here on earth, and make myself content with that. Have you also rockets to shoot their autogiros out of the air?"

Smith spread his hands regretfully. "No. Now that we are in contact with you, though, we may be able to manage a shipment—"

"It would be to your advantage if you did," Bogdan said earnestly. "The Croats and Germans use Serbia as a live-fire training ground for their men, you know. They are better soldiers for having trained in actual combat. And that our people are slaughtered—who cares what happens to backwoods Balkans peasants, eh? Who speaks for us?"

"The democracies speak for you," Smith said.

"Yes—to themselves." Bogdan's scorn was plain to hear. "Oh, they mention it to Berlin and Zagreb, but what are words? Wind! And all the while they go on trading with the men who seek to murder my nation. Listen, Englishmen, and I shall tell you how it is . . ."

The partisan leader did not really care whether Smith and Drinkwater listened. He talked, letting out the poison that had for so long festered inside him. His picture of Serbia reminded Smith of a fox's-eye view of a hunt. The Englishmen marveled that the guerrilla movement still lived, close to two generations after the *Wehrmacht* rolled down on what had been Yugoslavia. Only the rugged terrain of the interior and the indomitable ferocity of the people there kept resistance aflame.

"The Germans are better at war than the cursed Croats," Bogdan said. "They are hard to trap, hard to trick. Even their raw troops, the ones who learn against us, have that combination of discipline and initiative which makes Germans generally so dangerous."

Smith nodded. Even with Manstein's leadership, fighting the Russians to a standstill had been a colossal achievement. Skirmishes along the borders of fascist Europe—and in such hunting preserves as Serbia—had let the German army keep its edge since the big war ended.

Bogdan went on, "When they catch us, they kill us. When we catch them, we kill them. This is as it should be." He spoke with such matter-of-factness that Smith had no doubt he meant exactly what he said. He had lived with war for so long, it seemed the normal state of affairs to him.

Then the partisan's voice changed. "The Germans are wolves. The Croats, their army and the stinking *Ustashi*, are jackals. They rape, they torture, they burn our Orthodox priests' beards, they kill a man for having on his person anything written in the Cyrillic script, and in so doing they seek to turn us Serbs into their own foul kind." Religion and alphabet divided Croats and Serbs, who spoke what was in essence the same language.

"Not only that, they are cowards." By his tone, Bogdan could have spoken no harsher condemnation. "They come into a village only if they have a regiment at their backs, and either flee or massacre if anyone resists them. We could hurt them far worse than we do, but when they are truly stung, they run and hide behind the Germans' skirts."

"I gather you are coming to the point where that does not matter to you," Smith said.

"You gather rightly," Bogdan said. "Sometimes a man must hit back, come what may afterwards. To strike a blow at the fascists, I am willing to ally with the West. I would ally with Satan, did he offer himself as my comrade." *So much for his disbelief,* Smith thought.

"Churchill once said that if the Germans invaded hell, he would say a good word for the devil," Drinkwater observed.

"If the Germans invaded hell, Satan would need help because they are dangerous. If the Croatians invaded hell, he would have trouble telling *them* from his demons."

Smith laughed dryly, then returned to business: "How shall we convey to you our various, ah, pyrotechnics?"

"The fellow who bought your eels will pay you a visit tomorrow. He has a Fiat, and has also a permit for travel to the edge of Serbia: one of his cousins owns an establishment in Belgrade. The cousin, that swine, is not one of us, but he gives our man the excuse he needs for taking his motorcar where we need it to go."

"Very good. You seem to have thought of everything." Smith turned away. "We shall await your man tomorrow."

"Don't go yet, my friends." Agile as a chamois, Bogdan clattered down the steep steps of the mausoleum. He carried a Soviet automatic rifle on his back and held a squat bottle in his hands. "I have here *slivovitz.* Let us drink to the deaths of fascists." He yanked the cork out of the bottle with a loud pop. *"Zhiveli!"*

The harsh plum brandy burned its way down Smith's throat like jellied gasoline. Coughing, he passed the bottle to Drinkwater, who took a cautious swig and gave it back to Bogdan. The partisan leader tilted it almost to the vertical. Smith marveled at the temper of his gullet, which had to be made of something like stainless steel to withstand the potent brew.

At last, Bogdan lowered the *slivovitz* bottle. "Ahh!" he said, wiping his mouth on his sleeve. "That is very fine. I—"

Without warning, a portable searchlight blazed into the courtyard from the open gateway into Trsat Castle. Smith froze, his eyes filling with tears at the sudden transformation from night to brighter than midday. An amplified voice roared, "Halt! Stand where you are! You are the prisoners of the Independent State of Croatia!"

Bogdan bellowed like a bull: "No fucking Croat will take

me!" He grabbed for his rifle. Before the motion was well be-gun, a burst of fire cut him down. Smith and Drinkwater threw themselves flat, their hands over their heads.

Something hot and wet splashed Smith's cheek. He rubbed the palm of his hand over it. In the actinic glare of the search-light, Bogdan's blood looked black. The partisan leader was still alive. Shrieks alternated with bubbling moans as he writhed on the ground, trying to hold his guts inside his belly.

Jackboots rattled in the courtyard as men from the *Ustashi*, including a medic with a Red Cross armband, dashed in from the darkness. The medic grabbed Bogdan, stuck a plasma line in his arm. Bogdan did his best to tear it out again. A couple of or-dinary troopers kept him from succeeding. "We'll patch you up so you can sing for us," one of them growled. His voice changed to gloating anticipation: "Then we'll take you apart again, one centimeter at a time."

A rifle muzzle pressed against Smith's forehead. His eyes crossed as they looked down the barrel of the gun. "Up on your feet, spy," said the *Ustashi* man holding it. He had 7.92 millime-ters of potent persuasion. Smith obeyed at once.

An *Ustashi* major strode into the brilliant hole the searchlight had cut in the darkness. He marched up to Smith and Drinkwa-ter, who had also been ordered to his feet. Smith could have shaved on the creases in his uniform, and used his belt buckle as a mirror for the job. The perfect outfit served only to make him more acutely aware of how grubby he was himself.

The major studied him. The fellow had a face out of a fascist training film: hard, stern, handsome, ready to obey any order without question or even thought, not a gram of surplus fat any-where. An interrogator with a face like his could make a pris-oner afraid just by looking at him, and instilling fear was half an interrogator's battle.

"You are the Englishmen?" the major demanded. He spoke English himself, with a better public-school accent than Smith could boast. Smith glanced toward Drinkwater. Warily, they both nodded.

Like a robot's, the major's arm shot up and out in a perfect fascist salute. "The fatherland thanks you for your help in capturing this enemy of the state and of the true faith," he declared.

On the ground, Bogdan's groans changed tone as he realized he had been betrayed. Smith shrugged. He had a fatherland, too—London told him what to do, and he did it. He said, "You'd best let us get out of the harbor before dawn, so none of Bogdan's people can be sure we had anything to do with this."

"It shall be as you say," the major agreed, though he sounded indifferent as to whether Smith and Drinkwater gave themselves away to Bogdan's organization. He probably *was* indifferent; Croatia and England loved each other no better than Croatia and the Communists. This time, it had suited them to work together. Next time, they might try to kill each other. They all knew it.

Smith sighed. "It's a rum world, and that's a fact."

The *Ustashi* major nodded. "So it is. Surely God did not intend us to cooperate with such degenerates as you. One day, though, we shall have a true reckoning. *Za dom Spremni!*"

Fucking loony, Smith thought. If the major read that in his eyes, too bad. Croatia could not afford an incident with England, not when her German overlords were dickering with London over North Sea petroleum rights.

The trip down to Rijeka from Trsat Castle was worse than the one up from the city. The Englishmen dared not show a light, not unless they wanted to attract secret policemen who knew nothing of their arrangement with the *Ustashi* major and who would start shooting before they got the chance to find out. Of course, they ran the same risk on (Smith devoutly hoped) a smaller scale, traveling in the dark.

Traveling in the dark down a steep hillside also brought other risks. After Peter Drinkwater fell for the third time, he got up swearing: "God damn the Russians for mucking about in Turkey, and in Iraq, and in Persia. If they weren't trying to bugger the oil wells there, you and I wouldn't have to deal with the likes of the bloody *Ustashi*—and we'd not have to feel we needed a bath afterwards."

"No, we'd be dealing with the NKVD instead, selling out Ukrainian nationalists to Moscow," Smith answered. "Would you feel any cleaner after that?"

"Not bloody likely," Drinkwater answered at once. "It's a rum world, all right." He stumbled again, but caught himself. The path was nearly level now. Rijeka lay not far ahead.

The Phantom Tolbukhin

Most stories come to me character-first or situation-first.
This one didn't; it came to me title-first; those who know
my work know I *will* make puns like that every now and
again, or rather more often than every now and again.
Then, of course, I had to find a story to go with it. This
one looks at the Ukrainian town of Zaporozhye, too, but
in a world different from that of "Ready for the Fatherland."

General Fedor Tolbukhin turned to his political commissar.
"Is everything in your area of responsibility in readiness for the
assault, Nikita Sergeyevich?"

"Fedor Ivanovich, it is," Nikita Khrushchev replied. "There
can be no doubt that the Fourth Ukrainian Front will win another smashing victory against the fascist lice who suck the
blood from the motherland."

Tolbukhin's mouth tightened. Khrushchev should have addressed him as *Comrade General*, not by his first name and
patronymic. Political commissars had a way of thinking they
were as important as real soldiers. But Khrushchev, unlike
some—unlike most—political commissars Tolbukhin knew,
was not afraid to get gun oil on his hands, or even to take a
PPSh41 submachine gun up to the front line and personally pot
a few fascists.

"Will you inspect the troops before ordering them to the assault against Zaporozhye?" Khrushchev asked.

"I will, and gladly," Tolbukhin replied.

Not all of Tolbukhin's forces were drawn up for inspection, of course: too great a danger of marauding *Luftwaffe* fighters spotting such an assemblage and shooting it up. But representatives from each of the units the Soviet general had welded into a solid fighting force were there, lined up behind the red banners that symbolized their proud records. Yes, they were all there: the flags of the First Guards Army, the Second Guards, the Eighth Guards, the Fifth Shock Army, the 38th Army, and the 51st.

"Comrade Standard Bearer!" Tolbukhin said to the young soldier who carried the flag of the Eighth Guards Army, which bore the images of Marx and Lenin and Stalin.

"I serve the Soviet Union, Comrade General!" the standard bearer barked. But for his lips, he was utterly motionless. By his wide Slavic face, he might have come from anywhere in the USSR; his mouth proved him a native Ukrainian, for he turned the Great Russian *G* into an *H*.

"We all serve the Soviet Union," Tolbukhin said. "How may we best serve the motherland?"

"By expelling from her soil the German invaders," the young soldier replied. "Only then can we take back what is ours. Only then can we begin to build true Communism. It surely will come in my lifetime."

"It surely will," Tolbukhin said. He nodded to Khrushchev, who marched one pace to his left, one pace to the rear. "If all the men are as well indoctrinated as this one, the Fourth Ukrainian Front cannot fail."

After inspecting the detachments, he conferred with the army commanders—and, inevitably, with their political commissars. They crowded a tumbledown barn to overflowing. By the light of a kerosene lantern, Tolbukhin bent over the map, pointing out the avenues of approach the forces would use. Lieutenant General Yuri Kuznetsov, commander of the Eighth Guards Army, grinned wide enough to show a couple of missing teeth. "It is a good plan, Comrade General," he said. "The invaders will regret ever setting foot in the Soviet Union."

"I thank you, Yuri Nikolaievich," Tolbukhin said. "Your

knowledge of the approach roads to the city will help the attack succeed."

"The fascist invaders *already* regret ever setting foot in the Soviet Union," Khrushchev said loudly.

Lieutenant General Kuznetsov dipped his head, accepting the rebuke. "I serve the Soviet Union," he said, as if he were a raw recruit rather than a veteran of years of struggle against the Hitlerites.

"You have the proper Soviet spirit," Tolbukhin said, and even the lanternlight was enough to show how Kuznetsov flushed with pleasure.

Lieutenant General Ivanov of the First Guards Army turned to Major General Rudzikovich, who had recently assumed command of the Fifth Shock Army, and murmured, "Sure as the devil's grandmother, the Phantom will make the Nazis pay."

Tolbukhin didn't think he was supposed to hear. But he was young for his rank—only fifty-three—and his ears were keen. The nickname warmed him. He'd earned it earlier in the war— the seemingly endless war—against the madmen and ruffians and murderers who followed the swastika. He'd always had a knack for hitting the enemies of the peasants and workers of the Soviet Union where they least expected it, then fading away before they could strike back at his forces.

"Has anyone any questions about the plan before we continue the war for the liberation of Zaporozhye and all the territory of the Soviet Union now groaning under the oppressor's heel?" he asked.

He thought no one would answer, but Rudzikovich spoke up: "Comrade General, are we truly wise to attack the city from the northeast and southeast at the same time? Would we not be better off concentrating our forces for a single strong blow?"

"This is the plan the council of the Fourth Ukrainian Front has made, and this is the plan we shall follow," Khrushchev said angrily.

"Gently, gently," Tolbukhin told his political commissar. He turned back to Rudzikovich. "When we hit the Germans straight on, that is where we run into trouble. Is it not so, Anatoly

Pavlovich? We will surprise them instead, and see how they like that."

"I hope it won't be too expensive, that's all," Major General Rudzikovich said. "We have to watch that we spend our brave Soviet soldiers with care these days."

"I know," Tolbukhin answered. "Sooner or later, though, the Nazis have to run out of men." Soviet strategists had been saying that ever since the Germans, callously disregarding the treaty Ribbentrop had signed with Foreign Commissar Molotov, invaded the USSR. General Tolbukhin pointed to the evidence: "See how many Hungarian and Romanian and Italian soldiers they have here in the Ukraine to pad out their own forces."

"And they cannot even station the Hungarians and Romanians next to one another, lest they fight," Khrushchev added—like any political commissar, if he couldn't score points off Rudzikovich one way, he'd try another. "Thieves fall out. It is only one more proof that the dialectic assures our victory. So long as we labor like Stakhanovites, over and above the norm, that victory will be ours."

"Anatoly Pavlovich, we have been over the plan a great many times," Tolbukhin said, almost pleadingly. "If you seek to alter it now, just before the attack goes in, you will need a better reason than 'I hope.' "

Anatoly Rudzikovich shrugged. "I hope you are right, Comrade General," he said, bearing down heavily on the start of the sentence. He shrugged again. "Well, *nichevo*." *It can't be helped* was a Russian foundation old as time.

Tolbukhin said, "Collect your detachments, Comrades, and rejoin your main forces. The attack *will* go in on time. And we shall strike the fascists a heavy blow at Zaporozhye. For Stalin and the motherland!"

"For Stalin and the motherland!" his lieutenants chorused. They left the barn with their political commissars—all but Lieutenant General Yuri Kuznetsov, whose Eighth Guards Army was based at Collective Farm 122 nearby.

"This attack *must* succeed, Fedor Ivanovich," Khrushchev said quietly. "The situation in the Ukraine requires it."

"I understand that, Nikita Sergeyevich," Tolbukhin answered, as quietly. "To make sure the attack succeeds, I intend to go in with the leading wave of troops. Will you fight at my side?"

In the dim light, he watched Khrushchev. Most political commissars would have looked for the nearest bed under which to hide at a request like that. Khrushchev only nodded. "Of course I will."

"Stout fellow." Tolbukhin slapped him on the back. He gathered up Kuznetsov and his political commissar by eye. "Let's go."

The night was very black. The moon, nearly new, would not rise till just before sunup. Only starlight shone down on Tolbukhin and his comrades. He nodded to himself. The armies grouped together into the Fourth Ukrainian Front would be all the harder for German planes to spot before they struck Zaporozhye. Dispersing them would help there, too.

He wished for air cover, then shrugged. He'd wished for a great many things in life he'd ended up not receiving. He remained alive to do more wishing. *One day,* he thought, *and one day soon, may we see more airplanes blazoned with the red star.* He was too well indoctrinated a Marxist-Leninist to recognize that as a prayer.

Waiting outside Collective Farm 122 stood the men of the Eighth Guards Army. Lieutenant General Kuznetsov spoke to them: "General Tolbukhin not only sends us into battle against the Hitlerite oppressors and bandits, he leads us into battle against them. Let us cheer the Comrade General!"

"Urra!" The cheer burst from the soldiers' throats, but softly, cautiously. Most of the men were veterans of many fights against the Nazis. They knew better than to give themselves away too soon.

However soft those cheers, they heartened Tolbukhin. "We shall win tonight," he said, as if no other alternative were even imaginable. "We shall win for Comrade Stalin, we shall win for the memory of the great Lenin, we shall win for the motherland."

"We serve the Soviet Union!" the soldiers chorused. Beside Tolbukhin, Khrushchev's broad peasant face showed a broad peasant grin. These were indeed well-indoctrinated men.

They were also devilishly good fighters. To Tolbukhin's mind, that counted for more. He spoke one word: *"Vryed'!"* Obedient to his order, the soldiers of the Eighth Guards Army trotted forward.

Tolbukhin trotted along with them. So did Khrushchev. Both the general and the political commissar were older and rounder than the soldiers they commanded. They would not have lost much face had they failed to keep up. Tolbukhin intended to lose no face whatever. His heart pounded. His lungs burned. His legs began to ache. He kept on nonetheless. So did Khrushchev, grimly slogging along beside him.

He expected the first brush with the *Wehrmacht* to take place outside of Zaporozhye, and so it did. The Germans patrolled east of the city: no denying they were technically competent soldiers. Tolbukhin wished they were less able; that would have spared the USSR endless grief.

A voice came out of the night: *"Wer geht hier?"* A hail of rifle and submachine-gun bullets answered that German hail. Tolbukhin hoped his men wiped out the patrol before the Nazis could use their wireless set. When the Germans stopped shooting back, which took only moments, the Eighth Guards Army rolled on.

Less than ten minutes later, planes rolled out of the west. Along with the soldiers in the first ranks, Tolbukhin threw himself flat. He ground his teeth and cursed under his breath. Had that patrol got a signal out after all? He hoped it was not so. Had prayer been part of his ideology, he would have prayed it was not so. If the Germans learned of the assault too soon, they could blunt it with artillery and rockets at minimal cost to themselves.

The planes—Tolbukhin recognized the silhouettes of Focke-Wulf 190s—zoomed away. They dropped neither bombs nor flares, and did not strafe the men of the Fourth Ukrainian Front. Tolbukhin scrambled to his feet. "Onward!" he called.

Onward the men went. Tolbukhin felt a glow of pride. After so much war, after so much heartbreak, they still retained their revolutionary spirit. "Truly, these are the New Soviet Men," he called to Khrushchev.

A middle-aged Soviet man, the political commissar nodded. "We shall never rest until we drive the last of the German invaders from our soil. As Comrade Stalin said, 'Not one step back!' Once the fascists are gone, we shall rebuild this land to our hearts' desire."

Tolbukhin's heart's desire was piles of dead Germans in field-gray uniforms, clouds of flies swarming over their stinking bodies. And he had achieved his heart's desire many times. But however many Nazis the men under his command killed, more kept coming out of the west. It hardly seemed fair.

Ahead loomed the apartment blocks and factories of Zaporozhye, black against the dark night sky. German patrols enforced their blackout by shooting into lighted windows. If they hit a Russian mother or a sleeping child . . . it bothered them not in the least. Maybe they won promotion for it.

"Kuznetsov," Tolbukhin called through the night.

"Yes, Comrade General?" the commander of the Eighth Guards Army asked.

"Lead the First and Second Divisions by way of Tregubenko Boulevard," Tolbukhin said. "I will take the Fifth and Ninth Divisions farther south, by way of Metallurgov Street. Thus we will converge upon the objective."

"I serve the Soviet Union!" Kuznetsov said.

Zaporozhye had already been fought over a good many times. As Tolbukhin got into the outskirts of the Ukrainian city, he saw the gaps bombs and shellfire had torn in the buildings. People still lived in those battered blocks of flats and still labored in those factories under German guns.

In the doorway to one of those apartment blocks, a tall, thin man in the field-gray tunic and trousers of the *Wehrmacht* was kissing and feeling up a blond woman whose overalls said she was a factory worker. *A factory worker supplementing her income as a Nazi whore,* Tolbukhin thought coldly.

At the sound of booted feet running on Metallurgov Street, the German soldier broke away from the Ukrainian woman. He shouted something. Submachine-gun fire from the advancing Soviet troops cut him down. The woman fell, too, fell and fell screaming. Khrushchev stopped beside her and shot her in the back of the neck. The screams cut off.

"Well done, Nikita Sergeyevich," Tolbukhin said.

"I've given plenty of traitors what they deserve," Khrushchev answered. "I know how. And it's always a pleasure."

"Yes," Tolbukhin said: of course a commissar would see a traitor where he saw a whore. "We'll have to move faster now, though; the racket will draw the fascists. *Nichevo.* We'd have bumped into another Nazi patrol in a minute or two, anyway."

One thing the racket did not do was bring people out of their flats to join the Eighth Guards Army in the fight against the fascist occupiers. As the soldiers ran, they shouted, "Citizens of Zaporozhye, the hour of liberation is at hand!" But the city had seen a lot of war. Civilians left here were no doubt cowering under their beds, hoping no stray bullets from either Soviet or German guns would find them.

"Scouts forward!" Tolbukhin shouted as his men turned south from Metallurgov onto Pravdy Street. They were getting close to their objective. The fascists surely had guards in the area—but where? Finding them before they set eyes on the men of the Eighth Guards Army could make the difference between triumph and disaster.

Then the hammering of gunfire broke out to the south. Khrushchev laughed out loud. "The Nazis will think they are engaging the whole of our force, Fedor Ivanovich," he said joyfully. "For who would think even the Phantom dared divide his men so?"

Tolbukhin ran on behind the scouts. The Nazis were indeed pulling soldiers to the south to fight the fire there, and didn't discover they were between two fires till the Eighth Guards Army and, moments later, the men of the Fifth Shock Army and the 51st Army opened up on them as well. How the Hitlerites howled!

Ahead of him, a German machine gun snarled death—till grenades put the men handling it out of action. Then, a moment later, it started up again, this time with Red Army soldiers feeding it and handling the trigger. Tolbukhin whooped with glee. An MG-42 was a powerful weapon. Turning it on its makers carried the sweetness of poetic justice.

One of his soldiers pointed and shouted: "The objective! The armory! And look, Comrade General! Some of our men are already inside. We have succeeded."

"We have not succeeded yet," Tolbukhin answered. "We will have succeeded only when we have done what we came here to do." He raised his voice to a great shout: "Form a perimeter around the building. Exploitation teams, forward! You know your assignments."

"Remember, soldiers of the Soviet Union, the motherland depends on your courage and discipline," Khrushchev added.

As Tolbukhin had planned, the perimeter force around the Nazi armory was as small as possible; the exploitation force, made up of teams from each army of the Fourth Ukrainian Front, as large. Tolbukhin went into the armory with the exploitation force. Its mission here was by far the most important for the strike against Zaporozhye.

Inside the armory, German efficiency came to the aid of the Soviet Union. The Nazis had arranged weapons and ammunition so their own troops could lay hold of whatever they needed as quickly as possible. The men of the Red Army happily seized rifles and submachine guns and the ammunition that went with each. They also laid hands on a couple of more MG-42s. If they could get those out of the city, the fascists would regret it whenever they tried driving down a road for a hundred kilometers around.

"When you're loaded up, get out!" Tolbukhin shouted. "Pretty soon, the Nazis will hit us with everything they've got." He did not disdain slinging a German rifle on his back and loading his pockets with clips of ammunition.

"We have routed them, Fedor Ivanovich," Khrushchev said. When Tolbukhin did not reply, the political commissar added, "A million rubles for your thoughts, Comrade General."

Before the war, the equivalent sum would have been a kopeck. Of course, before the war Tolbukhin would not have called the understrength regiment he led a front. Companies would not have been styled armies, nor sections divisions. "Inflation is everywhere," he murmured, and then spoke to Khrushchev: "As long as you came in, Nikita Sergeyevich, load up, and then we'll break away if we can, if the Germans let us."

Khrushchev affected an injured look. "Am I then only a beast of burden, Fedor Ivanovich?"

"We are all only beasts of burden in the building of true Communism," Tolbukhin replied, relishing the chance to get off one of those sententious bromides at the political commissar's expense. He went on, "I am not too proud to load myself like a beast of burden. Why should you be?"

Khrushchev flushed and glared furiously. In earlier days—in happier days, though Tolbukhin would not have thought so at the time—upbraiding a political commissar would surely have caused a denunciation to go winging its way up through the Party hierarchy, perhaps all the way up to Stalin himself. So many good men had disappeared in the purges that turned the USSR upside down and inside out between 1936 and 1938: Tukhashevsky and Koniev, Yegorov and Blyukher, Zhukov and Uborevich, Gamarnik and Fedko. Was it any wonder the Red Army had fallen to pieces when the Nazis attacked in May 1941?

And now, in 1947, Khrushchev was as high-ranking a political commissar as remained among the living. To whom could he denounce Tolbukhin? No one, and he knew it. However furious he was, he started filling his pockets with magazines of Mauser and Schmeisser rounds.

Sometimes, Tolbukhin wondered why he persisted in the fight against the fascists when the system he served, even in its tattered remnants, was so onerous. The answer was not hard to find. For one thing, he understood the difference between bad and worse. And, for another, he'd been of general's rank when the Hitlerites invaded the motherland. If they caught him, they would liquidate him—their methods in the Soviet Union made even Stalin's seem mild by comparison. If he kept fighting, he might possibly—just possibly—succeed.

Khrushchev clanked when turning back to him. The tubby

little political commissar was still glaring. "I am ready, Fedor Ivanovich," he said. "I hope you are satisfied."

"Da," Tolbukhin said. He hadn't been satisfied since Moscow and Leningrad fell, but Khrushchev couldn't do anything about that. Tolbukhin pulled from his pocket an officer's whistle and blew a long, furious blast. "Soldiers of the Red Army, we have achieved our objective!" he shouted in a great voice. "Now we complete the mission by making our departure!"

He was none too soon. Outside, the fascists were striking heavy blows against his perimeter teams. But the fresh men coming out of the armory gave the Soviets new strength and let them blast open a corridor to the east and escape.

Now it was every section—every division, in the grandiose language of what passed for the Red Army in the southern Ukraine these days—for itself. Inevitably, men fell as the units made their way out of Zaporozhye and onto the steppe. Tolbukhin's heart sobbed within him each time he saw a Soviet soldier go down. Recruits were so hard to come by these days. The booty he'd gained from this raid would help there, and would also help bring some of the bandit bands prowling the steppe under the operational control of the Red Army. With more men, with more guns, he'd be able to hurt the Nazis more the next time.

But if, before he got out of Zaporozhye, he lost all the men he had now . . . *What then, Comrade General?* he jeered at himself.

Bullets cracked around him, spattering off concrete and striking blue sparks when they ricocheted from metal. He lacked the time to be afraid. He had to keep moving, keep shouting orders, keep turning back and sending another burst of submachine-gun fire at the pursuing Hitlerites.

Then his booted feet thudded on dirt, not on asphalt or concrete any more. "Out of the city!" he cried exultantly.

And there, not far away, Khrushchev doggedly pounded along. He had grit, did the political commissar. "Scatter!" he called to the men within the sound of his voice. "Scatter and hide your booty in the secure places. Resume the *maskirovka* that keeps us all alive."

Without camouflage, the Red Army would long since have become extinct in this part of the USSR. As things were, Tolbukhin's raiders swam like fish through the water of the Soviet peasantry, as Mao's Red Chinese did in their long guerrilla struggle against the imperialists of Japan.

But Tolbukhin had little time to think about Mao, either, for the Germans were going fishing. Nazis on foot, Nazis in armored cars and personnel carriers, and even a couple of panzers came forth from Zaporozhye. At night, Tolbukhin feared the German foot soldiers more than the men in machines. Machines were easy to elude in the darkness. The infantry would be the ones who knew what they were doing.

Still, this was not the first raid Tolbukhin had led against the Germans, nor the tenth, nor the fiftieth, either. What he did not know about rear guards and ambushes wasn't worth knowing. His men stung the Germans again and again, stung them and then crept away. They understood the art of making many men seem few, few seem many. Little by little, they shook off pursuit.

Tolbukhin scrambled down into a *balka* with Khrushchev and half a dozen men from the Eighth Guards Army, then struggled up the other side of the dry wash. They started back toward Collective Farm 122, where, when they were not raiding, they labored for their Nazi masters as they had formerly labored for their Soviet masters.

"Wait," Tolbukhin called to them, his voice low but urgent. "I think we still have Germans on our tail. This is the best place I can think of to make them regret it."

"We serve the Soviet Union!" one of the soldiers said. They returned and took cover behind bushes and stones. So did Tolbukhin. He could not have told anyone how or why he believed the fascists remained in pursuit of this little band, but he did. *Instinct of the hunted,* he thought.

And the instinct did not fail him. Inside a quarter of an hour, men in coal-scuttle helmets began going down into the *balka*. One of them tripped, stumbled, and fell with a thud. "Those God-damned stinking Russian pigdogs," he growled in guttural

German. "They'll pay for this. Screw me out of sack time, will they?"

"*Ja,* better we should screw their women than they should screw us out of sack time," another trooper said. "That Natasha in the soldiers' brothel, she's limber like she doesn't have any bones at all."

"Heinrich, Klaus, *shut up!*" another voice hissed. "You've got to play the game like those Red bastards are waiting for us on the far side of this miserable gully. You don't, your family gets a *'Fallen for* Führer *and Fatherland'* telegram one fine day." By the way the other two men fell silent, Tolbukhin concluded that fellow was a corporal or sergeant. From his hiding place, he kept an eye on the sensible Nazi. *I'll shoot you first,* he thought.

Grunting and cursing—but cursing in whispers now—the Germans started making their way up the side of the *balka.* Yes, there was the one who kept his mind on business. Kill enough of that kind and the rest grew less efficient. The Germans got rid of Soviet officers and commissars on the same brutal logic.

Closer, closer . . . A submachine gun spat a great number of bullets, but was hardly a weapon of finesse or accuracy. "Fire!" Tolbukhin shouted, and blazed away. The Nazi noncom tumbled down the steep side of the wash. Some of those bullets had surely bitten him. The rest of the German squad lasted only moments longer. One of the Hitlerites lay groaning till a Red Army man went down and cut his throat. Who could guess how long he might last otherwise? Too long, maybe.

"*Now* we go on home," Tolbukhin said.

They had practiced withdrawal from such raids many times before, and *maskirovka* came naturally to Soviet soldiers. They took an indirect route back to the collective farm, concealing their tracks as best they could. The Hitlerites sometimes hunted them with dogs. They knew how to deal with that, too. Whenever they came to rivulets running through the steppe, they trampled along in them for a couple of hundred meters, now going one way, now the other. A couple of them also had their canteens filled with fiery pepper-flavored vodka. They poured some on their trail every now and then; it drove the hounds frantic.

"Waste of good vodka," one of the soldiers grumbled.

"If it keeps us alive, it isn't wasted," Tolbukhin said. "If it keeps us alive, we can always get more later."

"The Comrade General is right," Khrushchev said. Where he was often too familiar with Tolbukhin, he was too formal with the men.

This time, though, it turned out not to matter. One of the other soldiers gave the fellow who'd complained a shot in the ribs with his elbow. "*Da,* Volya, the Phantom is right," he said. "The Phantom's been right a lot of times, and he hasn't hardly been wrong yet. Let's give a cheer for the Phantom."

It was another soft cheer, because they weren't quite safe yet, but a cheer nonetheless: "*Urra* for the Phantom Tolbukhin!"

Maybe, Tolbukhin thought as a grin stretched itself across his face, *maybe we'll lick the Hitlerites yet, in spite of everything.* He didn't know whether he believed that or not. He knew he'd keep trying. He trotted on. Collective Farm 122 wasn't far now.

Deconstruction Gang

This one was inspired by a ROAD CONSTRUCTION AHEAD freeway sign. I wondered what a ROAD DECONSTRUCTION AHEAD sign would mean, and how deconstruction would work if it were a real technology, not just a technique for literary analysis. Yes, it's in second person, present tense. When writing about deconstruction, daunting narrative technique sort of comes with the territory.

You have your degree. You are, as the piece of thick, creamy paper they handed you attests, a doctor of philosophy in English with all the rights and privileges thereto pertaining.

You need not have spent years studying literary theory to get to the outside of the text printed on that creamy paper, to understand what those rights and privileges thereto pertaining are: nothing.

You have other pieces of paper, not so thick, not so creamy as your diploma, but textually similar in what they offer: nothing. You know the polite phrases so well: *Thank you for your interest in the assistant professorship at the University, but . . . ; pleased to be in the position of choosing from among such a large number of highly qualified applicants; confident that with your outstanding record you will soon be able to find an appointment elsewhere; due to financial constraints, the Department will not be hiring this year.*

Critical theory makes continuity and meaning suspect, but you have trouble interpreting these polite letters as implying anything save *fuck you very much* and *up yours truly.*

No one wants you.

Along with your degree, you have an apartment, a car, a fiancée whose father suspects academics on general principles, unemployed academics in particular, and most especially the one unemployed academic who happens to be engaged to his one daughter. You also have no health insurance, which seems increasingly insane each day older than thirty you become. You know every possible way to make macaroni and cheese taste like something else. You know none of them works.

You never wanted to be anything but a scholar, to teach other budding scholars the ineffable difference between *différence* and *différance*, to show them that which appears in no text but lurks between the words of all texts. But too many have the same ambition. Too many of them have jobs; none is left for you.

You can't remember when you first thought about looking for work outside the university. That first time, you shook your head in indignation; such an indignity could never befall you. Your checking account was fuller then, your credit cards less overdrawn. Your landlord made no pointed remarks when you walked past her on the way to the laundry room.

After a while, you see your choice clearly: you can go forth and confront the Other, or you can sit tight, watch your savings slip through your fingers until nothing is left . . . and then go forth and confront the Other.

Put that way, it should be obvious. As a matter of fact, it is obvious. You wait a last week even so, hoping a miracle will happen. God must be busy somewhere else. The five dollars you waste on the lottery is just that, waste, and one more rejection letter adds insult to injury.

Tomorrow, you tell yourself, but you put it off again till the day after.

The last time you looked for work away from a campus was after your senior year of high school. That's a long time ago now. You wonder how much things have changed—you wonder how much you've changed—since then. You'll find out soon.

When the morning comes, you put on slacks, shirt, tie, the herringbone tweed jacket which irrevocably brands you an academic, the shiny black shoes that always start squeezing your toes after you wear them for fifteen minutes. You throw half a dozen copies of your vita into a manila folder, go downstairs to your car. You hope it starts. It does.

You have your list with you: addresses for three banks, an insurance company, a software outfit that needs someone who can write documentation, and a God-knows-what called Humanoid Systems, Inc., that needs a technical editor. None of them is what you had in mind when you decided to go into the graduate program. Were it happening to someone else, it might be funny in an existential way.

You soon see you won't get to any of your possibilities very soon. Traffic is a mess; the main street into downtown has only one lane open in each direction. You start, stop, go forward a few more feet, stop again. You watch the temperature needle creep upward and remember the garage man telling you your water pump won't last forever. Neon-orange diamond-shaped signs seem to hang from every street light and telephone pole: RIGHT 2 LANES CLOSED AHEAD alternates with ROAD DECONSTRUCTION IN PROGRESS. You have plenty of time to read them.

You creep forward another couple of blocks. Then, under a DECONSTRUCTION IN PROGRESS sign, you see a different one, a small black-and-white rectangle: ROAD CREW HIRING OFFICE, 2 BLOCKS EAST, complete with an arrow for the directionally challenged.

A nihilistic wind blows through you. If you're out to confront the Other, why not at its most Otherly? Besides, you'll break out of this godawful traffic jam. When you get to the corner, you turn right.

A line snakes toward a house with its front door open. You almost make a U-turn in the middle of the street when you see the people who are standing in that line: pick-and-shovel types, every one of them. You're not desperate enough to want calluses on your hands, not yet. But you've come this far. You may as well find out just who's getting hired. You park your car and walk over to the tail of the line.

With your jacket and tie, you are the Other here. A couple of workbooted musclemen elbow each other in the ribs and point your way. You pretend you don't notice them. They don't hassle you, though, for which you thank the God you can't quite believe in. They need work as badly as you do, and they've been in these lines before: they know they'll get thrown out if they give you a bad time.

The line slithers forward. Men fall into place behind you. Most of the people who come out the front door look glum. A few wear ear-to-ear grins. They've found jobs, so they'll be able to make the next payment on the Harley after all.

You make your slow way up the stairs, across the porch, and into the house. It's as tacky inside as you expected, maybe worse. Till this minute, you never believed anybody would actually frame a print of those poker-playing dogs and hang it in the living room. Again, you almost turn around and leave.

But by now you're only three men away from the hiring boss behind the office-style folding table sitting in the middle of the floor. You watch him, listen to him while he questions the guys ahead of you. He is the Other, all right: hard hat, cigar, beer belly with a black T-shirt stretched obscenely tight across it. On the T-shirt is a skeleton in a football helmet. The legend reads, KICK ASS AND TAKE NAMES.

The hiring boss talks as if he's been chewing rocks for the past couple of hundred years. "Sorry, bud, can't use you," he growls to the man in front of you. The fellow's longshoreman shoulders sag. He turns and shambles out of the house. Now it's your turn.

The hiring boss looks you over. The way he takes in everything at once makes you realize for the first time that, while he might not be educated, he's a long way from stupid. The cigar waggles in his mouth. "Well, well," he says. "What have we here?"

He hasn't seen anything like you in a while, that's for certain. If he sounded scornful, you'd walk away. But he doesn't; he's just honestly curious. Trying to make your voice somewhere near as deep as his, you answer, "I'm looking for work on your deconstruction crew."

"Are you?" He looks you over again, in a different kind of way. "Just so you know, kid, we call it a gang, not a crew." You want to glare; nobody's called you *kid* since you were one. But this fellow holds that greatest of all plums, a job, in the palm of his hand. Besides, if you annoy him, you have no doubt he'll kick your ass around the block now and worry about lawsuits later.

He holds out his hand. You give him a copy of your vita, meanwhile trying to decide which of your original targets you'll save for another day. The bank that's been having trouble with the FDIC over too many bad loans, probably. You say, "I'm a recent Ph.D. from—"

He grunts. It's not a *go on* grunt; it's a *shut up* grunt. He goes through your vita so fast you know he's not really reading it, then tosses it carelessly onto the table in front of him. "I see more bullshit on this job," he remarks to no one in particular. When he looks up at you again, cunning lights his narrow eyes. Around the fat cigar, he says, "Awright, kid, you're so damn smart, tell me something—*quick,* now—about Paul de Man."

For a second you just gape, astounded a dinosaur like this ever heard of de Man. Then you remember he bosses deconstruction crews (no, gangs; you'd like to trace the evolution of that text one day). He'd better have some idea of what his hired help is up to.

He's still watching you; you feel the same almost paralyzing attack of nerves you did in front of the committee for your doctoral exams. As you did then, you fight it down: "One of the things de Man talks about is the figurality that alters the way we perceive what a text means, the mechanism through which any text asserts the opposite of what it appears to say."

The hiring boss's heavy features light up in the sort of smile he'd give if he drew four nines to an ace kicker. "Goddamn! You know what you're talking about!" His handshake crushes your fingers, but you don't dare wince any more than you dared glare before. Then he says the magic words: "When do you want to start?"

You haven't asked about pay yet, or benefits. This was just supposed to be a nihilistic lark. Now all of a sudden it's serious, so you ask. The answers make you blink: better money than any assistant professor's job you've seen advertised, and *much* better bennies. You hear yourself say, "If you really need me, I can be here tomorrow morning."

The hiring boss squashes your hand again. "Kid, you're okay." He turns around, grabs a white hard hat from a pile behind him, reaches up and sticks it on your head. You feel as if you've just been knighted. He says, "Be right here at half past seven. We'll do your paperwork then, and I'll assign you to a gang. See you tomorrow."

Reality starts to set in as you head back to your car. What have you just done to yourself? When you get in, the first thing you do after you fasten your seat belt is take off the hard hat and throw it onto the mat under the glove compartment. Even if you can't find an academic job right now, do you want to work the *roads*?

You look at the manila folder still almost full of vitas, then at your watch. If you hustle, you can still spread your name around today. Then you look at the plastic hard hat. You have a job right there if you want it. What a funny feeling that is!

In the end, you drive back to your apartment instead of downtown. You call up your fiancée. She squeals in your ear when you tell her you found work, then says absolutely nothing after you explain what kind of work it is. You picture her by the phone with her mouth hanging open.

After a long, long pause, she asks, "Are you sure this is what you want to do with your life?" She sounds wary, as if she's wondering what else the you she thinks she knows has managed to hide for the past three and a half years.

"Of course it's not what I want to do with my life. But it's money, and we need that." When you tell her how much money it is, she inhales sharply: she's at least as surprised as you were. You say, "And you know what else?"

"No, what?"

"They gave me my very own hard hat, too."

That does it. You both start cracking up over the phone. She says, "I can't wait to see you in it. Are you going to start hanging out in cowboy bars, too?"

"Jesus, I hope not." If that isn't a fate worse than death, you can't think of one offhand. "Look, honey, if this turns out to be awful, I'll quit, that's all. But the pay is good enough that I ought to see what it's like."

"Okay. Dad'll be glad to hear you've gotten hired." She hesitates a split second too long, then says, "Do you want me to tell him what the job is?"

You can hear she doesn't want to. You can't really blame her, either. "No, you don't need to, not right away. We'll see how it goes."

"Okay," she says again, and yes, she is relieved. But before you can decide whether you're irked about it, she adds, "I love you, honey." In the face of that, irk can wait.

You microwave your favorite frozen entrée to celebrate, and wash down the herbed chicken with a glass of cheap white wine. You contemplate a second glass, but virtue triumphs. You're going to have to be sharp tomorrow. No David Letterman tonight, either.

At half past six, the alarm clock goes off right beside your head, like a car bomb when the timer reaches the hour of doom. You shower in a hurry, put on jeans and a T-shirt with the tweed jacket over it, throw a Pop-Tart into the toaster. You gulp a cup of muddy instant coffee, then head down to your car.

When you pull up in front of the hiring house, you start to get out, then remember the hard hat and plant it on your head. It's not light like a baseball cap. You wonder how your neck will like wearing it all day.

The hiring boss grins when you walk in. "Ha! You did come back. When I take on a guy out of college, I always wonder if he'll show up the next morning. Come here. I'm gonna need your signature about sixty thousand times."

You come. He's just barely kidding—you sign and you sign and you sign. It's a government job, after all. Your formal job title, you learn, is deconstructive analyst. You like it. It won't look half bad on your vita, so long as you're vague about exactly what it entails.

By the time you write your name for the last time, it doesn't look like yours any more. You might as well be signing traveler's checks. "All right," the hiring boss says when you're done. "I'm gonna put you on Gang 4; they've been a man short for a coupla weeks now. Here—" He points to one of the maps spread out on the table. "They're at 27th and Durant. You hustle, you'll be there by 8:45. Ask for Tony. I'll call him, let him know you're on your way. He'll show you where you need to go." He slaps you on the back. "Good to have you aboard."

You're still a long way from sure it's good to be aboard, but you go back to your car and head for 27th and Durant. The hiring boss knows how traffic works, all right; you get there at 8:43. Fellows in hard hats check you out as you head toward them. You're wearing yours, too, so you may be one of them, but they've never seen you before. You say, "I'm looking for Tony."

"I'm Tony." He's a big black guy, looks like he played defensive end at a medium-good college maybe twenty years ago. His handshake has the gentleness of controlled strength; his smile shows a mouthful of gold. "Hiring boss told me you were coming. Good to have you with us, man. We've been understrength too long. Come on, I'll take you over to the deconstruction gang. Watch where you step."

It's no idle warning. You step over boards and small pieces of pipe and tools, walk around other pieces of pipe almost big enough for you to go through them without stooping. Tony negotiates the chaos as effortlessly as a chamois bouncing up an Alp. He leads you to four men in hard hats sitting on dirt-strewn grass beside a trench that looks as if it escaped from World War I.

"Here's the new fish," Tony says.

They get up, shake your hand, give you their names: Brian, Louis, Pete, and Jerome. You all talk for a few minutes, getting to know one another. It turns out Brian, Louis, and Jerome are refugee academics like you; Brian, whose hair is gray, has been doing this for fifteen years now. You still find that a chilling thought, even if you're part of the gang now, too. Pete, who's almost the size of Tony, picked up deconstruction after he joined the road gang. He's not as smooth as the other three, but listening to him you can tell he knows enough to do the job.

Names flash back and forth through the chitchat: Derrida and de Man, Levinas and Bataille, Hegel and Heidegger, Melville and Taylor. You never thought you'd have to raise your voice to make them heard over the pounding roar of jackhammers and the diesel snarl of skiploaders. The world has done a lot of things to you that you never thought of till they happened.

Finally, Brian, who's the gang leader, says, "Enough chatter. Time for us to get busy and earn our day's pay."

You sit on the grass with the rest of the deconstruction gang. Everyone is quiet for a while, peering down into the trench. You begin to get a handle on the problem: traffic here has got heavier than the roadbed was designed to handle. You can see how things have shifted, how pipes are bent, how this stretch of Durant is going to be nothing but potholes and cracked asphalt unless you do something about it now. A proper deconstruction job when they first built the road would have saved a lot of trouble, but back then they'd never heard of deconstruction. Now you have to worry about fixing the old blunders.

Brian starts out by getting everybody into the proper frame of mind to do what needs doing. He says, "We are the instruments that change the world. Since we are here, we have to understand what's in front of us and act to transform the world and ourselves."

You look admiringly at him: it's good Hegel, translated into language anybody can understand. Listening to Brian, you start to see how someone like Pete can pick up an abstruse skill like deconstruction just by keeping his ears open and thinking about what he hears.

And it's Pete, in fact, who supports Brian and provides the framework for the heavy deconstruction that will follow: "Error isn't fatal, so long as it keeps a grasp on the problem at hand. Even when you say the opposite of what you should be saying, you're still addressing the proper issue."

The proper issue here, of course, is the roadbed, and the error its weakness. Back when it was built, Durant was a residential street. Now it leads to a big shopping district and an industrial park. There are generally more cars around these days, too.

Brian looks at you next. Your stomach knots; it's like the first time you're called on in class. Outside the spoken text, evasive but pervading as Derrida's *différance*, a single thought hangs in the air: *let's see what the new guy can do.*

You're ready, too. You've been thinking about this ever since you impressed the hiring boss yesterday. Even so, you take a deep breath before you say, "As far as I can see, the best approach to deconstructing this roadbed is to bear in mind that nothing, whether the idea or text or roadway, truly happens *in relation to* anything else, before, after, or contemporary. Things *do not* relate to one another; they just *are*. We have to reintegrate the things that are to suit our purposes, not those of the original road builders."

Silence for a few seconds. Then Brian reaches out with a closed fist and lightly taps you on your denim-covered knee. You grin. You've passed the test. Better—you've aced it.

From then on, the work flows smoothly. Your English professors always insisted deconstruction is a universally valid technique. In your undergrad days, you found historians using deconstructive concepts like demystification and privileged ideas. Now you truly involve yourself in the broader application of the technology.

From the framework Brian, Peter, and you have set up, the gang goes on as you thought it would, analyzing the textuality of the roadbed, considering all the implications of the opposition roadway/traveler.

In the old days, they would have been inextricably linked. Travelers went where and how the roadway allowed, and that was that. It's different now; deconstruction has established that the roadway possesses its own existence, independent of travelers and their purposes. Because events are just events, not related, deconstruction lets the gang reach back through the false connections of time and make the roadway into what it always should have been, regardless of the builders' original intentions.

It's the hardest work you've ever done. Sweat trickles down from under your hard hat, drips off your chin. You take off your jacket and lay it on the ground. But in the trench, you can see the progress you're making. Jerome pushes against the referential being of the roadbed. Just as the new figurality, the one you've been grinding toward, begins to take shape, the lunch whistle blows.

"We've got to keep at it," Brian says quickly, before anyone can get up and head for the catering truck that's just parked down the block. "If we knock off now, we'll get a regression to the opposite and we'll have to do most of the work all over again."

So on you go, though the savor of hot grease from the truck makes your stomach growl like an angry beast. Tony walks by, sees you're all too busy to go to lunch. He doesn't say anything; he knows deconstruction is delicate work and doesn't want to distract you. But when you get to a place where you can stop for a while, he comes back with a gray cardboard carton full of hamburgers, fries, and Cokes.

"Tony, you're a lifesaver," Brian says. Everybody else nods.

Tony just grins. "Keeping you folks doing your job is part of my job." He won't even let any of you pay for the food. He has other things to see to. With people like him in this business, you begin to understand why the rest of the academics in your gang aren't busting a gut trying to escape.

Then you unwrap your hamburger from its yellow waxed paper and sink your teeth in. It's burnt on the outside, raw and soggy in the middle, and it hasn't been hot, or even warm, for quite a while. "Dewishush," you say with your mouth full.

You eat fast. So does everyone else; the deconstruction you've established up to now is only metastable. If it regresses before you can establish and validate your new and strong synthesis, you'll be in deep *kimchi*, worse off than if you never started.

It tries to snap, too, not five minutes after you go back to work. It's Louis who saves the bacon with a beautiful adaptation from Derrida. Together, you force the road back toward the pattern unperceived by its designers, toward force and away from weakness, a signifying structure of the sort only deconstructive analysis can produce.

"De la Grammatologie," you say when you have a moment to catch your breath.

"Bet your ass." Louis sounds even more exhausted than you are. If he is, he has a right to be; he carried the ball when things were toughest. After that, you're going downhill. Deconstruction by its nature subverts what was authoritative and revises what has been accepted. The road will be, and indeed always *will have been*, as it should exist by your analysis, not as it was made—with good intentions, no doubt, but also with ultimate ignorance—by the authors of its design.

You keep close watch on the roadbed, tracking the progress your figurality makes in replacing its inadequate predecessor. For a long, tense moment, the deconstructive operation allows both versions of the roadbed to exist together. Then, as if in consummation, the veil is torn and the new figurality displaces the old for good.

Tony, naturally, is there when it happens. "Way to go," he says to Brian. "The night shift'll have to check out what you've done, of course, but it looks real good to me."

"Thanks." Brian points at you. "He pulls his weight. Glad you found him."

Tony nods. "I thought he looked good when I met him." You just stare down at your dirty Reeboks, but you feel nine feet tall, maybe ten. These guys are all right.

Brian glances at his watch. "My God, is it five o'clock already? We wouldn't have come close to finishing this stretch today without a whole gang." He turns to you. "Want to have a beer before you head home? I'll buy."

You're not much of a beer drinker, but you say, "Sounds wonderful. Thanks." Camaraderie counts.

Your joints creak as you stand up and stretch. All over the work site, men are putting away tools, heading for their cars or for the bus stop. *Quitting time,* you think. Fair enough—you've earned your day's pay, as Brian said when you started out what feels like a week ago.

A pretty redhead in *tight* jeans walks by across the street. Along with everyone else who notices her, you whistle like a steam engine. She just walks faster. A couple of guys laugh. You feel sheepish; you'd never have done that back on campus. But what the hell? You have to fit in with the gang.

The Green Buffalo

Sticking things in places and times where they don't belong is one of the standard techniques of science fiction. I had a lot of fun doing it in the context of a Wild West tall tale. John Hatcher was a real paleontologist, and also really was a good poker player. By all surviving accounts, there were times when he needed to be.

I'm stackin' sacks of beans in the back of my brother Pete's general store when the door through the false front opens up and hits the bell a whack. The beans can wait. I hustle out front to see who it is.

"Mornin', Mr. Hatcher," I says, and touch one finger to where my hat brim'd be if I was wearing a hat—Pete, he always says be polite. "What can I do for you today? You haven't come down to Lusk in a while."

"Hello, Joe," John Hatcher answers. He's a little skinny fellow, already mostly bald no matter that he can't be more than thirty. He looks like an undertaker, is what he looks like. Anyway, he goes on, "I came in to send a new shipment off to Professor Marsh, and I figured I'd telegraph to let him know it's on the way."

"Right you are." I go on over to the telegraph clicker off in one corner, set myself down. "Go ahead. You want to write your message out, or can you just talk it to me?"

"I'll talk it," he says, the way he usually does—he knows how to say what he thinks, does John Hatcher. "Let's see, today's the seventeenth, isn't it? All right, here we go, Joe: 'August 17,

1890. To Othniel Charles Marsh, Yale University, New Haven, Connecticut.' "

"Spell me 'Othniel,' " I say. I've sent the man a dozen telegrams, and I never can rightly remember how his name goes.

Hatcher spells it out, then goes on, " 'Coming east will be two skulls and other skeletal remains of *Triceratops brevicornus—*' "

"Of *what*?" I say, and I take my hand off the key. "You know you got to spell me out those funny names you throw around." He spells out TRICERATOPS BREVICORNUS, nice and slow, and I tap it out a letter at a time. Then I ask him, "Beggin' your pardon, Mr. Hatcher, but what the hell is a Triceratops brevi-whatever?"

"A dinosaur, Joe, a dinosaur with a skull as long as you are and ten times as heavy." John Hatcher's been out here for years, diggin' up old bones and shippin' 'em back East. Damn fool way for a grown man to spend his time if you ask me, especially for a man as good with a deck of cards as Hatcher. Anyways, he goes on, " '—excavated from the Upper Cretaceous' "—I had him spell that one, too—" 'Lance Creek beds. More to be forthcoming as discovered. John Bell Hatcher.' "

I send it off, then count up the words and say, "That'll be a dollar twenty, Mr. Hatcher." He tosses down a gold dollar and a couple of dimes. I ask him, "What else can I do for you today?"

"Well, we're running low on beans out at the camp," he says, and it's all I can do to keep from cheering. I'd sooner sell beans than stack 'em, any day. He wants some salt, too, and some flour, as much plaster of Paris as we have, and a couple of other things I misremember. Then he says, "If you want to help get my boxes down from the wagon over at the train station, there's two dollars gold in it for you."

"I'm your man," I say, and we both head out of the store. I shut the door after me, but Pete comes up just then, all fresh-shaved from the barber shop. "Got some stevedore work from Mr. Hatcher here," I tell him. He waves for me to go on, so I go.

Seems like half the menfolks in Lusk are already gathered round Hatcher's wagon by the time I get there. He needed us, too—we work and we work, and by the time we wrestle this big crate off it and down the ramp to the ground, we're licked, I tell

you. "What the devil you really got in there, anyways?" somebody asks Hatcher.

"Dinosaur bones," he answers, the same as he always does.
He's been shippin' the things east out of Lusk for years now.
'Most everybody in town's rode out to his digs one time or an-
other, to look things over. Ain't nobody ever caught him minin'
gold on the sly yet. Now he says, "I do thank you, gentlemen.
Drinks are on me."

Nobody tells him no, either. We're all sweaty from fightin' the
crate, and even if we hadn't been, who's going to turn down a
free shot? We all troop over to the Rebel Yell, and Hatcher buys,
just like he said he would. Then he sits himself down at one of
the tables, and five or six of the boys sit down with him.

Me, I knock back my whiskey and get on out of there, before
I'm fool enough to try playin' poker with John Hatcher again.
That's not a wise thing to do, and I learned it the expensive way.
So has every poker-playin' man in Lusk, but it don't stop some
of 'em from comin' back after him. Some folks purely ain't got
no sense, you ask me.

I go on back to the store and start stackin' up what Hatcher ordered from me. Pete asks me why I'm back so soon and I tell
him the same thing I just told you—"Hatcher's in a poker game."
Pete, he only grunts. He's stubborner'n me, my brother is, so
Mr. John Bell Hatcher won a deal more money off him than off
me before Pete figured out he couldn't lick him. You throw me in
the ocean, I'll tell you pretty damn quick I'm in over my head.
My brother, he'd sooner try to wade to China, he would.

Maybe there's some new suckers in the Rebel Yell that day,
maybe the cards are even hotter for Hatcher than usual, or
maybe he's just plain glad to be in town—even a pissant excuse
for a town like I know Lusk is—because he doesn't come in for
his supplies all afternoon long. Come to think of it, maybe he
went upstairs a time or two, too, instead of playin' cards all that
while. Women's another thing you'll find in town that's in short
supply diggin' old bones out by Lance Creek.

The sun's close to setting when the telegraph clicker starts to
chatter. Pete's closer to it than I am, so he gets the message

down. When it's done, he gives it to me. "It's for Hatcher," he says. "Why don't you take it on over to him?"

So I take it. Sure enough, he's still at the poker table when I walk back into the Rebel Yell, and sure enough he's got a nice stack of gold and silver in front of him. He's got a bottle in front of him, too, a bottle he's been workin' on, but it don't look to have made him lose his card sense, not one bit of it.

"Telegram for you, Mr. Hatcher," I says. "It's from New Haven, it is."

"I thank you kindly, Joe." Hatcher takes the telegram from me, reads it through, and then, so help me Hannah, he starts to howl like a coyote, he's laughin' so hard.

"What's funny?" I ask him. He's been comin' into Lusk three, four years now, and I ain't never heard him laugh like that before.

"Listen to this." He picks up the telegram from where he's dropped it on the table, reads it out loud to me and everybody else. It goes like this: " 'To John Bell Hatcher. The perfidious Cope may by pure luck have found and described in *Monoclonius* the first of the ceratopsian dinosaurs, but my own' (that's Marsh talking, not me, mind you) 'continued discoveries of these fine specimens of *Triceratops* serve to cast him into the shade which is his natural home. Signed, O.C. Marsh.' "

I'm not the only one inside the Rebel Yell scratchin' my head over all that. I say, "Beggin' your pardon, Mr. Hatcher, but I don't quite see the joke."

"Well, for one thing, Marsh and Cope have hated each other's guts for twenty years now. If Cope were in a firepit of hell and screaming out for water, Marsh would hand him a bottle of kerosene—and the other way round, too. So if I've found a bigger, fancier dinosaur that's related to one Cope found first, half the reason Marsh is tickled about it is that he gets to score points off Cope's hide."

"I always thought professors were quiet, peaceable sorts," I says.

Hatcher commences to laugh again, but this time he gets hold of himself before it runs away with him. He goes on, "For another thing, notice they're *his* dinosaurs, even if I'm the one who's excavating them and shipping them off to him. He named the strata—the rock formations—from which we're digging *Triceratops* the Ceratops bed, and traced them eight hundred miles along the flanks of the Rockies, and carefully explored them, too, all in the space of three and a half days' time in the field."

"He did?" I say.

"He says he did." Hatcher lays a finger alongside of his nose.

"This here's a professor? Sounds more like a snake-oil salesman to me."

"He is. And if he were selling, you'd buy, too. He's like that." Hatcher sets down the telegram again, picks up his cards, just like he's forgot what he's holding. He tosses a gold half-eagle and then an eagle onto the middle of the table, careless-like. "See your five dollars, Fred, and I'll raise you ten."

Long as I'm at the Rebel Yell, I figure I'll buy me a drink. So I do, and sure as hell Fred loses that hand. He stomps out, all disgusted, but somebody else with more money'n sense sits down in his seat. John Hatcher, he doesn't even smile.

I go on back to the store, work some more. Hatcher's stuff is all piled up nice and neat, but he doesn't come get it. The fellow who took Fred's seat must be one natural-born greenhorn. Finally Pete and me, we go on up to bed up above in the attic.

Hatcher finally shows up the next morning. I hear later he'd played poker all night long, but he doesn't look it. I help him and his people load up their wagon—believe me, what we throw in isn't near as heavy as them bones we'd took out the day before. He pays me off, starts to get up onto the wagon, then stops and rubs his chin like he's just thought of somethin'.

He had, too. He turns around, says to me, "Joe, how would you like to ride out to camp with us? We're short of fresh meat, but we've been too busy digging to do much in the way of hunting. Maybe you and a couple of other folks from Lusk can shoot some for us."

"Three dollars a day, like the last time?" I ask. He just nods. It doesn't faze him a bit. I don't know whether he's spending

Marsh's money or what he wins at poker, but he always seems to have plenty. I say, "Let me go in and ask Pete."

I do. Pete says, "Sure, go on. I'll do well enough alone for a few days, and you'll have yourself a good time." So I go get my Winchester and two, three boxes of shells, walk over to the livery stable for my horse, and I'm back to Hatcher's wagon inside half an hour. By then he's not there—he's off gettin' his other people. My pa, he fought in the States War. He always used to say soldierin' was like that—as soon as one thing's ready, another one ain't. So I light up a cigar and I wait.

Hatcher, he comes back before too real long, I will say. Then up ride Jake Snow and Clancy O'Doole, one after the other. Clancy works for his brother Charlie, the farrier. Jake, he just drifts. Sometimes he rides herd, sometimes he does odd jobs, sometimes he just sits in the Rebel Yell cadgin' drinks. Can't deny he's a good man with a gun, though.

We ride out of Lusk, must have been a little past eight. The sun's right nice that time o' day. It lights up the red cliffs west of town pretty as a penny postcard. And you know what else? The air's a sight fresher out of town, too, away from the chimneys and the stables and the privies. I ought to get out more often. I really should.

We rattle along, not in any tearin' hurry but makin' good time all the same. Somewhere around noon, Hatcher goes inside the wagon, lays down, and damned if he doesn't lay himself out on top of the beans and go to sleep. How he can have such a clear conscience after skinnin' so many folks at the card table is purely beyond me. But when he comes out a couple of hours later he's cheery as could be, might as well have slept the whole night long.

By the time the sun goes down, we're every one of us ready for bedrolls. We're still half a day out from where the rest of Hatcher's crew is digging. He wants to talk about his bones, but he's the one had a nap. The rest of us are too worn (and I'm too sore-assed; I hadn't been in the saddle all day for a while) to listen long.

Anyway, we get to Hatcher's camp a little past noon the next day. He set himself up by this outcrop of rock in the middle of nowhere, near as I can see, but seein' the way he knows poker, I figure he knows his own game, too. When we ride up, a couple of his people that was still there come runnin' over and shoutin' like they found gold or somethin' really good.

But it's only more bones. They're carryin' on somethin' fierce about a fibia and tibula or tibia and fibula or whatever the hell the right names of 'em are. Hatcher gets all excited, too. He jumps down from the wagon and goes runnin' over like wolves are after him. Over his shoulder, he says, "Joe, Jake, Clancy, this is what we spend our time doing out here, if you care to see it."

I get down from my horse and go on over after him. Sure as hell, his people've dug a couple of great big bones out of the rock. There's picks leaned up against the outcrop, and chisels, and little awls and things like a dentist uses to poke inside your mouth with.

John Hatcher, he's carryin' on like my sister Betty did after she had her baby. He's as careful with those bones as Betty was with Tyler, too—he touches 'em like they'd break if he looked at 'em sideways. Then one of the fellows who was there when we came in says, "We saved these so you could have a look at them. We'll protect them now."

Well, blast me if they don't start coatin' them old, dead bones with plaster, just like a sawbones would do if I busted an arm. Hatcher sees I'm kind of starin' like, so he says, "We don't want them to break either on the way to the train or going east on it. They can't grow back together again, you know." He's just about readin' my mind. No wonder he's such a blamed good poker player.

Jake hasn't even got off his horse. He shifts his chaw, spits, and says, "Let's get huntin', if we're gonna get huntin'. "

"Yeah," Clancy says. So I mount up and the three of us, we ride on out of that camp. When we're out of earshot, Clancy grins and says, "And if we take a little longer to find meat than we reckoned, well, at three dollars a day, who's gonna complain?"

"You got that right," Jake says, and spits again.

Twenty years ago, you ride around in this part of the country and you'd fall over buffalo, there was that many of 'em. They're a lot thinner on the ground nowadays, what with repeatin' rifles and all. Truth is, I wasn't lookin' to come onto a trail. Pronghorn, I figured, 'd be about the best we can do.

But I'd just stuck a cigar in my mouth late that afternoon when blast me if we don't come across a buffalo track runnin' east, and a fresh one, too. Jake looks at Clancy, Clancy looks at me. "If we take it kind of easy," I say finally, "we won't catch up to 'em tonight. We'll worry about 'em again come mornin'. "

"I purely like the way you think, Joe," Clancy says.

So we make ourselves a little fire and gnaw on some jerked beef and hard bread. I brew up a pot of coffee, we all drink some, then we draw straws for who gets first watch. I get the short one, worse luck for me. But what with Indians and outlaws and all, you don't have somebody up at night and you'll wake up with an extra eyehole right in the middle of your forehead.

I wake Clancy and go to bed. When Clancy wakes Jake, he's loud enough so he wakes me, too, but not for long. Next thing that wakes me is the sun. We eat some more bread, pour down some more coffee, and off we go.

The buffalo, they haven't been gallivantin' around in the night time either, so we know pretty soon we're gainin' on 'em. Up ahead we see the cloud of dust the herd is raisin'. I peer toward the cloud, tryin' to make out critters through that dust. I just about think I can when the goddamnedest thing happens. I don't hardly know how to put it into words.

One minute I'm ridin' along without a care in the world but for tryin' to spot buffalo, the next I'm so dizzy I almost fall off my horse. He snorts, too, like he don't like what's goin' on either, and damn near stumbles, which doesn't make stayin' in the saddle any easier. Jake cusses and Clancy yells, so I'm not the only one who feels somethin' peculiar.

The dizzies go away after a few seconds, thank you Jesus. I guess they do for Clancy, too, 'cause he says, "That was right strange."

And it gets stranger, let me tell you. My horse puts his head down to snatch a bite to eat. Everybody knows what Wyoming prairie's like—sagebrush and tumbleweed and grass, all of it dry and yellow by the time August rolls around. Well, may God strike me dead if my horse isn't chewin' on ferns like you'd see if you was by a streambank up in the mountains somewheres, and them just as fresh and green and pretty as ever you'd hope to find.

Not far away is a kind of plant like I never seen before. You take a palm tree—you know, one of those funny ones they have down near the Mexican border, looks like a feather duster for a giant—and forget about the trunk, just have the leaves comin' out of a knobby thing down low to the ground, and you'll get the idea.

Well, I could go on a while longer, on account of there's a lot more funny plants around, but I reckon you'd think I was just makin' it up, so I'll leave well enough alone. It was purely perplexin', I tell you that. Like I said, Jake, he's done a deal o' driftin', so I turn to him and say, "Did you ever see the like?"

"Not even close," he answers. Just then a lizard scurries out from under one fern and over to another. I'm not talkin' about some little fence lizard or horny toad, mind you; this critter's big as my arm and half again as thick.

When Jake sees it, I thought he was gonna swallow his chaw. That's always worth a laugh, watchin' a fellow puke up his guts, but he kept it where it belongs. He spits again, and says, "Let's us head on outa here." Nobody argues with him, no sirree.

We ride on about a quarter mile maybe, then the dizzies hit me again. This time, though, they're not so bad as they was before. My horse missteps, but I jerk his head up and he's all right, too. When I look down, the prairie's back to bein' the prairie, just like it ought to.

Jake and Clancy, they see that, too. Clancy says, "Next time I drink in the Rebel Yell, I'm gonna watch the barkeep closer. I think maybe he put locoweed in my whiskey."

"We all saw the same thing, Clancy," I tell him. Then I stop and think—how do I know that's so? So I say, "The ferns and funny kind of squashed-down palm and that big fat lizard—"

When I talk about the lizard, Jake spits again, so I know he seen it. Clancy nods, too. I tell you true, I'm right relieved. I wouldn't want to think I made that stuff up out of my own head.

We ride on after the buffalo. They'd gained some on us—I guess we spent a while gawpin' after we got dizzy the first time.

Pretty soon, though, we come close enough to 'em to really start pickin' 'em out one by one. We ride closer, lookin' 'em over. Finally we're within a couple hundred yards, and nobody's sayin' a thing. I got to know if Jake and Clancy see the same thing I do. I just got to, so I say, "Boys, ain't one of them buffalo *green*?"

Clancy, he ups and crosses himself and shouts out, "Jesus, Mary, Joseph, and all the saints be praised, I'm not the only one!" He must be plumb shook up—first time I ever heard him sound like an Irishman. Jake spits twice and nods, so I figure he sees it, too.

We don't none of us say anything again for a while, but we don't need to, either. We're all makin' for that green buffalo. The closer we come, the older it looks. I start to figure the green's some kind of nasty mange, on account of it don't look to have any hair anywhere, just the bare hide. That makes me want to forget about killin' it—the stuff might be catchin'. Then I figure I better kill it, so it can't spread the sickness to the rest of the herd, or to the cattle the ranchers run hereabouts.

And then I get a look at its horns. They're bigger'n any I've ever seen on a buffalo, the ones above its eyes, I mean. But on top of those—no, not on top, in front—oh, hell, you know what I mean—it had another horn, a third one, right on its snout. I'm not makin' that up, so help me. Never seen one like that before nor since. Never seen a green one before nor since, either, come to that.

The regular buffalo, it's like they don't know what to make of the green one any more'n me and Clancy and Jake do. There's considerable pushin' and snortin' and shovin'. Some of the bigger bulls, they jostle the green buffalo pretty hard. He jostles right back, too. He's as big as any of 'em, bigger if you count his tail, which you ought to do, 'cause it's bigger and fatter than a buffalo tail has any business bein'. A buffalo he jostles stayed jostled, if you know what I mean. Those horns have a lot to do with that—he pretty near outdoes the rest of the herd put together with 'em.

Those horns! I mean, you'd have to be a natural born fool not to want to kill somethin' with horns as fine as that. I swing up my rifle to my shoulder and fire off a round. Jake and Clancy, they're still right with me, so I don't know to this day if I fired first.

The buffalo, they commence to bellowin', the way buffalo do when you shoot at 'em, and they run like a freight train comin' down out of the Rockies with its brakes gone. I see dust puff up on the green buffalo's flank, so I know we hit him, but he don't go down. Sometimes buffalo, they're purely hard to kill.

Kill? Hell, far as I can tell, the green one isn't even fazed. He runs right along with the rest of the herd. The three of us are gallopin' alongside 'em. I chiefly hope my horse don't stick his foot in a prairie dog hole. If he does, he breaks his own fool neck and mine along with it.

The chase goes on longer than you'd think, because the green one stays in the middle of the herd for a while. Usually in a hunt like that you take whatever critter you can get. Me, Jake, and Clancy, though, we all want him. If we can't get a clear shot at him, we let the others go.

Finally, when I'm startin' to wonder who has more wind, the herd or our horses, the green buffalo commences to drop a little behind the rest. We start shootin' again soon as we see the chance. I reckon we miss a few times, too, or maybe more'n a few. You try aimin' from a runnin' horse at a runnin' buffalo, my friend, before you laugh at us for it.

But we make some hits, too. The green buffalo slows down some more, then comes to a stop. Blood's runnin' down his side in little red streams. His flanks heave like he can't get enough air. His head hangs down the way they do when they're hurt too bad to go on much farther. When he opens his mouth to pant, he drools pink. There's pink froth around his nostrils, too, so he must've been bleedin' in the lungs.

When they stop like that, the kill's easy. You gauge by the hump where to put the next shot right through the heart. But the green buffalo, even his hump isn't right, and he's got a bony frill, I guess you'd call it, that runs up from his neck over the fore part of his back. Growin' something that unnatural must've been a torment to him, so I'd say he's lucky we come along to put him out of his misery.

I ride up close to do what needs doin'. I guess the best I can where his heart is, take dead aim, and squeeze the trigger. I have guessed better, indeed I have. When the bullet hits him, the green buffalo lifts up that big old head of his and out comes a noise like a locomotive with a busted boiler. Then he wheels round and runs right at me.

He's bigger and meaner'n any longhorn you ever seen. I shoot at him again, but you got to be lucky with a head shot on a buffalo, hit him in the eye or somethin' like that. Otherwise the slug'll just bounce off his skull. That's just what happens here, too. I rowel my horse for all I'm worth. He springs forward like you wouldn't believe, and the buffalo can't quite shift fast enough to spike me with his horn.

He lets out that squealin' bellow again, tries to change the way he's goin' so he can make another run at me. All the while, though, Jake and Clancy keep on pumpin' bullets into him. He takes so many, I reckon when we butcher him he'll be as full o' lead as a shotgunned mallard.

I turn around to shoot some more, too, but this time I see it really isn't needful. That last charge of his took all the strength he has left in him. He wobbles like a drunk goin' out of the Rebel Yell, then kind of folds up on himself and falls over. He heaves out another breath or two, then he's finally done.

"Thought he was gonna use you for a pincushion there, Joe," Clancy says.

"You're not the only one," I tell him. "I thought he was through. When he came at me, I like to've pissed myself."

"Don't blame you a bit."

Jake says, "Let's cut him up." Jake, he takes care of what needs doin' first and worries about everything else afterwards.

I climb down from my horse, tether him to a clump of sagebrush that sticks up higher above the ground than anything else thereabouts. Then I pull out a knife and walk up to the green buffalo. I'm ready to run like hell, I tell you. After that last scare, I figure he might just be shammin'.

But he's not, not this time. The one eye I can see doesn't blink. It just stares up at the sky. Flies have already started walking along the tracks of blood on his flank. One ambles down into a bullet hole, comes back out a second later and starts wipin' its little thread of a neck with its legs the way they do.

I take out my knife, give the green buffalo a poke. The mange or whatever it is has the hide all rough and scaly, but it's not any thicker than the usual run of buffalo hide. You have to put some arm into what you're doin', but you can cut yourself a good slice.

Once they see I'm not trampled, Jake and Clancy give me a hand with the butchering. We hack off steaks and chops and roasts till we've got as much as we can carry with our pack horse and tied behind us. It's not as easy as it ought to be. Instead of havin' the ribs stop at what'd be the bottom of a man's chest, they keep right on going, down to the critter's hipbones—that green buffalo isn't normal any which way. We're bloody to the elbows and dead beat by afternoon, but we get the job finished.

By the time we're done, the buzzards are already circlin' overhead, waitin' for their share. Soon as we take off, I figure they'll argue it out with the coyotes. Before too long, even the bones'll be gone. That's the way the world is. If it wasn't like that, we'd all be ass-deep in bones, and then what would ornery professors like Hatcher's Marsh and Cope do for fun?

We ride on back the way we came. Followin' our own tracks is the easiest way to get on back to Hatcher's camp. It's gettin' close to sundown when Clancy says, "Ain't this about the place where we all got dizzy?"

I look around. He's right. But there's no ferns there now, no funny plants that look like squashed feather dusters. Just prairie, lots of it. Clancy points. "Look, there's our tracks, right?"

I nod. Sure enough, those are our outbound tracks. Jake spits. Clancy rides on a few more feet. I walk my horse up after him. He keeps pointin' down to the ground. All at once he says, "There!"

I see what he's pointin' at, too. Right at the spot where he said "There!" our tracks just up and disappear. It's not like the wind blew dust over 'em. It's like they never, ever happened. "That's queer, all right," I say. Jake nods.

Clancy looks west, points again, this time toward the horizon. "We came from that way, right?" he says. He knows he's right, and doesn't wait for an answer. He walks his horse real slow and easy westward, lookin' down every foot of the way. After a quarter mile or so, maybe a tad more, he rides a little ways south, then a little ways north, like a dog castin' about for a scent. Finally he says, "Ha!"

I'm right with him. He's picked up our outbound tracks again. He rides back east just a few feet and goes "Ha!" one more time, and then, "Goddamn!" I say "Goddamn!" myself, on account of he's found the other side of where our tracks disappear. It's like we didn't ride over the stretch between, the stretch with the ferns and all the other stuff that had no call bein' in the Wyoming prairie.

"Hell with it," Jake says. "Let's cook some of this here buffalo meat. We don't stop and cook it pretty soon, I'll eat it raw." Comin' out of Jake, that's a speech.

So we stop, we get a fire goin', and we carve off chunks of meat and toast 'em on sticks over the flames. Before long, my mouth gets to waterin' so hard I can't wait any more. I blow and I blow and I blow on my chunk, then I sink my teeth in.

I've had buffalo a good many times. It's not that far from beef, a little leaner, a little tougher, a little gamier. This green buffalo—not that his meat was green, you understand, or the buzzards and coyotes would've been welcome to it—he doesn't taste like any buffalo I ever ate before. But he's a long way from bad.

Clancy says what I'm thinkin': "Reminds me more of dark-meat chicken than any proper buffalo." Jake doesn't say anything. He just ups and cuts himself off another piece.

We ride out again next mornin', and have as peaceful a trip as you please back to Hatcher's camp. We get there late afternoon, and everyone's right glad to see us, and to see the meat we've fetched. Hatcher's boys, they cook some of it and start smokin' the rest so as it'll keep.

I wait for Clancy or Jake to come out with the story of the green buffalo, and I guess they wait for me, too, but nobody ends up tellin' it. I like a tall tale as well as the next fellow, but usually a tall tale, you know the one who's tellin' it is yarnin'. Speakin' not a word but the truth and having it taken for a tall tale, that'll just ruin your day.

Tall tale or no, though, the meat's still good. Me and Clancy and Jake, we sit down around a fire and fill ourselves up again. I'm at the teeth-pickin' stage when Hatcher comes over. He's chewin' on a roasted buffalo rib. While he pays us off, some of his boys start laughin' over by his wagon.

"What's funny?" I ask him.

"I picked up my mail in Lusk, along with supplies," Hatcher answers. "O. C. Marsh sent me a copy of *Punch* with a cartoon of himself in it."

"*Punch?* What's *Punch?*"

"It's a British comic magazine. It has a picture of Marsh as a circus ringmaster. He's standing on a *Triceratops* skull—doubtless one of the ones we've excavated hereabouts—and putting a whole troupe of dinosaur skeletons through their paces, as if they were so many trained bears or lions or elephants. Would you like to have a look?" He uses the rib bone to point back where the magazine is.

I think it over, then shake my head. "I thank you kindly, Mr. Hatcher, but I'll take a miss on that. You're the one knows about these here dinosaur things, not me."

"However you like, Joe. I thank you for the tasty meat you brought back." By now, he's gnawed everything off of that bone, so he tosses it on the ground. Then he reaches into his waistcoat pocket, comes out with a deck of cards. "Care for a little game to make the time go by?"

"I'll pass on that, too, Mr. Hatcher," I tell him. He's just tryin' to skin me out of the wages he paid so next time he needs me, he can give me the same money again. I'm wise to that one, I am. So are Clancy and Jake, when he tries it on them. We may not know these dinosaurs, but we're nobody's fools.

The Maltese Elephant

This one, of course, is a pastiche and parody of one of the really fine mysteries of the twentieth century. Writing pastiche is tremendously enjoyable; it lets a writer put on a mask and pretend to be someone else for a while, with a different style, different strengths, different weaknesses. There really were elephants on Malta like the one described, but they didn't survive down to historic times. Too bad. Making up the Greek and Latin quotes was fun to do, too.

Miles Bowman was a man built of rectangular blocks. His head was one, squared off with short-cut graying hair at the top and a sharp jaw at the bottom. His chest and shoulders made a thick brick, his belly below them a slightly smaller one. His arms and legs were thick, muscular pillars. He trimmed his nails straight across at the ends of his fingers.

His partner Tom Trencher, that smiling devil, was dead. In the hallway outside the office, a sign painter was using a razor blade to scrape BOWMAN & TRENCHER off the frosted glass. When he was done, he would paint Bowman's name there by itself in gilt. Centered.

The phone rang. His secretary answered it. Hester Prine was a tall, skinny, brown-haired girl. She wore good clothes as if they were sacks. But when she talked, any man who heard her had hungry dreams for days.

She covered the mouthpiece with her hand. "It's your wife."

Bowman shook his head. "I don't want to talk to Eva."

"She wants to talk to you about Tom."

"I figured she did. What else would she call me about here? I don't want to talk to her, I told you. Tell her I'm out on a case. I'll see her tonight. She can talk to me then."

His secretary's mouth twisted, but she took her hand away and said what Bowman had told her to say. She had to say it three times before she could hang up. Then she rose and walked over to Bowman's desk in the inner office. She looked down at him. "You're a louse, Miles."

"Yeah, I know," he said comfortably. His arm slid around her waist. He pulled her closer to him.

"Louse," she said again, in a different tone of voice. She hesitated. "Miles, she wants to talk to you because—" She ran down like a phonograph that needs winding.

"Because she thinks I killed Tom." His hand tightened on her hip. He smiled. His teeth were not very good. "Why would she think a thing like that?"

"Because you know she and—" Hester Prine ran down again. "You're hurting me."

"Am I?" He did not let go. "I know lots of things. But I didn't kill Tom. Eva won't pin that one on me. The cops won't, either."

Soft footsteps came down the hall. They paused in front of the office. The sign painter stopped scraping. Hester Prine twisted away from Bowman. This time he did not try to stop her.

The door opened. By then, Bowman's secretary was back at her desk. A woman walked into the office. The sign painter stared at her until the door closed and cut off his view. Then, with reluctant razor, he went back to work.

The woman was small and swarthy and perfect, with a heart-shaped face and enormous black eyes that could smile or sob or blaze or do all three at once in the space of a couple of heartbeats. Her crow's-wing hair fell almost to her shoulders in a straight bob. It was not what they were wearing this year, but on her it was right. So was her orange crêpe silk frock with a flared peplum skirt.

She strode past Hester Prine as if the secretary did not exist and went into Bowman's inner office. He got up from in back of his desk. "Miss Lenoir," he said. He shut the door behind her.

"Your partner," Claire Lenoir said in a broken voice. "It's my fault." Tears glistened in her eyes, but did not fall.

"Not all of it," he answered. "Tom knew what he was doing, and you told him the guy he was tailing—the guy who's been tailing you—was one rough customer. You don't get into this business if you think everything is going to be easy all the time. Or you better not."

Her hands fluttered. She wore two rings, of gold and emeralds. They glowed against her dark skin. "But—" she said.

Bowman waved dismissively. "You mean that story you told us before? That didn't have anything to do with anything. If Tom and I had believed it, it might have, but we didn't. So don't worry about that. But you're going to have to level sooner or later, if you want me to do whatever you really want me to do."

The outer door opened. Hester Prine talked with someone—a man—for a few seconds. The phone on Bowman's desk jangled. He picked it up. "A Mr. Nicholas Alexandria wants to see you right now," his secretary said. "He says it's worth two hundred dollars."

"Have you seen the money?" Bowman asked.

"He's got it," she answered.

Bowman mouthed the name "Nicholas Alexandria" to Claire Lenoir. She started violently. The blood drained from her face, leaving her skin the color of old newspaper. She shook her head so her hair for a moment flew across her face. One strand stuck at the corner of her red-painted mouth. She brushed it away with an angry gesture.

"Send him in, sweetheart," Bowman said placidly. He hung up the telephone.

The man who came through the door might have been born in the city that gave him his name. He was darker than Claire Lenoir. His nose curved like a saber blade. His mouth, a Cupid's bow, was red but not painted. He stank of patchouli.

His eyes, hard and shiny and black as obsidian, flicked to Claire Lenoir and widened slightly. Then they returned to Bowman. "Your secretary did not say you had—this woman here," he said in a fussy, precise voice.

"Did you ask her?" Bowman asked. Nicholas Alexandria's

eyes widened again. He shook his head, a single, tightly controlled gesture. Bowman said, "Then you've got no cause for complaint. I hear you're two hundred dollars interested in talking to me." He held out his hand, palm up.

Nicholas Alexandria's finely manicured hand drew from the pocket of his velvet jacket a wallet of tanned snakeskin. He removed from it four bills bearing the image of Ulysses S. Grant, held them out to Miles Bowman.

Bowman took them, studied them, put them into his own wallet, and stuck it back in his hip pocket. "All right," he said. He waved to a chair. "Sit. Talk."

Alexandria sat. His red mouth contracted petulantly. "I might have known Miss Tellini would be here, when I wished to discuss with you matters pertaining to the Maltese Elephant."

Bowman's head turned on its thick neck. "Miss Tellini?" he asked Claire Lenoir.

"Gina Tellini," Nicholas Alexandria said with a certain cold relish. "Why? Under what name do you know her?"

"It's not important," Bowman answered. He smiled at the girl. "Got any others?"

Her skin darkened. She looked away from him. Nicholas Alexandria said, "That is the appellation with which she was born in the district of New York known as, I believe, Hell's Kitchen, any representations to the contrary notwithstanding." Gina Tellini spat something in Italian. Nicholas Alexandria answered in the same language, his diction precise. Her mouth fell open. His smile was frigid. In English, he said, "You see, I can get down in the gutter, too."

Miles Bowman held up a meaty hand. "Enough, already," he said. He waved to Alexandria. "You wanted to talk about the Maltese Elephant. Go ahead and talk."

"You are already familiar with this famous and fabulous creature?" Nicholas Alexandria inquired.

"Never heard of it," Bowman said politely.

Nicholas Alexandria gave another of his tightly machined headshakes. "I am afraid I cannot believe you, Mr. Bowman," he said. He reached inside his jacket once more. His hand returned to sight with a snub-nosed chromed automatic. He pointed it at Miles Bowman's chest. "Place both your hands wide apart on the desk immediately."

"You stinking little pansy," Bowman said.

Nicholas Alexandria's red, full lips narrowed into a thin pink slash. His tongue darted out like a snake's. The hand holding the automatic did not waver.

Bowman lowered a shoulder, twisted his body a little to one side. Then he spoke with savage satisfaction: "All right, Alexandria, now you've got a gun and I've got a gun. But you've got that cheap .22 and I'm holding a .45. You shoot me, I spend some time in the hospital getting patched up. I shoot you, pal, you're not just history, you're archaeology." He laughed loudly at his own wit. "Now put your little toy away and we'll talk."

"I do not believe you have a weapon," Nicholas Alexandria said.

"The more fool you," Bowman answered. "My partner didn't believe in packing a gun, and now the fool is dead. I'm a lot of things, but I'm no fool."

"He has it," Gina Tellini said. "I can see his hand on it."

"You would say the same in any case." Nicholas Alexandria's eyes did not move toward her. To Bowman, he said: "Shooting through the front of your desk does not strike me as like to produce the results you would desire."

Bowman leaned back in his chair. One of his feet left the nubby, mustard-colored wool rug for a moment. It slammed against the inside of the center panel of the desk. The panel bowed outward. At the sudden crash, Nicholas Alexandria's finger tightened on the trigger. Then it eased again. Bowman's voice was complacent: "Cheap plywood, varnished to look like mahogany. A slug won't even know it's there."

Alexandria's mouth screwed tight, as if he were about to kiss someone he did not like. He slid the revolver back into the inner pocket of his jacket. As if he had never taken it out, he said, "Perhaps Miss Tellini did not see fit to tell you the Maltese Elephant— *a* Maltese elephant, I should say—is in San Francisco now."

"No, she didn't tell me that," Miles Bowman said. He looked Gina Tellini up and down. Now her eyes were as flat and opaque as Nicholas Alexandria's. Bowman turned back to the man in the velvet jacket. "So what do you want me to do about it? Find this elephant and sell it to the circus?"

Nicholas Alexandria rose and bowed. "I see I am being mocked. I shall return another time, in the hope of finding you alone and serious."

"Sorry you feel that way." Bowman also got up. He came around the desk and stood towering over Nicholas Alexandria as he opened the door to let the slighter man out of the inner office.

Alexandria raised one finger. "A moment. Did you truly have a pistol?"

Bowman reached under his jacket. The motion exposed a battered leather holster on his right hip. He pulled out the Colt Model 1911A and let it lie, heavy and ugly and black, in his palm. It bore no frill, no ornament, no chromium. It was a killing machine, nothing else. Nicholas Alexandria stared at it. He let out a small, gasping sigh.

"I never bluff," Bowman said. "No percentage to it." He shifted the pistol in his hand. His fingers closed on the checkered grip. With a motion astonishingly fast from such a heavyset man, he slammed the Colt's hard steel barrel against the side of Alexandria's face. "Remember that."

The blow knocked Alexandria back two paces. He staggered but did not fall. The raised foresight had cut his cheek. Blood dripped onto his jacket. Slowly he removed the silk handkerchief from his breast pocket. He dabbed at the jacket, then raised the handkerchief to his face. "I shall remember, Mr. Bowman," he whispered hoarsely. "Rely on it."

He walked past Hester Prine without looking at her, and out of the office.

Gina Tellini brought her hands together several times, clapping without sound. "Now I know you will be able to protect me— Miles." She lingered half a heartbeat over his Christian name.

He shrugged. "All in a day's work. You have anything you want to tell me about this Maltese Elephant?"

Those quicksilver eyes betrayed an instant's alarm. Then they were her servants again. She shook her head. "I can't, not yet," she said huskily.

"Have it your way." Bowman's thick shoulders moved up and down once more. "You're going to, or Alexandria will, or somebody." He watched her. She stood very still, like a small, hunted animal. He shrugged a third time, motioned for her to precede him out of the inner office. "See you later."

When her footsteps could no longer be heard in the hall, he turned to Hester Prine. "I'm going home." He checked his wristwatch. "Quarter past seven already. Jesus, where does the time get to?" He set his hand on her shoulder. "Go on back to your place, too. To hell with all this."

She did not look at him. "I have some more typing to do," she said tonelessly.

"Have it your way," Bowman said, as he had to Gina Tellini. He closed the outer door—now it read BOWMAN, in letters bigger than BOWMAN & TRENCHER had been painted—and strolled down the hall to the elevator.

As he walked, he whistled "Look for the Silver Lining." He whistled out of tune, and flat. The elevator boy looked at him as he got into the cage. He looked back. The elevator boy suddenly got busy with the buttons and took him to the ground floor.

He walked across the street to the garage where he kept his Chevrolet. He threw the kid on the corner a nickel. The kid handed him a copy of the *San Francisco News*. He tossed it into the front seat of the car. The starter whined when he turned the key. Coughing, the motor finally caught. He put the Chevrolet in gear and drove home.

The house on Thirty-third Avenue in the Sunset district needed a coat of paint. The houses to which it was joined on either side had been painted recently, one blue, the other a sort of rose pink. That made the faded, blotchy yellow surface look all the shabbier.

Bowman bounded up the steps two at a time. He turned the key in the Yale lock, mashed his thumb down on the latch. With a click like a bad knee, the door opened.

The interior was all plush and cheap velvet and curlicued

wood and overstuffed furniture. "Is that you, honey?" Eva's voice wafted out of the kitchen with the smell of pot roast and onions. She sounded nervous.

"Who else do you know with a key?" Bowman asked. He scaled his hat toward the couch. It fell short and landed on the fringe of the throw rug under the coffee table. He dropped the *News* onto the table.

Eva came out and stood in the kitchen doorway. He walked over, kissed her perfunctorily. They had been married thirteen years. She was ten years the younger. She was about the age Tom Trencher had been. Trencher would not get any older.

Eva's short red curls got their color from a bottle. They'd been the same color when he married her, and from the same source. They went well with her green eyes. She was twenty pounds heavier now than when they had walked down the aisle, but big-boned enough to wear the pounds well. She wore a ruffled apron over a middy blouse and a cotton skirt striped brightly in gold and blue.

Her smile was a little too wide. It showed too many teeth. "Do the police know anything more about—who killed Tom?" She looked at the point of his chin, not his eyes.

"If they do, they haven't told me. I didn't talk with 'em today." He shrugged. "Get me a drink."

"Sure, honey." She hurried away. She opened the pantry, then the icebox, and came back with a tumbler of bourbon on the rocks. "Here." That too-ingratiating smile still masked her face.

Bowman drank half the tumbler with two long swallows. He exhaled, long and reverently, and held up the glass to scrutinize its deep amber contents against the light bulb in the kitchen ceiling lamp. "This is the medicine," he announced, and finished the bourbon. He handed Eva the glass. "Fix me another one of these with supper."

"Sure, Miles," she said. "We ought to be just about ready." The pot lid clanked as she lifted it off to check the roast. She set it back on the big iron pot. The oven door hinge squeaked. "The meat is done, and so are the potatoes. I'll set the table and get you your drink."

Bowman buttered his baked potato, spread salt and pepper lavishly over the thick slab of red-brown beef Eva set before him. He ate steadily, methodically, without wasted motion, like a man shoveling coal into a locomotive firebox. Every so often, he sipped from the tall glass of bourbon next to the chipped china plate that held his supper.

Eva dropped her knife on the flowered linoleum floor. Bowman looked up for the first time since he'd seated himself at the table. Eva flushed. She flung the knife into the sink. Then she got up and took a clean one from the silverware drawer.

Before Bowman could resume his assault on the pot roast, she said, "Miles, honey, who do you think murdered Tom?"

"Had to be that guy he was shadowing," he answered. He speared another piece of meat with his fork, but did not raise it to his lips. "Thursday, that was his name. Evan Thursday." He ate the piece of meat. With his mouth full, he went on, "Couldn't have been anybody else." He swallowed, and smiled at Eva. "Could it?"

"No, I don't imagine it could," she said quickly. She bent her head over her plate. A moment later, her fork clattered to the floor. Her lips twisted. "I'm as twitchy as a cat tonight."

"Can't imagine why," Bowman said. He drank from the tumbler. Two ice cubes clinked against its side.

When supper was done, Bowman went out to the living room. He set what was left of his drink on the coffee table, then sat down on the sofa. The springs creaked under his weight. He bent over, grunting a little, untied his shoes, and tossed them under the table.

"Eva, get me my slippers," he said.

"What?" she called over the noise of running water in the kitchen. He repeated himself, louder. The water stopped running. Drying her hands on a dish towel, Eva bustled past him into the bedroom. She came back with the towel draped over her arm and the slippers in her hands. "Here they are." He slid them onto his feet. She returned to the dishes.

He smoked three cigarettes waiting for her to finish washing and drying them. When she came out, he handed her the tumbler. She washed it and dried it and put it away. He had opened the *News* by then, and was going through it front to back, as systematically as he ate.

Eva sighed softly and went over to a bookcase. She pulled out a sentimental novel and carried it into the bedroom. Bowman went on reading. When he came to the *Ships in Port* listing, he chewed thoughtfully on his underlip. He got up. In the clutter of papers and matchbooks in the top drawer of the hutch, he found a pencil. He underlined the names of four ships:

Daisy Miller from London
La Tórtola from Gozo
Admiral Byng from Minorca
Golden Wind from Bombay

After he read the advertisements on the other side of the page that held *Ships in Port*, he tore out the three-inch length of agate type and stuck it in his trouser pocket. Then he worked his way through the rest of the newspaper.

"Miles?"

Bowman looked up. Eva stood in the doorway that led to the bedroom. She was wearing a thin, clinging silk crêpe de chine peignoir. Bowman had given it to her for their anniversary a few years before. She did not wear it very often.

"It's getting late," she said. "Aren't you coming to bed?" She had not washed off her makeup and smeared her face with cold cream, the way she usually did at bedtime.

Bowman folded up the paper and tossed it on the floor. His fingers were stained with ink from the cheap newsprint. He rubbed them on the thighs of his pants, rose from the couch. "Don't mind if I do," he said.

A hard fist pounded on the front door. Bowman sat up in bed. The pounding went on. "Who's that?" Eva asked, her voice half drunk with sleep.

"Damned if I know, but I'm going to find out." Bowman groped for the switch on the lamp by the bed. He flicked it, and screwed up his eyes against the sudden flare of light. He peered at the alarm clock on the nightstand by the lamp. Midnight. Scowling, he got out of bed. He had hung his holster on a chair. He pulled out his pistol, clicked off the safety.

"What are you going to do?" Eva asked. The cold cream made her round cheeks glisten like the rump of a greased pig.

"See who it is," Bowman answered reasonably. "You stay here." He slid into his pajama bottoms and padded out toward the door. For a bulky man, he was surprisingly light on his feet. He closed the bedroom door after him.

The pounding had slowed when the light went on. Bowman yanked the door open. He pointed the pistol at the two men on the front porch. A moment later, he lowered it. "Jesus Christ," he said. "You boys trying to get yourselves killed? I knew cops were dumb, but this dumb?" He shook his head.

"We've got to talk to you, Miles," one of the policemen said. "Can we come in?"

"You got a warrant, Rollie?" Bowman asked.

"Not that kind of talk, I swear." Detective Roland Dwyer crossed himself to show he was serious.

Bowman considered. He nodded gruffly. "All right, come in, then," he said, and turned on the imitation Tiffany lamp on the table by the door. "But if you and the Captain here are playing games with me—" He did not say what would happen then, but left the implication it would not be pretty.

"Thanks, Miles," Dwyer said with an air of sincerity. He was a tall Irishman heading toward middle age. His hair had naturally the color to which Eva's aspired. His face was long and ruddy and triangular, with a wide forehead and a narrow chin. He wore a frayed shirt collar and pants shiny with wear at the knees: he was, on the whole, an honest cop.

Bowman waved him toward the sofa. The Captain followed him in. Bowman quickly closed the door. The night was chilly, and had the clammy dankness of fog. Bowman sat down in the rocking chair next to the table that held the lamp with the colored glass shade. His voice turned hard: "All right, what won't keep till morning?"

Dwyer and the Captain looked at each other. The latter was a short, pudgy man, a few years older than Bowman. He had a fringe of silver hair futilely clinging to the slopes of his pate, skin as fine and pink as a baby's, and innocent blue eyes. His suit was new, and tailored in the English fashion. He smelled of expensive Bay Rum aftershave lotion.

After a brief hesitation, the Captain said: "Evan Thursday's dead, Miles. One slug, right between the eyes."

"So?" Bowman said. "Good riddance to him is all I have to say, Bock."

Captain Henry Bock steepled his fingers. He pressed them so tight together, the blood was forced from their tips, leaving them pale as boiled veal. "Where have you been tonight, Miles?" he asked delicately.

Bowman heaved himself out of the rocker. He took two steps toward the Captain before he checked himself. "Get out of here," he snarled. "Rollie tells me everything's going to be jake, and you start with that—" He expressed his opinion with vehemence, variety, and detail.

Roland Dwyer spread his hands placatingly. "Come on, take it easy," he said. "This guy gets iced, we have to talk with you. We think he shot Tom, after all, and Tom was your partner."

"Yeah? Is that what you think?" Bowman made a slashing gesture of disgust with his left hand. "Looked like you were trying to pin Tom on me. Or do you figure I took care of both of 'em now?"

"Where have you been tonight?" Captain Bock repeated.

"At the office and here, dammit, nowhere else but," Bowman said. "Ask my secretary when I left, ask Eva when I got here. You want me to get her out so you can ask her?" He glanced over to the closed bedroom door. "Only take a minute."

"It's all right, Miles," Detective Dwyer said. "We believe you." He looked over at Henry Bock again. "Don't we, Captain?"

Bock shrugged. "Neither of those women is likely to tell us anything different from what Bowman says, anyhow."

The Captain had spoken quietly. Bowman glanced at the bedroom door again. When he answered, he, too, held his voice down, but anger blazed in it: "And what the hell is that supposed to mean? You come round here with one load of rubbish, and now you start throwing around more? I ought to—"

"Shut up, Bowman," Captain Bock said flatly. "What the women say doesn't matter, not this time. Thursday caught his right outside Kezar Stadium, in Golden Gate Park. If you'd arranged to meet him there, it wouldn't have been five minutes out of your way."

"And if pigs had wings—" Bowman stood up, opened the front door. "Get out," he growled. "Next time you come here, you bring a warrant, like I said. My lawyer'll be here with me, too."

"I'm sorry, Miles," Dwyer said. "We're doing our job, too, remember. You aren't making it any easier for us, either."

"Go do it somewhere else," Bowman said.

The two policemen got up and walked into the building fog. They got into their car, which they had parked behind Bowman's. The heavy, wet air muffled the sound of the motor starting. In the fog, the beams the headlamps cast seemed thick and yellow as butter.

Bowman shut the door and locked it. He went back into the bedroom, replaced the pistol in its holster. Eva was sitting up, reading the novel she'd abandoned earlier. "What—did they want?" she asked hesitantly.

"Somebody punched that Evan Thursday's ticket for him," Bowman answered.

"And they think it was you?" Eva's eyes widened. "That's terrible!"

"It's nothing to worry about," Bowman said, shrugging. "I didn't do it, so they can't pin it on me, right?" He lay down beside her, clicked off the lamp on his side of the bed. He yawned. "You going to look at that thing all night?"

"No, dear." Eva put down the book and turned off her lamp. Although she stretched out next to Bowman, she wiggled and fidgeted the way she did when she was having trouble going to sleep. Bowman shrugged once more, breathed heavily, then soon began to snore.

The telephone rang, loud in the night as a fire alarm. Bowman thrashed, twisted, sat up, and turned on the bedside lamp. The alarm clock said it was almost three. He shook his head. "I don't believe this."

The phone kept ringing. "Answer it," Eva told him. She pulled the pale blue wool blanket up over her head.

Muttering, he walked into the living room. He snatched the earpiece off the hook, picked up the rest of the instrument, and barked his name into the mouthpiece: "Bowman." The voice on the other end of the line spoke. "Now?" Bowman asked. "Are you sure? . . . Jesus Christ, it's three in the morning. . . . All right, if that's the way it's got to be. . . . Room 481, right? See you there. . . . Yeah, fifteen minutes if the fog's not too thick."

He slammed the mouthpiece down on his goodbye, stalked back into the bedroom. Eva had turned off the light. He turned it on again. He unbuttoned the shirt to his pajamas and walked naked to the dresser.

"What's wrong?" Eva asked as he pulled a clean pair of white cotton boxer shorts out of a dresser drawer. "Why are you getting dressed?" She sounded frightened.

"I'm going down to the station." He got into the same trousers he had worn the day before. "Bock and Dwyer, they have some more questions for me." He put on socks and shoes, got a fresh shirt from the closet, knotted a tie with a jungle pattern of hot blues and oranges and greens, shrugged a jacket over his wide shoulders. He ran a comb through his hair, then planted a curled-brim fedora on his head.

"Shouldn't you call your lawyer?" Eva said.

"Nah, it'll be all right." He started out. At the bedroom door, he stopped and blew her a kiss.

The fog was there, but not too thick. He had the roads all to himself. Once, his Chevrolet and a police car passed each other on opposite sides of the street. He waved to the men inside. One of them recognized him and waved back.

He turned right off Market onto New Montgomery. During business hours, no one could have hoped to find a parking space there. Now the curb was his to command. He walked over to the eight-story Beaux Arts building of tan brick and terra cotta at the corner of Market and New Montgomery. A man in uniform held the door open for him. He strode across the lobby to the bank of elevators.

"Fourth floor," he told the operator as he got into one.

"Fourth floor, yes, sir," the man answered. "Welcome to the Palace Hotel."

Bowman stood with his feet slightly spread, as if at parade rest. He looked straight ahead. The elevator purred upward. When it got to the fourth floor, the operator opened the cage. Bowman stepped out while the fellow was telling him the floor.

A sign on the wall opposite the elevator announced:

401–450	451–499
⇐	⇒

Bowman went ⇒. The carpet in the hall was so thick that the pile swallowed the welt of his shoe each time his weight came down on it. He paused a moment in front of room 481, then folded his thick hand into a fist and rapped on the door just below the polished brass numbers.

It opened. "Come in," Gina Tellini said. She looked as fresh as she had the afternoon before, but at some time between then and now had changed into a dark green velvet lounging robe of Oriental cut. The front of a Chinese dragon, embroidered in deep golds and reds, coiled across her breasts.

Bowman stepped into the hotel room. Gina Tellini closed the door after him. As she started back past him, he said, "Thursday's dead."

She stopped in her tracks. A hand started to fly up to her mouth, but checked itself. "How do you know that?" she asked in a shaken voice.

"Cops—how else?" He barked mirthless laughter. "They want to put that one on my bar tab, too, along with Tom." His lips thinned, stretching his mouth into a speculative line. "You could have done it. You would have had time, after you left the office."

"No, not me." She dismissed the idea in three casual words. "Here, sit down, make yourself comfortable." She waved Bowman to a chair upholstered in velvet two shades lighter than her gown. She sat down on the edge of the bed facing him. The bed had not been slept in since the maid last prepared it.

"All right, not you," Bowman said agreeably, crossing his legs. "Who, then?"

"It could have been Nicholas Alexandria," Gina Tellini said. "He carries a gun. You saw that."

"Yeah, I saw that. It could have been. But a lot of people carry guns. I carry one myself. 'Could have been' doesn't cut much ice."

"I know." Gina Tellini nodded. The motion made the robe come open, very slightly, at the neckline. "But somebody besides Alexandria wants the Maltese Elephant."

"Somebody besides Alexandria and you." Bowman's gaze focused on the point, a few inches below her chin, where velvet had retreated. "Thursday's dead. Who else is there?"

"A man named Gideon Schlechtman," she answered promptly. "Sometimes he and Alexandria work together, sometimes Alexandria is on his own, or thinks he is. But if he gets the elephant, Schlechtman will try to take it from him."

"I bet he will," Bowman said. "And what about you and Alexandria and what's-his-name, Schlechtman? I bet the three of you are one big happy family, right?"

"It's not funny, Miles," Gina Tellini insisted. "Schlechtman is—dangerous. If Evan Thursday is dead, that's all the more reason to believe he's come to San Francisco."

"Is that so?" Bowman said. "All I have is your word, and your word hasn't been any too real good, you know what I mean. And if this here Schlechtman is real and is in town, whose side are you on?"

"That's a terrible question to ask." Gina Tellini's eyes blazed for a moment. Then sudden tears put out the fire. "You don't believe a word I've told you. It's so—hard when you don't trust me. I'm here in your city all alone and—" The rest was muffled when she buried her face in her hands.

Bowman rose from the chair, sat down beside her on the bed. "Don't get upset, sweetheart," he said. "One way or another, I'll take care of things."

She looked up at him. Lamplight sparkled on the tracks two tears had traced on her cheeks. "I'm so damned tired of always being alone," she whispered.

"You're not alone now," he said. She nodded, slowly, her eyes never leaving his. He slipped his left arm around her shoulder, drew her to him. Her lips parted. They kissed fiercely. When they fell back to the mattress together, his weight pinned her against its firm resilience.

The rumble of a cable car and the clang of its bell outside the window woke Miles Bowman. The gray light of approaching dawn seeped through the thick brocaded curtains of Gina Tellini's room.

Moving carefully, Bowman slid out from under her arm. She stirred and murmured but did not wake. Bowman dressed with practiced haste. The door clicked when he closed it. He paused outside in the hall. No sound came from within. Satisfied, he walked back to the elevator.

More automobiles were on the street now, but not too many to keep Bowman from making a U-turn on New Montgomery. He turned right onto Market Street and took it all the way to the Embarcadero.

The Ferry Building was quiet. Its siren would not wail for another two hours, not until eight o'clock. Through the thinning fog, its high clock tower loomed, brooding and sinister. Man-o'-War Row and berths for passenger liners stretched south of the Ferry Building, commercial piers for foreign lines north and west around the curve of the shore. Bowman turned left, toward them, onto the Embarcadero. Between gear changes, his right hand grubbed in his trouser pocket. He pulled out the piece of newsprint he had torn from the *San Francisco News*.

He parked the car and got out. His nostrils dilated. The air was thick with the smells of rotting piles and roasting coffee, mud and fish and salt water. Sea gulls mewed like flying cats. He padded along, burly as the longshoremen all around but standing out from them by virtue of jacket and collar and tie.

The *News* listed ships in order of the piers at which they were docked. The *Daisy Miller* was tied up by Pier 7. Shouting dock workers loaded wooden crates onto her. Stenciled letters on the sides of the crates declared they held sewing machines. They were the right size for rifles. Bowman shrugged and walked on to Pier 15, where *La Tórtola* was berthed.

A handful of sailors worked on deck, swabbing and painting under the watchful eye of a skinny blond man in a black-brimmed white officer's cap and a dark blue jacket with four gold rings circling each cuff. He saw Bowman looking at him. "What do you want, you?" he called. He had a German accent, or maybe Dutch.

Bowman put hands on hips. "Who wants to know?"

"I am Captain Wellnhofer, and I have the right to ask these questions. But you—" The captain's face had been pale. Now it was red and angry.

"Keep your shirt on, buddy," Bowman said. He looked down at the scrap of newspaper in his hand. "This here the boat that's supposed to get another load of fodder today?"

Captain Wellnhofer's face got redder. "Do you not know in your own language the difference between a boat and a ship? And we have no need for fodder now. You are mistaken. Go away."

The *Admiral Byng* was docked at Pier 23. Nobody aboard her admitted any need for fodder, either. Bowman grimaced and hiked on to Pier 35, which held the *Golden Wind*. "Halfway to Fisherman's damn Wharf," he muttered. The only men visible aboard her were little brown lascars in dungarees. None of them seemed to speak any English. Bowman held a couple of silver dollars in the palm of his hand. A lascar hurried to the rail with a sudden white smile. Bowman tossed him one of the coins. He asked the same question he had before. The lascar didn't understand fodder. "Hay, straw, grain—you know what I mean," Bowman said.

"You crazy?" the lascar said. "We got tea, we got cotton, we got copra. We take away steam engines, petrol engines. You think maybe we feed them this grain?" He spoke in his own singsong language. The other lascars laughed.

"Yeah, well, just for that, funny guy—" Bowman jammed the other silver dollar back into his trouser pocket. The lascar's Hindustani oaths followed him as he strode down the pier toward the Embarcadero. He paused at the base of the pier to scribble a note: *Expenses—Information—$2.* Then he walked back along the curb of the harbor to his automobile.

He parked it in the garage across the street from his office. Lounging against the brick wall not far from the entrance was a burly middle-aged man with the cold, hard, angular features of a Roman centurion. With its wide, pointed lapels, padded shoulders, and pinstripes, his suit stood on one side or the other of the line between fashion and parody. Bowman looked him over, then started up the steps.

The lounger spoke: "You don't want to go in there. You want to come with me."

"Yeah? Says who?" Bowman dropped his right hand from the doorknob. It came to rest at his side, near waist level.

"Says my boss—he's got a business proposition to put to you," the fellow answered. He stood straighter. One of his hands rested in the front pocket of his jacket. "And says me. And says—" The hand, and whatever it held, moved a little, suggestively.

Bowman came down the steps. "All right, take me to your boss. I'll talk business with anybody. As for you, pal, you can get stuffed." He spoke the words lightly, negligently, as if he didn't care whether the hard-faced man followed through on them or not.

The hard-faced man took a step toward him. "You watch your mouth, or—"

Bowman hit him in the pit of the stomach. His belly was hard as oak. Against a precisely placed blow to the solar plexus, that proved irrelevant. He doubled over with a loud, whistling grunt. His suddenly exhaled breath smelled of gin. While he gasped for air, Bowman plucked a revolver from his pocket and put it in his own. He hauled the burly man back to his feet. "I told you— take me to your boss."

The man glared at him. Hatred smoldered in his eyes. He started to say something. Bowman shook his head and raised a warning forefinger. The burly man visibly reconsidered. "Come on," he said, and Bowman nodded.

The seventeen-story white brick and stone Clift Hotel on Geary Street was five blocks west of the Palace. The hard-faced man said nothing more on the way there, nor through the lobby, which was decorated in the style of the Italian Renaissance. He and Bowman took the elevator to the fourteenth floor in silence. He rapped at the door to suite 1453.

Nicholas Alexandria opened it. His chrome-plated pistol was in his hand. "Ah, Mr. Bowman, so good to see you again," he said in a tone that belied the words. His left hand rose to a sticking plaster on his cheek. The plaster did not cover all the bruise there. "Won't you come in?"

"Don't mind if I do," Bowman said, and stepped past him. The suite was furnished in spare and modern style. Gina Tellini sat on a chair that looked as if it might pitch her off at any moment. She sent Bowman a quick, nervous glance, but did not speak. Nicholas Alexandria closed the door, sat on a similar chair beside her.

The couch opposite them was low and poorly padded enough to have come from ancient Greece. On it, hunched forward as if not to miss anything, sat a thin, pale, long-faced man with a lantern jaw and gold-rimmed spectacles. He wore a suit of creamy linen, a Sea Island cotton shirt, and a burgundy silk tie whose bar was adorned with a small silver coin, irregularly round, that displayed a large-eyed owl.

"Schlechtman?" Bowman said. The pale man nodded. Bowman took the revolver out of his pocket. He handed it to him. "You shouldn't let your little chums play with toys like this. They're liable to get hurt."

The hard-featured man who had unwillingly brought Bowman to the Clift Hotel flushed. Before he could speak, Gideon Schlechtman held up a hand. His fingers were long and white, like stalks of asparagus. "Hugo, that was exceedingly clumsy of you," he said, his voice dry, meticulous, scholarly.

He glanced a question at Bowman. Bowman nodded. Schlechtman returned the revolver to Hugo. The burly man growled wordlessly as he received it.

Bowman said: "Your bully boy tells me you want to talk business."

Schlechtman shifted so he could draw a billfold from his left hip pocket. From the billfold he took a banknote with a portrait of Grover Cleveland. He set it on the black lacquered table in front of him. Four more with the same portrait went on top of it. "Do you care for the tone of the conversation thus far?" he enquired.

"Who wouldn't like five grand?" Bowman asked hoarsely. His eyes never left the bills. "What do I have to do?"

"You have to deliver to me, alive and in good condition, the Maltese Elephant currently in this fair city of yours," Gideon Schlechtman replied.

"If you'll pay me five thousand for it, it's worth plenty more than that to you," Bowman said. Schlechtman smiled. He had small white even teeth. Gina Tellini caught her breath. Bowman went on: "I ought to have something to work from. Give me two grand now."

Gideon Schlechtman pursed his lips. He took one bill from the top of the stack, held it out to Bowman between thumb and forefinger. Bowman seized it, crumpled it, stuffed it into the trouser pocket where he kept his keys. Schlechtman neatly replaced the rest of the banknotes in his wallet. The wallet returned to the pocket from which it had come. Nicholas Alexandria sighed.

"All right," Bowman said. "Next thing is, everybody here knows more about this damned elephant than I do. Even Hugo does, if Hugo knows anything about anything."

"Why, you lousy—" Hugo began.

Again Schlechtman held up his hand. Again Hugo subsided into growls. Schlechtman said, "Your request is a fair one, Mr.

Bowman. If you are to assist us with your unmatchable knowledge of San Francisco, you must also have some knowledge of the remarkable beast we seek.

"Though the Maltese Elephant has of course been known since haziest antiquity to the human inhabitants with whom it shares its island, it was first memorialized in literature in the *Periplus* of Hanno the Carthaginian, which was translated from Punic to Greek in the fourth century B.C. Hanno's is a bald note: *Thêridion ho elephas Melitês estin.*"

"It's Greek to me, by God," Bowman said.

Schlechtman continued his lecture as if Bowman had not spoken: "Aristotle, in the *Historia Animalium*, 610ᵃ15, says of the Maltese Elephant, *Ho elephas ho Melitaios megethei homoios tê nêsô en hê oikei.* And Strabo, in the sixth book of his geography, notes Maltese dogs shared a similar trait: *Prokeitai de tou Pakhynou Melitê, hothen ta kynidia te kai elephantidia, ha kalousi Melitaia, kai Gaudos,* Gaudos being the ancient name for Malta's island neighbor.

"The Maltese elephant retained its reputation in Roman days as well. In the first century B.C., Cicero, in his first oration against Verres, claims, *Et etiam ex insulolae Melitae elephantisculos tres rapiebat.* More than a century later, Petronius, in the one hundred thirty-second chapter of the *Satyricon*, has his character Encolpius put the curled and preserved ear of a Maltese Elephant to a use which, out of deference to the presence here of Miss Tellini, I shall not quote even in the original. And in the fifth century of our era, as St. Augustine sadly recorded in the *Civitas dei, Res publica romanorum in statu elephantis Melitae nunc deminuitur.* So you see, Mr. Bowman, the beast whose trail we follow has a history extending back toward the dawn of time. I could provide you with many more citations—"

"I just bet you could," Bowman interrupted. "But what does any of 'em have to do with the price of beer?"

"I am coming to that, never fear," Gideon Schlechtman said. "You were the one who complained of lack of background. Now I have provided it to you. In the foreground is the presence on Malta since 1530 of the Knights of St. John of Jerusalem. During the great siege by the Ottoman Turks in 1565, a Maltese Elephant warned of an attack with its trumpeting. Since that time, it has come to be revered as a good-luck totem not only by the Knights but also by the great merchants who, under the British crown, are the dominant force on Malta today. The return of one of these beasts to its proper home would be . . . suitably appreciated by these men."

"Yeah? If they're so much in love with these elephants of theirs, how'd one of 'em go missing in the first place?" Bowman demanded.

"Evan Thursday knew the answer to that question, I believe," Schlechtman answered. "He is, unfortunately, in no position to furnish us with it. Unless, that is, he conveyed it to Miss Tellini. Her involvement in this affair has been, shall we say with the charity Scripture commends, ambiguous."

"He didn't," Gina Tellini said quickly. "I have a cousin on Malta—in Valetta—who—hears things. That's how I found out."

Bowman shrugged. "It's a story. I've heard a lot of stories from her." His voice was cool, indifferent.

Her flashing eyes registered anger, with hurt hard on its heels. "It's true, Miles. I swear it is."

"Her word is not to be trusted under any circumstances," Nicholas Alexandria said.

"As if yours is," Gina Tellini retorted hotly.

Bowman turned back to Gideon Schlechtman. "The five grand is mine provided I find this Maltese Elephant for you, right?"

"Provided we do not find it first through our unaided efforts, yes," Schlechtman said.

"Yeah, sure, I knew you were going to tell me that," Bowman said, indifferent again. "But if you thought you could do it on your own, you never would've dragged me into it." He started for the door. Passing Hugo, he patted him on the hip. "See you around, sweetheart."

Hugo slapped his hand away, cocked a fist. Beefy face expressionless, Bowman hit him in the belly again, in the exact spot his fist had found before. Hugo fell against an end table of copper tubing and glass. It went over with a crash.

At the door, Bowman looked back to Gideon Schlechtman. "A smart man like you should get better help."

He closed the door on whatever answer Schlechtman might have made. Waiting for the elevator, he peered back toward suite 1453. No one came out after him. The elevator door opened. "Ground floor, sir?" the operator asked.

"Yeah."

Bowman stepped into his office. Hester Prine stared up from her typing. Relief, anger, and worry warred on her face. "Where have you been?" she demanded. "Your wife has called three times already. She asked me if you were under arrest. Are you?"

"No." Bowman hung his hat on the tree. "I'd better talk to her this morning. Anybody else call?"

"Yes," she said in her lascivious voice. She looked down at the pad by her telephone. "He said his name was Wellnhofer." She spelled it. "He said he'd already talked to you once today, and he wanted to see you by ten. I was sure you'd be in—I was sure then, anyhow."

"What did he sound like?" Bowman asked.

"He had an accent, if that's what you mean."

Bowman did not answer. He went into his inner office, closed the door. He sat down in the swivel chair, lit a cigarette, and sucked in harsh smoke with quick, savage puffs. After he stubbed it out, he picked up the phone and called. "Eva? . . . Yeah, it's me. Who else would it be? . . . No, I'm not in jail, for God's sake. . . . What do you mean, you called them up and they said they didn't have me? . . . What time was that? . . . I was gone by then. . . . No, I didn't see any point to coming home when I had to go in to the office anyway. I ate breakfast and did some looking around. Now I'm here. All right?"

He hung up, smoked another cigarette, and went back out of his private office. From his pocket he took the silver dollar he had not given to the lascar sailor. He dropped it on his secretary's desk. It rang sweetly. "Go around the corner and get me some coffee and doughnuts. Get some for yourself, too, if you want."

"I thought you already ate breakfast," she said. She picked up the cartwheel and started for the door.

Bowman swatted her on the posterior, hard enough to make her squeak. "I'm going to have to soundproof that door," he said gruffly. "Go on, get out of here."

He returned to his office, pulled the telephone directory off its shelf, pawed through it. "Operator, give me McPherson's Agricultural Supplies." He drummed his fingers on the desk. "McPherson's? Yeah, can you tell me if you've filled any big, unusual orders for hay the last couple of days? . . . No? All right, thanks." He went through the book again. "Let me have The Manger." He asked the same question there. He received the same answer, and slammed the earpiece back onto its hook.

The outer door opened. Hester Prine came in with two cardboard cups and a white paper sack. Grease already made the white paper dark and shiny in several places.

"I thought maybe you were Wellnhofer," Bowman said.

"No such luck." Hester Prine took a half dollar, a dime, and a nickel from her purse and gave them to Bowman. He dropped them into his pocket. She opened the bag and handed him a doughnut whose sugar glaze glistened like ice on a bad road. He devoured it, drained his coffee. She pointed to the bag and said, "There's another one in there, if you want it."

"Don't mind if I do." Bowman was reaching for it when several sharp pops, like firecrackers on Chinese New Year, sounded outside the office building. Down on the street, a woman screamed. A man cried out. Bowman snatched the doughnut from the bag. "That's a gun," he said, and ran for the stairs.

He gulped down the last of the doughnut as he burst out into the fresh air. The man who lay crumpled on the sidewalk wore a navy blue jacket with four gold rings at each cuff. His cap had fallen from his head. It lay several feet away, upside down. The brown leather sweatband inside was stained and frayed.

"I called the cops," a man exclaimed. "A guy in a car shot him. He drove off that way." The man pointed west.

Bowman squatted beside Captain Wellnhofer. The seaman had taken two slugs in the chest. Blood soaked his shirt and jacket. It puddled on the pavement. He stared up at Bowman. His eyes still held reason. "Warehouse," he said, and exhaled. Blood ran from his nose and mouth. With great effort, he spoke through it: "Warehouse near Eddy and Fillm—" He exhaled again, but did not breathe in. He looked blindly up at the pale blue morning sky.

Bowman was getting to his feet when a car pulled to a screeching stop in front of him. Out sprang Detective Dwyer and Captain Bock. Bock looked from Bowman to the corpse and back again. "People have a way of dying around you," he remarked coldly.

"Go to hell, Bock," Bowman said. "You can't pin this on me. Don't waste your time trying. I was upstairs with Hester when the shooting started." He pointed to the man who had said he had called the police. "This guy here saw me come out."

"What were you doing up there with Hester?" Dwyer asked, amusement in his voice.

"Eating a doughnut. What about it?"

"You've got sugar on your chin," Dwyer said.

Bowman wiped his mouth on his sleeve. Bock asked several questions of the man who had called the police. His mouth curling down in disappointment, he turned back to Bowman. "Do you know the victim?" he asked.

"His name's Wellnhofer," Bowman answered unwillingly. "He was coming to see me. He had a ten o'clock appointment." He looked at his watch. "He was early. Now he's late."

"You were down there by him when we drove up," Dwyer said. "Did he say anything to you before he died?"

"Not a word," Bowman assured him. "He must have been gone the second he went down."

"Two in the chest? Yeah, maybe," Dwyer said.

"Are you going to take a formal statement from me, or what?" Bowman asked. "If you are, then do it. If you aren't, I'm going back upstairs." He jerked a thumb in the direction of Wellnhofer's body. "A hole just opened up in my schedule."

"You're a cold-blooded so-and-so," Dwyer said. He and Captain Bock walked over to their car and put their heads together.

When they were done, Dwyer came back to Bowman. "Go on up, Miles. We've got enough from you for now. If we need more later, we know where to find you."

"Yeah, I know," Bowman said bitterly.

Hugo pushed the room-service cart to the door of Gideon Schlechtman's suite in the Clift Hotel. He opened the door, pulled the cart through, left it in the hall. Then he closed the door and returned to the others in the ever so modern living room.

To Schlechtman, Bowman said: "Much obliged. Lobster and drawn butter, baked potato. I usually like my liquor hard, but that wine was tasty, too."

"That was a Pouilly-Fumé from the valley of the Loire, Mr. Bowman, and a prime year, too," Gideon Schlechtman replied, steepling his long, thin, pale fingers.

"Didn't I say it was good?" Bowman asked equably. "Now, before we go any further, we have to figure out who gets thrown to the wolves. There's three bodies with holes in 'em lying on slabs in the morgue. That kind of business gets the cops all up in arms. They're going to be looking for somebody to blame. If we give 'em somebody, they won't do any real digging on their own. Cops, they're like that."

"Whom do you suggest, Mr. Bowman?" Schlechtman enquired.

"Hugo's just hired muscle," Bowman answered. "Turn up a flat rock and you'll find a dozen like him. Dwyer and Bock'll see it the same way."

The hard-faced man snarled a vile oath. He yanked out his revolver and pointed it at Bowman's chest. Schlechtman raised his hand. "Patience, Hugo. I have not said I agree to this. What other possibilities have we?"

Bowman shrugged. "Alexandria there's a squiff. With three strapping men dead, that might do. Rollie Dwyer, he's got seven kids."

"You are an insane, wicked man," Nicholas Alexandria cried shrilly. His hand darted inside his coat. Lamplight glittered from his chromed automatic. He aimed the little gun at Bowman's face. Hugo still held his pistol steady.

"Nicholas, please." Schlechtman held up his hand again. "We do have a problem here which merits discussion. Everything is hypothetical." He turned back to Bowman. "Why not Miss Tellini?"

"We could work the frame that way, for Tom and Thursday, anyhow," Bowman said. "A guy plugged Wellnhofer, though. We'd have to drag in Hugo or Alexandria any which way."

Gina Tellini sent Bowman a Bunsen burner glance. "Why not Schlechtman?" she demanded.

"Don't be stupid, darling," Bowman answered. "He's paying the bills."

"Whoever finds the Maltese Elephant can pay the bills," she said.

"If we find the elephant, we shall be able to pay the attorneys' fees to keep us from the clutches of the intrepid San Francisco police, as well," Gideon Schlechtman said. He pointed to Hugo and to Nicholas Alexandria in turn. "Put up your weapons. We are all colleagues in this matter. And, as the saying has it, if we do not hang together, we shall hang separately."

"You're the boss," Hugo said. He put the gun back in his pocket. His muddy eyes raked Bowman once more. Nicholas Alexandria bit his lip. Purple and yellow bruises still discolored his cheek. He had taken off the sticking plaster that covered the dried-blood scab on the cut Bowman's pistol had made there. At last, the little chromed automatic disappeared.

Schlechtman smiled. The stretch of lips was broader and more fulsome than his rather pinched features could comfortably support. "Shall we be off, Mr. Bowman?" he said.

Bowman got to his feet, went to the window, pulled aside the curtain. He looked at the night, then at his watch. "Give it another half hour," he said. "I want it good and dark, and the fog's starting to roll in, too."

"How fitting," Schlechtman remarked. "This whole business of the elephant has been dark and foggy."

At the hour Bowman had chosen, they left suite 1453 and rode down to the Clift's elegant lobby. Outside, the fog had thickened. It left the taste of the ocean on the lips. Defeated streetlamps cast small reddish-yellow puddles of light at the foot of their standards. Automobile headlamps appeared out of the mist, then were swallowed up once more. Walking in the fog was like pushing through soaked cotton gauze.

Hugo looked around nervously. His hand went to the pocket where the revolver nestled. "I don't like this," he muttered.

"We've got three guns with us—at least three," Bowman amended, glancing from Schlechtman to Gina Tellini. "You don't like those odds, go home and play with dolls."

"You're pushing it, Bowman. Shut your stinking mouth or—"

"After the elephant is in our hands, these quarrels will seem trivial," Gideon Schlechtman said. "Let us consider them so now."

They walked four blocks down Taylor to Eddy, then turned right onto Eddy. "It's a mile from here, maybe a little more," Bowman said. He lit a cigarette. Fog swallowed the smoke he blew out.

As they passed Gough, shops and hotels and apartments fell away on their left. The mist swirled thickly, as if it sprang from the grass in the open area there. A few trees grew near enough streetlamps to be seen. "What is this place?" Hugo said.

Bowman rested a hand on his pistol. "It's Jefferson Square," he answered. "In the daytime, people get up on soapboxes and make speeches here. Nights like this, the punks come out." He peered warily into the fog until they left the square behind. Then, more happily, he said, "All right, three-four blocks to go."

He turned right on Fillmore, then left into an alley in back of the buildings that fronted on Eddy. The alley had no lights. Gravel scrunched under the soles of his shoes.

"I don't trust him," Nicholas Alexandria said suddenly. "This is a place for treachery."

"Shut up, dammit," Bowman said. "You make me mess up and you'll get all the treachery you ever wanted." He walked with his left hand extended. Like a blind man, he brushed the bricks of the buildings with his fingertips to guide himself. "Stinking fog. Hell of a lot easier to find this place this afternoon," he muttered, but grunted a moment later. "Here we are. These are stairs. Come on, everybody up."

The stairway and handrail were made of wood. They led to a

second-floor landing. The door there wore a stout lock. Gideon Schlechtman felt for it. "I presume you have some way to surmount this difficulty?" he asked Bowman.

"Nah, we're all going to stand around here and wait for the sun to come up." Bowman pulled a small leather case from his inside jacket pocket. "Move. I've got picks." He worked for a few minutes, whistling softly and tunelessly between his teeth. The lock clicked. He pulled it from the hasp and laid it on the boards of the landing. He opened the door. "Let's go."

Bowman waited for his comrades to enter first. When he went in, he closed the door. It was no darker inside than out. The air was different, though: drier, warmer, charged with a thick odor not far from that of horse droppings. Again, he ran his hand along the wall. His fingers found a light switch. He flicked it.

Several bare bulbs strung on a wire across the warehouse ceiling sprang to life. He pointed from the walkway on which he and the others stood down to the immense gray-brown beast occupying the floor of the warehouse proper. Its huge ears twitched at the light. Its trunk curled. It made a complaining noise: the sound of a trumpet whose spit valve has not worked for years. "There it is, right off *La Tórtola*." Bowman stood tall. "The Maltese Elephant."

Gina Tellini, Schlechtman, Nicholas Alexandria, and Hugo stared down at the elephant. Then their eyes swung to Bowman. The same expression filled all their faces. Hugo drew his pistol. He pointed it at the detective. "He's mine now," he said happily.

"No, mine." The chromium-plated automatic was in Nicholas Alexandria's right hand.

Gina Tellini fumbled in her handbag. "No, he's mine." She, too, proved to carry a small automatic, though hers was not chromed.

"I am sorry, but I must insist on the privilege." Gideon Schlechtman had worn a .357 magnum in a shoulder holster. His stance was like an army gunnery sergeant's, left hand supporting right wrist. The pistol was pointed at a spot an inch and a half above the bridge of Bowman's nose.

Bowman stared down the barrel of the gun. His eyes crossed

slightly. His right hand stayed well away from the gun at his belt. "What the hell is the matter with you people?" he demanded. "I find your damned elephant, and this is the thanks I get?"

"Let's all fill him full of holes, boss," Hugo said. His finger tightened on the trigger.

"No, wait," Schlechtman said. "I want him to die knowing what an ignorant idiot he is. Otherwise he would not understand how richly he deserves it."

"This stupid ox? It is a waste of time," Nicholas Alexandria said.

"Possibly, but we have time to waste," Gideon Schlechtman replied. "Mr. Bowman, that great lumpish creature down there—in that it bears a remarkable resemblance to you, eh?—is an elephant, but not a Maltese elephant, not *the* Maltese Elephant we have sought so long and hard."

"How do you know?" Bowman said. "An elephant is an elephant, right?"

"An elephant is an elephant—wrong," Schlechtman answered. "A Maltese elephant is easily distinguished from that gross specimen by the simple fact that a grown bull is slightly smaller than a Shetland pony."

"Yeah, and rain makes applesauce," Bowman said with a scornful laugh. "Go peddle your papers."

"The old saw about he who laughs last would seem not to apply in your case, Mr. Bowman," Schlechtman said. "I spoke nothing but the truth. For time immemorial, Malta has been the home of a rare race of dwarf elephants. And why not? Before man came, the island knew no large predators. An elephant there had no need to be huge to protect itself. Natural selection would also have favored small size because the forage on Malta has always been less than abundant; smaller beasts need smaller amounts of food. The Maltese and their later conquerors preserved the race down to the present as an emblem of their uniqueness—and you tried to fob off this great, ugly creature on us? Fool!"

The elephant trumpeted. The noise was deafening. The beast took a couple of steps. The walkway trembled, as if at an earthquake. Nicholas Alexandria nearly lost his balance. Almost involuntarily, Gina Tellini and Hugo glanced toward the elephant for an instant. Even Gideon Schlechtman's expression of supreme concentration wavered for a moment.

Bowman jerked out his .45 in a motion quicker than conscious thought. "Come on," he snarled. "Who's first? By God, I'll nail the first one who plugs me—and if you don't shoot straight, I'll take out two or three of you before I go."

The tableau held for perhaps three heartbeats. The elephant trumpeted again. The door to the warehouse opened. "Drop the guns!" Detective Roland Dwyer shouted. His own pistol covered the group impartially. Behind him came Henry Bock, and behind him two men in uniform. All were armed. "Drop 'em!" Dwyer repeated. "Hands high!"

Nicholas Alexandria let his little automatic fall. It clattered on the walkway. Then Hugo threw down his gun. So did Gina Tellini. At last, with a shrug, Gideon Schlechtman surrendered.

Bowman stepped back against the wall, the heavy pistol still in his hand. Captain Henry Bock might have had something to say about that. Before he could speak, Dwyer asked Bowman, "Just what the hell is going on here, Miles?"

Bowman pointed to Gina Tellini and said: "She's the one who fingered Wellnhofer. Had to be: I visited the docks right after I saw her, and I had the list of ships I was going to check in my trouser pocket then."

"How'd she have a chance to find out what was in your trouser pocket without you knowing it?" Bock demanded, leering.

"You said you loved me," Gina Tellini hissed.

"Loved you?" Bowman shook his head. "You must have heard wrong, sweetheart. I'm a married man." He went on talking to Detective Dwyer: "She may have fingered Tom for that Evan Thursday item, too. I don't know that for a fact, but you knew Tom. He wouldn't have been easy to take down, not unless somebody recognized him who wasn't supposed to. Or she may have shot him herself. Tom would go after anything in a skirt."

"Yeah," Dwyer said. One of the uniformed policemen behind him nodded.

"I figure laughing boy here probably canceled Wellnhofer's

stamp." Bowman jerked a thumb at Hugo. "Gina and Schlecht-man knew each other pretty well, and Hugo's Schlechtman's hired gun."

"So who did Thursday?" Roland Dwyer asked.

"Could have been Hugo again," Bowman answered, shrugging. "Or it could have been sweetheart here"—he grinned at Nicholas Alexandria, who returned a hate-filled glare—"on account of I'm not sure if Hugo was in town yet."

Dwyer pointed to Gideon Schlechtman. "What about him?"

"The hell with it," Captain Bock said. "He's in it some kind of way. We'll take 'em all in and sort it out later." He gestured to the uniformed policemen. They advanced with their handcuffs. The one who cuffed Gina Tellini shoved her lightly in the middle of the back. She stumbled out of the warehouse. The others glumly followed.

"You almost got too cute for your own good, Miles," Detective Dwyer said. "If that witness hadn't heard Wellnhofer spill to you—and if he hadn't decided to tell us about it—you wouldn't have had yourself a whole lot of fun, didn't look like." He stared down at the elephant. It pulled hay from a bale with its trunk and stuffed it into its mouth. "What the devil were you doing here, anyway?"

"Who, me?" Bowman replaced his Colt in its holster. "I was just on a wild elephant chase, Rollie, that's all."

"Yeah?" Dwyer's eyes swung to the door through which Gina Tellini had just gone. "You going to tell Eva all about it?"

"I'll tell her what she needs to know: I got paid."

Dwyer shook his head. "You're a louse, Miles."

"That's what everybody tells me." Miles Bowman laughed. "Thanks," he said.

Vermin

What made this piece interesting to do was that the main character's beliefs and emotions are so different from mine. Writing convincingly about someone who isn't like you is one of the harder tricks to pull off; I hope I've done it well here. I wrote "Vermin" not least to make my wife, who isn't fond of bugs, squirm a little. There, I know I succeeded.

The heavy but familiar weight of the water jar pressed into Victoria Griffin's left hip as she walked back from the stream toward her husband's cabin. Sweat slithered down her face, prickled in her armpits, greased the crevice between her buttocks so that she was unpleasantly aware of her own flesh sliding against itself. The heavy wool dress that covered all of her but head, hands, and feet made her want to scratch everywhere at once, as if it were a hair shirt.

She forced facial muscles into an expression of determined serenity. Serenity was the expression most often seen along the paths of New Zion. The Holy Mission Church taught that, since the body was the chief source of sin, all its sensations were to be mistrusted, and ignored as far as possible. On a steambath of a planet like Reverence, that was not always easy.

Serenity sagged toward exhaustion. Endless jungle heat and humidity made the task of building Reverence into a perfect world all the more daunting. Once in a great while, as now, the devil tempted Victoria to wish the Church had enjoyed the secular wealth to pick a more salubrious planet on which to pasture

179

its flock. She knew the wish was sinful. Later, she would spend hours on aching knees repenting of it. But the water came first.

The path was muddy (the path was always muddy). One of Victoria's feet flew out from under her. "Jesus' name!" she cried in the moment before the ground slammed her backside. Even as she fell, she grabbed for the water jar. Too late. It hit a rock and smashed. A sharp sherd sliced her thumb, almost to the bone.

Filthy, bleeding, and crying, she staggered to her feet. Wet, slimy earth glued her dress to her haunches. Normally, that would have disgusted her. Now she hardly noticed. She squeezed the torn flesh of her thumb together, trying to stem the flow of blood. Drawn by the iron smell, the animated pinheads that were vermin scuttled down her arm.

Victoria let go of her thumb to smash a couple of the tiny pests, but more soon took their place. She hated bugs of every description; they made her cringe inside. But bugs of every description was what Reverence had. She looked daggers in the direction of the Haldol village a couple of miles away. Like all Haldol villages, it was awash in offal, a perfect breeding place for the crawling horrors that were only too happy to infest New Zion as well. The settlers fumigated their cabins again and again. It did no lasting good, not with the Haldols and their corruption so close.

One of the vermin bit her on the inside of the thigh, so high up that even her husband's touch there felt wicked. On top of everything else that had just happened, that was too much. She let out a high, piercing note of pure outrage. And exactly then, of course, Cornelia Baker came round the corner with an empty jug.

Cornelia's big blue eyes went round and wide. "Why, Victoria!" she gasped. "*Are* you all right?"

"I think so," Victoria said through clenched teeth. Cornelia Baker somehow managed perfect cleanliness and perfect neatness on a raw colonial world. Even the sheen of sweat that glistened on her face might have been taken for a virtuous glow. It was impossible to imagine a bloodsucking bug being so rude as to bite her high up on the thigh. She boasted every Christian virtue, and flaunted them as well.

Now she took efficient charge of Victoria. She brushed the

worst of the muck from Victoria's dress, threw a strong (and somehow, even after that tidying job, not particularly dirty) arm around her shoulder, and half led, half supported her back to New Zion. All the while she chattered on with such aggressively sincere sympathy that Victoria wanted to claw out those big blue eyes.

Victoria wanted to claw at herself as well. The biting bug, or perhaps a different biting bug, had decided to pierce her right between her legs. To scratch herself there made Victoria's cheeks flame crimson even when she was alone. To scratch herself there in front of anyone would have been lewd and indecent, and possibly good for time in the pillory. To scratch herself there in front of Cornelia Baker was hideously unimaginable.

But the biter would not relent. To make matters worse, it kept looking for new, tender spots; she felt it crawling slowly through her secret hair. She could also feel the gooseflesh rising on her arms and legs at every new motion of the bug, no matter how tiny. The horrible anticipation of its next move brought her worse pain than any from her torn thumb or bruised behind.

At last, in front of Victoria's cabin, Cornelia said, "Here we are, my dear. I do hope you'll be better soon. God bless you."

"God bless you, Cornelia, and thank you for all your help," Victoria said, when she would sooner have screamed, *Just go away!*

Finally, Cornelia did go away. Victoria bolted inside the cabin, locked the door behind her. She shuttered the two small windows, pausing at the second one to dip her head in the direction of the church steeple she could see through it.

With all openings closed, the inside of the cabin turned night-dark. That suited Victoria. She hardly saw and deliberately did not look at the pale flesh she revealed when she stripped off her soiled and soaked dress. She did her best not to notice the puff of air that cooled her for a moment as the dress went off over her head.

Both her other dresses were dirty. She'd intended to wash them after she brought the water home. Now, instead, she quickly picked one and threw it on. Only when she was properly clothed did she wrap a rag around her thumb. And only after that did she look to the ceiling so she would not have to watch her unhurt hand as it tried to rout the biter from her private parts.

She gasped in relief, then gasped again when she thought how the first gasp might sound—no one could possibly hear it, but it shamed her all the same. Then the barred door rattled and she gasped again. Someone was trying to get into the cabin. "Who's there?" she called shrilly.

"Only me, Mrs. Griffin," a deep voice replied. "May I please come in?"

She ran to the door, threw up the bar. "Of course, Mr. Griffin," she answered, and stood aside to let her husband by. "I didn't expect you back from the fields so soon."

"Broke my hoe handle," he answered, scowling. He pointed to the path outside, where he'd dropped the ruined tool. "Have to shape myself a new one." Then he finally seemed to take a good look at Victoria. "By the hope of heaven, Mrs. Griffin, what's befallen you?"

Victoria went through the whole sorry tale (leaving out only Cornelia Baker's attitude, which no man could be expected to understand). When she finished, her husband's gaze flicked toward the kitchen. The cabin was too dark for him to see what was there, but he knew anyhow. He said, "We have no other water jar."

"No, Mr. Griffin, we don't." Victoria fought down a flare of resentment—he might have spoken of her hurts before the household's. But he was right. "I've been meaning to go into the Haldol village to dicker for another one, but—" She could not continue. She hated hiking to the Haldol village, not on account of the walk itself but because the village and all the Haldols in it crawled with vermin.

"No buts," her husband said firmly. "Tomorrow you must get a new one. Now you will excuse me, I hope. I have a great deal of work still to do this day."

He went out behind the cabin. Victoria heard him rummaging through the sticks piled there, then the *snick-snick* of his knife cutting the end of one of them to fit the shank of the hoe blade. After a while, he grunted in satisfaction. His footsteps receded down the path.

Sighing, Victoria bundled up the two dresses she was not wearing—water from the wet, muddy one promptly soaked her breasts and belly all over again—with some of her husband's overalls and carried them down to the stream to wash. She hadn't planned to do the washing for another couple of days, but she hadn't planned to fall in a puddle, either.

Her knees clicked and complained as she knelt by the bank of the stream. She scrubbed the clothes against a wooden washboard, rasping her knuckles with every stroke. Gooey lye soap burned the raw patches and slowly, so slowly, worked dirt free from wool. In New Zion's ever-humid air, the clothes would dry even more slowly.

She looked upstream. It was only a quick glance, but she muttered a prayer of contrition as she averted her eyes. Upstream from New Zion, only a few miles away in distance but centuries in technology and light-years in attitude, lay the new Federation research base on Reverence—*the godless Federation's godless research base,* she thought. Its gleaming metal walls, the whip and bowl antennae that linked the base to the thousands of other worlds in the Federation—all were anathema to the way of life the Holy Mission Church had worked for the past three generations to build here.

She picked up the bundle of clean, wet clothes. By now she was so soaked herself that a little more water no longer bothered her. She made sure, though, to carry the bundle in front of her as if it were a shield, so no one in the village could see how immodestly the damp dress she was wearing clung to her.

Once she'd spread dresses and overalls out to dry by her cabin, she went back to the stream yet again with a couple of small jars to get enough water for the night's cooking. She had to make two trips, which left her gloomy as she began chopping turnips. Mr. Griffin was right, without a shadow of a doubt. Tomorrow, no matter how she loathed them, she would have to get a new jar from the Haldols.

Her husband came in from the fields again not long before sunset. He spoke a long grace over supper; Victoria bent her head and prayed with him. When they were finished, she carried the dishes into the kitchen. He ignited a stick of punk at the fire-place; in their desire for a life of Biblical simplicity, those who followed the way of the Holy Mission Church eschewed electricity.

Victoria came out, sank wearily into a chair. The hard seat was a trial to her sore backside, but she tried to will away the discomfort. The day had been long and taxing. But Mr. Griffin said, "Why are you sitting in idleness, with plates and pots yet to clean?"

"With our jug broken, I haven't the water here to wash them, and I am too worn to travel to the stream two or three more times to fetch it. I shall clean them tomorrow, when I have a new jug, if that is pleasing to you, Mr. Griffin." She did her best to make her voice sweet and persuasive.

Her husband would have been within his rights to order her into action, but he only grunted. He was tired, too. After a while, he said, "If you like, Mrs. Griffin, I will read you a passage of Scripture, that the idleness may be improved."

"Yes, thank you," Victoria said eagerly, glad he had decided not to make an issue of the dishes.

The Bible was the only book in the cabin. Her husband kissed the wooden cover that protected the precious pages from long-ago Earth. He held the volume close to the fattest candle. Twilight was already gone from the sky; night at New Zion fell with tropical swiftness. "This is the Book of Judges, the second chapter, the first verse," he said, and paused to scratch his thick brown beard before he began: " 'And the angel of the Lord came up from Gilgal to Bochim. And he said . . .' "

Leaning a little to one side on her chair to favor her bruised hindquarter, Victoria listened to Mr. Griffin read. They had not been married long; this was only their second trip through the Holy Scriptures together. Older couples in New Zion read the sacred words twelve, fifteen, even twenty times, and always seemed to find something new and rewarding in them.

After several chapters, Mr. Griffin caught himself in a yawn. "That's enough for tonight, I think," he said, shutting the Bible and setting it back on its stand on the mantel. He went around the room blowing out candles, picked up the one by whose light he'd read. "Shall we go to bed, Mrs. Griffin?"

"As you say, Mr. Griffin." Victoria got up and followed him into the bedroom. He set the candle in a stand on the small chest of drawers by the bed. Then he and Victoria knelt side by side and prayed the day's last prayers.

He turned his head and blew out the candle. The small, hot bedroom plunged into darkness. Victoria could not see her hand in front of her face as she lay down.

Her husband joined her in bed a moment later. As they had prayed side by side, so they lay side by side. She felt the mattress shift, heard the small, soft sounds of fasteners opening as he undid part of his overalls. *So,* she thought, and spread her legs for him.

He rolled onto her without a word, his weight and the heavy smell of him a familiar burden. His right hand pulled her dress up to her waist, bundled it between them. His left, for a moment, closed on her right breast. After a couple of squeezes that brought hurt and pleasure mixed, he took it away. Then, brusquely, he thrust himself into her.

That hurt, too; she was still dry. The rough cloth of his overalls chafed against her inner thighs, and against the new bites there. She opened her legs wider. The motion, though intended as one of escape, helped ease his way. A few more thrusts and he was lodged to the hilt.

His harsh exhalations stirred the soft down of her cheek. His passage in and out of her grew smoother. She felt herself tighten around him. Of itself, her back arched as she awaited the gathering sweetness of each new thrust.

He grunted above her, quivered briefly, and stopped. All his weight came down on her, so she could hardly breathe. As he withdrew, she felt a pang of frustrated longing. Congress between man and wife was one of the few pleasures the Church of the Holy Mission sanctioned. To have that pleasure cut short before its peak— Victoria sighed. It usually was.

Mr. Griffin flopped back to his side of the bed. Victoria rearranged her dress so it decently covered her once more. "May

God grant us a child," she said. They'd had a daughter a year and a half before, but she'd died inside of three months. The empty place she left still ached inside Victoria.

Her husband did not answer. He had already started to snore. She sighed again—quietly, so she would not disturb him. She lay on her back, staring up at the blackness of the ceiling. Of itself, her hand pressed at the place where her legs joined, this time not to scratch but to finish what Mr. Griffin had begun. But the first twinge of sensation made her guiltily snatch it away. "Sinful," she whispered, reminding herself. "Shameful."

After a long while, she slept.

Breakfast was a heel of bread. The butter was going bad; in Reverence's climate, it would not keep no matter what she did. The rancid taste lingered in Victoria's mouth as she loaded iron tools into her basket for the trip to the Haldol village. Having to make that trip left a bad taste in her mouth, too.

At the edge of the jungle, she turned to look back at New Zion. She felt like one of the Hebrews doomed to wander in the desert for forty years. No help for it, though. Treading carefully to keep from falling again, she started down the narrow, winding track that led from the human settlement to that of the Haldols.

Reverence's jungle was far more alien to her than the long-ago desert of Sinai had been to the Hebrews. Even the green of the foliage was brighter, shinier, a touch more yellow than the honest green of the Earthly plants that fed New Zion. When she brushed into them, the leaves felt velvety against the skin of her hands and face. Smells went in swift succession from lasciviously sweet to stinks worse than any outhouse.

Bugs were everywhere—bugs on the velvety leaves, bugs on the ground, bugs flying through the air. Victoria swatted at herself, but she might as well have been Pharaoh, trying to hold back the inrushing Red Sea. Even in New Zion, bugs were a torment. In the jungle, they were a plague. She thought again of

Pharaoh as many-legged wriggling things tickled between her breasts, ran up and down her legs, tried to crawl into her ears and nostrils. By the horror they raised in her, they might have been Satan's imps.

The closer she drew to the Haldol village, the thicker the bugs became and the more of them were the pinhead-sized biters that particularly afflicted Reverence's natives—and Victoria. She was all but trembling when the jungle abruptly ended and the clearing round the village began. A tall yellow Haldol spotted her and let out a high, trilling yeep that momentarily silenced the racket in the market square.

Everyone in the square came rushing toward her, yeeping and whistling and calling out "Good day! God bless you!" in shrilly accented English. The Haldols resembled nothing so much as stick people whose ancestors had been salamanders. Their skins were hairless and as slick and moist as the inside of her cheek, their eyes huge and round and altogether black. They wore no clothes. Their genitals looked enough like those of human beings to make Victoria's cheeks heat on seeing them.

Worse even than those shamelessly and openly displayed genitals were the red warty patches on the sides of the males' necks. Not only did they look creviced and diseased, but a faint odor of rotting meat came from them. The Haldols never seemed to notice it, but it twisted Victoria's stomach and brought a flow of nauseous saliva to her mouth.

And worst of all were the vermin. She watched them crawl blithely over the Haldols' smooth, shiny skins, now and then pausing to feed. The Haldols paid no special attention to them, not even when they came to rest on their private parts. She squirmed, remembering her own torments of the day before.

The vermin seemed fond of the Haldols' privates. *Why not?* she thought—they were filthy creatures, and had to be naturally drawn to filthy places. They also congregated around the males' warty, stinking neck patches. And from the Haldols, they were happy enough to crawl onto Victoria. She squirmed again, this time at the feather touch of tiny feet.

"What you want, *pisquaa*?" one of the males squealed. The Haldol epithet for humans meant something like *silly person wrapped up in big leaves*. Haldols thought humans endlessly amusing. It wasn't mutual, not to the serious folk who went about God's work at New Zion.

"I need a new water jug," Victoria answered. She spoke no Haldol; few colonists did. The male who had asked her the question translated her reply into his own high-pitched speech.

His companions chattered excitedly. A water jug was serious business. "I show you!" the male said. "No, I!" another one broke in. A third, one evidently without English, pointed to his own skinny chest. Victoria vowed she would never chaffer with him.

Several more of the tall yellow natives darted into their huts, to emerge in moments with jugs to thrust into Victoria's face. The Haldols were such excellent potters that no one at New Zion followed that trade any more. But the natives were ignorant of metalwork. They squawked in delight when Victoria displayed the assortment of nails, knife blades, and other iron tools she'd brought with her.

She quickly waved away a couple of would-be jug sellers whose wares were obscenely decorated. The Haldols had no sense of decency; they believed anything that was right to do was also right to depict. Anyone in New Zion depraved enough to buy such wares would spend time in the stocks.

Some of the potters were greedy. They wanted more tools than she was willing to part with. After a while, she was down to dickering with only three males. She liked all their pots. One in particular had lines of almost perfect smoothness. When she lifted it and set it against her hip, it fit as if it had grown there. But she did not want the Haldol to know she was especially fond of his pot, so she also made sure to admire the jugs the other two set before her.

The haggling went on most of the morning. That was partly because New Zion was not rich enough in iron to waste it for no good cause, and partly because Victoria hated to get the short end of a bargain, even if accepting it would have let her sooner leave the village she loathed.

The Haldols not directly involved in the haggling returned to their own pursuits, as unselfconsciously as if she had not been there. Some went out into the jungle to forage for the animals and fruits on which they lived. A disappointed potter, one with whom Victoria had chosen not to deal, began to shape a clay coil into a new vessel. Young Haldols scampered here and there, screaming at one another; they were even louder and shriller than their elders. A female spitted a still-writhing lizardy creature on a sharp stick and held it over the fire.

Haldols casually relieved themselves in the open. Victoria tried not to look, lowering her eyes to the water jugs and to the metal she was offering in exchange (that last was a sensible precaution in any case, as knife blade or nails might otherwise inexplicably ascend to heaven). But the sharp, foul stink of the natives' droppings fought against the burnt-meat smell of the roasting (and *still* squirming) lizard.

She finally shook her head once too often at one of the Haldol potters. With dignity, he picked up his jug and walked away. Now she faced only two males, the one whose pot she really wanted and one whose work she would take if the other kept insisting on an exorbitant price.

Sensing that the dicker was heating up, more Haldols strolled over to watch and to be in at the climax. Just behind her preferred potter, a male Haldol ran his hands down the flanks and over the breastless chest of the female beside him. The female's mouth took the "O" shape that was a Haldol's smile. She turned toward the male, reached out and took his member in her hand.

Again, Victoria lowered her eyes to the pots—again and again. Of themselves, they kept returning to the Haldol couple, who went about coupling as nonchalantly as if they were the only souls (damned souls, surely, for their heathen lack of shame, but souls nonetheless) for miles about. She'd seen animals mate countless times, back in New Zion, but animals were only animals, and only slightly embarrassing. Haldols were people, of a sort.

The female sank gracefully to her knees in the mud. Her mouth closed on the male's organ. Victoria's cheeks were incandescent. Any woman who performed such lewdness—any man base or lascivious enough to demand it—the stocks or the pillory could not be enough. They would kick their lives away on the gibbet . . . if they did not burn.

Then the female went down on all fours. The male knelt beside her. They joined like dogs. The Haldols, used to such horrid sights, found the bargaining over the water jar more interesting than their linked fellows. Victoria's cheeks grew hotter still as she watched the couple's slow, deliberate movements. Unexpectedly, mortifyingly, she also knew heat in her loins, the same frustrating, incomplete warming Mr. Griffin sometimes brought her in the darkness.

More anxious than ever to escape this cesspit of iniquity, she closed the deal with the Haldol potter she preferred faster than she might have. He beeped and squeaked his glee as she passed him nails and blades and fish hooks. The other potter glumly walked away, no doubt wishing the human would have been so generous to him.

The copulating Haldols finished at last. They got up, pulled some green leaves off a vine to wipe the mud from their lower legs and from the female's hands. They ignored the vermin crawling over the rest of their bodies, which would have distressed Victoria worse than any mud. Vermin even crept inside the female's distended genital slit. The sight made Victoria's stomach churn. So did the way the Haldol did nothing to drive them away, but went right on talking to the male with whom she'd just mated.

Victoria snatched up the water jug and fled. "Goodbye, *pisquaa*," the Haldol potter called after her. "God bless you."

At that moment, she was convinced God would bless her most if He arranged for her never to have to set foot in the Haldol village again.

"They are *dirty* creatures," Victoria said to Cornelia Baker when she walked by the next morning.

"Who, the Haldols?" Cornelia's mouth narrowed into a thin, disapproving line. "Of course they are, my dear. They reject the true and living God, the only true morality. Why do you think we go so seldom to their villages?" Her eyes widened in perfectly realistic sympathy. "But then you had to visit them yesterday, didn't you? The water jug. I do hope you're better from your fall."

"Yes, thank you." Victoria ground her teeth. Somehow it seemed impossible to imagine Cornelia Baker with vermin crawling through her pubic hair, with bloodsucking vermin piercing her glazed, flawless skin—what would they find for nourishment under there? But she was not only a human being but of the flock of the Church of the Holy Mission, and Victoria's repugnance at all she'd witnessed among the Haldols came out: "They are *so* vile. Public filth, public lewdness—"

Cornelia looked at her avidly. "*What* did you see?"

"I cannot even bring myself to describe it," Victoria said. She was so full of disgust that she did not notice Cornelia's expression change to one of disappointment. "And the Haldol vermin were everywhere. How can they live that way?"

"They are dirty, as you said," Cornelia answered. "Another good reason to avoid them when we can. Is that a new bite on your cheek?"

Victoria's hand flew up to the injured spot. "Er—yes," she said, and knew she risked eternal damnation for the lie. Mr. Griffin had put that bruise there. He was not a hard man; he'd only hit her once for not having their home in proper order when he returned from the fields. Getting the new water jug from the Haldols had taken up too much of the day for her to finish the rest of the chores. But it was her own fault that the old jug had broken, so how could she complain?

"I do wish we could be rid of the Haldols' vermin, I will say that," Cornelia said. "Even the Haldols would benefit thereby. Surely they suffer worse from disease for being so constantly afflicted with those cursed crawling pinheads."

Victoria did not care whether the base and lewd Haldols benefited; by her best guess, the vermin that swarmed over them were a judgment like unto that which God had visited upon the sinful Egyptians. But how was divine justice served by having

New Zion also suffer for the natives' vile profligacy? Try as she might, she could see no answer to that question.

No more, however, could she see how to be rid of the vermin. She said as much: "The Holy Mission Church long ago forswore the devilish arts we would need to kill off the bugs." As if to remind her they were still there, one of them bit her on the inside of the ankle. She rubbed the wounded part against her other leg. Sometimes that crushed the little pests. More often, as now, the bug simply shifted its attack.

Cornelia Baker's voice went soft and sly: "We have not the devilish arts, but those at the Federation base may well."

"But they are as godless as the Haldol," Victoria gasped, trying again—and again without success—to kill the biter that was tormenting her. "They are worse, for, being human, they should be of His flock." The folk of New Zion had had no intercourse with the base in the two years since it was established. They had also firmly made it known that no one not of the Holy Mission Church was welcome in their town.

"How better and more just to overthrow the devil than through his own instruments?" Cornelia asked.

That was sound dogma. Victoria knew it. She also knew Cornelia was tempting her, trying to get her to be the one to step beyond the bounds of what was proper. "Mr. Griffin would never permit me to seek out the ones who have turned their backs on the Lord," she said. The bug bit her leg again, this time in the fold of skin at the back of her knee. A drop of blood—or maybe it was just sweat—slid wetly down her calf.

"Will you let him keep you from serving the greater glory of God?" Cornelia said.

"Proper obedience—" Before Victoria could say anything further, the biter sank its piercing beak into her flesh once more. It was not a sign like the burning bush, or like Paul's conversion on the road to Damascus, but she was no great prophet or saint, to deserve a great sign. She took the small one for what she thought it meant, and said, "Perhaps I will go after all."

"God will bless you for it," Cornelia exclaimed fervently, her eyes glowing at the prospect of His work being done . . . and also at the prospect of its being done at no risk to herself.

The Federation research base was farther from New Zion than the Haldol village. If she went there, she would surely be gone the greater part of a day. Mr. Griffin would probably hit her again, maybe more than once this time. She rubbed her cheek, wondering if she really wanted to take that chance.

Better a beating now and then, she thought, *than this constant torment from vermin.* As if to underscore the point, the Haldol pinhead crawling up her leg probed her again with its red-hot needle of a snout.

"Yes, perhaps I shall go after all," she said, swatting at herself. Cornelia Baker smiled.

The Haldol village, while disgusting, was at least disgusting in a comprehensible way. Victoria's knees wobbled from fear as much as from fatigue as she finally drew near the Federation research base. For all she knew, the godless scientists inside were waiting to strip her soul from her body with one of their machines and send it straight to the eternal fire. She didn't know whether they could do that, but she thought they might be able to. Why would the Holy Mission Church so completely have rejected science if it did not emanate from Satan? Only the thought of getting rid of the vermin that constantly tortured her, that she hated and feared, kept her going forward.

A woman's voice spoke from out of the air. "Hello, there. You're one of the Churchies, aren't you? What are you doing here? We thought you people didn't want anything to do with us."

Victoria had trouble following the quick, sharp accent, so different from that of her own folk. After a moment, she managed to stammer out an answer: "I—I need to talk with you people about—about something to help the Haldols."

"Do you?" the unseen woman said. Victoria thought she sounded dubious. "Well, come on, then. No reason we can't talk about it."

The research base was a single low, immense building, taking up almost as much space on the ground as the entire village of New Zion. A pair of big glass panes were in the size and shape of a double door, but Victoria saw no handle. "How do I go in?" she asked.

Without warning, and with no human agency she could detect, the glass panes hissed apart from each other. Startled and alarmed, she drew back a pace. "Come in if you're coming," the woman said, sharply now. "Don't just stand there letting out all our nice, conditioned air."

Muttering a prayer, Victoria walked into the base. The doors closed behind her with another soft hiss. She shivered. No wonder the Holy Mission Church had turned its back on technology, if technology could make ordinary objects like doors behave as if they were infused with life.

She shivered again. She'd lived all her life in Reverence's tropical humidity. Now, for the first time, she felt air that wasn't hot and sticky. It seemed chilly and wrong, but only for a moment. After that, it was delicious—*seductive* was another word that sprang into her mind. This was technology, too, she realized, technology luring man away from honest reality and into luxurious indolence.

The people inside the research base did not seem indolent. They bustled back and forth, going into a doorway here, popping out of one there. Despite the unnaturally cool air, they wore only brightly colored singlets and shorts. Victoria needed most of a minute to realize that some of the people so dressed were women. She blushed and cast her eyes to the floor at the indecent display of flesh. It was almost as bad as what she'd witnessed at the Haldol village—almost. *Nothing* could be that bad.

"Good heavens, dearie, when *did* you last bathe?" By the voice, it was the woman Victoria had heard outside. Victoria had to look at her. She was in her late twenties, a few years older than Victoria, with light brown hair cut shorter than any woman in New Zion wore it, gray eyes, and open, friendly features. From the neck up, she looked like a nice person. From the neck down . . . an orange singlet that clung to the bosom tightly enough to reveal the outlines of nipples, green shorts that molded themselves to buttocks, had to be devices of the devil to incite sensuality.

And the question she'd asked, and the way she'd asked it—"A few days ago," Victoria answered, more than a little defiantly. She didn't smell any different from anyone else in New Zion; she smelled the way a person was supposed to smell. Gathering her spirit, she looked the strange woman in the face, asked, "When did you last pray?"

The woman blinked. "It's been longer than a few days, I'll tell you that. But I already knew your priorities were different from mine. Fair enough. My name is Janice; who are you?" She held out her hand as if she were a man.

Scandalized yet again, Victoria took it. She gave her own name. Then she blurted, "Can you help me? I've come on account of the vermin."

"The vermin?" Janice frowned. A tiny vertical line appeared between her eyebrows. "I think you need to tell me more. Why don't you come along into my office so we can talk?"

Victoria followed her. A whole wall of the office was filled with—at first she thought they were windows. Then she realized they had to be something more. One showed the way she had come—this Janice must have seen her as she approached. The woman waved her to a chair. It was softer and conformed more closely to her shape than any that would have been tolerated in New Zion. Its very comfort made her want to squirm. Janice gave her a glass of something cold. "Is it spirituous?" she asked suspiciously.

"Is it what?" Janice asked. She spoke to something on her desk. Victoria almost got up and left when the desk answered. But Janice turned to her and said, "No, it has no alcohol."

Partially reassured, she took a small sip. Whatever it was, it was sweet and very cold, colder than stream water ever got. She felt it slide all the way down inside her when she swallowed. She took another sip, and another. Pretty soon the glass was empty. Victoria set it aside and said, "Now. About the vermin."

"Go ahead," Janice said. "Tell me about the vermin."

Victoria told her, not so much about the vermin themselves as

about her trip to the Haldol village. She even found herself
stammering out the story of what the male and female Haldol
had done right before her eyes, and how the vermin ambled over
their slick, moist skins while they did it. (She would never have
spoken of such things back in New Zion, but Janice, by the way
she dressed and by the fact that she did not belong to the Holy
Mission Church, seemed a harlot herself, and thus unlikely to be
offended.) Victoria finished, "It's just—disgusting. It can't be
healthy for them—the Haldols, I mean—either."

"You surprise me, you really do," Janice said. "From all I'd
ever heard, none of you Churchies gave a damn about the Haldols."

"They *are* damned," Victoria said. *So are you,* she added to
herself.

"Never mind; that's not quite what I meant." Janice frowned,
considering. "We probably could get rid of their parasites for
you, if that's what you want. Are you really sure that's what you
want?"

Something in the way she asked the question warned Victoria
it had teeth (after a moment, she figured out what it was: this
Janice woman sounded like Cornelia Baker). She asked, "Why
shouldn't it be what I really want?"

"Well, what do you think will happen with the Haldols if they
aren't constantly pestered by disease-carrying vermin?" Janice
asked.

"They'll be healthier, like I said. Why shouldn't I want them
to be healthier?" Victoria wondered if she and Janice were
speaking the same language.

Janice said, "Yes, I think you're right; I think they will be
healthier. Not only that, I think their children won't die young so
often. I think they'll grow up and have lots of little Haldols of
their own."

"Good. Maybe, God willing, we'll be able to convert them to
proper love for Jesus Christ." Babies who died young—even
Haldol babies—touched Victoria's heart.

Janice studied her as if she were a bug herself. "You really
don't understand, do you?"

"Understand what?"

"If we fix it so the Haldols don't die young, there are going to be more and more Haldols. They'll need more and more land, too. What will you Churchies do then? They're native to this world and you're not. Odds are, they'll overwhelm you in a few generations. That's how evolution works, you know."

Victoria didn't know. Evolution was evil; she was certain of that. The certainty was the beginning and end of her knowledge on the subject. Of one thing, however, she was even more certain. "The Lord will provide for us," she said confidently. A pinhead bit her, just below her left breast. She shuddered. She was also sure that having those accursed vermin dead now mattered more to her than anything a few generations down the road. Her great-grandchildren, if she ever had any, could take care of themselves. All she wanted was to be free of welts.

"The Lord will provide, will he, dearie?" Janice no longer seemed open and friendly. Again, she reminded Victoria of Cornelia—Cornelia looking for a way to get someone else into trouble at no expense to herself. "If that's what you want, I'm willing to give it to you. Far as I can see, it'll serve you right. You people have no business on this planet in the first place."

"Why do you hate us so much?" The hostility of the Federation research worker's response rocked Victoria. "What did we ever do to you?"

"You know-nothings have been holding back the advance of knowledge for the last two thousand years," Janice said. "If you had your way, all of humanity would be back on Earth, living in filthy huts like yours, starving one year in three, and going off to war over the nature of God. As far as I'm concerned, the faster people who think like you die out, the better off we'll all be. So I'll do just what you asked, because I think that's the quickest way to be rid of you for good."

Shaking, Victoria started to tell her to forget the whole idea. Then she realized it was too late for that; Janice was certain to try to get rid of the vermin now, just to hurt the Church of the Holy Mission as much as she could. Victoria's voice wobbled as she said, "You seem just as sure you have the only right way to do things as we are. We at least have faith to sustain us. What sustains you?"

Before Janice could answer, she happened to glance down at her arm. Like a wandering pinhead, a Haldol bug crawled through the fine hair there. With a cry of disgust, she crushed it between thumb and forefinger. "I should have had you fumigated before I ever let you in here."

"What does fumigated mean?" Victoria asked.

"You sure wouldn't know, would you, Churchie? You just go on home now. We'll take care of the bugs for you, I promise you that." When Janice got to her feet, she carefully examined herself to make sure no other vermin from Victoria had attached themselves to her. Victoria averted her eyes, not caring for the sensual thoughts roused by the sight of Janice's hands sliding over her smooth flesh (how did the woman have no hair on her legs?). She knew Janice was not caressing herself for the pleasure of it, but that was still how it looked.

"Go on," Janice said again. "Out of here. I'll clean up after you." As Victoria left the office and headed for the door by which she'd entered, the woman from the research base followed her with a metal tube that sent forth a sweetly noxious vapor. "Want me to spray you, too?"

"No, thank you," Victoria said with as much dignity as she could muster. She didn't mind smelling the way she smelled, and going back to New Zion literally reeking of technology was unthinkable.

"Keep your vermin, then," Janice said. "I don't know why I bothered to ask; you'd just pick up another set of them on the way home. And we will get rid of them in a bit—just remember, you asked for it." With that, she touched a button. The glass doors hissed open. Victoria stepped through. The doors closed. Inside the base, Janice sprayed where she had stood.

The outside air smote her like a warm, wet fist. She'd found the climate trying enough, living in it every moment of her life. Now, after an hour or two in—what had Janice called it?—conditioned air, she realized just how dreadful the weather was.

By the time she got back to New Zion, sweat plastered her heavy wool dress to her until it was almost as obscenely tight as Janice's outfit had been. The rough fabric prickled against the soft skin of her belly and flanks. She tugged at the dress, trying to pull it away, but no sooner did she let go than it stuck again.

She did not see Cornelia Baker anywhere about. That, she thought, was as well. She turned off the central street toward her own cabin. It would be good to get home. Then her stomach did a flipflop and she felt cold in spite of the weather. Her husband stood outside the front door waiting for her, his thick arms folded across his chest. His fists were clenched.

She dipped her head to him. "Good even', Mr. Griffin."

"Where have you been?" His voice seemed to rumble out from somewhere deep inside him. "Nothing's done here. Have you been slothfully idling again?"

"No, Mr. Griffin, I've not been idling," Victoria said, deciding not to notice that unjust *again*. "I'm sorry I didn't do as much here as I might have today; the walk to and from the Federation research base took longer than I thought it would."

He stared at her. She'd given him an answer he'd not looked for. It was not, however, one he approved of. "Did Satan possess you, to make you want to visit that godless place?"

"I don't think so, Mr. Griffin," she said. *I will not fear him,* she told herself uselessly. "I thought they might have a way to rid the Haldols—and us—of the crawling vermin that torment our lives. They said they did—they said they would." She did not repeat what else the woman named Janice had said. She trusted God to know who His true followers on Reverence were, and to protect them.

"Technology," he said in that rumbling, fateful voice. "You went seeking technology. Technology is the Whore of Babylon, as well you know."

"Yes, Mr. Griffin," she whispered. The elders of the Church of the Holy Mission drummed that into every child on New Zion. Still, though, she tried to defend herself: "I did not seek it for us, Mr. Griffin, only for the Haldols, so that—" She broke off. *—so that I wouldn't be sickened by seeing the vermin crawl on them, sickened near to madness by the feel of them on me* was what was true. She had gone looking for technology for her own sake, then. She could not lie. That sin was even worse. She stared at the ground between her feet. "I'm sorry, Mr. Griffin."

He turned, opened the door. "I think we'd better go inside, Mrs. Griffin." Numbly, she followed him into the cabin. He closed the door behind them. The sound of the bar thudding home was dreadfully final. Jonah might have heard that sound when the jaws of the whale closed on him.

"Please, Mr. Griffin—" Victoria began. He hit her then. Whatever she'd been about to say was lost in the pain. He hit her again, and again. She cowered and endured it as best she could. At first he was dispassionate about the beating, as if he were simply training an animal to do what he required.

But soon he began to breathe hard. The blows he rained on her grew harder and less calculated. "Whoring with the Whore of Babylon," he panted. "I'll teach you about whoring. See if I don't!" He grabbed her by the shoulders and hurled her to the ground. One of her outflung arms slammed against a footstool, sent it spinning away.

He threw himself atop her. Even then, she did not understand what he was about until he jerked her dress up toward her waist. "No, Mr. Griffin," she exclaimed. "Not in the daylight!"

"Shut up, whore!" He backhanded her. Clumsily, one-handed, he unbuttoned his overalls, yanked them down. She shut her eyes tight so she would not have to see the swollen organ that slapped against the inside of her thigh.

He always took her roughly. But for the fact that she was down on the floor instead of in their bed, this was hardly different from any other time. But he did it now to punish her further, not to join them as man and wife. She knew that—how well she knew it. But somehow, even though she knew it, his harsh thrusts made her body kindle, transmuting pain to pleasure.

She opened her eyes. His were closed, his face but a couple of inches from her own. Before her pleasure mounted to a peak— too soon as usual—he turned red and grunted like a pig. Then he abruptly pulled himself out of her. She did not want to be empty of him, not yet. But he rolled away, rearranged his overalls. "Cover yourself," he growled.

"Yes, Mr. Griffin." She tugged at her dress until it went decently down to her ankles once more. She watched her husband warily as she got to her feet, fearful he wanted to beat her again.

But he seemed sated. He stayed on the floor longer than she had. When he did get up, all he said was, "Fix me some supper."

"Yes, Mr. Griffin," Victoria said again. She went back into the kitchen. The places where he had hit her ached at every step. Only a small part of her minded the pain, the animal part concerned solely with bodily well-being. She knew she deserved what he'd given her.

The animal part of her also still wished he'd stayed atop her another minute longer. Her cheeks and ears heated in shame as she took out an onion and began to slice it. He hadn't intended her to enjoy his body; he'd intended to humiliate her with it. And he had—but the humiliation itself was sweet. It almost tempted her to sin again, so that she might be chastised. . . .

"Get thee behind me, Satan," she whispered as she reached for the loaf of bread on the counter. She threw away the stale slice at the end. That waste of food was in its own way also sinful, but she wanted supper to be as fine as it could, to show Mr. Griffin she truly was contrite.

Her husband was in his own way a fair man, and not one to hold a grudge—and perhaps that splendid supper did help mollify him. He read Scripture to her afterwards. And he spoke no more of her trip to the Federation research base. Their life together healed along with her bruises.

Two weeks after the day he beat and raped her, her courses failed to come. When she was certain what that meant, she got down on her knees and praised the Lord: "Truly all things work together for good."

They named the baby Lavinia, after Mr. Griffin's mother who was in heaven. She was a fussy child, and squawked for Victoria's breast at all hours of the day and night. Between the baby and everything else she still had to do, Victoria stumbled about in a gray haze of fatigue. But Lavinia flourished, which made up for any amount of exhaustion.

When Lavinia was asleep during the day, Victoria would some-times steal a moment to stand by the cradle and look down at her. Part of that was the normal pride any mother knew, part the extra concern of a mother who'd already lost one child. And part was the urgent need she felt to keep the vermin away from her baby.

Every so often, one of the round, revolting little bugs crawled out from under Lavinia's swaddling and walked across her smooth cheek or through her thin, fine light brown hair. Then Victoria's hand would swoop down like a stooping hawk, nab the pest, and crush it between the nails of thumb and forefinger. A couple of times, after she'd killed two or three vermin in the space of a couple of minutes, she cried because it was her daughter's blood that stained her hand.

She also found and destroyed a great many biting pinheads while she was changing the baby's soiled linen: that only made a revolting task more so. The vermin seemed especially fond of Lavinia's most tender places. Victoria wished she did not have to touch her in those parts, but had no choice. Once she satisfied herself no vermin remained on the baby, she would avert her eyes from what her hands were doing.

The pests also seemed drawn to her breasts. In the moments before she dropped the privacy shawl over Lavinia and her bosom, she would flick away vermin one by one. Whatever she did was never enough. The bugs kept biting her and kept biting Lavinia, too.

She laughed at the promise she'd got from the Federation re-search base, the promise to eliminate the vermin and with them the settlements of the Church of the Holy Mission. The vaunted technology that had seduced so much of humankind must have stumbled here, when confronting the true elite of God. Progress in the material world was a snare and a delusion, anyhow. Where were Babylon, Rome, New York? Gone, gone, gone.

Victoria was tempted to go back to the research base and tell Janice just that, throw it in her face. Whenever she thought about leaving the baby with a friend for a day and making that long walk, she felt a curious stirring in her privates. That was a temptation, too, but one she managed to resist. She conceived again, but miscarried, which slowed her down for half a year.

The baby grew. She began to walk, to talk, to lisp her first hymns. She got into everything, came home covered in every kind of filth. Victoria washed Lavinia far more often than she washed herself. She always used the baths as an occasion to get rid of as many vermin on her daughter as she could. By the time Lavinia turned three, she found fewer of them than she had before. By the time Lavinia was four, the blood-filled pinheads were almost gone. She noticed she wasn't getting bitten so often herself, either. She did not know whether to rejoice or be afraid.

When in doubt, she found out what her husband thought. "Fewer vermin lately, seems to me," she said one evening after Lavinia had gone to sleep. She spoke cautiously, lest he remember how that might have come to pass.

Mr. Griffin grunted. He was tired from another in the endless string of days out in the fields. "Can't say I miss 'em," he answered, and let it go at that. Victoria had been sitting at the edge of her chair, stiff with tension. She relaxed—not that the hard chair permitted much relaxation. Her husband truly forgave her long-ago transgression, then.

The glow of relief sustained her only a couple of days. It turned to dread when Lavinia, trying to be helpful, knocked over the water jar and smashed it. She gave the child a sound switching and sent her to bed without supper, but that did not bring back the water jar. She would have to go to the Haldol village and dicker for another one.

She prepared for the ordeal as best she could. She cooked double the next day, so she would only have to reheat the stew the day after that: God willing, Mr. Griffin would find no excuse to set hands on her. She arranged for her neighbor to take care of Lavinia. None of that, though, kept the real panic, the panic that sprang from having to witness Haldol depravity, from making her heart pound and race.

When she finally got to the village, it was as bad as she remembered. In fact, it was worse. Two Haldols were mating in the middle of the street as she came up. They paid no attention to her; the rest of the Haldols paid no attention to them. They found the arrival of a *pisquaa*, a human, far more diverting.

"Pot? Water jar?" one of them said in his squeakily accented smattering of English. "We have pot, water jar, God bless you. What you have, *pisquaa*?"

The haggling started there. Victoria was glad to focus on the noisy Haldol potters rather than the lazily copulating couple behind them. Round Haldol eyes stared back at her from round Haldol faces. The red, rough patches on the sides of the males' necks still reminded her of meat that had gone over.

But the vermin were gone! Not a single biting pinhead crawled across smooth, slimy Haldol skin. The Haldols themselves took no special notice of that, but then, they had never seemed to mind the vermin anyhow. Victoria minded them. Not having to look at them wandering over Haldol bodies, not having to feel their tiny legs on her own flesh and in her hair, left her so relieved that she almost managed not to think about the open lewdness constantly on display in the village.

One by one, the potters picked up their jugs and carried them away. At last Victoria was quietly bargaining with a single male, each of them sure goods would change hands, each intent they should do so on the best possible terms. Quietly bargaining . . . no sooner had the phrase crossed Victoria's mind than she looked up (no risk to her sensibilities now, for the mating couple had long since finished). One of the reasons the Haldol village was quieter than she remembered from her last visit was that fewer immature Haldols were about, and no little yellow toddlers that she could see.

"Where are all the children?" she asked the Haldol potter, who could use her language fairly well. "Are they out in the forest today for some reason?"

The Haldol stuck out his tongue, a gesture of uncertainty. "Not so many childs, *pisquaa*. Few borns. Think maybe forest gods angry. Plenty pray them, plenty—" He pumped his arm in an obscene gesture that made Victoria blush. "But females, they no get childs."

"Your gods are false," Victoria said. "Surely Jesus would hear your prayers. The true God gave His only-begotten Son that mankind might live forever. Accept Him and He will help you— you are His creatures, too."

Members of the Holy Mission Church had been preaching the Gospel to the Haldols since the day they landed on Reverence. Ever since that day, the Haldols had ignored them or, worse, laughed at them: all they'd taken was the *God bless you* that larded their speech. But now the potter stuck out his tongue and said, "Maybe we talk to this God of yours. Ours not hear."

Exultation filled Victoria's body. It was sweeter than beet sugar, sweeter than anything she'd known save the spasm of her flesh when, as occasionally did happen, Mr. Griffin mounted her long enough to take her out of herself. She bit the inside of her lip, hard, at having the temerity to compare the carnal to his infusion of divine joy.

She gave the potter an extra knife blade, above and beyond the price they'd finally settled on. "God bless you, you *pisquaa* really crazy," he said. She did not care. Had he been only a little less repellent to her, she would have kissed him.

Even her husband said, "If they truly do come over to Christ, you have done well, Mrs. Griffin." That made her hold her head proud and high until she remembered vanity was also sinful. She hoped Mr. Griffin would choose that night to lie with her. When they were in bed, she even went so far as to brush her thigh against his, as if by accident, shamefully forward though that was. But he was already asleep. The day had been long. She soon joined him in slumber.

Victoria was used to getting up at dawn. From sun to sun never seemed time enough to get through a day's chores. But she was not used to being blasted out of bed by a horn that sounded as if Satan himself would wind it come Judgment Day. "That's technology," Mr. Griffin shouted, trying to make himself heard above the hellish din. "What are the damned Federation people playing at, using their accursed technology here?"

Victoria did not answer. Lavinia was screaming in terror from the next room. She ran to comfort her daughter, who cried, "Make it stop, Mommy! Make the bad noise stop!" But Victoria could not make the bad noise stop.

In fact, the noise got worse, for it turned to bellowed words, and terrifying words: "Victoria Griffin! Where are you, Victoria Griffin? Come out!"

From the other bedroom, Mr. Griffin yelled, "Don't you go, Mrs. Griffin! I'll fetch the axe to protect you."

All at once, Victoria felt a warm burst of affection for her husband. She also felt fear for him—what could an axe do against the demonic dangers of technology?

"We need to talk with you, Victoria Griffin," the impossibly loud voice went on. "No harm will come to you; you have our promise."

"Don't believe them, Mrs. Griffin," Mr. Griffin said. "Those from outside the Church are by nature liars and cheats."

Now that the horn was no longer blaring, Victoria found she could think again, after a fashion. She said, "Let me go out, Mr. Griffin. How can they have any reason to wish me harm? And even if they should, well, as a martyr for the faith I will sit at the right hand of God and His Son. And besides," she added, slipping from the spiritual to the purely pragmatic, "if I talk with them, maybe they'll quit roaring."

Her sudden switch jerked a startled chuckle from her husband. "All right, Mrs. Griffin. God go with you."

"God go with you, Mommy," Lavinia echoed as Victoria walked out of her room and went to the front door. Despite her brave words, her legs were fear-light, ready to turn and bolt the instant her will released them. She took a deep, determined breath and kept walking.

Several men and women of New Zion were already out of doors, staring in disbelief and horror at the smoothly curved metal device that floated a couple of feet above the grass of the village square, and at the wantonly dressed man and woman sitting inside the device. Cornelia Baker's avidly curious glance flicked from the flying machine to Victoria and back again. Victoria looked away, sick at heart. Cornelia would never let her live down such scandal.

She decided the quickest way to be rid of the scientists (even thinking such a filthy word made her lips purse in dismay) would be to let them have their say. She forced herself to take a step toward the flier. "Here I am."

"That's her, all right." Victoria recognized Janice more by voice than by face. Janice jumped down from the flying machine. Even Cornelia Baker gasped at the sight of her uncovered legs. Several New Zion doors slammed shut as the folk who lived in those cabins protected themselves from the shocking spectacle.

Janice strode toward Victoria. "I ought to knock your stupid, hymn-singing teeth down your throat, you stinking Churchie," she snarled.

Victoria stared at her. "How have I offended you? How could I have offended you, when we've not so much as seen each other these past five years?"

"You didn't do much then, either, did you?" Janice said bitterly. "All you did was set in motion the extinction of a whole intelligent species."

"What? The vermin?" Victoria said. "You *are* mad."

"Not the vermin—the Haldols. There won't be any more Haldols after the last of this generation dies, and it's all your fault."

"All I wanted to do was to get rid of the vermin, so the Haldols wouldn't suffer so much from them." *And so they wouldn't crawl on me,* Victoria thought, recalling too well the feel of tiny legs moving through her body hair, of needlelike mouthparts jabbing through her skin to suck her blood.

"So you asked us, and we did it. We took care of the bugs, all right—turn three tailored retroviruses loose on them at once and they go, go fast. Trouble was, we moved too fast. I'm going to hate myself every day for the rest of my life for that, and I'm not the only one. When the Haldols stopped having little Haldols, we tried to find out why. Turns out the vermin aren't just vermin—the Haldols need them to reproduce."

"That's the most disgusting thing I ever heard," Victoria said with a shudder. "Besides, how could it be true? To my shame, I've seen what the Haldols do. It's not—" Hot blood rose from her throat to the crown of her head, but she made herself go on, though her voice fell to a whisper: "It's not that different from what passes between men and women."

"It doesn't *look* that different," Janice corrected her. "But male Haldols don't put sperm into females when they fuck, they—"

"When they what?" Victoria broke in.

Janice clapped a hand to her forehead. "Churchies! When they mate, I mean. Anyway, they don't put sperm in. They just prime the females'—organs. Is that all right? Do you understand what I'm talking about?"

"Yes. Go on," Victoria said. The sooner this was over, the better.

"I am." Janice glared at her. She still didn't understand what she'd done wrong. The woman from the research base continued, "They prime them, they make them secrete a mucus loaded with pheromones that— Why am I bothering? Anyway, then the vermin that have been wandering over their bodies, the vermin that have picked up sperm from the males' throat patches, those vermin go inside to feed on the mucus and incidentally to put the sperm where they'll do the most good."

Victoria remembered watching vermin crawl into the female Haldol's private parts after she was done mating, remembered how sick the sight had made her. Now, knowing why they did it, she felt even sicker. She said, "You're telling me that without the vermin—"

"No more baby Haldols, not ever again. That's right, Churchie. How do you like being responsible for wiping out a whole race?"

The weight of the accusation was crushing, a weight like the one Jesus had accepted when He assumed the burden of mankind's sins. But He was the Son of God, Victoria a mere human being. *I didn't mean it,* she thought. That wasn't good enough. She tried, "You're the ones who killed the vermin, not me." That wasn't good enough, either; she knew it the moment the words passed her lips.

"We never would have done it if you hadn't suggested it," Janice said.

The coldness in her voice brought back to Victoria how cold it had been inside the research base; it was the only time in her life, save after an infrequent bath, that she hadn't been filmed with sticky sweat (and, she recalled, Janice had said something rude about how often, or rather how seldom, she bathed). Thinking of that unnatural chill helped her remember what had gone on in there, remember it with almost word-for-word clarity, as if it had happened yesterday, not five years before. She said, "You didn't get rid of the vermin to do New Zion and the Church of the Holy Mission a favor. You did it for the Haldols—you thought your lying evolution would make them prevail over us. I told you then that the Lord would provide. Now I see that He has." She dropped to her knees and clasped her hands so she could properly thank God for His blessing.

Deep in her throat, Janice made a noise that would have seemed better suited to the killing beasts that haunted the jungles of Reverence. "Better it would have been you," she ground out. "You deserve to be extinct. We're going to try to figure out a way to keep the Haldols going without their vermin, but God— and I don't mean yours—only knows if we'll be able to do it before all their females get too old to breed. With a research budget that just about keeps us in paper clips, it won't be easy."

"I will pray for you and the Haldols both, you for delivery from your false idol of technology, and them for being delivered from the affliction it has brought." Victoria shut her eyes to do just that. She slid into the near-trance state that marked true communion with God. In it, she was only dimly aware of Janice stomping away, of the aircar *whoosh*ing out of New Zion, of the gasps from some of the more impressionable folk there at the sight of that marvel.

When at last she came back to herself, Cornelia Baker was

standing in front of her. The other woman helped her to her feet, brushed at her dress to get out the mark of the dirt in which she'd knelt. "You drove them away, Victoria," Cornelia said. "How ever did you do that?"

It was, Victoria thought, the first time in her life that she'd succeeded in impressing Cornelia Baker. "I told them the Lord's truth, Cornelia," she answered proudly.

"Was she—the slut, I mean—was she talking with you about the Haldols'—their—their—" Cornelia Baker was the boldest woman in New Zion. Not even she could make herself discuss prurient matters straight on.

Victoria understood her well enough. "Her name is Janice. Yes, we talked about that." What the Haldols did, she thought, was so vile it made the way of man and woman, squalid as that was, seem perfection and purity beside it. "She says they'll probably die out after this generation, and leave the whole world of Reverence to us."

"Oh." Cornelia thought about that. "Where will we get our pots, then?"

"It won't happen tomorrow," Victoria assured her. "Our great-grandparents knew how. I expect we'll have time to learn again. It's just what I told Janice—the Lord will provide. He always has."

Cornelia Baker nodded confidently. "Amen," she said.

Ils ne passeront pas

One thing the twentieth century taught us was that man could be inhuman to his fellow man on a scale previously unimagined. It's not the only lesson we take from those hundred crowded years, but it's one of the big ones. Set alongside what the French and Germans really were doing to one another at Verdun in 1916, St. John the Divine's vision of the Apocalypse all of a sudden isn't so much of a much.

As the sun rose from the direction of Germany, Sergeant Pierre Barrès rolled out from under his filthy, lousy blanket. His *horizon bleu* uniform was equally lousy, which he loathed, and equally filthy, which he minded not at all, for it made him a harder target for the *Boche*.

He yawned, rubbed his eyes, scratched his chin. Whiskers rasped under his fingers. When had he last shaved? Two days before? Three? He couldn't remember. It didn't much matter.

Under the blanket next to his in the muddy trench, his loader, Corporal Jacques Fonsagrive, was also stirring. *"Bonjour, mon vieux,"* Barrès said. "Another lovely morning, *n'est-ce pas?"*

Fonsagrive gave his opinion in one word: *"Merde."* He always woke up surly—and stayed that way till he fell asleep again.

"Any morning I wake up and I am still breathing is a lovely morning," Barrès said. He pulled his water bottle off his belt and shook it. Half full, he judged: maybe a liter in there. He pulled out the cork and drank. *Pinard* ran down his throat. The rough red wine got his heart beating better than coffee had ever dreamt of doing.

"Well, then, odds are there won't be many more lovely mornings left in the world," Fonsagrive said. "Fucking miracle we've had this many." He scratched himself, then stuck a *Gitane* between his lips. His cheeks hollowed as he sucked in smoke. He coughed. "Christ on His cross, that's worse than the chlorine the *Boche* shoots at us. What's for breakfast?"

"Ham and eggs and champagne would be nice, especially if an eighteen-year-old blonde with big jugs brought it to me," Barrès answered. Fonsagrive swore at him. Unperturbed, he went on, "What I've got is *singe*. How about you?"

"*Singe* here, too, and damn all else," Fonsagrive said. "I was hoping you had something better."

"Don't I wish," Barrès said fervently. The company field kitchen—like about half the company field kitchens in the French Army—was unserviceable. Some capitalist well back of the line had made a profit. If the troops who tried to use the worthless stoves went hungry . . . well, *c'est la guerre.*

Glumly, the two men opened tins of *singe* and stared down at the greasy, stringy beef. "Goddamn monkey meat," Fonsagrive said. He started shoveling it into his face as fast as he could, as if he wanted to fuel his boiler while enduring as little of the taste as he could. Barrès followed suit. Even washed down with more swigs of *pinard*, the stuff was vile.

He flung the empty tin out of the trench, almost as if it were a grenade. It didn't clank when it came down, which probably meant it landed on a corpse. There were more corpses around than anything else, he often thought. The stench was all-pervasive, unbelievable, inescapable—a testament to what all flesh inevitably became. He wanted to delay the inevitable as long as he could.

And how likely was that? He spat. He knew the answer too well. "Verdun," he muttered under his breath. "World's largest open-air cemetery."

Jacques Fonsagrive grunted. "Visitors always welcome," he said, taking up where Barrès had left off. "Come on in yourself and see how you'd make out as a stiff." He sounded like an advertising circular filled with a particular sort of repellent good humor.

"Heh," Barrès said—more acknowledgment that the words were supposed to be funny than an actual laugh.

Cautiously, he reached up and plucked the cork from the muzzle of the Hotchkiss machine gun he and his partner served, then pulled away the oily rag that covered the machine gun's cocking handle. He and Fonsagrive could get soaked and maintain their efficiency. The machine gun was more temperamental—and, in the grand scheme of things, more important to the French Army.

Even more cautiously, he peered over the edge of the parapet. Ahead and over to the north lay what had been the Bois des Fosses. It was a wood no more, but a collection of matchsticks, toothpicks, and bits of kindling. Like gray ants in the distance, Germans moved there now.

Sharp cracks behind him announced that the crews of a battery of 75s were awake, too. Shells screamed overhead. They slammed down in the middle of the wood, scattering the gray ants and sifting the remains of the timber one more step down toward sawdust.

"Nice to see the artillery hitting the other side for a change," Fonsagrive remarked. Like any infantryman who'd ever been under fire from his own guns, he had an ingrained disdain for cannons and the men who served them.

Barrès said, "Those 75s are too close to bring their shells down on our heads."

"Merde," Fonsagrive said again. "With those bastards, you never say they're too close to do anything."

The sun rose higher. The day was going to be fine and mild, even warm. Barrès faced the prospect with something less than joy. Heat would make the stench worse. And it would bring out the flies, too. Already they were stirring, bluebottles and greenbottles and horseflies not too finicky to feast on human flesh as well.

Thunder in the east made Barrès turn his head in that direction. Dominating the terrain there, Fort Douaumont was one of the keys to Verdun—and a key now in the hands of the *Boche*. Barrès neither knew nor cared how the fort had been lost. That it had been lost, though, mattered very much, for with its loss the Germans held the high ground along this whole stretch of front.

French artillery was doing its best to make sure the *Boche* did not rest easy on the heights. A gray haze continually hung about Fort Douaumont. Black shellbursts from a battery of 155s punctuated the haze. Below and around the fort, nothing at all grew. The ground was bare and brown and cratered, like astronomical photographs of the moon.

More thunder boomed, this closer. German 77s and 105s were replying to the French guns harassing the *Boche* in the Bois des Fosses. The French field pieces defiantly barked back.

Some of the German shells fell short, a few falling only a couple of hundred meters beyond the trench in which Barrès stood. He did not deign to look back at them, but remarked, "Back when the war was new, misses that close would have put my wind up."

"Back when the war was new, you were stupid," Fonsagrive answered. "And if you'd got any smarter since, you wouldn't be here."

That held too much truth to be comfortable. Sighing, Barrès said, "When the battalion has taken seventy-five percent casualties, they'll pull us out of the line. That's the rule."

"When the battalion has taken seventy-five percent casualties, odds are three to one you'll be one of them," his loader said. Fonsagrive punctuated the words with a perfect Gallic shrug. "Odds are three to one I'll be another."

Barrès nodded. No one had shot him yet, though not for lack of effort. He didn't know why not. His belief in luck had grown tenuous—had, to be honest, disappeared—from seeing so many comrades wounded and slain around him. He had no reason to believe he was in any way different from them. Yes, he'd lasted a little longer, but what did that mean? Not much.

He said, "The one good thing about fighting is that then you don't think about all the things that can happen to you. You just fight, and that's all. It's before and after that you think."

"There is no good thing about fighting." Fonsagrive spoke with authority a general might have envied. "There are some that are bad, and some that are worse. If I kill the *Boche*, it is bad. If the *Boche* kills me, that, I assure you, is worse. And so I kill the *Boche*."

For the *Boche*, of course, the pans of that scale were reversed. The German trenches lay only a couple of hundred meters away. They had been French trenches till the field-gray tide lapped over them. The field-gray tide had briefly lapped over the trench in which Barrès and Fonsagrive stood, too, but a French counterattack had cleared it again. Some of the rotting corpses and chunks of corpses between the lines wore field-gray, others *horizon bleu*. In death, they all smelled the same.

Behind their rusting barbed wire, the Germans were awake now, too. Here and there along the trench, riflemen started shooting up the slope toward the French position. *Poilus* returned the fire. Their rhythm was slightly slower than that of the *Boche*; they had to reload rounds one by one into the tubular magazines of their Lebels, where the Germans just slapped fresh five-round boxes onto the Mausers they used.

Sighing, Barrès said, "There are quiet sections of the front, where for days at a time the two sides hardly shoot at each other."

"Not at Verdun," Fonsagrive said. "No, not at Verdun."

"Tu a raison, malheureusement," Barrès said. A moment later, he added, not unkindly, *"Cochon."*

And Fonsagrive was indeed right, however unfortunate that might have been. In front of Verdun, France and Germany were locked in an embrace with death—a *Totentanz*, a German word the French had come to understand full well. The town itself, the white walls and red-tiled roofs four or five kilometers back of the line, had almost ceased to matter. In the bit more than a month since the Germans swarmed out of their trenches on 21 February, the battle had taken on a life of its own. It was about itself, not about the town at all: about which side would have to admit the other was the stronger. And it was about how many lives forcing such an admission would cost.

As if to underscore that point, a German Maxim gun snarled to life. The *Boche* was a good combat engineer; a concrete emplacement protected the machine gun from anything short of a direct hit from artillery. Sandbags protected Barrès' Hotchkiss. He envied his counterparts in field-gray their snug nest.

But, regardless of his envy, he had a job to do. "If they are feeling frisky, we had better pay them back in kind," he said to Jacques Fonsagrive.

The loader already had one of the Hotchkiss gun's thirty-round metal strips of ammunition in his hands. He inserted it in the left side of the weapon. Barrès used the cocking handle to chamber the first round, then squeezed the trigger and traversed the machine gun to spray bullets along the German trenches like a man watering grass with a hose.

As soon as the strip had gone all the way through the gun, Fonsagrive fed in another one. Barrès chambered the first round manually; the Hotchkiss gun, again, did the rest. It didn't have quite the rate of fire of the German Maxim with its long, long belts of ammunition, but it was more than adequate for all ordinary purposes of slaughter, as a good many of the German dead could have attested.

Barrès had no idea whether any individual bullet he fired hit any individual *Boche*. He didn't much care. If he fired enough bullets, some of them would pierce German flesh, just as, if he played roulette long enough, the ball would sometimes land on zero, missing both red and black.

Unfortunately, the same applied to that Maxim down the slope. A *poilu* perhaps fifty meters from Barrès let out an unearthly shriek and fell writhing to the bottom of the trench, clutching at his shoulder.

Fonsagrive spat. "In most factories, it is an accident when someone is hurt—an accident that causes work to stop. What we make in this factory is death, and when someone is hurt it is but a death imperfectly manufactured. I hope the *Boche* who fired that round gets a reprimand for falling down on the job."

One more casualty, Barrès thought as a couple of men helped the wounded soldier up a zigzagging communications trench toward a medical station. *One more casualty that is neither Jacques nor I. One casualty closer to the three-quarters who have to be shot or blown up before they take this battalion out of the line.* That was a revoltingly cold-blooded way to look at a man's agony and probably mutilation. He knew as much. Being able to help it was something else again.

He did his best to return the disfavor to the *Boche*. Methodical as any factory worker, Fonsagrive fed strip after strip of bullets into the Hotchkiss gun. Barrès knew from long experience just how hard to tap the weapon to make the muzzle swing four or five centimeters on its arc of death. Had the Germans come out of their trench, they would not have lived to reach his.

Presently, the doughnut-shaped iron radiating fins at the base of the barrel began to glow a dull red. Over in the trench the *Boche* held, the mirror image of his own, the water in the cooling jacket surrounding the Maxim gun's barrel would be boiling. The Germans could brew coffee or tea with the hot water. All Barrès could do was remember not to touch those iron fins.

After a while, the German machine gun fell silent, though rifles kept on barking. Barrès turned to Fonsagrive and asked, "Have we got any of that newspaper left?"

"I think so," the loader answered. His words seemed to come from far away; Barrès' hearing took a while to return to even a semblance of its former self after a spell of firing. Fonsagrive rummaged. "No newspaper, but we've got this." He held out a copy of *L'Illustration*.

"It will do," Barrès said. Taking the magazine, he scrambled up out of the trench and into a shell hole right behind it. A couple of bullets whipped past him, but neither came very near; he'd had much closer calls. He unbuttoned his fly to piss, then yanked down his pants and squatted in a spot that wasn't noticeably more noisome than any other. In some stretches of the line, trenches had latrine areas soldiers were supposed to use. The trenches around Verdun had been shelled and countershelled, taken and retaken, so many times, they were hard to tell from the shell holes in front of and behind them.

As Barrès did his business, he glanced at an article about the fighting in which he was engaged. He needed only a couple of sentences to be sure the writer had never come within a hundred kilometers of Verdun or, very likely, any other part of the front. *Confident hope rings a carillon of bells in our hearts,* the fellow declared.

"I know what hope would ring a carillon of bells in my heart, *salaud*," Barrès muttered: "the hope of trading places with you."

Slowly and deliberately, he tore that page from the copy of *L'Illustration* and used it for the purpose for which he had requested the magazines of Fonsagrive. Then he used another page, too; like a lot of the men on both sides here, he had a touch of dysentery. A lot of men had more than a touch.

He set his pants to rights and then, clutching the magazine, dove back into the trench. He drew more fire this time, as he'd known he would. "The *Boche* would sooner assassinate a man answering a call of nature than do battle when both sides have weapons at hand," he said.

"So would I," Fonsagrive replied. "The pigdogs"—he liked the feel of the German *Schweinhund*—"are just as dead that way, and they can't shoot back at me."

Barrès thought it over. "It could be that you have reason," he said at last.

"And it could be that all the world has gone mad, and that reason is as dead as all the other corpses in front of us in no-man's-land," Fonsagrive said. "That, I think, is more likely. If there were a God, these would be the last days."

"I was, once, a good Catholic," Barrès said. "I went to Mass. I took communion. I confessed my sins." He scratched his head. Something popped wetly under his fingernail. "I wonder where the man who did those things has gone. The man I am now . . . all that man wants to do is to kill the *Boche* and to keep the *Boche* from killing him."

"All I used to want to do was get drunk and fuck," Fonsagrive said. "I still want to do those things. Like you, I also want to keep the *Boche* from killing me, especially when I have my pants down around my ankles. What do you say that you feed our friends down there another couple of strips, to show them you were not taken up to heaven while answering nature's call?"

"And why not?" Barrès peered over at the German trenches. He was very careful not to lift his head above the parapet in the same spot twice in a row. *Boche* snipers knew their business. The Germans would not have been where they were, would not have been doing what they were doing, had their soldiers not known their business.

His eyes slid past motion out in no-man's-land, then snapped sharply back. Any motion out there was dangerous. But this was not a *Boche*, sneaking from shell hole to shell hole to lob bombs into the French trench. It was a couple of rats, fat and sleek and sassy and almost the size of cats, on promenade from one favorite dining spot in field-gray or *horizon bleu* to the next. Rats thrived at Verdun—and why not? Where else did men feed them so extravagantly?

Barrès was tempted to knock them kicking with a burst from the Hotchkiss. In the end, he didn't. There would only be more tomorrow, eating of their obscene meat. And these were as likely to go down and torment the Germans as they were to come up and molest his comrades and him.

Then Barrès spotted motion *in* the trenches of the *Boche*. A man so incompetent as to give away his position to a machine gunner did not deserve to live. Barrès squeezed the Hotchkiss' trigger. The German crumpled. "I got one," Barrès told his loader. "I saw him fall."

"One who won't get us," Fonsagrive replied.

The Germans promptly replied, too. Their riflemen picked up their pace of fire. The Maxim gun came back to life, flame spurting from its muzzle as if from the mouth of a dragon. And, a few minutes later, the *Boche* artillery began delivering presents to the French trenches. Barrès scuttled into the little cave he had scraped out of the front wall of the trench. The Germans—and, he understood, the English, too—forbade their soldiers from digging such private shelters. If a shell landed squarely on one, it would entomb the soldier huddling there. But a man in his own little cave enjoyed far better protection from splinters than one simply cowering at the bottom of the trench.

Some of the rounds—77s, 105s, and 150s—exploded with a peculiar muffled burst. Even before *poilus* started banging on empty shell casings—carillons of dread, not hope—Barrès yanked his gas helmet out of its case and pulled it down over his head. He got a quick whiff of chlorine, enough to make his throat scratchy and bring tears to his eyes, before he could secure the helmet.

He took several anxious breaths after that, fearing the pain would get worse. But he'd protected himself fast enough; it eased to a bearable discomfort. He stared out at the world through round windows, filthy as the portholes of a cabin in steerage. Wearing the helmet, he had to move more slowly and carefully, for he wasn't getting enough air to do anything else. A man who exerted himself too strenuously in a gas helmet was liable to burst his heart.

But when the *Boche* used gas, he was liable to send assault troops as soon as the barrage ended. And so, regardless of the high-explosive shells, still coming down with the ones carrying chlorine, Barrès got out of his shelter and took his place at the Hotchkiss gun again. Better the risk of a shell fragment piercing him than the certainty of a bayonet or a bullet if the *Boche* got into his trench.

He spied no special stirring in the German trenches. Jacques Fonsagrive peered over the parapet with him. "Nothing," Barrès said. "Nothing at all, not this time."

"Not quite." When Fonsagrive spoke, his voice, heard through two thicknesses of varnished cloth, sounded as if it came from the bottom of the sea. The laugh that followed seemed even worse, almost demonic. "Look at the vermin."

Out between the lines, several rats kicked and frothed as chlorine seared their lungs. They were enough like men to sneak about. They were enough like men to steal. They were enough like men to prey on the dying and the dead. But they were not quite enough like men to invent such ingenious ways of murdering one another, or to come up with defenses against that deadly ingenuity.

"I don't miss them a bit," Barrès said.

"Nor I," the loader agreed. "As when you shot that German earlier today, I merely think, *There are a couple who will not gnaw my bones.*"

"Even so," Barrès said. The gas shells were still raining down. "I hope we do not have to wear these cursed helmets too much longer."

"Ah, to hell with a mealy-mouthed hope like that," Fonsagrive said. "What I hope is that the wind will shift and blow the gas back on the pigdogs"—yes, he was enamored of that word—"who sent it to us. They deserve it. They are welcome to it. Hope for something worth having."

"That is a better hope," Barrès said after due reflection. "It is also a hope that could come true without much difficulty." The German trenches lay downhill from the one in which he stood, and chlorine was heavier than air. Even a little breeze would give the *Boche* a taste of his own medicine.

"Do you want to feed them a few strips?" Fonsagrive asked. "Let them know they have not put paid to us?"

"I had in my mind that thought," Barrès said, "but then I thought again, and I decided I would rather not. If they know they have not gassed us, they are likely to drop more ordinary shells on our heads, are they not?"

Behind the gas helmet, Fonsagrive's expression was as hard to read as the unchanging countenance of a praying mantis. After a little while, though, he nodded. "That is a good notion. We can give them a nasty surprise if they come at us, and by then their men will be too close for them to shell us."

"I wish they would give it up soon," Barrès said. "I would like another swig of *pinard*. Even a tin of monkey meat might not taste bad right now."

"My poor fellow!" Fonsagrive exclaimed. "You must have inhaled more of the gas than you think, for your wits have left you altogether."

"It could be," Barrès admitted. "Yes, it could be. Did I truly say I wanted to eat *singe*? No one in his right mind—no one who is not starving, at any rate—would be so foolish."

"I wonder if we will be starving before too long," Fonsagrive said. "The *cuistots* will have a hellish time bringing supplies to the line through this."

"That is a duty for which I would not care," Barrès said—no small statement, coming as it did from a machine gunner at the front. The *cuistots* walked, or more often crawled, to the front festooned with loaves of bread as if with bandoliers, and with bottles of *pinard*. They paid the butcher's bill no less than anyone else—more than many—and had not even the luxury of shooting back.

And, if the bread arrived covered with mud and loathsome slime, if some of the wine bottles got to the front broken . . . why, then the weary, hungry, thirsty, filthy *poilus* cursed the *cuistots*, of course. And if the bread and wine did not arrive at all, the *poilus* still cursed the *cuistots*, though in that case the bearers were more often than not in no condition to take note of curses.

"Bread and wine," Barrès muttered. "The communion of the damned." He'd had that thought before, as no doubt many Catholics at the front had done, but it struck him with particular force today.

"What is it you say?" Fonsagrive asked. The gas helmet muffled voices and hearing both. Barrès repeated himself, louder this time. Fonsagrive gestured contemptuously. "You and your God, *mon vieux*. How important you think you are—how important you think we are—to merit damnation. I tell you again: if there is a God, which I doubt, as what man of sense could not, then we are not damned. We are merely forgotten, or beneath His notice."

"You so relieve my mind," Barrès said. Through the gas helmet, Fonsagrive's chuckle sounded like the grunting of a boar. Barrès cocked his head to one side, listening not to the loader but to the German bombardment. "It is easing off." He might have been speaking of the rain. Indeed, he had so spoken of the rain many times; in the trenches, rain could be almost as great a nuisance as gas, and lasted far longer.

After another hour or so, Jacques Fonsagrive cautiously lifted his gas helmet from his head. He did not immediately clap it back on. Neither did he topple to the ground clutching at his throat with froth on his lips. He had done that once for a joke while Barrès was taking off his own helmet, and had laughed himself sick when his partner on the machine gun pulled it back down in a spasm of panic. Barrès had not known he could curse so inventively.

Now he pulled off the gas helmet with a sigh of relief. The air still stank, but the air around Verdun always stank. If anything, the chlorine that remained added an antiseptic tang to the ever-present reek of decay. Behind him, the sun was sinking toward the battered horizon. "Another day at the shop," he remarked.

"But of course," Fonsagrive said. "Now we go home to our pipes and slippers." They both laughed. They might even sleep a little tonight, as they had the night before, if the *Boche* proved to be in a forgiving mood. On the other hand, they might stay awake three, four, five days in a row—if they stayed alive through the end of that time. Barrès had done it before.

Fonsagrive did light a pipe, a stubby little one filled with tobacco that smelled as if it were half dried horse dung. All French tobacco smelled that way these days. For lack of anything better—the only reason a man with a tongue in his head would do such a thing—he and Barrès opened tins of *singe* and supped as they had breakfasted. Even in the twilight, the preserved beef was unnaturally red.

"Poor old monkey," Barrès said. "A pity he got no last rites before he died." He took another bite and chewed meditatively. "He tastes so bad. . . . Maybe he was a suicide, and they found his body two or three days later and stuffed it in a tin then. That would account for the flavor, to be sure, and for his getting no rites. Yes," he went on, pleased with his own conceit, "that would account for a great many things."

"Would it account for your being an idiot?" Jacques Fonsagrive enquired. Barrès chuckled to himself. *He is jealous,* Barrès thought. *Usually, such foolishness falls from his lips, and I am the one who has to endure it.* But then Fonsagrive continued, "We are all suicides here, and none of us shall receive the last rites. It is true, is it not? Of course it is true. We are suicides, and the *Boche*, he is a suicide, and the whole cursed world, it is a suicide, too, throwing itself onto the fire as a moth will hurl itself into the flame of a gas lamp."

Pierre Barrès dug into the tin of *singe* and ate without another word till it was empty. It was not that he disagreed with his loader. On the contrary: he felt exactly as did Fonsagrive. But some things, no matter how true they were—indeed, because of how true they were—were better left unsaid.

Fonsagrive seemed to sense the same thing, for when he spoke again, after flinging his own empty tin out of the trench, what he said was, "Perhaps the two of us will succeed in botching our own suicides. We have botched so many things since this *tragédie bouffe* began, what is one more?"

"Maybe we will," Barrès said, glad for any excuse not to contemplate what was far more likely to happen to him.

And then, from down the trench, voices were raised in simultaneous greeting and anger. That could mean only one thing. "The *cuistots* have got here at last," Fonsagrive said, spelling out that one thing, "and the bread is even filthier than usual. Either that, or they have no wine at all."

"Fuck you and fuck all your mothers, too, the ugly old bawds," a *cuistot* was saying furiously in a voice that broke every fourth word: he couldn't have been above seventeen. "I suppose you stand up and wave when the *Boche* drops shells on *your* heads. If you think my job is so easy, come do it."

"If you think fighting up here while you're starving is so easy, *you* come do it," one of the *poilus* retorted. But his voice held less outrage than those of the front-line troops had before; the *cuistot*'s answering fury had quelled theirs, as counterbattery fire reduced the damage gun crews could do. None of the soldiers cared for the notion of becoming a *cuistot* himself: no, not even a little.

Eventually, Barrès and Fonsagrive got bread and wine for themselves. Barrès' share of the wine did not quite fill his water bottle, and he had to use his belt knife to cut away several muddy, filthy spots from the chunk of bread. Even after he'd done that, it still stank of corruption and death. Or perhaps it was only his imagination, for the whole battlefield stank of corruption and death.

Fonsagrive gave the bread such praise as he could: "Lord knows it's better than *singe*." He drank some of the *pinard* the *cuistot* had brought forward. "And this is better than horse piss, but not much."

With his belly full, Barrès was inclined to take a somewhat more charitable view of the world. "Let it be as it is, Jacques," he said. "All the grousing in the world won't make it any better."

"To hell with the world," the loader replied. "If I grouse, *I* feel better." His eyes glittered in the gathering darkness.

Barrès decided not to push it any further. What the devil was the use? What the devil, for that matter, was the use of anything up here at the front line? Survival was the most he could hope for, and his odds even of that weren't good. "Let me have a cigarette, *mon vieux,* will you?" he said. "Either that or some tobacco for my pipe. I'm just about all out."

"Here." Fonsagrive handed him a leather pouch. "Help yourself." Tobacco got to the front even less reliably than *pinard* and bread. A few days before, he'd been the one who was low, and Barrès had kept him smoking.

A brimstone reek, as of a fumigation or an exorcism, rose from the match Barrès struck. He got his pipe going and sucked smoke into his mouth. It was vile smoke, but less vile than everything else around him. He leaned back against the wall of the trench, savoring the pipe. The *Boche* must have been at his supper, too, for there was silence in the trenches about the space of half an hour.

He looked up. The stars were coming out, as if all the world beneath them were at peace. He always marveled at that. The stars did not care. Maybe it was just as well.

From high above, cold and thin in the distance, came the sound—Barrès dug a finger in his ear, for his mind at first would not credit what he heard—of a brazen trumpet blowing a long blast. "That is not a call of ours," he said, repose dropping from him like a hastily donned cloak. "That is surely some thing of the *Boche*."

"Bugger the *Boche*," Fonsagrive said, but he, too, scrambled to his feet. Barrès set his finger on the trigger of the Hotchkiss gun. If the Germans wanted to pay a call on his stretch of trench by night, as they had been known to do, he would give them a warm reception. Fonsagrive went on, "I think they mean to bombard us from above: that horn must surely be coming from an *avion*."

"So it must." Barrès shrugged and sighed. "If only our own *avions* were worth something more than an arse-wipe article from *L'Illustration*."

"If only, if only, if only," the loader mocked him. "If only you did not say 'If only' so much. The *Boche* has more artillery, he has more men, and he has more *avions* as well. Such is life. We shall go on killing him anyway, until we are killed ourselves."

Down in the German trenches a couple of hundred meters away, men were shouting and stirring, as the French soldiers were to either side of Barrès' machine gun. Barrès thought he saw movement, and started firing. The German Maxim gun answered instantly, and riflemen on both sides also opened up. Muzzle flashes stabbed the night.

Then the aerial bombardment Fonsagrive had feared began. It was like no bombing raid Barrès had ever known: hail and fire rained out of the sky together. "Mother of God!" Barrès shouted, diving for shelter. "The *Boche* has learned how to take his cursed flamethrowers up into *avions*."

"So he has," Fonsagrive answered. "What he has not learned to do, the stinking pigdog, is to aim his flying fire. Listen to them howl down the slope, roasted in their own ovens!" He chuckled in high good humor.

"Might as well be our artillery," Barrès said, laughing, too. The Germans *were* howling when hail smote or fire burned, and the bombardment seemed to be falling on them and the French almost impartially. Barrès cocked his head to one side. "Truly their pilots are great cowards, for they are flying so high, one cannot even hear the sound of their engines."

"As you say, might as well be our own artillery." Fonsagrive got to his feet. "And this bombardment is not so much of a much, either. Shells or bombs would do far worse than these drippy wisps of fire." A hailstone clattered off his helmet.

Barrès did not think the *Boche* could come out of his trenches and attack, not when he was being bombarded, too. Nonetheless, the Frenchman peered toward the enemy's line. The rain of fire had started blazes in the wrecked and battered woods, although, thanks to the hail, they weren't spreading very fast.

Fonsagrive stuck up his head, too. He shrugged. "One part in three of the forest on fire, more or less," he said. "I had not thought the Germans to be such a slovenly people. If they have this weapon that burns, they would do better to bring it all down on *our* heads, not scatter it about as a running man with dysentery scatters turds." He sounded rather like a critic explaining why a dramatist had ended up with a play worse than it might have been.

After a while, the rain of hail and fire eased, both ending at about the same time. Never once had Barrès heard the buzz of an *avion*'s motor. The woods and such dry grass as remained on the ground burned fitfully. They would, Barrès judged, burn themselves out before long: so many of those trees had already burned, not much was left on which flames could support themselves.

He said, "With any luck at all, the next time the *Boche* trots out his fire, he will use it against the English farther north."

"It could be," Fonsagrive said. "He honored them with poison gas before he gave us our first taste of it, but now he shares it with them and us alike. He is a generous fellow, the *Boche*, is he not?"

"To a fault," Barrès said. "I wonder when he will do us another favor of this sort. Not soon, I hope."

In that hope he was disappointed, as he discovered within minutes. He had been disappointed a great many times since the war began, and was hardly surprised to have it happen again. As if proud of their ingenuity, the Germans heralded the new onslaught with another of those trumpetlike blasts that seemed to come from everywhere and nowhere at the same time.

"Look up in the sky!" Fonsagrive exclaimed. "One of their *avions* must have walked into a shell, for it is burning, burning."

"That is a very huge bastard of an *avion*, to be sure," Barrès replied. "I wonder—I wonder most exceedingly—how such a machine could even so much as hope to get off the ground. Look at it, Jacques. Does it not seem like a great mountain burning with fire?"

"So it does," Fonsagrive said. "And may all the Germans inside it burn with fire, too. There it goes, by God! It will crash in the river."

Crash in the Meuse it did, behind the French lines and to the west of the trench in which Barrès and Fonsagrive huddled. The ground shook under Barrès' boots. "Good!" he said savagely. "All the bombs and all the fire the *salauds* still had with them have gone up. Now there can be no doubt they are dead."

"They are dead, yes, and probably one fish in three in the Meuse with them," Fonsagrive said. "That was a formidable explosion."

"A pity the *avion* did not crash into the trenches the *Boche* holds," Barrès said. "It would have been sweet, having him hoist by his own petard."

"So it would," Fonsagrive said. "It would also be sweet if, having made a nuisance of himself in the first part of the evening, the *Boche* would roll up in his covers and go to sleep for the rest of the night. As you said, another favor like the falling fire we do not need."

But the respite the two Frenchmen got did not last long. For the third time that evening, the horn sounded not behind the German line but, as best Barrès could tell, above it. "What *is* the *Boche* playing at?" he demanded in a cross voice. "When he does strange things, I grow nervous, for then I do not know what he is likely to try next."

Even as he spoke, a great searing white light sprang into being above him. "Parachute flare!" The cry rose from up and down the line. Barrès ducked down below the lip of the parapet. In that pitiless glare, the Germans would have had an easy time picking him off.

He waited for the Maxim gun in the trench down the slope to take advantage of the flare and start potting *poilus* less cautious than he. But the enemy's machine gun stayed quiet, as did his own Hotchkiss. He wondered why. When he said so aloud, Fonsagrive answered, "Could it be that no one told the *Boche* machine gunners the flare was going up? Could it be they think it is ours, and wait for us to shoot at them?"

"It could be, I suppose," Barrès said dubiously, "but it sounds like something our own officers are more likely to do than those of the Germans." He had a healthy, indeed almost a fearful, respect for the men who wore field-gray and coal-scuttle helmets, and for their commanders. They had come too close to killing him too many times for him to feel anything but respect for them.

Slowly, slowly, the parachute flare sank. It was an extraordinarily fine one. It scarcely flickered or dimmed as it came down, staying so bright, Barrès could not even make out the 'chute supporting it in the air.

It lit in a muddy puddle—a water-filled shell hole, no doubt— off to the right, in the direction of Fort Douaumont. Even after it sank into the puddle, its light still shone for a moment. The *Boche* remained in his trenches. "Whatever he was supposed to do, he has buggered it up," Fonsagrive said.

"So it would seem," Barrès agreed. "Who would have thought it of him?"

From that muddy puddle, and perhaps from all the other sodden shell holes nearby, of which there were a great many, rose a bitter odor penetrating even through the horrid stench of the battlefield of Verdun. "What the devil is that?" Fonsagrive said. "Some new German gas?" He grabbed for his gas helmet.

But Barrès held up a hand. "No, that's not a gas," he said. "Don't you recognize it? That's the smell of wormwood."

"Wormwood?" The loader frowned. "The stuff that goes into absinthe?"

"The very same," Barrès replied.

Fonsagrive snorted. "And what do you know of wormwood, of absinthe, eh, *mon vieux*? I suppose you are going to tell me you were one of those Paris dandies who knocked back the stuff by the beaker before they made it against the law because it drove some of those dandies mad?" As Barrès' eyes readjusted to the night, he saw Fonsagrive gesture airily, as he guessed a Parisian dandy might do. Whatever effect the gesture might have had from a Paris dandy, it altogether failed of its purpose when coming from a filthy, unshaven corporal.

"Oh, yes, I used to guzzle absinthe by the tumblerful," Barrès said.

His loader snorted again, louder and more rudely this time. "The truth, if you please. Do you know what the truth is?"

"Better than Pontius Pilate. Better than you, too," Barrès retorted. But then he sighed. "Oh, very well. The truth. Back when the war was new, my company commander used to drink the stuff. Every day, at noon and in the evening, he would pour some absinthe into the bottom of a glass, hold a perforated spoon filled with sugar above it, and drip a little water through the sugar and into the absinthe. Then he'd drink it down. I don't know where he got the stuff, but he had plenty."

"What sort of officer was he?" Fonsagrive asked, interest in his voice. "Did the absinthe make him crazier than those who don't drink it?"

"Not so you'd notice," Barrès answered. "He was just a soldier, like any other. He's dead now, I heard."

"As who is not, these days?" Fonsagrive said. "It's almost a fucking dishonor to stay alive, if you know what I mean."

"Only too well, *mon ami*—only too well." Sadly, Barrès shook his head. After he'd done it, he wished he hadn't. "Those cursed fumes of wormwood are giving me a hangover, and I didn't even get to enjoy the drunk."

"Life is full of tragedies," Fonsagrive said. "Shall I weep for you?"

"If you would be so kind," Barrès answered. His loader rolled his eyes. Both men laughed. After a little while, Fonsagrive began to complain that his head hurt, too. "Ah, *quel dommage,*" Barrès said, his voice full of lachrymose, even treacly, sympathy. "How I grieve that you suffer!"

"How I grieve that you lay it on with a trowel," Fonsagrive remarked. The two soldiers laughed again.

Barrès said, "The *Boche* has been trying all sorts of strange and curious things tonight. I wonder whether he is finished, or whether he will show us something else new and interesting."

That made Jacques Fonsagrive stop laughing. But then, after some thought, the loader said, "The *Boche* has shown us strange and curious things tonight, *oui,* but I cannot see that he has hurt us very badly with them. His fire did him as much harm as it did us, and if he somehow turned water into absinthe—well, so what? Jesus Christ turned water into wine, and look what happened to *Him.*"

"If a priest heard you say that, he would swell up and turn purple, like a man stung by many hornets," Barrès said. "But, since it is my ears you assail . . ." As Fonsagrive had earlier in the day, he shrugged a fine French shrug.

A fourth trumpet blast sounded, above and beyond the battlefield. Barrès tensed, but not so much as he had done when that strange horn call first sounded. These German attacks were strange and curious, true, but, as his loader had said, they were less dangerous than most of the things the Germans had done before.

For some time, he wondered if this trumpet blast were merely sound and fury, signifying nothing. But then Jacques Fonsagrive asked, "Where has the moon gone?" By his tone, he suggested that Barrès was hiding it in one of the pockets of his uniform tunic.

Looking east, Barrès saw that the waning crescent moon which had crawled up above the German-held land in that direction—without his noticing, the hour had got well past midnight—was now vanished. He spied no cloud behind which it could have disappeared . . . and, for that matter, the stars in that part of the sky also seemed to have gone.

"Absinthe fumes," he said again. "What else could it be? They poach your wits like the eggs in eggs Benedict."

"Hmm." Fonsagrive pondered the phrase as if he'd seen it in some new essay from Anatole France. "Not bad," he said at last. "Soon the sun will be up. If you see strange things in the light of day, you will know your wits are not poached, but as addled as the eggs a Picard peasant sells you for fresh."

A good many of the infantrymen in the trench with them were Picard peasants. If they heard, if they thought the comment a slander on their habits, they gave no sign. *Probably laughing up their sleeves,* Barrès thought.

And the sun gave no sign of coming up. When a waning crescent moon rises, the sun cannot be far behind. So a lifetime of experience had taught Barrès. But, even though the sun did not rise and did not rise, he refused to let it fret him. After all, among all the other stenches, the stench of wormwood remained strong in the air. "A few minutes seem like an hour," Barrès remarked after some time had passed.

"True: time marches on hands and knees," Fonsagrive said, adding, "It could be that we should put on our gas helmets, to clear these fumes from our heads. The sun should have risen long ago."

"To the devil with that," Barrès said. He waved out across no-man's-land. "The *Boche* is in the same state we are. The *Boche* must be in the same state we are, or he would have come over here and done us a mischief." He leaned against the wall of the trench and closed his eyes. "I am going to sleep for a bit, while I have the chance."

"Not the worst idea in the world," Fonsagrive agreed, and he stretched out, too. They knew they could be up and firing in a couple of seconds if the Germans had been rendered less nearly insensible than seemed to be the case.

When Barrès opened his eyes, he was prepared to swear on a stack of Bibles two meters high that he had dozed only a few minutes. But the sun, that suddenly treacherous beast, stood high in the sky, having somehow traveled a third part of its journey across the heavens while he lay snoring.

Ever so cautiously, he sniffed. Yes, the odor of absinthe lingered. If it had thrown him into such a stupor, maybe he should have thrust the gas helmet over his head in the darkness. But, while it might save his life, he hated it, just as he hated donning a rubber that might save him from disease.

Fonsagrive woke up a couple of minutes later. "What's going on?" he demanded, pointing toward the sun. "Where'd that little bugger sneak out from while we weren't looking?"

"Damned if I know," Barrès answered. "But there he is, and we just have to make the best of it."

They weren't the only ones who'd taken advantage of what still felt like unnaturally extended darkness. All up and down the line, *poilus* who'd just awakened were exclaiming in wonder at how the sun had come out of nowhere. Barrès spoke no German past *"Hände hoch!"*—which he mispronounced abominably—but he knew surprise when he heard it. By the noises the *Boche* was making down in his trenches, he was as surprised as his French foes.

Before Barrès had a chance to marvel at that, the aerial trumpet sounded again: the fifth time overall, the first in daylight. Fonsagrive made a disgusted noise, then said, "Ahh, I thought we were done with that weird crap."

Then, together, he and Barrès exclaimed not in disgust but in fright. A shell—it had to be a shell, though it glowed like a star even in broad daylight—was falling from the sky, seemingly straight toward them. Barrès had seen plenty of German 420s and flying mines: half the terror of those things was that you *could* see them as they fell. The same held true here. This was no parachute flare, like the one that had somehow brought with it the reek of absinthe. This one plunged to earth unimaginably faster than any stooping hawk.

Barrès barely had time to dive into his cave before the starlike shell burst in no-man's-land. By the way the ground shook beneath him, it had landed not far in front of his Hotchkiss gun. Dirt and gobbets of decayed man's-flesh rained down on the trench, as they did after any near miss from a big shell. He gritted his teeth, bracing himself for the storm of steel sure to follow that first shot.

But the storm of steel did not come. When it didn't come, Barrès scrambled to his feet and seized his machine gun's trigger instead of sheltering in the hole he'd scraped for himself in the front wall of the trench. Maybe something had gone wrong with the *Boche*'s artillery signals, and footsoldiers in field-gray were about to swarm out of their trenches and up the slope toward him.

He saw no swarming footsoldiers, for which he heartily thanked God. He did see the enormous hole the shell had dug, about halfway between his line and the forwardmost German positions. From that hole, a great smoke rose: perhaps the star shell had been of armor-piercing make, and had penetrated deep enough into the soft earth to ignite a stock of cooking oil or motor oil merely buried by all the other thousands of rounds that had slammed into the slope. The smoke spread quickly, all but blotting out the light of the sun that had so mysteriously reappeared in the sky.

Something stirred, there at the edge of the hole. Barrès' finger tightened on the trigger of the Hotchkiss gun. But then, frantically, he jerked his hands away from the weapon, snatched the gas helmet off his belt, and stuffed it down over his head. "Holy Virgin Mary Mother of God," he gasped, almost as if the phrase were but a single word. "The absinthe fumes were ever so much worse than I thought."

Beside him, Fonsagrive was also putting on his gas helmet with desperate haste. "Tell me what you see," the loader begged.

"I will not," Barrès said firmly. "In no way will I do that. You would think I was mad. I would think I am mad, did I put into words what my fuddled brain makes of what my eyes see."

Locusts the size of horses? Locusts the size of horses with the tails of scorpions and the faces of men? Locusts the size of horses with iron breastplates, with wings that rumbled as they shook them out? Locusts with women's hair streaming out from under golden crowns, with the fierce teeth of lions huge in their jaws?

Though Barrès breathed clean air now, the absinthe fumes had already fuddled him, and the hallucinations—for such they had to be—did not resume their proper form, which could be nothing but men in field-gray with coal-scuttle helmets on their heads.

"I do not care what they look like to me," he declared as the impossible things began to advance on the trench. He was lying. He knew he was lying, but saying the words helped him control his fear, even if he could not banish it. And what he said next was surely true: "If I can see them at all, I can kill them."

He squeezed the machine gun's trigger and sent a strip of ammunition into the Germans who did not to his mind look like Germans. Mechanical as if powered by steam, Jacques Fonsagrive fed the Hotchkiss another thirty-round strip, and another, and another. All along the trench, *poilus,* some wearing gas helmets, some not, emptied their rifles at the advancing enemy as fast as they could.

The slaughter was gruesome. The *Boche* had to be throwing in raw recruits, for they knew nothing—less than nothing—about taking cover. Barrès had heard that the Germans were trying out armor like that which knights of old had worn. Maybe the breastplates he thought he saw on the giant locusts were in fact breastplates on Germans. If they were, they weren't proof against machine-gun bullets.

And then Barrès laughed out loud, a huge, delighted laugh. Some—perhaps even half—the Germans in no-man's-land, unable to stand up against the withering French fire, started back toward their own line. And the Germans in that line, as fuddled from wormwood fumes as Barrès was himself, opened fire on their comrades as if they were Frenchmen. The Maxim and Mausers worked an execution as ghastly as the Hotchkiss and Lebels.

A few got into the trenches on either side. None lasted long, not against bullets and bayonets and grenades. Then one more rose out of the pit. Maybe the fumes were fading from Barrès' head, for this one looked like a man. But *what* man he looked like kept changing from moment to moment. Now he had lank, dark hair, a small mustache, and wore what looked something like a German uniform, save with a red armband bearing some kind of symbol on his left arm. Then again, he might have been a short, pockmarked fellow with iron-gray hair and a large mustache, wearing a suit halfway between military and civilian cut, with a gold star hanging from his left breast pocket. Or—

Barrès waited to see no more. He fired at the man who shifted shape. So did the German Maxim gunner. They both started shooting at essentially the same instant. They both scored hits, too, a great many hits. The man—a German officer?—went down and stayed down. He didn't look now like one man, now like another, not any longer. He just looked dead.

"Is that the end of it?" Barrès asked.

"Am I God, that I should know such things?" Fonsagrive returned. "I will tell you what I think, though. What I think is, it will never be over for us, not until we are killed. In the meanwhile, we are obliged to make ourselves as difficult for the *Boche* as we can."

Since Barrès thought the same thing, he did not argue with his loader. Down the trench, someone was screaming, "It burns! Aii, it burns! The sting, the horrible sting!" Barrès wondered what the absinthe fumes had made that poor *poilu* imagine he was fighting.

And then, clearly audible even through the varnished cloth of his gas helmet, Barrès heard that trumpet sound for a sixth time. *"Merde alors!"* he exclaimed angrily. "Has the *Boche* not yet realized that, whatever his wormwood-filled gas shell may have done to us, it has done likewise to his own men?"

"If our generals are fools, why should the *Boche*'s generals not be fools as well?" Fonsagrive said.

Whatever the wormwood-filled gas shell had done to Barrès, its effects had not left him. Nor, as he'd thought, had they diminished. Rushing hard toward him came a host of cavalry straight from the imagination of a madman. The horses wore breastplates of fire and brimstone; their heads looked like those of lions. Instead of tails, snakes grew from the end of their spines, snakes with great poisonous fangs. The lion heads breathed out flames and smoke. Some of the riders had wings.

"Gas!" Fonsagrive shouted. "Horsemen with poison gas!" Barrès nodded. His gas helmet kept him safe. And he had before him a target of which machine gunners could commonly but dream. He fired and fired and fired, till the cooling fins on the Hotchkiss gun glowed red. Fonsagrive fed him strip after strip of ammunition.

"The *Boche* is mad, to attack us with cavalry," Barrès said. "But however mad he is, they shall not pass!"

That he, too, was mad, to see the German *Uhlans* as he did, went without saying. But a man who had spent so long breathing absinthe fumes could hardly be expected to remain in his right mind. And anyone on the front lines at Verdun was apt to be mad anyhow. He was sane enough to keep the machine gun pointed in the right direction, and that was the only thing that really mattered.

Some of the improbable-looking cavalry charged back toward the German lines, as had some of the footsoldiers who'd looked to him like giant locusts. The Germans shot them down as cheerfully as Barrès did. He laughed. They were making his work easier for him.

He did not think any of the horsemen got into either set of trenches. Both the Empire and the Central Powers kept cavalry divisions behind their lines, awaiting breakthroughs that never came. Cavalry, in any case, melted under machine-gun fire like frost melting under hot sunshine. To anyone who'd spent time in the trenches, that was obvious. Generals on both sides, though, had a way of staying back at nice, comfortable headquarters. What was obvious to the soldiers who did the fighting and dying must not have seemed so plain ten or twenty kilometers behind the line.

At last, Barrès stopped shooting. "Have we got a jam?" Fonsagrive asked anxiously.

"Not at all," Barrès replied. "The gun performs splendidly. But I see nothing more alive in front of me. Why, then, should I waste cartridges I shall need to try to beat back the next German attack?"

Rain mixed with sleet—Verdun surely had the most abominable climate in all of France, and yesterday's warmth was forgotten—began pelting down. A great clap of thunder sounded, and another, and another, until there were seven in all. Jacques Fonsagrive laughed. "Do you know, *mon ami*," he said, "that I used to be frightened of thunder, and would hide under my bed during a storm?"

"Artillery fire will cure one of that, *n'est-ce pas?*" Barrès said. "I would like to hide under my bed when the *Boche* shells us. I would like to have a bed under which to hide when the *Boche* shells us."

"An iron bed, by choice," Fonsagrive said. "But yes, after artillery, how is one to lose one's nerve over thunder?" He shook his fist at the sky. "If there is a God up there, which, as I have said, I do not believe, how could He do worse to us than what the Germans and our own officers have visited upon us here? Such a thing would not be possible."

Barrès scratched himself. "It could be that you are right. But it could be that you are wrong, too. After all, when the *Boche* shelled us with poison gas yesterday, he did kill a great many rats, as we both noted."

"I beg your pardon." Fonsagrive's nod was full of exquisite, understated irony. "If God is as all-powerful as most fools say, no doubt He could give us rats and poison gas at the very same time. Or He might simply give the rats gas helmets, which would save Him a miracle."

"Very good. Oh, very good indeed." Barrès clapped his hands. "I wish we had a chaplain here, to listen to these brilliant blasphemies."

"Chaplains are no fools," Fonsagrive said. "Nothing requires that they come to the front line, and so they do not. If nothing required me to come to the front line, I would not either, I assure you."

"Nor I," Pierre Barrès answered. He shrugged. "But the nations are angry. It is the time of the dead. And so we are here: the dead, but not quite yet." The ground shook under his feet. "Is that an earthquake?"

"What a fool you are," Fonsagrive said. "That's someone's ammunition dump going up. I hope very much it is an ammunition dump of the *Boche* going up." He cocked his head to one side, to hear from which direction the roar of the explosion would come.

So did Barrès. He heard no explosion, though, only the endless patter of the rain. And then, through the rain, high and thin, came a seventh trumpet blast. He glanced over to Jacques Fonsagrive. The loader nodded: he had heard it, too. They both braced themselves for whatever the Germans might throw at them next.

"We are not dead yet," Barrès repeated. "We have heard six of these horn calls, and endured them. What is one more?"

"Perhaps one too many," Fonsagrive said. "But then again, perhaps not, also."

The ground shook again. There were lightnings and thunderings. The sleet turned to hail. After shell fragments, hail was at worst a minor nuisance. But, little by little, the foul weather eased. The sun came out once more—not by stealth, as it had before, but simply because the wind blew away the clouds.

Barrès and Fonsagrive both nodded. "It is done," they said together.

They looked at each other. Somehow, it should not have been their voices saying those words, but Another's. They both shrugged. Who had time to think of Another, here in the man-made hell of Verdun? And, as Jacques Fonsagrive had said, what even from the last of days could be worse than that which soldiers endured here?

Barrès took off his gas helmet. A last few raindrops fell, though the sky seemed clear. They tasted of salt, almost as if they were tears.

A buzzing in the air swiftly swelled to a mechanical roar. With a grunt of fright, Barrès threw himself into the hole he'd scraped in the trench. Bullets from the machine guns of several low-flying *avions* decked with black crosses chewed up the French entrenchments. Men screamed as they were wounded.

As soon as the *avions* had passed, Barrès emerged and sent what ammunition was left in his machine gun after them. He did not think he scored any hits. A man on the ground with a Hotchkiss gun knocked down an *avion* only by luck. He knew it. He accepted it. But if a man on the ground did not bet, how could he hope to win?

Maybe his puny act of defiance angered the Germans. Whatever the reason, their artillery opened up on the position his regiment occupied. A man on the ground with a Hotchkiss gun could do nothing whatever against artillery. Barrès knew that, too. He had trouble accepting it. That was one of the reasons he hated gunners so much.

Slow as usual, the French artillery eventually got around to responding to the *Boche* bombardment. That tardiness was another reason why Barrès hated gunners, even gunners in *horizon bleu*. Also as usual, all too many of the French shells fell short and landed on the same trenches the Germans were pounding. That gave Barrès—and every other *poilu*—a most excellent reason for hating his own gunners.

By the time the two rival sets of artillerymen (so Barrès supposed they were, even if they sometimes seemed joined in a malign alliance against the French infantry) had finished plowing up the trenches and the ground between them, no one could have told from what manner of creature the chunks of flesh out there had come. Germans? Very likely. Horses? Very likely. Giant locusts with scorpion stings? No one could not have proved otherwise.

Little by little, the shelling slowed. Barrès came out of his hole, wondering if the *Boche* intended rushing up the slope at him. But the men in field-gray seemed content for the time being to stay where they were. He took out a tin of *singe*, opened it, and stared resignedly at the red, red meat inside.

Jacques Fonsagrive was opening some tinned beef, too. "I

wonder if the *cuistots* will be able to get more bread up here any time soon," he said.

"Whether they do or not, we'll get by," Barrès answered. "We still have monkey meat and we still have *pinard*. We can go on a while longer."

"You have reason, *mon vieux*," Fonsagrive said. "And the fighting's been a little quieter the last couple of days, eh?"

"Yes, I think so." Barrès nodded, then shrugged. "Who knows? I would not care to bet on it, but we might even live. You have any more tobacco?" Fonsagrive passed him a *Gitane*. He lit it and took a long drag. "Ahh. Thanks. That's good, by God."

In This Season

Here is another tale of man's inhumanity to man in our century, this one set in the Second World War rather than the First. There are powers, and then again, there are powers—and there are also Powers. "In This Season" is the story of a collision between them. I owe Marty Greenberg a thank-you for this one, for letting me put a Chanukah story in an anthology of Christmas tales.

Sunset came early to the little Polish town of Puck as winter began. The Baltic slapped in growing darkness against the shelving, muddy beach. The Poles grubbed clams and cockles and whelks from the mud and fried them or ate them in soups. For Puck's three families of Jews, shellfish were, of course, forbidden food.

The hunger that gnawed Berel Friedman's belly made him wonder with increasingly urgent curiosity what fried clams tasted like. In the three months since the Germans overran Poland, Puck's Poles had come to know hunger and want. As for the town's Jews—well, falling under Hitler's yoke made Friedman long to be ruled by Poles again, and what comparison could be worse than that? None he could think of.

A soft knock on the door distracted him from his gloomy reflections. His wife, Emma, said, "That will be the Korczaks. We're all here now."

"Yes." He opened the door, nodded to Jacob and Yetta Korczak, chucked their two little boys under the chin. "Welcome, all," he said. "*Gut yontif*—happy holiday."

"Gut yontif." Deep lines of worry lost themselves in Jacob Korczak's graying beard. He laughed bitterly. "As if there are any happy holidays any more."

"We go on day by day, as best we can," Friedman said. "What else can we do?" Behind him, Isaac Geller nodded, not so much from conviction (for his nature was less sunny than Friedman's) as from despair at finding any better course.

Friedman made sure the curtains were tightly shut before he took down the silver menorah and set it on the mantel. For the Poles to see him lighting Chanukah candles would be bad enough. For the Germans to see him would be catastrophic.

He set a slim orange candle in the leftmost space in the menorah, then took another from the box and laid it on the mantel for a moment. He got out a match, scraped it against the sole of his boot. The match caught. Coughing a little at the sulfurous smoke, he picked up the candle from the mantel, lighted it, and used it to kindle the one already in the menorah. Then he put the *shamas* candle in the menorah's centermost place, which was higher than the four to either side of it.

That done, he chanted in Hebrew the blessings over the candles, then translated them into Yiddish for the women and children: "Blessed art thou, O Lord our God, king of the universe, who hast sanctified us with thy commandments and commanded us to light the lights of dedication . . ." ("Which is what 'Chanukah' means, after all," he added in an aside.) "Blessed art thou, O Lord our God, king of the universe, who wrought miracles for our fathers in those days and in this season . . . Blessed art thou, O Lord our God, king of the universe, who hath preserved us alive and brought us to enjoy this season."

Though Friedman was in most circumstances a man far from imaginative, the irony of the Chanukah blessing struck him with almost physical force. God might have helped the Jews against Antiochus long ago, but what was He doing about Hitler, whose venom was enough for twenty Antiochuses? Nothing anyone could see.

Shaking his head, Friedman read and then translated the explanatory passage that followed the blessings in the prayer book: "These lights we light to praise thee for the miracles, wonders, salvations, and victories which thou didst perform for our fathers in those days and in this season, by the hands of thy holy priests. Therefore, by command, these lights are holy all the eight days of Chanukah; neither are we permitted to make any other use of them save to view them, that we may return thanks to thy name for thy miracles, wonderful works, and salvation."

All the adults in the crowded little living room exchanged troubled glances above the heads of their children. Where were the victories? The wonderful works? As for salvation, who under the Nazis had even the hope to pray for it?

If there were miracles, they lay in the hearts of the children. As soon as Friedman stepped away from the menorah, his daughter Rachel, the two Korczak boys, and the Gellers' son and daughter all squealed, "It's Chanukah!" so loud that their parents looked alarmed. Children didn't worry about hard times, but they made the most of celebrations. In a moment, three or four dreidels, some of wood, others baked from clay, were spinning on the floor and on the low, battered table in front of the fireplace.

"Here, here," Jacob Korczak said gruffly. "If you're going to play with dreidels, you need some Chanukah *gelt*, don't you?" He dug in his trouser pocket, took out a handful of mixed German and Polish small change, and passed the little coins to all the children. Friedman and Geller did the same.

The letters on the four sides of the dreidels began the Hebrew words that meant "a great miracle happened here." The sounds of joy from the children as they played, the delight when the person who spun won the pot on a *gimel*, the moan when *shin* landed face up and the spinner had to add to the pile, made the house sound like all the Chanukahs Friedman remembered. In these times, that was not the smallest of miracles itself.

It even began to smell like Chanukah. The rich odors of hot grease and onions flooded in from the kitchen as Emma fried potato *latkes*: a man could still come by potatoes. But the *latkes* would be the entire Chanukah feast. No fat goose, no brisket marinated in wine, not this year. Friedman could count on the fingers of his hands the times he'd tasted meat since the swastika flag replaced Poland's red and white banner over the town hall.

"We'll just stuff ourselves the fuller with *latkes*, then," he declared. Jacob Korczak glared at him. He just smiled in return. If your children were happy, could you stay grim for long?

Someone knocked on the door.

In an instant, the house was silent. The children looked frightened. The adults looked terrified. All the Jews in Puck were gathered together here. Whoever stood outside had to be a *goy*, then: maybe a Pole; maybe, worse, a German. The Germans were deporting Jews from this part of Poland now that they'd annexed it to their country. Ice in his veins, Friedman waited for the harsh cry, *"Juden, heraus!"*

The knock came again. But for that, silence.

Emma poked her head out of the kitchen. "What shall I do?" Friedman mouthed in her direction. Opening the door and not opening it were equally appalling choices.

"Open it," she said without hesitation. "It's Chanukah, after all. Feeding the stranger is a *mitzvah*."

If the stranger outside was a cruelly grinning SS man in a coal-scuttle helmet, Friedman did not think even God would reckon feeding him a blessing. Of course, if it was an SS man outside, he had better things to eat than the poor fare a handful of Jews could offer him.

Whoever it was knocked for a third time, not loudly but with persistence. The slow, steady raps helped hearten Friedman. Surely an SS man would not politely knock three times; an SS man would hammer down the door with a rifle butt.

Friedman raised the bar, threw the door wide. Outside stood the tallest, widest man he'd ever set eyes on, dressed in rags far too small for him. Friedman had never seen him, or anyone like him, before. He looked as though he could have ripped the door off its hinges with his little finger.

The big man did nothing of the sort. He just stood quietly, looking down at Friedman even though the living room floor was a tall step above the street. His eyes reflected the flickering glow of the Chanukah candles like a cat's.

Seeing those candles, even if at second hand, reminded Friedman why he'd opened the door. He forced his voice not to wobble as he said, "Will you come in, friend, and take supper with us? We have an abundance of good *latkes*, so help yourself to all you can eat." He knew he'd lied—no one but Germans had an abundance of anything in Poland these days—but it was not the sort of lie God recorded in his book of judgments.

The stranger looked at him a moment more. He did not answer, not with words. All at once, though, he nodded. He had to go sideways through Friedman's door, and duck his head to get under the lintel. When he straightened up inside the house, the hairless crown of his head just missed scraping the ceiling.

Rachel Friedman was only four years old, too little to be perfectly polite. She stared up and up and up at the stranger, then started to cry. Through her tears, she wailed, "If he eats all he can eat, the rest of us won't have any!" That set a couple of the other children crying, too. They'd all been hungry too often of late to think of losing a promised feast.

As host, Berel Friedman did what he could to repair the damage. He knew with a certain somber pride that his chuckle sounded natural. "Don't worry about the children, my friend. What do children know? As I said, we have plenty. And Emma"—he raised his voice—"bring out the plum brandy for our guest, will you?"

The big man did not speak. David Korczak, Jacob's older boy, was twelve. His *bar mitzvah* would have come next summer, had the Germans not come first. Now he nudged his father and said, "Why does the stranger—"

"The guest," his father hissed, also mindful of the proprieties.

"The guest, I mean," David corrected himself, then went on, not quite quietly enough, "Why does the guest have *emes* written across his forehead?"

"What nonsense are you bleating?" Jacob Korczak made as if to cuff his son. But he was just, as well as stern, and looked before he struck. Friedman looked, too. He'd taken the brown patches above the stranger's eyes for a birthmark, about which any comment or even apparent notice would have been rude. Now, though, he saw David was right. The marks did spell out the Hebrew word for truth.

For a moment, he accepted that as a freak of nature. Then he remembered the Talmudic teaching that the word *emes* was the Seal of God, which had also adorned Adam's forehead when he and the world were newly created things.

Since Adam, no man had borne that sign. It was instead the mark of a thing newly created, though not by God: the mark, in short, of the *golem*. Fear all but froze Friedman's heart. There were other terrors than Germans loose in the world—and he had just invited one of them into his house!

A low choking noise from Jacob Korczak said he'd come to the same dreadful realization. Isaac Geller hadn't, but Isaac Geller, while a good man and a good Jew, was not overly burdened with brains.

What to do? What to do? Friedman didn't dare even moan, for fear of angering the undead creature. He wanted to command it to leave, but feared its wrath since he knew he had no authority over it. Besides, having accepted it as a guest, he could not turn it out when it had done no wrong without incurring sin himself.

That left him no choice but to treat the thing as if it were a man like any other. He waved to the table. When it sat, he said, "Will you honor us by leading prayers this evening?"

The *golem* shook its head, pointed to its throat with a massive index finger, shook its head again. *Of course,* Friedman thought: *it can't speak—only true divine creations can do that.* He racked his fear-frozen wits for other bits of lore, but it was as if he were trying to get money from a bank that had failed.

As if with a magic of her own, Emma had set an extra place for the *golem*, shifted her husband's chair to it, and found him an old splintery stool, all without being noticed. Now, red-faced and beaming, she placed a big tray of *latkes* on the table. With her spatula, she filled the *golem*'s plate. Berel poured *slivovitz* into its glass.

Since the *golem* had declined, Isaac Geller led the prayers.

After the final *omayn*, he lifted his snifter of brandy and made the usual toast: "*L'chayim*—to life!"

Friedman was more convinced than ever that his friend had rocks in his head. Of all the things that might enrage a *golem*, he couldn't think of one more likely to infuriate than praise for something it would never have.

But the *golem* only raised its glass along with the rest of the adults. It let the potent plum brandy moisten its lips, but whatever passed them did not lower the level of the *slivovitz* by a hair's breadth. It used its fork to cut a tiny crumb from one *latke*, then put the rest of that potato pancake and all the others back on the platter.

That was too much for Emma. She could extend hospitality to a *golem* with aplomb, but to see the hospitality refused roused her ire. "You're not eating," she said sharply, as if in the one accusation she condemned the creature for crimes uncounted.

The *golem* obediently dipped its head to her, then lifted the scrap of fried potato to its mouth. It chewed but, Friedman saw, did not swallow. *What need has a thing of clay for nourishment?* he asked himself, and found no answer. Politely nodding once more to Emma, the *golem* put both hands on its belly, as if to show it was stuffed to overflowing. She let out a loud, unimpressed sniff but otherwise held her peace.

With the *golem* so abstemious, the *latkes* were enough to feed everyone. Friedman had trouble remembering the last time he'd been so pleasantly full—not since the Germans came, that was certain. He sipped his brandy, savored the heat spreading from his middle. Even that heat, though, was not enough to keep him from wondering when he'd enjoy a fully belly again.

After the last pancake had vanished, Emma started carrying dishes back into the kitchen. She let Yetta Korczak and Bertha Geller help, but when the *golem* started to do likewise, she stopped in her tracks and looked so scandalized that even the undead creature got the message. It sat back down; Berel's chair creaked under its weight.

He didn't let that worry him. He'd had food and drink; now he lit his pipe and blew a happy cloud toward the ceiling. Then, emboldened and perhaps a trifle *shikker* from the *slivovitz*, he turned to the *golem* and said expansively, "What shall we call you, my friend?"

The moment the words were out of his mouth, he felt a fool for forgetting the thing of clay was mute. But it answered him even so: it pointed with one finger to the letter written on its forehead.

"*Emes?*" Friedman said. The *golem* nodded. Friedman raised his own forefinger, something he did only when he'd had a bit to drink. "All right then, Emes, show us some of the truth you are."

"Berel—" Jacob Korczak began. He stopped there, but Friedman could fill in what he'd meant: *Berel, shut up, you damned fool, before you ruin us all.* It was good advice; he wished he could have taken it.

Too late for that—the *golem* was nodding again. Friedman's vision suddenly blurred, or rather doubled strangely. He could still see the room in which he sat, the *golem* next to him, Korczak and Geller across the table, the children back to playing with dreidels.

But set side by side with the familiar, homely scene, he also saw other things, the *golem*'s truth he had so rashly requested. He saw Jews jammed insanely tight into a tiny corner of a great city he somehow knew to be Warsaw. He saw Germans smirking as they clipped Jews' beards, more Germans holding their sides and howling laughter as they dipped other beards into oil and set them ablaze. He saw twelve-year-old girls selling their bodies for half a crust of bread. He saw the starved corpses of others who perhaps had not sold themselves enough, leaning dismally against battered buildings. He saw Jews walk by the corpses without so much as glancing at them, as though they'd grown numb even to death.

As if at the cinema, the scene shifted. He saw a big pit gouged out of the ground. Under German guns, a line of naked people walked up to the edge of the pit. All the men and boys among them were circumcised. The Germans shot them from behind. They tumbled into their ready-made mass grave. The Germans led up another line.

The scene shifted again. He saw a wrought-iron gate, and

above it, in letters of iron, the words ARBEIT MACHT FREI. He saw more naked people, these mostly women and children, slowly walking toward a low, squat building. Signs in Yiddish, Polish, and German said TO THE SHOWERS. He saw endless piles of bodies fed into what looked like enormous bake ovens. He saw black, greasy smoke rise from the stacks above those ovens.

Slowly, slowly, the other seeing faded. He was altogether back in his own warm room in his own little house. But a chill remained, a chill in his heart no fireplace could touch. He looked across the table to his friends. Both men were pale and stunned and looking at him. They'd shared the vision, then.

He looked at the *golem*, hating it. If it had given him the truth, how much more comforting a lie, any lie, would have been! He'd looked into the open grave of his people. What man could do that and then go on as if he'd seen nothing? He hated himself, too, for asking the undead creature into his home.

While he berated himself, simple, practical Isaac Geller said, "If that's how it's going to be, what do we do about it?" Having less imagination than either Friedman or Korczak, he yielded less readily to horror.

"Dear God, what can we do?" Korczak said. But Geller had not asked him; he'd spoken to the *golem*.

That second sight returned, this time blurrily, as if the thing of clay presented not truth but only possibility. In fragmented visions, Friedman saw the Jews of Puck walking down the main street of town, saw them approaching a fishing boat, saw them in the boat with sea all around. The compass showed they were sailing northwest.

Again he was back only at his own table. "That's *meshuggeh*!" he cried. "The Germans would shoot us for breaking curfew. Nobody among us knows how to run a fishing boat, and the boats have almost no fuel anyhow. The fishermen spend more time complaining than they do fishing."

As usual, though, Isaac Geller looked at things differently. He asked the *golem*, "What happens if we don't try, Emes?"

Friedman saw that wrought-iron gate again. He shuddered, though the vision lasted but a split second. Set against what lay beyond that gate, any risk at all seemed worth trying. He found his own question for the *golem*: "You'll help us?"

The undead creature nodded. That was enough to satisfy Friedman. He twisted in his chair, called into the kitchen. "Emma!"

"What is it?" She stood in the doorway, the sleeves of her dress rolled up past her elbows, soapy water dripping from her fingers onto the floor. "What is it that won't wait till I finish washing?"

Our lives, he thought. But that would have taken explanation and argument. He just said, "Get coats for the children and for yourself, too. We're going out."

"What?" Her eyes went wide. "The curfew, the Nazis—"

"I don't care," he said, and her eyes went wider still. He turned to the *golem*. "Show her, too, Emes. She needs to see."

He never figured out precisely what the thing of clay showed his wife, but she gasped and put a hand to her mouth. Without a word, she walked over to the closet and pulled out coats. "Come here this instant, Rachel, Aaron! This instant, do you hear me? We need to dress warmly."

Bertha Korczak and Yetta Geller came out of the kitchen to find out what was going on. Like Emma, they started to protest when they learned they'd be out and about in the night. Then the *golem* looked at each of them in turn, mud-colored eyes somber in his great ugly face. Argument was cut off as abruptly as a chicken's head when the *shochet* wielded his cleaver. Friedman wondered if he could learn that trick himself. But no, it was probably supernatural.

A few minutes later, he stood outside his home. Even wrapped in his coat, he was cold. The *golem* started down the street, toward the docks. The three families of Jews followed. Friedman looked back at the house where he'd lived his whole life. To abandon it suddenly seemed insane. But even more insane were the visions Emes had granted him. Life away from everything he'd known would be strange and hard, but it would be life, for him and his children. Even without the *golem*'s power, he saw again in his mind's eye naked Jews standing at the mouth of their ready-dug grave.

•

The main street was almost eerily quiet. Nothing moved—no cars, no bicycles, no people on foot. The town of Puck might have been cast headlong into the strange space from which the *golem* drew its visions. Berel Friedman shook his head. The Germans had powers of their own, chief among them fear.

Every step he took seemed to echo from the houses, from the solid stone front of the Catholic church that was much the biggest building in town. Every time one of the children coughed or stumbled or complained, he expected a division of panzer troops to burst from an alley, engines bellowing, cannon and machine guns all pointed straight at him and his. But the silence held.

Puck was anything but a big city; even the main street, the one straight street it boasted, was only a couple of hundred meters long. Soon most of the houses were behind the Jews, the dockside fish market straight ahead. Hope rose in Friedman. The *golem*, after all, was a creature of might. No doubt its spell lay on the Germans, lulling them into taking no notice of the families it was spiriting away.

He had no doubt—until the German patrol came out of the market, heading back toward town. Then fear flooded into him, all the more fiercely for having been held at bay. His legs turned to jelly, his bowels to water. He started to gasp out the *Shma yisroayl* so he would not die with the prayer unsaid: "Hear, O Israel, the Lord our God, the Lord is one!"

Even as the harsh cry *"Halt!"* rang in the air, the *golem* ran straight for the Germans. They were not first-quality troops: who would waste such on a fleabag town like Puck? They were not expecting trouble, so their reactions were slower than they might have been. But they were soldiers, and they did carry guns. Before the *golem* reached them, a couple flung Mausers to their shoulders and started shooting.

Amidst screams from women and children, Friedman's head filled with a sudden urgent vision: the *Pilsudski*, Tadeusz Czuma's fishing boat. As usual, it was the one moored farthest north in the little harbor. "This way!" he shouted, and the rest of the Jews followed—incidentally, he thought some time later, taking themselves out of the line of fire.

Muzzle flashes from the Germans' rifles gave them flickering light, like small lightning bolts, as they ran. Bullets slapped into the *golem*, one, two, three. The impacts were shockingly loud. A man would have been down and dead, maybe cut in two, with such wounds in him. But the thing of clay had never been alive, so how could rifle fire kill it?

All the Germans were shouting, in terror now, as their prey refused to fall. Then the *golem* was among them. It might not have been alive, but it was immensely strong. Its great fists smashed ribs, caved in steel helmets and the skulls beneath them. The Germans' shouts turned to screams that shut off one by one.

Friedman leaped from the pier down into the *Pilsudski*, then whirled to catch his wife and children as they sprang after him. Korczak and Geller were doing the same for their families. Faster than he could have imagined, everyone was on board. Only then did he remember he hadn't the faintest idea how to sail the fishing boat.

Isaac Geller was already in the cabin. "Cast off the lines, you two," he called to Friedman and Korczak. Friedman dashed to the bow, Korczak to the stern. By the time they'd obeyed, Geller had the noisy old engine going.

Booted footsteps pounded toward the fishing boat—the last German soldier, running for his life. Behind him came the *golem*, gaining with every enormous stride. The German whirled round in desperation, dropped to one knee, and fired at point-blank range straight into the *golem*'s face.

Maybe he'd intended to hit it between the eyes. Friedman knew even less about matters military than he did about sailing, but he had a vague idea that was what you were supposed to do. If it *was* what the German had in mind, he didn't quite succeed. The muzzle flash showed that his bullet smashed into the *golem*'s forehead just above its left eye.

In so doing, it destroyed the letter *aleph*, the first letter of the word *emes*. *Mes* was also a word in Hebrew; it meant *death*. Just as a man would have, the *golem* ceased when that bullet struck it. But its heavy body smashed into the kneeling German just the same. Friedman heard bones snap, the soldier's last cry abruptly cut off. Two corpses lay unmoving a few meters from the *Pilsudski*.

The racket from the fishing boat's engine got louder. The boat pulled away from the dock. Friedman had hardly ever been on the water despite a lifetime by the sea, and wondered if he'd be seasick. For now, he didn't think so. The motion wasn't that unpleasant; it reminded him of bouncing up and down on the back of a mule.

He went into the cabin to see if he could do anything to help Isaac Geller. Geller didn't seem to need help. Despite his long black coat and big black hat, he looked surprisingly nautical. Maybe it was the cigar he'd stuck in the corner of his mouth.

"I didn't know you could handle a boat," Friedman said.

The cigar twitched. Geller grunted. "I may not be much for *pilpul* about the Talmud, Berel my friend, but give me something with a motor in it and I will make it work."

"This is also a *mitzvah*," Friedman said, adding, "especially now." He looked around the cabin. Once he'd seen it, he couldn't imagine what sort of help he'd thought to give Geller. For all he could make of the instruments, they might have been printed in Chinese. The only thing he recognized was the compass. He studied that for a while, then said hesitantly, "Excuse me, Isaac, but are we not sailing south and east?"

"Yes," Geller said. *"Nu?"*

"In the vision Emes granted us, were we not supposed to go northwest?"

Geller laughed so hard, the cigar jerked up and down in his mouth. "Berel, not even the help of a *golem* will make this boat sail across the dry land of the Hela Peninsula."

"Oh," Friedman said in a very small voice.

"Let me get around the peninsula before I make for Sweden," Geller went on, "not that we have much real chance of getting there."

"What? Why not?"

Geller poked a finger at one of the incomprehensible gauges.

"You see how much fuel we have there. It isn't enough. It isn't nearly enough. God only knows what will happen when it's gone. I'm sure of only one thing: whatever it is, it will be better than what the *golem* showed us."

"Yes," Friedman said. "Oh, yes."

He went out on deck. Emma came rushing up to him. "Will it be all right, Berel?" she demanded fiercely. "Will the children get away from—that?"

He still didn't know what the *golem* had showed her. He didn't want to know; Emes had shown him too much for him to want to find out more. He shook his head, blew out a long sigh. "I just don't know, Emma," he answered, thinking first of the fuel gauge Geller showed him and then of what his friend had just said. "But whatever we find on the sea, how can it be worse?"

His wife nodded. "This is true enough."

Friedman walked over to Jacob Korczak, who was watching the low, flat coast of the Hela Peninsula flow by. Every few kilometers, lights defined the land: though there was a war on, no British or French planes could reach Poland, and as for Russia—Russia had helped Hitler carve up his neighbor. So the lights kept burning.

Korczak might have been reading Friedman's mind: "With the kind of pilot Isaac is liable to be, he'll need all the help he can get."

"He's better than either of us," Friedman answered, to which Korczak replied with a cough. After a moment, Berel went on, "I had thought—I had hoped—the *golem* might save more of our people before it met its fate. For a moment, I had even hoped it might save all our people. For what other purpose could it have been made?"

"I asked myself this very question." By his slightly smug tone, Korczak had come up with an answer, too. "My thinking is this: the *golem* is a power in the world, not so?"

"Indeed," Friedman said, nodding vigorously. "A very great power. This is why I hoped it might accomplish more than freeing us alone—not that I am not grateful to the Lord for preserving us, but what are we among so many?" He had another queasy flash of

memory from the *golem*'s vision. That camp with ARBEIT MACHT
FREI on the gate had been *huge*—and were there more like it?

"The *golem* is a power," Korczak repeated. "But—the Germans, are they not also a power? Ten years ago, who had heard
of that *mamzer* Hitler? And when power meets power, who that
is not a power can say which of them will break?"

Friedman thought it over. "Whether this is *the* answer, Jacob,
I cannot say: *I* am no power, as we both know. But *an* answer you
definitely have, one good enough for mortal men. I will say *kaddish* for Emes on his *yortzeit* each year."

"And I," Korczak agreed. He returned to more immediate matters. "Does Isaac truly know enough to keep from drowning us?"

"I think he may." Friedman hesitated, then told his friend what
he had not mentioned to his wife: "He says we are low on fuel."

"*Oy.*"

Since that one word summed things up as well as anything
Friedman could say, he kept quiet. The *Pilsudski* passed another
light. Emma found some grimy wool blankets. She and the other
mothers wrapped the children in them. Before long, in spite of
the terrifying excitement of the day—maybe even because of
it—the youngsters fell asleep.

Another light, this one higher and brighter than any of the rest.
In its blue-white glare, Friedman saw that the long spit of the Hela
Peninsula ceased. Isaac Geller saw that, too. The fishing boat
heeled in the water as it changed course. *Northwest now,* Friedman thought, and remembered what the *golem* had shown him.

Northwest now, but for how long? He had to know. He went into
the cabin, waited for Geller to notice him—who could say how
complicated steering a boat was? After a while, Geller turned his
head. Feeling as if he were asking a rabbi to explicate a thorny passage of the Talmud, Friedman said, "How do we stand for fuel?"

Geller scowled. "Not very well. I think the gauge is broken.
It's scarcely changed from when we set out."

"That may be good news," Friedman said. He was looking for
good news. "Maybe it lies when it says we have only a little.
Maybe we have a great deal."

"We don't," Geller said flatly. "When I saw the gauge seemed stuck, I put a stick down into the tank to find out how much it held. What the stick says comes near enough to agreeing with what the gauge says."

"Then—" Friedman quavered.

"Yes, then," Geller agreed. "Then we will run out of fuel and the boat will stop. If God is kind, a Swedish ship or a Danish one or even a Russian one will find us and pick us up. If God is less kind, no one will pick us up and we will die. If God is most unkind, a German ship will find us."

"A German ship." Friedman hadn't thought of that. Geller was right—it would be most dreadful to come so close to freedom only to have it snatched away by a ship flying the swastika banner. "Surely God would not permit it."

"After what the *golem* showed us, Berel, who are we to say what God would and would not permit?"

"How can I answer that? How can anyone answer that?" Friedman left the cabin; between them, the rolling of the boat in the open sea and the stink of Geller's cigar were making his stomach churn. So was worry. Back in Puck, running had seemed the only possible thing to do. Now when it was too late, he wondered whether running had been wise.

The last lighthouse faded astern. Friedman cast himself into the hands of God—not that he hadn't been in them all along, but now he abandoned the usual human feeling that he had some control over his own fate. Whatever would happen would happen, and there was nothing he could do about it.

The fishing boat chugged along. After a while, a thick, clammy bank of fog rolled over it. It left damp droplets in the tendrils of Friedman's beard. When he held his hand out at arm's length, he could not see it. Maybe God was stretching His hand over the *Pilsudski*. No German ship would ever find them in this soup. Of course, no Swedish or Danish or Russian ship would, either.

Of course, likeliest of all was that no ship of any nation would come anywhere near. The Baltic Sea all around had seemed incomprehensibly vast, as if the fishing boat were traveling the dark of space between the stars. Somehow the fog intensified the effect rather than diminishing it.

And then, from out of nowhere, felt and heard rather than seen through the mist, a huge shape, vaster than the great fish that had swallowed Jonah, flowed blindly past the bow of the boat. From the cabin came Isaac Geller's startled exclamation: *"Gevalt!"* Friedman had not even the wit for that. He waited, heart in his throat, for the brusque hail that might mean rescue or disaster. No hail came. The big ship sailed away, intent solely on its own concerns.

Friedman said, "That was close."

From out of the fog somewhere close by, Jacob Korczak answered, "That was very close." He called to Geller, "How are we doing for fuel?"

"I'll check," Geller said from out of the pale, milky smudge that marked the cabin's place. After a pause, he went on, "We still have—about what we set out with." He sounded surprised, but far from displeased.

"How could we?" Korczak demanded. "We set out quite a while ago, so surely we've burned some."

"You'd think so, wouldn't you?" Geller said. "I'd think so, too. But the gauge doesn't think so, and the stick doesn't think so, either. The gauge may be mistaken. How the stick could be mistaken, I tell you I do not see."

"It makes no sense," Korczak complained. "Fuel burns, it burns just so fast. When so much time is gone, so is the fuel."

"Tell it to my stick," Geller said. Korczak subsided with a wounded sniff.

Northwest, northwest, northwest . . . Friedman hoped it was northwest, hoped Geller was minding the compass. For all he could tell, the *Pilsudski* might have been sailing in circles. He recognized Emma's footsteps on the deck before she came close enough to be seen. "Berel, are you here?" she called. "Oh, you are here. Good. Look—I found more blankets."

"Thank you." He took one and draped it over his shoulders like a huge prayer shawl. It smelled of wool and stale tobacco and even staler sweat; Friedman's opinion of Tadeusz Czuma's cleanliness, already low, fell another notch. Emma was already swaddled against the chill and fog. He turned to her. "You ought to sleep if you can."

"So should you," she retorted. He nodded; he knew she was right. Neither of them lay down. She moved a step closer to him, lowered her voice. "Berel . . . is it going to be all right? Why is Geller going on about how much fuel we have?" He heard the undercurrent of reproach in her voice: *why didn't you tell me about this?*

He answered the undercurrent, not the question: "I didn't want to worry you."

She amazed him by starting to laugh. "I had a *golem* come into my living room, I ran from the house where I lived since I was married to you and the town where I lived all my life, German soldiers shot at me and I watched them die, and you didn't want to worry me about *fuel*?"

"All right, all right." He started laughing, too; looked at from that direction, it was funny. But his self-conscious chuckles quickly faded. "The trouble with the fuel is, we don't have much."

"We've come this far," Emma said.

"Already it's farther than Geller thought we could."

"If it's already farther, then what does Geller know?" she said, and nodded decisively, as if she'd just won a subtle point of logic. "We'll sail as far as we'll sail, and please God it will be far enough."

"All right, Emma," Friedman repeated. Oddly, her reasoning reassured him. If he was in God's hands, then God would take care of things. And if God would take care of things, then Berel Friedman didn't need to stay awake to watch. He redraped the blanket so it covered all of him. "Maybe I will try and rest."

"This is sensible," Emma agreed. They stretched out side by side on the hard planks of the deck. He took off his hat and gave it to her for a pillow. She shook her head. "I'll ruin it."

"If everything turns out all right, I can get another hat. And if everything does not turn out all right, what difference will a ruined hat make?"

She put it under her head. "Sleep well, Berel."

"And you."

He didn't think he would sleep at all, let alone well. But when his eyes opened, the black mist surrounding the *Pilsudski* had turned gray. His neck, his back, his legs were stiff; everything crackled like breaking ice as he painfully got to his feet.

The children were already awake. They'd adapted to life on the fishing boat faster than their parents; they sat in a circle round a spinning dreidel one of them must have stuffed into a pocket when they fled the house. *"Gimel!"* Friedman's daughter Rachel shouted. She couldn't read, but she knew her Yiddish letters, and they sprang from the Hebrew ones. She knew something else, too: "I win!"

Smiling, Friedman stepped around the game. In the cabin, Isaac Geller still stood at the wheel. His face was as gray as the fog all around him, gray with fatigue. The cigar in his mouth had gone out; Friedman didn't think he'd noticed. But he steered on.

Friedman said, "The fuel hasn't run out, I see."

Geller jerked violently; he'd forgotten everything but the wheel, the compass, and the window that barely showed him the boat's bow. "Oh, it's you, Berel," he said, as if reminding himself. "No, the fuel hasn't run out. Ask God why; I've given up trying to figure it out." He sounded indignant; maybe he held Friedman responsible for the engine's still chugging along, or maybe his friend just made an easier target than the Lord.

Outside in the mist, Rachel Friedman squealed, "Another *gimel*! I win again!"

"If she keeps on like that, she'll end up owning this boat," Friedman said, hoping the feeble joke would help keep Geller alert and ease his burden. He went on, "The little one, she's always been lucky with a dreidel. I remember once when she—"

He stopped. Thinking about dreidels made him think about the letters on them, about what those letters stood for, and about the nature of the miracle they commemorated.

"You remember when she what?" Geller snapped. "Don't just stand there like a cow, with your mouth hanging open. Say something if you're going to talk. Otherwise, go away."

"Isaac, last night was the first night of Chanukah," Friedman said softly.

"Nu?" Geller said: "So what? I take it back. You shouldn't talk if you're going to wander all over creation and confuse me."

"I'm sorry," Friedman said, bowing his head. "I just thought to wonder whether God, who made one day's worth of pure oil burn for eight days in the Temple, might not let a tiny bit of fuel take a few of His people farther than anyone would guess. You said to ask God why it hadn't run out. I think I just have. On that night, with what happened that night . . . what do you think, Isaac my friend?"

Geller slowly turned his head. Now his mouth fell open. The dead cigar fell out. He nodded, once, twice, his eyes wide. Then he gave his attention back to the *Pilsudski*.

Less than a minute later, the fishing boat came out of the fog bank. All at once, the winter sun sparkled off the ocean, cold and bright and clear. Ahead—not far—lay the Swedish coast. The engine kept running.

Honeymouth

I've written a fair number of werewolf stories. I've written a fair number of vampire stories. Doing strange things while staying within the conventions and traditions of such tales is a challenge for a writer; it makes one think left-handed, so to speak. "Honeymouth" is the only unicorn story I've ever done. I take a certain modest pride in noting that it's one of the raunchier unicorn stories ever written.

The charge of unicorn cavalry would be the most deadly tool of war, were it not for one small difficulty.

The Emperors of the East try to get round the problem by mounting eunuchs on their special steeds, but western knights reckon this company lacking in courage. "No balls," they say, and laugh at their own wit.

Yet the westerners' efforts to use unicorns to their best advantage are makeshifts, too. The Duke of Hispalis used to maintain a Stripling Squadron, a hundred youths ages fourteen to seventeen. They did well enough, but lacked the experience (and often the bulk) that would have ensured success against seasoned troops on more ordinary mounts. And, youths fourteen to seventeen being what they are, the Duke often found the unicorns would not let half of them ride when they set out on campaign.

For a while the Kings of Gothia raised an Amazon Corps, but it suffered from the same problems of size and inexperience as the Stripling Squadron. Further, should anyone think women immune to the calls of the flesh, let him examine the rosters of the Amazon Corps year by year.

In every generation arose one or two warrior-saints who genuinely were immune to sensual allure, but unicorns bear such more gladly than princes. Armored in righteousness, they obeyed only their own consciences, and so hardly made pleasant company for the usual run of ruler. They also had the unfortunate habit of telling the truth as they saw it.

That unfortunate habit was one of the two things they had in common with Coradin the mercenary, called Honeymouth. Coradin was a warrior, but no saint he. His every third word was an oath, foul enough to account for his ironic nickname. When he was not swearing, he was mostly drinking. He betrayed whomever he pleased, whenever he pleased. Like too many such rogues, he had more than his share of luck with women. They fell all over him, and he did nothing to discourage them.

This Coradin rode a unicorn.

"Are you sure it's Coradin, my lord?" Milo the seneschal of the County of Iveria asked without much hope when his suzerain summoned him to the audience hall one fine spring morning. He was a big, dark, stolid man with wide shoulders and a slow walk.

Count Rupen, by contrast, was short, lean, handsome in a foxy way, and red-headed to boot. He also had a waspish temper. He scorched Milo with a glare as he paced quickly up and down the hall. "Who tethers a unicorn outside a whorehouse?"

"Coradin," Milo said. His head started to ache. Sometimes he wished his father had been a serf; he would have inherited a simpler calling. He suspected this was going to be one of those times.

"Huzzah," Rupen said sourly. He rubbed his little chinbeard. After a bit, he went on in a musing tone, "Milo, I have a task for you."

Milo had a bad feeling he knew what the task was going to be. "Sir?" was all he said. He might have been wrong.

He wasn't. "Get yourself down to that brothel and find out how this cursed Coradin can wench and wench without a thought in the world past his prick and keep a unicorn, where everyone else loses the beast with his cherry. If I can learn his secret and pass it to my knights, then let my neighbors beware." Rupen's eyes were foxy, too, the exact shade of amber; they had a greedy gleam in them, like a fox's when he spots a henroost.

Knowing it would not help, Milo protested, "People have been trying to learn Coradin's secret for a dozen years now. No one has yet. What makes you think I'll have better luck than the wisest— to say nothing of the sneakiest—men in the western realms?"

"Because I told you to," Rupen snapped. "Do whatever you have to. Hire him into the army, bribe him—pay him as much as he asks."

Milo's bushy eyebrows rose. Rupen was serious—he squeezed every piece of bronze till the copper and tin separated. The seneschal, however, was unhappily aware that richer treasuries than Iveria's had opened for Coradin. With characteristic skill, the mercenary had collected from several of them—and kept his secret.

Milo sighed. "Which crib is he at?"

"The Jadeflower."

"Can't fault his taste." The Jadeflower was the best—and the most expensive—joyhouse Iveria boasted. Milo sighed again. "All right, I'll see what I can do."

"Just do what I told you," Rupen said, but he was talking to the seneschal's back.

"Make way! Make way, there!" Milo elbowed through the milling crowd in front of the Jadeflower.

"Watch it!" someone snarled, whirling angrily. When he saw who was behind him, his face cleared. "Oops—sorry, sir." The fellow raised his voice. "It's the lord count's seneschal."

That helped clear the path; if not widely loved, Milo had earned solid respect in Iveria. He squeezed up to the Jadeflower's hitching rail and gaped with the rest of the throng at the unicorn.

He had seen the magnificent beasts only two or three times;

Rupen did not keep a squadron of them. To find one tied in front of a whorehouse was like finding a nightingale singing from a dungheap.

Snow, milk: those were the comparisons that sprang into the seneschal's mind. He gave them up. The unicorn was past comparison. It was simply *white*. It gazed at Milo with absolute unconcern for its surroundings. The man it had chosen was somewhere near, and that sufficed.

The crowd whooped when Milo, tearing himself away from the unicorn's perfection, strode up the broad marble steps toward the Jadeflower's door. Someone shouted, "Rupen's bumped his pay!"

Several people made it into a chant: "Bump, bump, bump!" Milo felt his ears grow hot. He was happily married, and not given to straying.

The door swung open on silent hinges. When it closed behind the seneschal, the ribald noise outside vanished as if it had never been. Standing in the vestibule waiting for him was the Jadeflower's proprietress. Her name, he knew, was Lavria. She was plump now, and her hair silver, but it was easy to see she had been a famous beauty not so many years ago.

"What an unexpected pleasure," she said with the slightest hint of malice. She knew he was faithful, then.

He covered his discomfiture with brusqueness. "Where's Coradin?"

"Why, upstairs, of course." Lavria's manner changed subtly; this was business, too, but of a different sort. "Come into the parlor and wait, if you care to. He's paid enough not to be disturbed." She held the brocaded curtain wide in invitation.

The Jadeflower's reception chamber lived up to the place's reputation. Panes of gold- and rose-colored glass gave the entering light the texture of thick velvet. The paintings on the wall were erotic without being blatant. A lutanist better than the one at Rupen's castle sat on a tall stool in one corner of the room, playing softly. Even the bouncer bathed. And when Milo picked a chair, he thought the soft goosedown cushions would swallow him up.

A few seconds later, a servant appeared at his elbow with a

goblet of wine. The goblet was cut crystal. At the first taste of the wine, his eyebrows shot up. "Rincian!" Maybe every other year, a handful of bottles of the precious stuff reached Iveria.

The banister of the stairway that led up to the girls' rooms had to be polished brass, he decided. It could not be gold . . . could it? That he wondered showed how much the place intimidated him.

A door closed upstairs, with a slam that rattled the stained-glass windows. Someone howled out a snatch of bawdy song in an off-key bass voice. That sounded like the kind of racket Coradin might make. Milo mouthed the name, looked a question to the lute player, who nodded. The seneschal rose expectantly.

Coradin appeared at the head of the stairs, a blond bear of a man, even bigger than Milo, and at the moment mightily rumpled. The seneschal hardly gave him a glance—he was not alone up there. No fewer than three of Lavria's choicest girls were seeing him off. Transparent silk that displayed rather than hid the softly rounded flesh beneath held Milo transfixed. He was happily married, but a long way from blind.

Three—! And every one of them gazed at Coradin with a satisfied languor that was a million miles from the hard, bright professional smiles of their trade.

Milo ground his teeth. He had expected to dislike the mercenary, but not to hate him on sight.

Coradin kissed all the girls thoroughly, gave them a pat or two, and started down the stairs. He noticed Milo staring up at him. "Do you want something with me, you vinegar-faced bastard? Gods, in a place like this how can a man look like he's just had a live crab pounded up his arse?"

Milo's first impulse was to find out how good Coradin was with the sword that swung at his belt—but then he would have to explain to Rupen. That did not bear thinking about.

Instead, he drew himself up to his full height. Voice icily formal, he proclaimed, "Coradin Honeymouth"—he could not resist that much of a gibe; the girls at the top of the stair giggled—"I am charged by Rupen, lord of Iveria, to offer you employment with the Count's army at a rate to be set by mutual agreement, and further to offer you a reward of your own choosing for the secret of your ability to ride the unicorn currently outside this establishment."

Coradin was close enough for the seneschal to smell the wine on his breath, but he turned alert even so. "Another snoopy bugger, eh?" Mischief kindled in his eyes, which were almost as blue as his mount's. "I tell you what—we can dicker later, but I'll solve the mystery for you now, for free."

Milo waited, sure it was not going to be that easy. "What's this?" Coradin said in mock surprise. "You don't want the answer after all?"

"Tell me," the seneschal said wearily. As well have the foolishness over with, he thought, so we can get down to serious haggling.

"All right, then, though you don't sound much interested." Coradin struck a pose. "You know not what bribes I have declined for this shameful secret out of my darkest past." His voice sank to a dramatic whisper. "You see, I'm a virgin."

He laughed so hard he almost fell over the banister. Above him, the courtesans clung to each other while tears of mirth ran down their cheeks. The lutanist missed a note.

Milo swore in disgust. "If you're quite through, let's head for my lord Rupen's hall. I told him he was giving me a sleeveless errand, but he still wants you to fight for him."

"So you can keep prying, of course," Coradin said.

Milo looked at him. "Of course."

"Maybe he is a virgin," the seneschal said a couple of weeks later. "He's never left any byblows behind that I've been able to track down."

Count Rupen stared at him as if he were an idiot. "By the gods, it's not from lack of effort. There's not a tavern wench in town hasn't had her skirts rucked up or her bodice torn. He's not shy about getting 'em alone, either. And the worst part is, they love it. Honeymouth, Honeymouth, Honeymouth—it's all you hear in the bloody town these days." That infuriated Rupen as much as it had Milo; the count snarled every time he saw Coradin riding through the streets on his unicorn.

"He'd best be good at more than friking, if he's to earn what you're giving him."

Rupen snarled all over again. Coradin was profane and drunken, but drunk or sober he knew to the half-copper what his unique services were worth. "Pay what I ask or go piss yourself," he'd said. "It doesn't matter a fart to me. If you don't, plenty of others will." Rupen had paid.

The count brought himself back to the business at hand. "That's why you're going along, to make sure he earns it and doesn't decide to pick old Gui's side instead." Rupen and Gui had been quarreling about their border for years. With Coradin available, the count of Iveria had chosen direct action.

As Rupen's war party rode south, Milo marveled anew at the unicorn. It paced the knights' brawny horses with effortless ease. The seneschal was sure it could have left them in the dust as easily, though Coradin was as heavily accoutered as any of the warriors.

Milo soon saw the mercenary was in his element on campaign. Coradin swapped rough jokes with Rupen's troopers, and howled laughter at the few he hadn't heard. When they camped that night, he produced a lute from his saddlebag and led the men in a series of songs that started foul and ended fouler. His playing wasn't up to the standard of the lutanist at the Jadeflower, but he was far from bad, and his big bass voice covered a lot of fluffs. The knights took to him without reservation. Milo kept his own counsel.

Somehow Gui had heard Rupen was about to have a go at the valley they both claimed. Archers shot at the war party from ambush as it splashed through the little creek that, Gui claimed, marked the rightful boundary. They hit two horses and a man. Arrows flew all around Coradin, but, with what Milo was coming to think of as his customary luck, he escaped unscathed.

Lances couched, the knights thundered into the brush after the bowmen. They flushed three snipers and rode them down. That must have been the lot, for the shooting stopped. But Rupen's warriors had little chance to rejoice. Coming from the other side of the valley was a band of knights at least as big as theirs, all wearing Gui's dark green surcoats.

Milo quickly re-formed his own troop. They spurred toward

the foe. Out of the corner of his eye the seneschal saw Coradin dart ahead of the battle line, but he had no time to spare for the mercenary. All his attention was on one knight in the line rumbling at them, a knight whose gleaming lancehead pointed straight at his chest. He brought his own lance down.

They met with a crash like an accident in a smithy. The enemy knight's lance shivered against Milo's shield. His own stroke was better aimed. Gui's man flew over his horse's tail and thudded to the ground. He lay there, out cold.

The first impact between the two lines expended the momentum of their charge. The fight became a wild melee, knights on both sides hacking away at one another with swords and warhammers and swinging broken lances club-fashion. Unhorsed men, those who could, clambered to their feet and did their best to help their comrades. The ones who could not rise were soon trampled under the iron-shod hooves of the knights' war-horses.

In the melee, Coradin truly came into his own. He slid away from the blows of Gui's men as if he were made of shadow, and struck his own from places where he had no right to be. Foes tumbled from their mounts like ninepins. The unicorn was so much faster and more agile than the knights' snorting chargers that they might as well have been riding oxen.

But the unicorn was not faster than a flung stone. One of Gui's unhorsed men hurled a fist-sized rock at Coradin from behind. It caught the mercenary just below his helmet, on his chainmail neckguard. Stunned, he crashed to the ground, sword flying from nerveless fingers.

The unicorn screamed, a high, keening sound like a woman in pain. The anguished cry was all but drowned by the triumphant roar from Gui's knights. Three of them closed in to finish Coradin. The unicorn attacked furiously, but not even its speed and gleaming horn could hold off three knights for long.

Milo was charging to the mercenary's rescue before he wondered why. His instinct, or so he would have thought, would have been to say good riddance to Coradin. But there was the matter of Rupen's temper, and something more. A thoroughly stubborn man, he was still working away at the puzzle Coradin posed, and could hardly expect to solve it with him killed.

The seneschal's sword crunched into a hauberk. The iron rings kept the blade from his opponent's flesh, but the fellow grimaced and went white all the same; the force of the blow was enough to break ribs. Gui's knight wheeled his horse and fled. The unicorn routed a second enemy, goring him in the thigh and his mount in the flank. Wild with pain, the horse bucketed away, out of the fight.

But the third knight was on Coradin, who groggily tried to rise. He lurched away from a swordstroke that would have taken his head; luckily, Gui's trooper had shattered his lance, or he would have pinned the mercenary to the ground like a bug. Then Milo and the unicorn attacked the knight together. The fellow was a good swordsman. He matched Milo blow for blow. But the added threat of the unicorn distracted him. Milo felt the jar all the way to his shoulder as his sword made a bloody mask of his opponent's face. Gui's knight died before his feet slid from the stirrups.

That was enough to send his comrades, already wavering, into headlong retreat. Rupen's men chased them a little way, then let them go. Milo turned back to see how Coradin was. The unicorn was anxiously nuzzling its master, who did not seem badly hurt. "The father and mother of all headaches, but I'll live," he told the seneschal. He watched Gui's warriors disappear. "We won, eh? Good. Now to serious business—where do we celebrate?"

The disputed valley held a small village: a few houses, a smithy, a mill, a three-story tavern that was much the most impressive structure there. The villagers gave Rupen's troops a warm welcome—for a while, at least, they would only pay taxes to one overlord, not two. Coradin's unicorn didn't hurt, either. No one remembered the last time the village had seen such a beast. Children shyly stroked it; their parents wished they could.

The tavern served bad wine and surprisingly good ale. The knights filled the taproom to overflowing. A good half of them sat outside on the steps or in the street, which had only a little less grass in it than the meadow where the cows grazed back of the village.

Milo climbed to the two little attic rooms to see if he could spot Gui's men—and to make sure they were not trying to return stealthily and take revenge on his troopers while they roistered. A long way away, the setting sun glinted from chainmail. Trimming fingernails he had broken in the fighting, Milo grunted in satisfaction. He took a long pull at the jack of ale beside him, went downstairs again. The steps seemed to wobble under his feet: it was not the first jack he'd had.

Down below, Rupen's followers were giving Coradin his due. Not even Milo begrudged him that; his work with the unicorn had done a lot to beat Gui's warriors. The knights bought him round after round, and cheered when he made what was obviously going to be a successful play for the tavern's prettiest serving girl.

As the evening wore along, some of the knights who had been drinking hard fell asleep in their chairs. Others stretched out on bedrolls outside. Milo thought he would join them. On a fine mild night like this, sleeping indoors held no appeal for him.

He broke another nail, this one on the buckle of the belt that held his bedroll closed. He reached down to his belt for his dagger to pare it, and discovered that the little scabbard was empty. He could have borrowed anyone else's, but by then his ale-soaked wits had room for only one thought at a time: nothing would do but his own. He wearily climbed the stairs to the attic again, and fuzzily wondered why the job seemed so much harder than it had the last time.

He had forgotten to bring along a candle, and had also forgotten which room he'd been in. Searching on hands and knees, at last he found the dagger. "There!" he said, and carefully trimmed the broken nail. He started to get up, but rolled over and fell asleep instead.

The noise of someone shutting the door to the other attic room did not wake him, but Coradin's deep voice did. It pierced the thin wall as if that were made of gauze: "Here we are, my pretty, all the privacy we need—"

Other noises followed, rustlings and wrestlings and bumps and thumps and squeals of delight. Milo made a noise of his own, a groan; his head was already beginning to pound. The pair in the other room ignored it.

The amatory racket went on and on. Milo had not intended to listen, did not want to listen, but had little choice but to listen. After a while he sat bolt upright (sending a spear of pain through his skull) and exclaimed, "So that's it!" Being a cautious sort, he added, "I think."

Exclamation and addition passed unnoticed on the far side of the wall. The seneschal did not care. He did not think Rupen could use the answer, but he didn't care about that, either. He had it. Racket or no, he lay down and went back to sleep.

Milo woke the next morning feeling exactly like death. When he went downstairs for hot porridge, he found Coradin already there, looking much less crapulent than he should have. Even so, the seneschal gazed at him with something approaching benevolence.

Coradin noticed. "What's *your* problem?" he demanded.

"None at all, except for too much ale last night. I own I could use some fresh air, though. Shall we wander outside?"

"Mm." The mercenary packed a world of suspicion into a grunt. He lifted his tankard, tossed down what was left in it. "Why not?"

The unicorn gave a happy whicker as its master came out of the tavern. He fed it half a dried apple. It licked his fingers, looking for more. "Later," he chuckled. The beast's feelings mattered much more to him than Milo's did.

Coradin and the seneschal wandered out of the village and down a twisting lane. After a minute, Coradin said, "This is charming and all, but piss or get off the pot."

So much for benevolence, Milo thought. He came back bluntly, "I have your precious secret."

The mercenary laughed in his face. "If I got a goldpiece for every time I've heard that, I'd be too rich to fight. What's *your* version?"

"Just what you told me at the Jadeflower: you're a virgin—in a manner of speaking, anyway."

Coradin was still laughing. "Go ask Vylla back there—she'll sing you a different tune."

"I don't need to ask her. Truly I hadn't intended to spy that way, but you weren't as private as you thought last night." He told the mercenary what he'd heard, and what it meant. From the way Coradin scowled, he knew he had it right. "One way or another, that's all you do, eh?"

"Yes, curse you." Coradin turned purple, because the seneschal had started to laugh. "What's so funny, you beetle-headed blackguard?"

A little vindictiveness went a long way with Milo. "Sorry," he said. "It just now hit me."

"What did?" Coradin looked as if he wanted to hit Milo himself.

"Now I know why they really call you Honeymouth."

Myth Manners' Guide to Greek Missology #1: Andromeda and Perseus

This one turns a well-known Greek myth upside down, backwards, and inside out. Proving I have no shame whatsoever, I've read it aloud several times at science-fiction conventions. The same line, toward the end, always gets the biggest laugh. It's not the line *I* thought was the funniest. Only goes to show an author doesn't always know quite what he's doing.

Andromeda was feeling the strain. "Why *me?*" she demanded. She'd figured Zeus wanted something from her when he invited her up to good old Mount Olympus for the weekend, but she'd thought it would be something else. She'd been ready to play along, too—how did you go about saying no to the king of the gods? You didn't, not unless you were looking for a role in a tragedy. But . . . this?

"Why you?" Zeus eyed her as if he'd had something else in mind, too. But then he looked over at Hera, his wife, and got back to the business at hand. "Because you're the right man— uh, the right person—for the job."

"Yeah, right," Andromeda said. "Don't you think you'd do better having a man go out and fight the Gorgons? Isn't that what men are for?—fighting, I mean." She knew what else men were for, but she didn't want to mention that to Zeus, not with Hera listening.

And Hera *was* listening. She said, "Men are useless—for fighting the Gorgons, I mean." She sounded as if she meant a lot of other things, too. She was looking straight at Zeus.

No matter how she sounded, the king of the gods dipped his head in agreement. "My wife's right." By the sour look on his face, that sentence didn't pass his lips every eternity. "The three Gorgons are fearsome foes. Whenever a man spies Cindy, Claudia, or Tyra, be it only for an instant, he turns to stone."

"*Part* of him turns to stone, anyway," Hera said acidly.

"And, so, you not being a man, you being a woman—" Zeus went on.

"Wait a minute. Wait just a linen-picking minute," Andromeda broke in. "You're not a man, either, or not exactly a man. You're a god. Why don't you go and take care of these Gorgons with the funny names your own self?"

Zeus coughed, then brightened. "Well, my dear, since you put it that way, maybe I ought to—"

"Not on your immortal life, Bubba," Hera said. "You lay a hand on those hussies and you're mythology."

"You see how it is," Zeus said to Andromeda. "My wife doesn't understand me at all."

Getting in the middle of an argument between god and goddess didn't strike Andromeda as Phi Beta Kappa—or any other three letters of the Greek alphabet, either. Telling Zeus to find himself another boy—or girl—wouldn't be the brightest thing since Phoebus Apollo, either. With a sigh, she said, "Okay. You've got me." Zeus' eyes lit up. Hera planted an elbow in his divine ribs. Hastily, Andromeda went on, "Now what do I have to do?"

"Here you are, my dear." From behind his gold-and-ivory throne, Zeus produced a sword belt. He was about to buckle it on Andromeda—and probably let his fingers do a little extra walking while he was taking care of that—when Hera let out a sudden sharp cough. Sulkily, the king of the gods handed Andromeda the belt and let her put it on herself.

From behind her throne, Hera pulled out a brightly polished shield. "Here," she said. "You may find this more useful against Cindy, Claudia, and Tyra than any blade. Phallic symbols, for some reason or other, don't much frighten them."

"Hey, sometimes a sword is just a sword," Zeus protested.

"And sometimes it's *not*, Mr. Swan, Mr. Shower-of-Gold, Mr.

Bull—plenty of bull for all the girls from here to Nineveh, and I'm damned Tyred of it," Hera said. Zeus fumed. Hera turned back to Andromeda. "If you look in the shield, you'll get some idea of what I mean."

"Is it safe?" Andromeda asked. As Zeus had, Hera dipped her head. Her divine husband was still sulking, and didn't answer one way or the other. Andromeda cautiously looked. "I can see myself!" she exclaimed—not a claim she was likely to be able to make after washing earthenware plates, no matter the well from which the house slaves brought back the dishwashing liquid. A moment later, her hands flew to her hair. "Eeuw! I'm not so sure I want to."

"It isn't you, dearie—it's the magic in the shield," Hera said, not unkindly. "If you really looked like that, loverboy here wouldn't be interested in feeling your pain . . . or anything else he could get his hands on." She gave Zeus a cold and speculative stare. "At least, I don't *think* he would. He's not always fussy."

A thunderbolt appeared in Zeus' right hand. He tossed it up and down, hefting it and eyeing Hera. "Some of them—most of them, even—keep their mouths shut except when I want them to be open," he said meaningfully.

Hera stood up to her full height, which was whatever she chose to make it. Andromeda didn't quite come up to the goddess's dimpled knee. "Well, I'd better be going," she said hastily. If Zeus and Hera started at it hammer and tongs, they might not even notice charbroiling a more or less innocent mortal bystander by mistake.

Just finding Cindy, Claudia, and Tyra didn't prove easy. Minor gods and goddesses weren't allowed to set up shop on Olympus; they lowered surreal-estate values. Andromeda had to go through almost all of Midas' Golden Pages before getting so much as a clue about where she ought to be looking.

Even then, she was puzzled. "Why on earth—or off it, for that matter—would they hang around with a no-account Roman goddess?" she asked.

"What, you think I hear everything?" Midas' long, hairy, donkeyish ears twitched. "And why should I give a Phryg if I do hear things?" His ears twitched again, this time, Andromeda judged, in contempt. "You know about the Greek goddess of victory, don't you?"

"Oh, everybody knows about *her*." Andromeda sounded scornful, too. Since the Greeks had pretty much stopped winning victories, the goddess formerly in charge of them had gone into the running-shoe business, presumably to mitigate the agony of defeat on de feet. Nike had done a gangbanger business, too, till wing-footed Hermes hit her with a copyright-infringement suit that showed every sign of being as eternal as the gods.

"So there you are, then," Midas said. "I don't know what Victoria's secret is, and I don't give a darn."

"That's my shortstop," Andromeda said absently, and let out a long, heartfelt sigh. "I'll just have to go and find out for myself, won't I?"

Thinking of Hermes and his winged sandals gave her an idea. Back to the high-rent district of Mount Olympus she went. The god raised his eyebrows. He had a winged cap, too, one that fluttered off his head in surprise. "You want *my* shoes?" he said.

"I can't very well walk across the Adriatic," Andromeda said.

"No, that's a different myth altogether," Hermes agreed.

"And then up to Rome, to see if the gods are in," Andromeda went on.

"They won't be, not when the mercury rises," Hermes said. "They'll be out in the country, or else at the beach. Pompeii is very pretty this time of year."

"Such a *lovely* view of the volcano," Andromeda murmured. She cast Hermes a melting look. "May I *please* borrow your sandals?"

"Oh, all right," he said crossly. "The story would bog down if I told you no at this point."

"You'd better not be reading ahead," Andromeda warned him. Hermes just snickered. Gods had more powers than mortals, and that was all there was to it. When Andromeda put on the winged sandals and hopped into the air, she stayed up. "Gotta be the shoes," she said.

"Oh, it is," Hermes assured her. "Have fun in Italy."

As she started to fly away, Andromeda called back, "Do you know what Victoria's secret is?"

The god dipped his head to show he did. "Good camera angles," he replied.

Good camera angles. A quiet hostel. A nice view of the beach. And, dammit, a lovely view of the volcano, too. Vesuvius *was* picturesque. And so were Cindy, Claudia, and Tyra, dressed in lacy, colorful, overpriced wisps of not very much. As soon as Andromeda set eyes on them, she started hoping the mountain would blow up and bury those three in lava. Molten lava. Red-hot molten lava. The rest of Pompeii? So what? Herculaneum? So what? Naples, up the coast? Who needed it, really?

But Vesuvius stayed quiet. Of course it did. Hephaestus or Vulcan or whatever name he checked into motels with locally was probably up at the top of the spectacular cone, peering down, leering down, at some other spectacular cones. "Men," Andromeda muttered. No wonder they'd given her this job. And they wouldn't thank her for it once she did it, either.

As Andromeda flew down toward the Gorgons with the spectacularly un-Hellenic names, Victoria flew up to meet her, saying, "Whoever you are, go away. We're just about to shoot."

Shooting struck Andromeda as altogether too good for them. "Some victory you're the goddess of," she sneered, "unless you mean the one in *Lysistrata*."

"You're just jealous because you can't cut the liquamen, sweetheart," Victoria retorted.

Andromeda smiled a hemlock-filled smile. "Doesn't matter whether I am or not," she answered. "I'm on assignment from Zeus and Hera, so you can go take a flying leap at Selene."

"Uppity mortal! You can't talk to me like that." Victoria drew back a suddenly very brawny right arm for a haymaker that would have knocked the feathers right off of Hermes' sandals.

"Oh, yes, I can," Andromeda said, and held up the shield Hera had given her.

She didn't know whether it could have done a decent job of stopping the goddess's fist. That didn't matter. Victoria took one brief look at her reflection and cried, *"Vae! Malae comae! Vae!"* She fled so fast, she might have gone into business with her Greek cousin Nike.

A grim smile on her face, Andromeda descended on Cindy, Claudia, and Tyra. They were lined up on the beach like three tenpins—*except not so heavy in the bottom,* Andromeda thought resentfully. Had they been lined up any better, she'd have bet she could've looked into the left ear of the one on the left and seen out the right ear of the one on the right.

They turned on her in unison when she alighted on the sand. "Ooh, I like those sandals," one of them crooned fiercely. "Gucci? Louis Vuitton?"

"No, Hermes," Andromeda answered. She fought panic as they advanced on her, swaying with menace—or something.

"I wonder what she's doing here," one of the Gorgons said. She waved at the gorgeous scenery, of which she and her comrades were the most gorgeous parts. "I mean, she's so plain."

"Mousy," agreed another.

"Nondescript. Utterly nondescript," said the third, proving she did have room in her head for a three-syllable word: two of them, even.

And the words flayed like fire. Cindy, Claudia, and Tyra weren't even contemptuous. It was as if Andromeda didn't rate contempt. That was their power; just by existing, they made everyone around them feel inadequate. *Zeus wanted me,* Andromeda thought, trying to stay strong. But what did that prove? Zeus wanted anything that moved, and, if it didn't move, he'd give it an experimental shake.

Andromeda felt like curling up on the beach and dying right there. If she put the shield up over her, maybe it would keep her from hearing any more of the Gorgons' cruel words. The shield . . . !

With a fierce cry of her own, Andromeda held it up to them. Instead of continuing their sinuous advance, they fell back with cries of horror. Peering down over the edge of the shield, Andromeda got a quick glimpse of their reflections. The shield had given her and Victoria bad hair. It was far more pitiless to Cindy, Claudia, and Tyra, perhaps because they had farther to fall from the heights of *haute couture*. Whatever the reason, the three Gorgons' hair might as well have turned to snakes once the shield had its way with them.

"Plain," Andromeda murmured. "Mousy. Nondescript. Utterly nondescript."

How the Gorgons howled! They fell to their knees in the sand and bowed their heads, trying to drive out those images of imperfection.

Still holding the shield on high, Andromeda drew her sword. She could have taken their heads at a stroke, but something stayed her hand. It wasn't quite mercy: more the reflection that they'd probably already given a good deal of head to get where they were.

Roughly, she said, "Stay away from Olympus from now on, if you know what's good for you. You ever come near there again, worse'll be waiting for you." She didn't know if that was true, but it would be if Hera could make it so.

"But where shall we go?" one of them asked in a small, broken voice. "What shall we do?"

"Try *Sports Illustrated*," Andromeda suggested, "though gods only know what sport you'd be illustrating."

"Been there," one said. Andromeda had no idea which was which, and didn't care to find out. The other two chorused, "Done that."

"Find something else, then," Andromeda said impatiently. "I don't care what, as long as it's not in Zeus' back yard." *And mine,* she thought. Thinking that, she started to turn the terrible shield on them again and added, "Or else."

Cindy, Claudia, and Tyra cringed. If they weren't convinced now, they never would be, Andromeda judged. She jumped into the air and flew off. That way, she didn't have to look at them any more, didn't have to be reminded that they didn't really look the way Hera's shield made them seem to. Plain. Mousy. Nondescript. Utterly nondescript. Her hand went to the hilt of the sword. *Maybe I should have done a little slaughtering after all.* But she kept flying.

She took the scenic route home—after all, when would she be able to talk Hermes out of his sandals again? She saw Scylla and Charybdis, there by the toe of the Italian boot, and they were as horrible as advertised. She flew over the Pyramids of Egypt. Next door, the Sphinx tried his riddle on her. "Oh, everybody knows *that* one," Andromeda said, and listened to him gnash his stone teeth.

She admired the lighthouse at Alexandria. It would be very impressive when they got around to building it—when there was an Alexandria. Then she started north across the wine-dark sea toward Greece.

When she got to the coast near Argos, she saw a naked man chained to the rocks just above the waves. He was a lot more interesting than anything else she'd seen for a while—and the closer she got, the more interesting he looked. By the time she was hovering a few feet in front of him, he looked mighty damn fine indeed, you betcha. "I know it's the obvious question," she said, "but what are you doing here?"

"Waiting to be eaten," he answered.

"Listen, garbagemouth, has it occurred to you that if I slap you silly, you can't do thing one about it?" Andromeda said indignantly. "Has it?"

"No, by a sea serpent," he explained.

"Oh. Well, no accounting for taste, I suppose," she said, thinking of Pasiphaë and the bull. Then she realized he meant it literally. "How did that happen?" Another obvious question. "And who are you, anyway?"

"I'm Perseus," he said. "My grandfather, Acrisius, is King of Argos. There's a prophecy that if my mother had a son, he'd end up killing Gramps. So Mom was grounded for life, but Zeus visited her in a shower of gold, and here I am."

"And on display, too," Andromeda remarked. Zeus had been catching Hades from Hera ever since, too—Andromeda remembered the snide *Mr. Shower-of-Gold*. But that was neither here nor there, and Perseus was definitely here. "The sea serpent will take your granddad off the hook for doing you in?"

"You got it," Perseus agreed.

"Ah . . . what about the chains? Doesn't he think those might have something to do with him?"

Perseus shrugged. Andromeda admired pecs and abs. The chains clanked. "He's not *real* long on ethics, Acrisius isn't."

"If you get loose, you'll do your best to make the prophecy come true?" Andromeda asked.

Another shrug. More clanks. More admiration from Andromeda. Perseus said, "Well, I've sure got a motive now, and I didn't before. But I'm not in a hurry about it. Omens have a way of working out, you know? I mean, would you be here to set me free if I weren't fated to do Gramps in one of these years?"

"I'm not here to set you free," Andromeda said. "I just stopped by for a minute to enjoy the scenery, and—"

Perseus pointed. He didn't do it very well—he was chained, after all—but he managed. "Excuse me for interrupting," he said, "but the sea serpent's coming."

Andromeda whirled in the air. "Eep!" she said. Perseus hadn't been wrong. The monster was huge. It was fast. It was hideous. It was wet (which made sense, it being a sea serpent). It had an alarmingly big mouth full of a frighteningly large number of terrifyingly sharp teeth. Andromeda could have rearranged those adverbs any which way and they still would have added up to the same thing. Trouble. Big trouble.

She could also have flown away. She glanced back at Perseus and shook her head. That would have been a waste of a great natural resource. And, no matter what Hera had to say about it, Zeus wouldn't be overjoyed if she left his bastard son out for sea-serpent fast food.

She drew her sword—Zeus' sword—and flew toward the monster. One way or another, this story was going to get some blood in it. Or maybe not. She held up Hera's mirrored shield, right in the sea serpent's face. It might figure it was having a bad scales day and go away.

But no such luck. Maybe the shield didn't work because the sea serpent had no hair. Maybe the serpent had already maxed out its ugly account. Or maybe it was too stupid to notice anything had changed. Andromeda shook her head again. If Cindy, Claudia, and Tyra had noticed, the sea serpent would have to.

No help for it. Sometimes, as Zeus had said, a sword was just a sword. Andromeda swung this one. It turned out to cut sea serpent a lot better than her very best kitchen knife cut roast goose. Chunk after reptilian chunk fell away from the main mass of the monster. The Aegean turned red. The sea serpent really might have been dumber than the Gorgons, because it took a very long time to realize it was dead. Eventually, though, enough of the head end was missing that it forgot to go on living and sank beneath the waves. If the sharks and the dolphins didn't have a food fight with the scraps, they missed a hell of a chance.

Chlamys soaked with seawater and sea-serpent gore, Andromeda flew back toward Perseus. "I would applaud," he said, "but under the circumstances . . ." He rattled his chains to show what he meant. "That was very exciting."

Andromeda looked him over. He meant it literally. She could tell. She giggled. Greek statues always underestimated things. Quite a bit, here. She giggled again. Sometimes a sword wasn't just a sword.

She looked up toward the top of the rocks. Nobody was watching; maybe Acrisius' conscience, however vestigial, bothered him too much for that. She could do whatever she pleased. Perseus couldn't do anything about it, that was plain enough. Andromeda giggled once more. She flew a little lower and a lot closer.

Perseus gasped. Andromeda pulled back a bit and glanced up at him, eyes full of mischief. "You said you were here to be eaten," she pointed out.

"By a *sea serpent*!"

"If you don't think this is more fun . . ." Her shrug was petulant. But, when you got down to the bottom of things, what

Perseus thought didn't matter a bit. She went back to what she'd been doing. After a little while, she decided to do something else. She hiked up the clammy chlamys and did it. Though she hadn't suspected it till now, there were times when the general draftiness of Greek clothes and lack of an underwear department at the Athens K-mart came in kind of handy. Up against the side of a cliff, winged sandals didn't hurt, either. A good time was had by all.

Afterwards, still panting, Perseus said, "Now that you've ravished me, you realize you'll have to marry me."

Andromeda stretched languorously. A *very* good time had been had by all, or at least by her. She wished for a cigarette, and wished even more she knew what one was. "That can probably be arranged," she purred.

"First, though, you'll have to get me off," Perseus said.

She squawked. "Listen, mister, if I didn't just take care of that—"

"No, off this cliff," he said.

"Oh." Andromeda dipped her head in agreement. "Well, that can probably be arranged, too." She drew the sword again and swung it. It sheared through the metal that imprisoned Perseus like a divine sword cutting cheap bronze chains. After four strokes—considerably fewer than he'd been good for—he fell forward and down. They caught each other in midair. Hermes' sandals were strong enough to carry two. Andromeda had figured they would be. She and Perseus rose together.

After topping the rocks, they flew north toward Argos. Perseus said, "Can I borrow your sword for a minute?"

"Why?" Andromeda looked at him sidelong. "I like the one you come equipped with."

"It won't cut through the manacles on my ankles and wrists," Perseus said.

"Hmm. I suppose not. Sure, go ahead."

Divine swords had a lot going for them. This one neatly removed the manacles without removing the hands and feet they'd been binding. Thinking about all the times she'd sliced herself carving wild boar—those visiting Gauls could really put it away—Andromeda wished she owned cutlery like that.

Perseus said, "Can you steer a little more to the left?"

"Sure," Andromeda said, and did. "How come?"

"That's Acrisius' palace down there." Perseus pointed. "Who knows? Maybe I can make a prophecy come true." He dropped the manacles and the lengths of chain attached to them, one after another. He and Andromeda both watched them fall.

"I can't tell," Andromeda said at last.

"Neither can I." Perseus made the best of things: "If I did nail the old geezer, Matt Drudge'll have it online before we get to Olympus."

The wedding was the event of the eon. Andromeda's mother and father, Cepheus and Cassiopeia, flew up from their Ethiopian home in their private Constellation. Acrisius' cranium apparently remained undented, but nobody sent him an invitation. Danaë, Perseus' mother, did come. She and Hera spent the first part of the weekend snubbing each other.

Zeus dishonored two maids of honor, and, once in his cups, seemed convinced every cupbearer was named Ganymede. After he got into the second maid of honor, he also got into a screaming row with Hera. A couple of thunderbolts flew, but the wedding pavilion, though scorched, survived.

Hera and Danaë went off in a corner, had a good cry together, and were the best of friends from then on out. A little later, Zeus sidled up to Andromeda and asked in an anxious voice, "What is this *First Wives' Club* my wife keeps talking about? Do you suppose it is as powerful as my sword?"

"Which one, your Godship, sir?" she returned; she was in her cups, too. Zeus didn't answer, but went off with stormy, and even rather rainy, brow. Before long, he and Hera were screaming at each other again.

And then Andromeda and Perseus were off for their wedding night at the Mount Olympus Holiday Inn. In her cups or not, Andromeda didn't like the way the limo driver handled the horses.

Perseus patted her knee. "Don't worry, sweetie," he said. "Phaëthon hasn't burned rubber, or anything else, for quite a while now."

She might have argued more, but Perseus' hand, instead of stopping at the knee, kept wandering north. And, with all the gods in the wedding party following the limo, odds were somebody could bring her back to life even if she did get killed.

Ambrosia—Dom Pérignon ambrosia, no less—waited on ice in the honeymoon suite. The bed was as big as Boeotia, as soft as the sea-foam that spawned Aphrodite. Out in the hallway, the gods and demigods and mortals with pull who'd been at the wedding made a deityawful racket, waiting for the moment of truth.

They didn't have to wait very long. Perseus was standing at attention even when he lay down on that inviting bed. Wearing nothing but a smile, Andromeda got down beside him. At the appropriate time, she let out a squeal, pretending to be a maiden. Everybody in the hallway let out a cheer, pretending to believe her.

After the honeymoon, things went pretty well. Perseus landed an editorial job at *Argosy*. Andromeda spent a while on the talk-show circuit: Loves Fated to Happen were hot that millennium. They bought themselves a little house. It was Greek Colonial architecture, right out of Grant Xylum, and they furnished it to match.

When Andromeda sat down on the four-poster bed one night, she heard a peculiar sound, not one it usually made. "What's that?" she asked Perseus.

"What's what?" he said, elaborately casual.

"That noise. Like—metal?"

"Oh. That." Elaborately casual, all right—too elaborately casual. Perseus' face wore an odd smile, half sheepish, half . . . something else. "It's probably these." He lifted up his pillow.

"Chains!" Andromeda exclaimed. "Haven't you had enough of chains?"

"Well—sort of." Perseus sounded sheepish, too, sheepish and . . . something else. An eager something else. "But it was so much fun that first time, I, I . . . thought we might try it again."

"*Did* you?" Andromeda rubbed her chin. You don't find out

everything right away about the person you marry, especially if it's a whirlwind courtship. Gods knew she hadn't expected *this*. Still . . . "Why not?" she said at last. "Just don't invite that damn sea serpent."

And a good time was had by all.

Goddess for a Day

This one is taken from a real incident related by the Greek historian Herodotos. One of the more interesting challenges here was finding out what the Akropolis of Athens looked like in the sixth century B.C., before the Persian invasions and before the great building program that followed them. Everything here is as authentic as I could make it—which is, of course, not the same as saying it's true.

The driver held the horses to a trot hardly faster than a walk. Even so, the chariot jounced and pitched and swayed as it rattled down the rutted dirt track from the country village of Paiania to Athens.

Every time a wheel jolted over a rock, Phye feared she'd be pitched out on her head. She couldn't grab for the rail of the car, not with a hoplite's spear in one hand and a heavy round shield on the other arm. The shield still had the olive-oil smell of fresh paint. Before they'd given it to her, they'd painted Athena's owl over whatever design it had borne before.

Another rock, another jolt. She staggered again. Peisistratos, who rode in the car with her, steadied her so she didn't fall. She was almost big enough to make two of the *tyrannos*, but he was agile and she wasn't. "It will be all right, dear," he said, grinning at her like a clever monkey. "Just look divine."

She struck the pose in which he'd coached her: back straight so she looked even taller than she was (the Corinthian helmet she wore, with the red-dyed horsehair plume nodding above it, added to the effect), right arm out straight with the spear grounded on the floorboards of the chariot (like an old man's stick, it helped her keep her balance, but not enough), shield held in tight against her breast (that took some of the weight off her poor arm—but, again, not enough). She stared straight ahead, chin held high.

"It's all so *uncomfortable*," she said.

Peisistratos and the driver both laughed. They'd really fought in hoplite's panoply, not just worn it on what was essentially a parade. They knew what it was like.

But they didn't know everything there was to know. The bell corselet they'd put on Phye gleamed; they'd polished the bronze till you could use it for a mirror. That corselet would have been small for a man her size. Mashed against hard, unyielding metal, her breasts ached worse than they did just before her courses started. The shield she carried might have been made of lead, not wood and bronze. One of her greaves had rubbed a raw spot on the side of her leg. And, of course, she stared straight ahead; the cheekpieces and noseguard on the helmet gave her no other choice. The helm was heavy, too. Her neck ached.

She itched everywhere.

A couple of people—a man with a graying beard and a younger woman who might have been his daughter or his wife—stood by the side of the track, staring at the oncoming chariot. Phye envied them their cool, simple mantles and cloaks. A river of sweat was pouring down her face.

Peisistratos waved to the couple. He tapped Phye on the back. They couldn't see that. She couldn't feel it, either, but she heard his nails rasp on the corselet. "The gods love Peisistratos!" she cried in a loud voice. "The gods ordain that he should rule once more in Athens!"

"There! You see?" the man said, pointing at Phye. "It *is* Athena, just as those fellows who went by the other day said it would be."

"Why, maybe it *is*." The woman tossed her head to show she thought he was right. "Isn't that something?" She raised her voice as the chariot clattered by: "Hurrah for Peisistratos! Good old Peisistratos!"

"It's going to work," the driver said without looking over his shoulder.

"Of course it will." Peisistratos was all but capering with glee. "We have ourselves such a fine and lovely goddess here." He patted Phye on a bared thigh, between the top of her greave and the bottom of the linen tunic she wore under the corselet.

She almost smashed him in the face with her shield. Exposing her legs to the eyes of men felt shockingly immodest. Having that flesh out there to be pawed showed her why women commonly covered it.

She didn't think she'd given any sign of what was passing through her mind, but Peisistratos somehow sensed it. He was no fool: very much the reverse. "I crave pardon," he said, and sounded as if he meant it. "I paid your father a pound of silver for you to be Athena, not a whore. I shall remember."

The village lads made apologies, too, and then tried to feel her up again whenever they got the chance. After that once, Peisistratos kept his hands to himself. Whenever the chariot passed anyone on the road—which happened more and more often now, for they were getting close to Athens—Phye shouted out the gods' love for the returning *tyrannos*.

Some of those people fell in behind the chariot and started heading into Athens themselves. They yelled Peisistratos' name. "Pallas Athena, defender of cities!" one of them called out, a tagline from the Homeric hymn to the goddess. Several others took up the call.

Phye had not thought she could get any warmer than she already was under helm and corselet and greaves. Now she discovered she was wrong. These people really believed she was Athena. And why not? Had she been walking along the track instead of up in the chariot, she would have believed it was truly the goddess, too. To everyone in Paiania, the Olympians and other deities were as real and close as their next-door neighbors. Her brother, for instance, swore he'd seen a satyr in the woods not far from home, and why would he lie?

But not to Peisistratos and his driver. They joked back and forth about how they were tricking the—*unsophisticated* was the word Peisistratos used, but Phye had never heard it before, and so it meant nothing to her—folk of the countryside and of the city as well. As far as they were concerned, the gods were levers with which to move people in their direction.

That attitude frightened Phye. More and more, she wished her father had not accepted Peisistratos' leather sack full of shiny drachmai, even if that pound of silver would feed the whole family for a year, maybe two, no matter how badly the grapes and olives came in. Peisistratos and his friend might imagine the gods were impotent, but Phye knew better.

When they noticed what she was doing, what would *they* do—to her?

She didn't have much time to think about that, for which she was grateful. The walls of Athens drew near. More and more people fell in behind the chariot. She was shouting out the gods' will—or rather, what Peisistratos said was the gods' will—so often, she grew hoarse.

The guards at the gate bowed low as the chariot rolled into the city. Was that respect for the goddess or respect for the returning *tyrannos*? Phye couldn't tell. She wondered if the guards were sure themselves.

Now the road went up to the akropolis through hundreds upon hundreds of houses and shops. Phye didn't often come in to Athens: when you used a third of the day or more walking forth and back between your village and the city, how often could you afford to do that? The sheer profusion of buildings awed her. So did the city stink, a rich, thick mixture of dung and sweat and animals and stale olive oil.

"Athena! Pallas Athena!" the city people shouted. They were as ready to believe Phye was the goddess as the farmers outside the walls had been. "Pallas Athena for Peisistratos!" someone yelled, and in a moment the whole crowd took up the cry. It echoed and reechoed between the whitewashed housefronts that pressed the rutted road tight on either side, until Phye's head ached.

"They love you," the driver said over his shoulder to Peisistratos.

"That sound—a thousand people screaming your name— that's the sweetest thing in the world," the *tyrannos* answered. "Sweeter than Chian wine, sweeter than a pretty boy's *prokton*, sweeter than anything." Of the gods, he'd spoken lightly, slight- ingly. Now his words came from the heart.

Men with clubs, men with spears, a few men with full hop- lite's panoply like that which Phye wore, fell in before the char- iot and led it up toward the heart of the city. "Just like you planned it," the driver said in admiration. Peisistratos preened like a tame jackdaw on a perch.

Phye stared up toward the great buildings of wood and lime- stone, even a few of hard marble, difficult to work, that crowned the akropolis. They were hardly a stone's throw from the flat- land atop the citadel when a man cried out in a great voice: "Re- joice, Peisistratos! Lykourgos has fled, Megakles offers you his daughter in marriage. Athens is yours once more. Rejoice!"

The driver whooped. Unobtrusively, Peisistratos tapped Phye on the corselet. "Athens shows Peisistratos honor!" she called to the crowd. "Him Athena also delights to honor. The goddess brings him home to his own akropolis!"

At the man's news and at her words, the cheering doubled and then doubled again. From under the rim of her helmet, she looked nervously up toward the heavens. Surely such a racket would draw the notice of the gods. She hoped they'd note she'd spoken of Athena in the third person and hadn't claimed to be the goddess herself.

Past the gray stone bulk of the Hekatompedon, the temple with a front a hundred feet long, rattled the chariot. At Peisis- tratos' quiet order, the driver swung left, toward the olive tree sacred to Athena. "I'll speak to the people from the rock under that tree," the *tyrannos* said. "Seems fitting enough, eh?"

"Right you are." The driver reined in just behind that boulder. The horses stood breathing hard.

Peisistratos hopped down from the chariot. He *was* nimble, even if no longer young. To Phye, he said, "Present me one last time, my dear, and then you're done. We'll put you up in the shrine for the night"—he used his chin to point to the plain little

wooden temple, dedicated to both Athena and Poseidon, standing behind the olive tree—"get you proper woman's clothes,
and send you back to Paiania in the morning." He chuckled.
"It'll be by oxcart, I fear, not by chariot."

"That's all right," Phye said, and got down herself. She was
tempted to fall deliberately, to show the crowd she was no goddess. But she had taken on the outer attributes of Athena, and
could not bring herself to let the goddess fall into disrepute from
anything she did. As gracefully as she could, she stepped up
onto the rock.

"See gray-eyed Athena!" someone exclaimed. Phye's eyes
were brown. The Corinthian helm so shadowed them, though,
that people saw what they wanted to see. Thinking that, she suddenly understood how Peisistratos had been so sure his scheme
would work. She also discovered why he spoke of an adoring
crowd as sweeter than wine. Excitement flowed through her as
the crowd quieted to hear what she would say. She forgot the
squeeze and pinch of armor, the weight of the shield, everything
but the sea of expectant faces in front of her.

"Athena delights in honoring Peisistratos!" she cried in a
voice so huge it hardly seemed her own. "Let Athens delight in
honoring Peisistratos. People of Athens, I give you—Peisistratos!"

She still had not said she was Athena, but she'd come closer,
far closer, than she'd intended. She got down from the boulder.
The *tyrannos* hopped up onto it. Most of the roar that rose from
throats uncounted was for him, but some, she thought, belonged
to her.

He must have thought so, too. He leaned down and murmured,
"Thank you, O best of women. That was wonderfully done."
Then he straightened and began to speak to the crowd. The late-
afternoon sun gleamed from his white mantle—and from the
crown of his head, which was going bald.

Phye withdrew into the temple and set down her spear and
shield with a sigh of relief. She was out of sight of the people,
who hung on Peisistratos' every word. She did not blame them.
If he accomplished half, or even a fourth part, of what he prom-

ised, he would make Athens a better substitute for Zeus than Phye just had for Athena.

He must have memorized his speech long before he returned to the akropolis. It came out as confidently as if he were a rhapsode chanting Homer's verses. He made the people laugh and cheer and cry out in anger—when he wished, as he wished. Most of all, he made them love him.

Just as the sun was setting, Peisistratos said, "Now go forth, O men of Athens, and celebrate what we have done here today. Let there be wine, let there be music, let there be good cheer! And tomorrow, come the dawn, we shall go on about the business of making our city great."

A last cheer rang out, maybe louder than all those that had come before. The Athenians streamed away from the akropolis. Here and there, torches crackled into life; when night fell, it fell sudden and hard. Someone strummed a lyre. Someone else thumped a drum. Snatches of song filled the air.

Phye waited in the temple for someone to bring her a woman's long mantle. She wanted to go forth, not to revel but back to her quiet home in Paiania, and could hardly do that in the panoply of the goddess. Peisistratos had promised one of his men would take care of her needs. She waited and waited, but the man, whoever he was, did not come. Maybe he'd already found wine and music and good cheer, and forgotten all about her.

The akropolis grew quiet, still—deserted. Down below, in the agora, in the wineshops, people did indeed celebrate the return of Peisistratos: no *tyrannos* had ever given a command easier to obey. The noise of the festivity came up to Phye as the smoke of a sacrifice rose to the gods. Like the gods, she got the immaterial essence, but not the meat itself.

She muttered under her breath. Tomorrow, surely, they'd remember her here. If she spoke to Peisistratos, she could bring trouble down on the head of whichever henchman had failed her. She sighed. She didn't care about that. All she wanted was to go home.

Her head came up. Someone up here on the akropolis was playing a double flute—and coming closer to the temple where she sheltered. Maybe she hadn't been forgotten after all. Maybe Peisistratos' man had just paused for a quick taste of revelry before he took care of her. She wondered whether she should thank him for coming at all or bawl him out for being late.

He played the flutes very well. Listening to the sweet notes flood forth, Phye marveled that she didn't hear a whole band of men—and loose women, too—following, singing to his tune and stomping out the rhythms of the *kordax* or some other lascivious dance.

As far as her ears could tell, the fluteplayer was alone. Cautiously, she stepped forward and peered out through the entryway to the temple, past the sacred olive and the boulder on which she and then Peisistratos had spoken. She remained deep in shadow. Whoever was out there would not be able to spy her, while she—

She gasped, gaped, rubbed at her eyes, and at last believed. Daintily picking his way toward her, his hooves kicking up tiny spurts of dust that glowed white in the moonlight before settling, was a satyr.

No wonder he plays the flutes so well, Phye thought dizzily. He looked very much as her brother had described the satyr he saw, as the vase-painters showed the creatures on their pots: horse's hind legs and tail; snub-nosed, pointed-eared, not quite human features; phallos so large and rampantly erect, she wanted to giggle. But neither her brother's words nor the vase-painters' images had come close to showing her his grace, his strange beauty. Seen in the flesh, he wasn't simply something made up of parts of people and animals. He was himself, and perfect of his kind.

He lowered the double flute from his mouth. His eyes glowed in the moonlight, as a wolf's might have. "Gray-eyed Athena?" he called, his voice a slow music. Phye took a step back. Could he see her in here after all? He could. He did. He laughed. "I know you are in your house, gray-eyed Athena. Do you not remember Marsyas? You gave me the gift of your flutes." He brought them to his lips once more and blew sweetness into the night air.

"Go away," Phye whispered.

No man could have heard that tiny trickle of sound. Marsyas did, and laughed again. "You gave me a gift," he repeated. "Now I shall give you one in return." Altogether without shame, he stroked himself. He had been large. He got larger, and larger still.

Phye groped for the spear and shield she had set aside. The shield she found at once, but the spear—where was the spear? She had leaned it against the wall, and—

She had no time to search now. Past the boulder Marsyas came, past the sacred olive tree, up to the very threshold of the shrine. There he paused for a moment, to set down the flutes. Phye dared hope the power of the goddess would hold him away. Athena was a maiden, after all, as Phye was herself. Surely Athena's home on earth would be proof against—

Marsyas stepped over the threshold. "Goddess, goddess," he crooned, as easily befooled as any Athenian, "loose yourself from that cold hard bronze and lie with me. What I have is hard, too, but never cold." He touched himself again and, incredibly, swelled still more.

"Go away," Phye said, louder this time. "I do not want you." Would Athena let a woman, a virgin, be raped on the floor of her temple? *Why not?* a cold voice inside Phye asked. *What better punishment for a woman who dared assume the person of the goddess?*

And the satyr Marsyas said, "But I want you, gray-eyed Athena," and strode toward her.

Almost, Phye cried out that she was not the goddess. She would have cried out, had she thought it would do any good. But, to a satyr, female flesh would be female flesh. Even in the deep darkness inside the temple, his eyes glowed now. He reached out to clasp her in his arms.

She shouted and interposed the shield between them. If he wanted her maidenhead, he would have to take it from her. She would not tamely give it to him. All right: for Peisistratos' sake, she had pretended to be Athena. Now she would do it for herself. She'd have to do it for herself. Plainly, the goddess was not about to do it for her.

Marsyas shoved aside the shield. Phye's shoulder groaned; the satyr was stronger than a man. Marsyas laughed. "What have you got under that armor?" he said. "I know. Oh yes, I know." Like an outthrust spear, his phallos tapped at the front of her corselet.

"I do not want you!" Phye cried again, and brought up her leg, as hard as she could.

In her grandfather's time, greaves had covered only a hoplite's calves. These days, smiths made them so bronze protected the knee as well. She was a big woman—Peisistratos would never have chosen her had she been small—she was frightened, and, if not so strong as a satyr, she was far from weak.

Her armored kneecap caught Marsyas square in the crotch.

Just for an instant, his eyes flamed bright as a grass fire seen by night. Then, all at once, the fire was quenched. He screamed and wailed and doubled over, clutching at his wounded parts. His phallos deflated like a pricked pig's bladder.

"Go!" Phye said. "Never think to profane Athena's temple again." When the satyr, still in anguish, turned to obey, she kicked him, right at the root of his horse's tail. He wailed again, and fled out into the night.

That was well done.

Phye's head swiveled round. Had the thought been her own, or had it quietly come from outside her? How could it have? She was all alone, here in Athena's temple. But if you were alone in the house of the goddess, were you truly alone?

Peisistratos would think so.

"Thank you," Phye whispered. She got no response, real or imagined. She hadn't expected one.

A little while later, a man bearing a torch in one hand and carrying a bundle under his other arm came up onto the akropolis. He lurched as he walked, as a man with a good deal of wine in him might do. Almost like a windblown leaf, he made his erratic way toward the temple where Phye waited.

"Lady?" he called—he could not be bothered remembering Phye's name. "I've got your proper clothes here." He jerked the bundle up and down to show what he meant. "I'm sorry I'm late but—*hic!*" To him, that seemed to say everything that needed saying. "Here, what's this?" Just outside the temple, he bent and picked up the double flutes Marsyas had forgotten in his flight. "Are these yours, lady?"

"They are Athena's," Phye answered. "Close enough."

After the Last Elf Is Dead

From Tolkien on, many, many fantasies have dealt with the struggle between Good and Evil (capital letters are deliberate there), and with Good's eventual triumph. But, as we see after living in the world for a while, Good doesn't always win, however much we wish it would. What would the triumph of Evil look like in a high-fantasy world? Something like this, maybe?

The city of Lerellim burned. Valsak reckoned a good omen the scarlet flames and black smoke mounting to the sky: black and scarlet were the colors of the Dark Brother the high captain served.

An ogre came up to Valsak, bent savage head in salute while it waited for him to notice it. "Lord, the quarter by the river is taken," it reported.

The man nodded. "Good. Only the citadel left, then." His eyes narrowed as he studied the great stone pile ahead. Atop the tallest tower, the Green Star still flew, the proud banner snapping defiance in the breeze. Men and elves shot from the battlements at the Dark Brother's ring of troops as it tightened around them.

Valsak rubbed his chin. The citadel would be expensive to take. The high captain's mouth widened in a tight-lipped smile. He knew the difference between expensive and impossible.

Thunderbolts lashed out from the fortress, spears of green light. Valsak swore, and had to wait for his vision to clear to see what damage the enemy's magic had done. He smiled again: almost none. The Dark Brother put forth all his might now, to end once and for all the pretensions of these bandits who had for so long presumed to style themselves High Kings in his despite.

Valsak turned to his lieutenant. "Gather a storming party, Gersner. We will go in through the main gate, once our wizards have thrown it down."

"It shall be done, High Captain." Gersner was small, thin, and quiet; anyone who did not know him would have had trouble imagining him as any kind of soldier. Valsak knew him, and knew his worth. Within minutes, men and ogres began gathering before the main gate. A proper murderous crew, Valsak thought, almost fondly. The warriors brandished swords, spears, maces. Whatever the butcher's bill they would have to pay, they knew they stood on the edge of victory.

Two black-robed wizards, one with a bandage on his head, made their way through the storming party. Soldiers stepped back fearfully, letting them pass. They, in turn, bowed before Valsak. To wield their magic, they had to stand high in the Dark Brother's favor. He stood higher, and they knew it.

He pointed. "Take out the gates."

They bowed again, and stayed bowed, gathering their strength. Then they straightened. Crimson rays shot from their fingertips; crimson fire smote the metal at the top of the gates and ran dripping down them, as if it were some thick liquid. Where the fire stuck and clung, the metal was no more.

Then the clingfire slowed, nearly stopped. The bandaged wizard staggered, groaned, gave back a pace.

"Counterspell!" his comrade gasped hoarsely. He cried out a Word of power so terrible even Valsak frowned. That Word was plenty to occupy the men or elvish wizards trapped in the citadel. With them distracted thus, the other black-robe recovered himself, stepped up to stand by his colleague again. The fire began to advance once more, faster and faster.

Soon the gates were burned away. The harsh smoke from them made Valsak cough. He drew his sword, picked up his shield. "Forward!" he shouted. He charged with his warriors.

No officer could make troops dare anything they thought him unwilling to risk himself.

Archers appeared in the blasted doorway. Elf-shot shafts flew far, fast, and straight. Men and ogres behind Valsak fell. An arrow thudded against his buckler. The shield was thin and looked flimsy, but the magic in it gave better protection than any weight of wood or metal. Not even elf-arrows would pierce it, not today.

The archers saw they were too few to break up Valsak's attack. Those his own bowmen had not slain darted aside, to be replaced by heavily armored men and elves.

"If their gates can't hold us out, their damned soldiers won't!" Valsak yelled. His storming column's cheers rose to the skies, along with the smoke from falling Lerellim.

Recognizing the high captain as his foes' commander, an elflord sprang out to meet him in single combat. The elf was tall and fair, after the fashion of his kind, with gold hair streaming from beneath his shining silvered helm. Not a hint of fear sullied his noble features; more than anything else, he seemed sorrowful as he swung up his long straight blade. Even in mail, he moved gracefully as a hunting cat.

Valsak killed him.

Cunning alone had not raised the high captain to his rank. As happened often in the Dark Brother's armies, he had climbed over the bodies of rivals, many of them slain by his own hand. And in the wars against the High Kings and their elvish allies, he fought always at the fore.

He would never be so fluid a warrior as the elflord he faced, nor quite as quick. But he was strong and clever, clever enough to turn his awkwardness to advantage. What seemed a stumble was not. His shield turned the elf's blow; his own sword leaped out to punch through gorget and throat alike.

The elflord's fine mouth twisted in pain. His eyes, blue as the sky had been before the fires started, misted over. As his foe crumpled, Valsak felt something sigh past him: the elf's soul, bound for the Isle of Forever in the Utmost West. Flee while you can, the high captain thought—one day the Dark Brother may hunt you even there.

The fall of their leader threw the gateway's defenders into deeper despair than had been theirs before. With some, that increased their fury, so they fought without regard to their own safety and were sooner killed than might otherwise have been true. Others, unmanned, thought of flight, weakening the stand still more. Soon Valsak and his warriors were loose in the citadel.

He knew where he wanted to take them. "The throneroom!" he cried. "Those who cast down the last of this rebel line surely will earn great rewards from our master!" The cheers of men and ogres echoed down the corridors ahead of them as they stormed after Valsak. Some might have dreamed of lordships under the Dark Brother; some of loot beyond counting; some of women there for the taking; the ogres, perhaps, just of hot manflesh to eat. All their dreams might turn real now, and they knew it.

There was plenty more fighting on the way. Desperate parties of men and elves flung themselves at Valsak's band. The high captain got a slash on his cheek, and never remembered when or how. But the defenders were too few, with too many threats to meet: not only was the gate riven, but by this time the Dark Brother's armies had to have flung ladders and towers against the citadel's walls. Like the city outside, it was falling.

"Ha! We are the first!" Gersner called when the invaders burst past the silver doors of the throneroom and saw none of the Dark Brother's other minions had come so far so fast.

In front of the guards around the High King's throne, a white-robed, white-bearded wizard still incanted, calling on the Light. "Fool! The Light has failed!" Valsak shouted. The wizard paid no heed. Valsak turned to Gersner. "Slay him."

"Aye." The smaller man sprang forward. The wizard tried to fling lightning at him, but the levinbolt shriveled before it was well begun. Laughing, Gersner sworded the old man down.

Valsak's warriors flung themselves on the guards. The high captain saw they had the numbers and fury to prevail. That left only the High King. His sword was drawn, but he still sat on the throne, as if while his fundament rested there he remained ruler of the Western Realm.

Maybe that sort of mystic tie had existed once, but the Dark Brother's rise broke all such asunder. Watching his guards, men and elves die for him, the High King must have realized that. He sprang to his feet, crying to Valsak, "I'll not live, for your filthy master to make sport of!"

To Valsak's disappointment, the High King did fight so fiercely he made his foes kill him. "Miserable bastard," Gersner muttered, a hand to his ribs; one of the High King's slashes had almost pierced his mailshirt and the leather beneath it, and must have left a tremendous bruise. By then, though, the last guards were down, with men and ogres taking turns shoving steel into the corpse as it lay sprawled on the steps before the throne.

Above the royal seat, the air began to shimmer and twist, as if being kneaded by unseen hands. Then the Dark Brother, in all his dreadful majesty, assumed the throne he had coveted through the five ages since the First Beginning. His warriors bent the knee before him as, smiling, he surveyed the carnage in the throneroom.

He spoke then, and Valsak knew his words echoed from the Frozen Waste in the north to the deserts and steaming jungles of the Hotlands. "The world is mine!" he said.

"The world may be the Dark Brother's, but some folk have yet to believe it," Valsak said sourly as his long column of horsemen and footsoldiers moved slowly toward the mountains looming ahead. His backside ached from a week in the saddle.

Gersner frowned. "Our job is to teach them," he said, a touch of reproof in his voice.

"Aye," Valsak said. "Teach them we are." His eyes went to the fields to one side of the road. Bands of marauders wearing the Dark Brother's black surcoats were plundering the farms there. Some farmers must have been resisting from one stout building, for several raiders were working toward it with torches.

Valsak swung up a mailed hand. "Column left!" he called, and trotted toward the farm building. Riders followed. "Nock arrows," he added, and fit his own action to word.

The Dark Brother's irregulars cheered to see reinforcements riding to their aid. But Valsak led his troopers to cordon the farm building away from the raiders, and his men faced out, not in.

The marauders' leader, a man with features so dark and heavy he might have been a quarter ogre, angrily rushed up to Valsak. "Who do you think you are, and what in the name of the Dark Brother's dungeons are you playing at?" he shouted.

"I am the high captain Valsak, and if you invoke the Dark Brother's dungeons in my hearing again, you will earn the chance to see what you have called upon," Valsak said. He sat quiet upon his horse, coldly staring down as the fellow in front of him wilted. Then he went on, "I will give you back the second part of your question: what are you playing at here?"

"Just having a bit of sport," the other said. "We won, after all; why not take the chance to enjoy it?"

"Because if you go about burning farms, we will all be hungry by and by. I have fought for the Dark Brother more years than you have lived"—a guess, but a good one, and one calculated to put the marauder in fear, for Valsak looked no older than he—"and I have never known his soldiers to be exempt from the need to eat. The war we fought took out enough farms on its own. I do not think the Dark Brother would thank you for wantonly destroying more of what is his."

He expected that to finish demoralizing the irregular, but the fellow had more to him that Valsak had expected. He put hands on hips and said, "Hoity-toity! You talk like that, why weren't you on the other side at Lerellim? You—"

He never got further than that. Valsak nodded to the archer at his left. A bowstring thrummed. The irregular clutched at the arrow that suddenly sprouted in his chest. Still wearing a look of outraged disbelief, he toppled.

"Does anyone else care to question my loyalty?" Valsak asked quietly. No one did. "Good. I suggest you move on then, and if you want a bit of sport, try a brothel." The irregulars, outnumbered and outfaced, perforce moved on. Their leader lay where he had fallen.

One of the farmers came out of the stronghouse, looked from the corpse to Valsak and back again. "I thank you," he said at last.

"I did not do it for your sake," the high captain answered, "but for the Dark Brother's. You and yours are his, to be used as he sees fit, and not to be despoiled by the first band of armed men that happens by."

"I don't care why you did it. I thank you anyway," the farmer said. " 'Twas nobly done."

Valsak scowled. In his rude way, and no doubt all ignorant of what he meant, the rustic was saying the same thing the marauder had. Nobility! Valsak knew where his loyalty lay, and that was that. He jerked a thumb at the raider's body. "Bury this carrion," he told the farmer, then turned back to his troop. "Ride on!"

Gersner knew better than to question his commander in front of the men. But when they camped that night, he waited till most of them were in their bedrolls, then asked, "Did you really feel you had to set out on our own? After the war we fought against the cursed High Kings, that may not sit well."

" 'After' is the word, Gersner," Valsak said, as patiently as he could. "Except for mopping-up jobs like this one we're on, the war is over. This is not enemy territory, to be ravaged to hurt the foe. It *belongs* to the Dark Brother now."

Gersner grunted. "And if he chooses to send it to ruin?"

"Then his will be done. But it is not done, as you and I know, through a band of small-time bandits who happen to have coats the same color as ours. Or do you think otherwise?"

"Put that way, no." Gersner let it drop. He did not seem altogether happy, but Valsak wasted no time fretting over whether subordinates were happy. He wanted them to obey. Gersner had never given him cause to worry there.

The mountain keep looked strong enough. Before the war was won, it might have held up Valsak and his forces for weeks or even months. Now, with the Western Realm's heart torn out, he knew he could take it. It would still cost. Valsak had spent lives lavishly to take the citadel of Lerellim. He was not, however, a wasteful man. The need had been great then. Now it was less. And so, while Gersner and the troopers waited behind him and carefully said nothing, he rode forward alone, to parley.

The sentry above the gate shouted, "Go back, black-coat! My lord Oldivor has taken oath by the Light never to yield to wickedness, or let it set foot here."

"They swore that same oath in Lerellim, and the Dark Brother sits on the throne there. What has your precious lord to say to that? Will he speak with me now, or shall I pull his castle down around his ears and then see what he has to say? Now fetch him"—Valsak let some iron come into his voice—"or I will make a point of remembering *your* face as well."

The sentry disappeared fast enough to satisfy even the high captain.

The man who came to peer down from the gray stone walls at Valsak was tall and fair and, the high captain guessed, badly frightened: had he been in the other's boots, he would have been. The local lord made a game try at not showing it, though, shouting, "Begone, in the name of the High King!"

"The High King is dead," Valsak told him.

"Aye, you'd say that, wouldn't you, black-coat, to make us lose heart. Well, your tricks and lies are worthless here." Several men on the battlements shouted agreement.

"There are no tricks or lies. Along with others here, I was one of those who killed him. Should you care to share that honor with him, I daresay it can be arranged."

Appalled silence fell in the castle. Valsak let it stretch. Fear worked only for the Dark Brother. When Oldivor spoke again, he sounded less bold. "What would you have of me?"

"Yield up your fortress. You have not yet fought against the Dark Brother's servants, so no offense exists save failing to leave here when the High King, ah, died. I am high captain of the Dark Brother; I have the power to forgive that small trespass if you make it good now. You and yours may even keep your swords. All you need do is swear your submission to the Dark Brother, and you shall depart in peace. In his name I avow it."

"Swear submission to evil, you mean," the man on the battlements said slowly.

"The Dark Brother rules now. You *will* submit to him, sir, whether or not you swear the oath. The choice is doing it before your castle is sacked and you yourself—if you are lucky—slain." Valsak paused. "Do you need time to consider your decision? I will give it to you, if you like."

Oldivor stood suddenly straighter. "I need no time. I will stand by my first oath, and will not be forsworn. If the High King and his line have failed, then one day, with the aid of the elves, a new line will rise up to fight again for freedom."

"The elves are dead," Valsak said. "If you have anyone in your keep with the least skill at magic, you will know I tell no lies."

That knocked some of the new-come spirit out of the noble on the walls above the high captain. "So Velethol was right," he said. Valsak thought he was talking more to himself than to anyone else. But then Oldivor gathered himself again. "I will fight regardless, for my honor's sake," he said loudly. He had the backing of his men, if nothing else: they cheered his defiance.

Valsak shrugged. "You have made your choice. You will regret it." He rode back to his own line.

"A waste of time?" Gersner asked.

"A waste of time." Valsak turned to the lesser of the two wizards who had seared away the gates of Lerellim's citadel. "Open the keep for us."

The wizard bowed. "It shall be done, High Captain." He summoned his powers, sent them darting forth. This mountain keep's gates were not elf-silver, only iron-faced wood. They caught at once, and kept on burning despite the water and sand the defenders poured on them from the murder-holes above. Soon the gateway stood naked for Valsak's warriors.

As at the citadel, warriors rushed to fill the breach in the fortifications. "Shall I burn them down, High Captain?" the wizard asked. "They have scant sorcery to ward them."

Valsak rubbed his chin. "Burn a couple, but only a couple—enough to drive the others away from the portal," he said judiciously. "If we take some alive, the Dark Brother's army will be better for it. These are no cowards we face."

The wizard sniffed, but at Valsak's scowl he said, "It shall be as you wish, of course." It was also as Valsak guessed: after two men turned to shrieking fireballs, the rest drew back. The high captain's warriors had no trouble forcing an entrance.

Once inside the keep, Valsak spied Oldivor not far away, still leading what defense he could make. "Now will you yield?" the high captain shouted. "Your men have fought well enough to satisfy any man's honor. The Dark Brother would smile to gain the loyalty you show now for a cause that is dead."

Afterwards, he realized he should not have mentioned his master's name. His foe's haggard face twisted into a terrible grimace. "So long as we live and fight, the cause is not dead!" he shouted. "But you soon will be!" He came rushing toward Valsak, hewing down one of the high captain's men who stood in his way.

Valsak soon took his foe's measure: as a warrior who had slain an elf, he was in scant danger from this petty border lord, who had ferocity but no great skill. Still, the high captain looked to beat him as quickly as he could. He was not the sort of man to toy with any opponent—who could say when the fellow might get lucky?

And indeed, luck intervened, but not on Oldivor's side. When Valsak's sword struck his, the blow sent the blade spinning out of his sweaty hand. "Take him alive!" Valsak shouted. Three black-coated soldiers sprang on the castle lord's back and bore him to the ground.

After that, resistance faded rapidly. Only Oldivor's will had kept the fortress's warriors fighting once the gates went down. As they gave in, Valsak's troops gathered them into a disgruntled crowd in the courtyard.

"Shall we slaughter them?" Gersner asked. "That will make the next holding we come to think twice about fighting us."

"Or make it fight to the death," Valsak said. "Let's see first if we can spend fewer of our own troopers than we would on that path."

His lieutenant sighed. "As you wish. What then?"

Valsak strode up to the prisoners. "You, you, you, you, and you." He beckoned. None of the five men at whom he had pointed came forward willingly. His soldiers shoved them out. Fear on their faces, they eyed the captain, waiting for his decree.

"You are free," he told them. "Go on; get out of here. Go where you will."

Now both they and his own followers were gaping at him. Gersner, he saw out of the corner of his eye, looked about ready to explode. "What's the catch?" asked one of the five. "The Dark Brother and his never give anything for free—we know that." The others nodded.

"Who does?" Valsak retorted. "Here, though, the price is small. Wherever you go, tell the folk you meet that so long as they raise no insurrection and obey the Dark Brother's officers, they'll have no trouble. If they plot and connive and resist, they will suffer what they deserve. Anything else? No? Then leave, before I think twice of my own softness."

The five soldiers wasted no time. They ran for the gates. Valsak's warriors stood aside to let them pass. They might doubt the high captain, but they feared him.

"What about the rest of us?" a prisoner called. Gersner, who had been talking quietly with the wizard, looked up at the question.

"You have resisted in arms the Dark Brother, the overlord of all the world," Valsak said in a voice like ice. "You will serve him henceforth in the mines, fit punishment for your betrayal." He turned to his lieutenant. "Tell off a section to bind them and guard them on their journey to the mines."

"Aye, my lord." Gersner sounded happier than he had since the beginning of the campaign. Mine slaves seldom lasted long. Gersner chose a junior officer and his small command. They hurried up to begin chaining the captives in long lines.

Valsak held up a hand. "A moment. I want them first to hear my judgment for their leader." Oldivor lay before him, trussed up like a chicken. "Let him be brought before the Dark Brother's throne, to be dealt with as our master thinks proper. That is as it should be, for it was the Dark Brother himself he treacherously opposed here, after twice being offered the opportunity to yield."

A sigh ran through all the warriors in the courtyard, from winners and losers alike. The Dark Brother's revenge might last years, and even then leave its victim alive for more suffering.

"I betrayed no one, offered treachery to no one!" Oldivor shouted. "I stood by the loyalties I have always held."

"They are the wrong ones," Valsak said, "especially now."

"I hold to them, even so. What would you have done, were our positions reversed?"

"I chose the winning side, so the problem does not arise." The high captain turned to his warriors. "Take this stubborn blockhead away."

Pass by pass, castle by castle, raider band by raider band, Valsak scoured the mountain country clean. With the Dark Brother and his power immanent in the world, the fighting was never hard. But it came, again and again: no matter how hopeless the struggle, few yielded tamely to the new order of things.

"Strange," Valsak mused after yet another keep had fallen to his magician and his soldiers. "They know they cannot prevail against us, yet they will try, time after time." He watched another line of prisoners, many wounded, trudge off into captivity.

Gersner made a dismissive gesture. "They are fools."

"*Can* they be such fools as that? Truly, I doubt it. I tell you, Gersner, I begin to admire them. They cling to their dead cause, never caring about the cost. The Dark Brother would cherish such steadfastness, would they only direct it toward him."

"You've wasted enough time, trying to convince them of that," his lieutenant said.

Valsak frowned. Gersner's tongue was running rather free these days. "They, too, are possessions of the Dark Brother, could they be made to see it. Wantonly slaying troops of such potential wastes his substance. I will not do that without exploring other choices first, as I have said, lest I anger him by my omission."

"As you have said, sir," Gersner agreed. The high captain nodded to himself. Yes, that had the proper tone of respect to it.

The last prisoners limped by. Valsak shook his head. Such a shame that soldiers of such bravery could not—or rather, would not—see sense. When the campaign began, he had thought Oldivor an aberration. Since then, he had seen too many warriors stubborn unto death to believe that any longer.

Obstinacy, however, sufficed no more than courage. The campaigning season had some weeks left when Valsak told the wizard, "Send word to our master, the Dark Brother, that I have subjected all this country to his rule, and have stamped out the last embers of rebellion that lingered here."

The wizard bowed, supple as a snake. "It shall be as you desire."

"Come over here a moment, wizard," Gersner called from beside his tent. "I, too, have a message for you to give to our master."

The wizard's hooded eyes went to Valsak. The high captain nodded permission.

Valsak set garrisons in some of the fortresses his troops had not damaged too badly. Then, with the balance of the army, he turned back toward Lerellim. "A triumphal procession will be in order, I dare say," he told Gersner. "We have earned it."

"I am sure, my lord, the Dark Brother will reward you as you deserve," his lieutenant said.

A day and a half outside what had been the High Kings' capital and was now the Dark Brother's, a pair of riders on matched black stallions came up to the approaching army. One of them displayed the Dark Brother's sigil; the red axe glowed, as if aflame, on a field of jet. "High Captain," that messenger said, "you are bidden to precede your host, that the Dark Brother may learn from you of your deeds."

"I obey," was all Valsak replied. He turned to Gersner. "I will see you in Lerellim. Care well for the army till then, as if you were high captain."

"Rest assured I shall," Gersner said.

Valsak urged his horse ahead, trotting with the two riders toward the city. He gratefully sucked in cool, clean air. "A relief to be away from the dust and stinks of the army," he remarked to one of the messengers.

"Aye, my lord, it must be," the fellow agreed. His comrade leaned over to touch the Dark Brother's sigil to the back of Valsak's neck. Instantly the high captain lost all control of his limbs. He tumbled to the ground in a heap. The messengers dismounted, picked him up and slung him over his horse's back like a sack of beans, then took chains from their saddlebags and bound his wrists to his ankles under the beast's belly.

His mouth was still his. "What are you doing?" he shouted, trying to show anger rather than fear.

"Obeying the Dark Brother's command," one of the men said stolidly. After that, the terror was there. Valsak knew it would never leave him for whatever was left of his life. He still tried not to show it. If Oldivor could go to his fate still shouting defiance, Valsak's pride demanded no less of him.

Unfortunately, he knew more than the fortress commander. That made a bold front harder to maintain before these underlings. Before the Dark Brother, no front would hold, not for long.

It was mid-afternoon the next day when the messengers dropped him, still chained, in front of the Dark Brother's throne. Those terrible yellow eyes pierced him like a spear.

"I—I am yours, my master," he stammered.

"Of course you are mine, worm beneath my feet." The soundless voice echoed in his skull like the tolling of a great bronze bell. "The world is mine."

"But I am yours willingly, my master, as I have always been." Had he not been telling perfect truth, Valsak would never have dared protest.

"Are you indeed?" Valsak felt mental hands riffling through his mind. He cried out in torment; who was there to beg the Dark Brother to be gentle? After some while that might have been forever or might have been a heartbeat, the Dark Brother's voice resounded once more: "Aye, you are. It is not enough."

"My master?" Valsak cried in anguish, though his anguish, he saw, was just beginning.

"Fool!" The Dark Brother flayed him with words. "Do you think I rooted out nobility in my foes only to see it grow among those who are my own? So you admire the doomed rebels you beat for holding so stubbornly to their worthless cause, do you?"

"They thought they were right." Now that Valsak realized nothing would save him, he spoke without concealment.

"And so they opposed me." Infinite scorn rode the Dark Brother's voice. "What idiocy would you essay, simply for the sake of doing what you thought was right?"

"My master, I—" Valsak had to stop then, for the Dark Brother squeezed his mind for truth like a man squeezing an orange for juice. "—I do not know," was what came out of his mouth, and what, he knew, sealed his fate.

"Nor do I," the Dark Brother rumbled, "and I have no wish to be unpleasantly surprised. Gersner will make a good high captain—he thinks only of his own advantage, which lies with me alone. Thus he betrayed you. A mind like that I can understand and use. As for you—" The Dark Brother paused a while in thought. Then he laughed, and his laughter was more wounding even than his speech. "I have it! The very thing!"

Valsak found himself gone from the throneroom, in a space that was not a place. Yet the Dark Brother's eyes were on him still, and the torment he had known in his interrogation as nothing beside what he felt now. It went on and on and on. In that torment, he took some little while to notice he was not alone.

Next to him, twisting in that not-place, was Oldivor. Their eyes met. Valsak saw the satisfaction that filled the other's face. So did the Dark Brother. Satisfaction was not why the castle lord was here. An instant later, his anguish matched Valsak's again.

They watched each other hurt a long, long time.

The Decoy Duck

I've done only three pieces of short fiction set in the Videssos universe, where things Byzantine meet things fantastic. "The Decoy Duck" is set about nine hundred years before the events described in *The Misplaced Legion*, at the time when the Empire of Videssos was at the peak of its power. The story originally appeared in *After the King: Stories in Honor of J.R.R. Tolkien*, a placement reflected in its closing line. It's also influenced by the work of the late, great Poul Anderson, a man I was privileged to call my friend.

The Videssian dromon centipede-walked its oared way into Lygra Fjord. Something about it struck Skatval the Brisk as wrong, wrong. Wondering what, the Haloga chief used the palm of a horn-hard hand to shield eyes against morning sun as he stared out to sea.

He reluctantly decided it was not the imperial banner itself, gold sunburst on blue, that fluttered from the top of the dromon's mast. He had seen that banner before, had clashed with those who bore it, too often to suit him.

Nor was it the twin suns the Videssians drew to help the warship see its proper path, though his own folk would have painted eyes instead. Coming from the far south, the Videssians naturally had more confidence in the sun than Halogai could give it. Hereabouts, in the ice and dark and hunger of winter, the sun seemed sometimes but a distant, fading memory. Not for the first time, Skatval wondered why the Empire of Videssos, which had so much, sought to swallow Halogaland and its unending dearth.

But that thought led him away from the mark he had set for himself. He peered further, sought once more for strangeness, something small, something subtle . . .

"By the gods," he said softly, "it's the very shadows." The northern men, who had to contend with the wild seas and savage storms of the Bay of Haloga, always built their boats clinker-style, each plank overlapping the one below and pegs driven through both for surer strength. The planks on the dromon were set edge to edge, so its sides seemed indecently smooth—*rather like the Videssians themselves,* Skatval thought with a thin smile.

The men he led could fill half a dozen war galleys. The arrogant dromon had already sailed past the inlets where four of them rested. Let the fightfire be kindled—and torches lay always to hand—and that brash captain would never hie back to his hot homeland. Skatval had but to say the word.

The word went unsaid. For one thing, in the bow of the dromon stood a white-painted shield hung on a spearshaft, the Videssian sign of truce. For another, the dromon was alone. If he sank it and slew its sailors, a swarm would sally forth for vengeance. Stavrakios, the man who sat on the Empire's throne, was very like a Haloga in that.

The dromon halted perhaps a furlong from the end of the fjord. Skatval watched the loincloth-clad sailors (his lips twisted in a scornful smile as he imagined how they would fare in such garb here, more than a month either way from high summer) lower a boat into the gray-blue water. Four men scrambled down a rope into the boat. The ragged way they worked the oars told him at once they were no sailors. Now the corners of his mouth turned down. What were they, then?

As they moved out of the dromon's shadow, the sun shone off their shaven pates. For a moment, Skatval simply accepted what he saw. Then he cursed, loud, long, and fierce. So the Videssians were sending another pack of priests to Halogaland, were they? Had they not yet learned the northern folk cared nothing for their god? Or was it that their Phaos sometimes demanded blood sacrifice?

Skatval chewed on the new thought some little while, for it made the Videssian god more like those he venerated. But in the end he spat it out. He had seen imperials at worship. They gave their effete god hymns, not gore.

With the boat gone, the dromon turned almost in its own length (there was oarwork worth respect) and made to the outlet of the fjord. Skatval frowned again. Not even the bloodless Videssians were in the habit of leaving priests behind to perish.

Instead of beaching, the boat paused half a bowshot from shore. The blue-robed priests began to chant. One stood, looked up at the sun, and sketched a circle above his breast. Skatval knew that was a gesture of respect. The other priests raised their hands to the heavens. The chant went on. The standing blue-robe sketched the sun-circle again, then made a quick pass, and another, and another.

A broad bridge of sunlight suddenly sprang from boat to beach. The priests swung knapsacks over their shoulders and strode across it as confidently as if they walked on dry land. When the last of them had crossed, the bridge vanished. The boat bobbed in the fjord, lonely and forgotten.

So, Skatval thought, *they are sorcerers.* The magic, which likely awed any watching crofters, impressed him as well, but only so far: he would have thought more of it had it brought the boat in, too. Still, the Halogai also boasted wizards, though their craft was earthier, often bloodier, than this play with light itself. Skatval refused to be awed. He had no doubt that was what the blue-robes sought, else they simply would have rowed ashore.

"Like to brag of themselves, do they?" he muttered. "I'll choke their brags in their throats, by the gods."

He set hand on swordhilt and strode shorewards. Should he slay the blue-robes now, he wondered, or was that Stavrakios' purpose, to seek to incite him and give the Empire excuse to turn loose its ships and soldiers? Videssos played a slipperier game of statecraft than most. Perhaps it was wiser to let the priests first commit some outrage, as they surely would, to justify their slaughter.

The unwelcome newcomers saw him tramping down the track from the longhouse. As one, they turned his way. *As one indeed,* he thought. Videssian priests were like so many peas in a pod. Before he drew near enough to make out faces, he was sure what he would find. Some would be older, some younger, but all small and slight and swarthy by his standards.

Three of the four priests fit the expected pattern. Even their ages were hard to judge, save by the grayness of their untrimmed beards: as much as their matching robes, their naked, gleaming skulls made them seem all the same.

Perhaps because he foresaw uniformity, Skatval needed longer than he should have to note the fourth man out of the boat broke the mold. Robed he was like his companions, and shaven, but the beard that burgeoned on cheeks and chin was neither black nor gray, but rather a golden tangle that reached halfway down his chest. His face was square; his nose short; his eyes not dark, heavy-lidded, and clever but open, friendly, and the exact color of the waters of Lygra Fjord.

Skatval's firm step faltered. He tugged at his own beard, more neatly kept than that of the fourth priest but of the same shade. Here was something unlooked for. How had Videssos made a Haloga into a priest of Phaos? More to the point, what sort of weapon was he?

All the priests had been praying since they left *Merciless* for the boat that had brought them to this inhospitable shore. But now Antilas, Nephon, and Tzoumas stood silent, watching the barbarian approach. They knew martyrdom might lie only moments away, knew their fate rested in Phaos' hands alone, knew the good god would do with them as he willed.

Kveldulf knew all those things, knew them as well as his brethren. Nevertheless, he recited the creed yet again: "We bless thee, Phaos, lord with the great and good mind, watchful beforehand that the great test of life may be decided in our favor."

"Your piety, as always, does you credit, Kveldulf," Tzoumas said. Like all imperials, the old priest pronounced Kveldulf's name as if it were a proper Videssian appellation: *Kveldoulphios*. He had grown so used to hearing it thus that it was nearly as if he'd borne it that way since birth. Nearly.

Not wishing to contradict his superior, he modestly lowered his eyes. He'd spoken Phaos' creed not so much to beg favor from the good god as to anchor himself, to recall what he'd willed himself to become, in a world where he needed such anchor as much as a shipwrecked sailor needed a spar to support himself in a sea suddenly turned all topsy-turvy.

Though he'd not set foot in Halogaland for twenty years and more, everything here smote him with a familiarity the stronger for being so unexpected: the way the land sloped sharply up from the sea; the grim gray of bare rock; the air's cool salt tang; the dark cloaks of arrow-straight fir and pine that covered the shoulders of the hills; the turf walls of the chief's longhouse and the way those walls turned in toward each other to accommodate the shape of the roof, which was not in fact a roof by original intention, but rather an upside-down boat outworn for any other use. He'd passed his boyhood in just such a longhouse.

But he was a boy no more. Taken back to the Empire as a prize of war, he'd grown to manhood—grown to priesthood—in its great cities, in golden Skopentzana and in the mighty imperial capital, Videssos the city itself. Now he saw through the eyes of a man who better knew a different world from what he had taken for granted as a child.

"They're so poor," he whispered. The green fields were brave with growing barley and beans, but pitifully narrow. And the crops, by Videssian standards, could not help being scanty. Under the smiling southern sun, some favored provinces brought in two harvests a year. Here in the north, getting one was by no means guaranteed. The kine were small, the pigs scrawny; only the sheep seemed as fine and woolly as he remembered. They had need for fine wool here, wool to ward against winter.

Even the longhouse was at the same time a match for his memories and less than he had looked for it to be. This chief was richer than Kveldulf's father had dreamed of being; his home was bigger and stronger than that from which Kveldulf had fled, nose running and throat raw from smoke, as the imperials set it ablaze. Yet beside a score of homes, palaces, temples in Skopentzana, beside a score of scores in Videssos the city, it was but a hovel, and a filthy hovel at that.

The chief himself still stumped toward the priests. He was a big, broad-shouldered man with the same pale hair, fair skin, and light eyes as Kveldulf's. The massive gold brooch that closed his cloak also declared his rank. But his baggy wool trousers had dirt-stained knees, perhaps from stooping in the fields but as likely from the earthen floor of the longhouse. Recalling his father's holding burning over his head made Kveldulf notice the chief's red-tracked eyes, the soot forever ground into the lines of his forehead: the Halogai knew of chimneys, but in winter they often chose not to let heat flee through them.

The chief paused about ten feet in front of the priests, spent a full minute surveying them. Then he said, "Why came you here, where you know your kind are not welcome?" His deep, slow voice, the sonorous, mouth-filling words he spoke, made Kveldulf shiver. Not since boyhood had he heard anyone save himself speak the pure Haloga tongue; he had taught it to his comrades here, but they gave it back with a staccato Videssian intonation.

Just the sound of the chief's voice set Kveldulf's heart crying to reply, but that was not his proper place. Modestly, he cast his eyes to the ground as Tzoumas, senior and most holy of the four, answered in the northern speech: "We come to tell you of the good god Phaos, the lord with the great and good mind, whom you must worship for the sake of your souls."

"Here is a new thing," the chief said, raising straw-colored eyebrows. Suddenly, he shifted into Videssian: "Not a few of us know your language, but few southern men have bothered learning ours."

Behind Kveldulf, Nephon nudged Antilas, whispered, "Few of Videssos would waste their time on this barbarous jargon." Antilas grunted agreement. The Haloga chief could not have

heard him. Kveldulf frowned anyhow, though Nephon was far
from wrong; only a direct order from the patriarch had produced
even three to learn the northern tongue and the ways of the
Halogai. Most Videssians assumed anyone unwilling to take on
their own ways was not worth saving.

The chief went on, still in Videssian, "I dare say this decoy
duck taught it to you." His gaze swung to Kveldulf and he returned to his birthspeech as he asked, "Who are you, and how
came you among the southrons?"

"By your leave, holy sir?" Kveldulf murmured to Tzoumas,
who dipped his head in assent. Only then did Kveldulf speak directly to the Haloga: "I am Kveldulf, a priest of Phaos like any
other."

"Not like any other, by the gods," the chief said. "And Kveldulf *what*? Are you a slave or a woman, that you have neither
ekename nor father's name to set beside your own?" He
thumped his chest with a big fist. "Me, I am Skatval the Brisk,
otherwise Skatval Raud's son."

"Honor to you and yours, Brisk Skatval," Kveldulf said, giving the chief proper greeting. "I am—Kveldulf. It is enough. If
you like, I am a slave, but a willing slave to the good god, as are
all his priests. We have no other titles, and need none."

"You—own yourself a slave?" Skatval's sword slid from its
sheath. "And you would fain enslave the free folk of Halogaland?"

"To the good god, yes." Kveldulf knew death walked close.
Among themselves, the Halogai kept no slaves. Videssos did.
Kveldulf had been a slave of the most ordinary sort until his fer-
vent love for the god of whom he learned within the Empire per-
suaded his master, a pious man himself, to free him to serve
Phaos. He unflinchingly met Skatval's glare. "Slay me if you
must, sir. I shall not flee, nor fight. But while I live, I shall preach."

The Haloga chief began to bring up his bright blade. Then, all
at once, he stopped, threw back his head, and roared laughter till
it echoed from the hills. "Preach as you will, where you will,
nithing of a priest. Let us see how many northern men would
willingly shackle themselves forever to anything, even a god."

Kveldulf felt angry heat rise from his throat to the top of his head. With his pale, almost transparent skin, he knew how visible his rage had to be. He did not care. Of themselves, his hands curled into clumsy, unpracticed fists. He took a step toward Skatval. "Hold!" Tzoumas said sharply.

Skatval laughed still, threw aside his sword. "Let him come, Videssian. Perhaps I can pound sense into his shaven head, if it will enter there in no other way."

"Hold, holy sir," Tzoumas told Kveldulf again, and waited for him to obey before turning back to Skatval. To the chief, he said, "Pick up your weapon, sir, for in the battle about to be joined, you will find Kveldulf well armed."

"Well armed? With what?" Skatval jeered.

"With words," Tzoumas answered. Skatval suddenly stopped smiling.

Kveldulf preached in a pasture, a clump of cow dung close by his sandals. From everything Skatval knew of Videssians, that in itself would have been plenty to put them off stride. But Kveldulf noticed no more than any of the chief's smallholders might have. And too many of those smallholders to suit Skatval stood in the field to listen.

Skatval watched from the edge of the woods that lay by the pasture. He had called Kveldulf a woman for bearing an unadorned name. Now, as if in revenge for that taunt, women flocked to hear the Haloga unaccountably turned Videssian priest. When he thought to be so, Skatval was just enough. Much as he despised Kveldulf, he could not deny the blue-robe made a fine figure of a man, save for his naked skull. And even that, repulsive as it still seemed on the Videssian clerics, might be reckoned but an exotic novelty on one who was in every other way a perfect northerner. By the sighs from the womenfolk, they reckoned it so, which only annoyed Skatval the more.

Among those womenfolk was his own daughter Skjaldvor; he saw her bright gold hair in the second row of the crowd around Kveldulf. He rumbled something discontented, down deep in his throat. If Skjaldvor took this southron nonsense seriously, how could he hope to rid himself of Kveldulf when the time

came for that? He rumbled again. His daughter should have
been wed two years ago, maybe three or four, but he'd indulged,
indeed been flattered by, her wish to stay in his own longhouse.
Now he wondered what sort of price he would have to pay for
that indulgence.

He could all but hear his own stern, bloodthirsty gods laughing at him. They knew one always paid for being soft. He
scowled. Would they willingly let themselves be supplanted, just
for the sake of teaching him a lesson he already had by heart?
They might. Halogai who went after vengeance pursued it for its
own sake, without counting coins to see if it was worth the cost.

The summer breeze, so mild as to befool a man who did not
know better into thinking such fine days would last forever, blew
Kveldulf's words to Skatval's ears. The priest had a fine, mellow
voice, a man's voice, and was no mean speaker: to northern di-
rectness he married a more sophisticated Videssian style, as if
he were holding up ideas in his hands and examining them from
all sides.

He paused. His listeners, who should have been making the
most of the short summer season instead of standing around listening to sweet-tasting nonsense, broke into applause. Skatval
saw Skjaldvor's hands meet each other, saw in profile her bright
eyes aimed straight at Kveldulf, her mouth wide and smiling.

He began to worry in earnest.

After some days' preaching, Kveldulf began to worry in
earnest. The Halogai, once his people—*still* his people if blood
counted as well as dwelling, as it surely did—flocked to hear
him. They listened to him with greater, more serious attention
than a crowd of Videssians would have granted; every imperial
fancied himself a theologian, and wanted to argue every shade
of meaning in Phaos' holy scriptures. The Halogai listened respectfully; they nodded soberly; they declined to convert.

It was not that they had no questions for him; they had many.
But those questions did not spring from the holy scriptures; they
did not assume those scriptures were true, and argue from or
about their premises. To the Halogai, everything pertaining to

Phaos, even his existence, was open to debate. Kveldulf had been warned of that before he sailed for his birthland. Only now, though, was he discovering what it meant.

No Videssian, for instance, would have asked, as did a herder whose rawhide boots were stained with sheepshit, "Well, just how d'you ken this Phaos o'yours is what you say he is?"

"Things act for good in this world, and others for evil," Kveldulf answered. "Phaos is the architect of all that is good, while Skotos works without pause to pull down all he does." He spat between his feet in rejection of the dark god.

The shepherd spat, too. "So you say. Who said so to you?"

"So say the good god's own holy words, written down in ancient days." Kveldulf nodded to Tzoumas, who held up a copy of the scriptures. The words within meant nothing to the watching Halogai; they did not write their own language, let alone Videssian. But the cover, of brass polished till it gleamed like gold and decorated with precious stones and an enamelwork portrait of Phaos' stern, majestic countenance, promised that what lay within was worthy of consideration. As the Videssian proverb put it, *a robe is revealed in advance by its border*.

But the stubborn shepherd said, "Did your god speak these words straight to you?" Kveldulf had to shake his head. The shepherd went on, "Then why put faith in 'em? When I hear the thunder, or see the grain spring green from the ground, or futter my woman, these are things whose truth I know for myself; I feel no shame to worship the gods that shaped them. But a god who spoke long ago, if he spoke at all? Pah!" He spat again.

Behind Kveldulf, one of his Videssian colleagues—he thought it was Nephon—softly said, "Blasphemy!" Kveldulf himself felt brief heat run through his body, heat warmer than that which the watery sunshine of Halogaland could engender. Along with their hair, Videssian priests gave up carnal congress as a mark of their devotion to the good god. Kveldulf had worn his celibacy a long time now; it rarely chafed him. But imperials did not talk about futtering as casually as the shepherd had, either. The naked word made Kveldulf feel for a moment what he had given up.

He said, "If the good god's holy words will not inspire you, think on the deeds of those who follow him. They hold sway from the borders of Makuran far in the southwest, round the lands which touch the Videssian Sea and the Sailors' Sea, and sweep up along the edge of the Northern Sea till their lands march with yours as well. And all this under the rule of one man, the mighty Emperor Stavrakios, Avtokrator of the Videssians, where small Halogaland is split among countless chiefs. Does this not speak for the strength of Phaos?"

Behind him, Nephon said, "This argument is unscriptural. The barbarians must come to Phaos' faith because of the glory of the good god, not that of those who follow him."

"Don't call them barbarians," Antilas said quietly. "He's one of them, remember?"

Nephon grunted. Tzoumas said, "How worshipers find Phaos matters little; that they find him matters much. Let Kveldulf go on, if he will."

The byplay had been in Videssian. The Halogai to whom Kveldulf preached took no notice of it. And now, for the first time since he'd come to Halogaland, he had hearers who listened seriously. He wondered why, for Nephon was right: an argument from results was weaker than one from doctrine. But the men of the north respected strength; perhaps reminding them of the power of Videssos had not hurt.

"Cast forth the evil from your own lives!" he called. "Accept Phaos into your hearts, into your spirits. Turn toward the good which rests in each of you. Who will show me now that he is ready to cleave to the lord with the great and good mind, and reject evil forevermore?"

He'd asked that before at the close of every sermon, and been answered with stony silence or with jeers. The Halogai were happy enough to listen to him; it gave them something unusual and interesting to do with their time. But hearing and hearkening were two different things, and for all his passionate exhortation, he'd not convinced anyone, not until today. Now a woman raised her hand, then another, and then a man.

Kveldulf sketched the sun-sign over his heart. As he looked

up to the heavens to thank Phaos for allowing him to be persuasive, his eyes filled with grateful tears. At last the good god had given a sign he would not forsake the folk of the north.

Skatval slashed the horse's throat. As the sacrificial beast staggered, he held the *laut*-bowl under its neck to gather the gushing blood. The horse fell. From the *laut*-bowl he filled *laut*-sprinklers and stained the wooden walls of the temple with shining red. He also daubed his own cheeks and hands, and those of the clansfolk who had gathered with him for the offering.

As he moistened men and women with the holy blood, his priest, Grimke Grankel's son, declared, "May goodness flow down from the god as the gore goes out of the offering."

"So may it be," Skatval echoed. So did his warriors and their women—those that were here. He did his best to hide his unease as he began to butcher the horse, but it was not easy. Sacrifice should have brought together the whole of the clan, to receive the gods' blessing and to feast on horseflesh and ale afterwards. Most of his people had come, but far too many were missing.

Among the missing was Skjaldvor. Skatval's eyebrows came together above his long, thin nose. Of all the people who might listen to this southron twaddle about Phaos, he'd expected his daughter to be one of the last.

He glanced over at Ulvhild, his wife. After they'd lived together in that longhouse the whole of their grown lives, she picked thoughts from his head as if he'd shouted them aloud. Now she shrugged, slowly and deliberately, telling him there was nothing she could do about Skjaldvor: his daughter was a woman now. He snorted. No one could do anything with a girl once she turned into a woman. Ulvhild heard the snort and glared at him—she'd stolen that thought, too.

Hastily, he turned back to roasting horseflesh. The first pieces were done enough to eat. Someone held out a birchwood platter. He stabbed a gobbet, plopped it onto the plate. Beside him, Grimkel plied a dipper, filled a mug with ale. "The gods bless us with their bounty," he intoned.

Some time later, his belly full of meat and his head spinning slightly from many mugs of ale, Skatval strode out of the temple. He was one of the last folk to leave: not least of his chiefly requirements was being able to outeat and outdrink those he outranked. The rich taste of hot marrow still filled his mouth.

He thumped his middle with the flat of his hand. Life was not so bad. The fields bore as well as they ever did; no murrain had smote the flocks, nor sickness his people. No raiders threatened. Winter would be long, but winter was always long. The gods willing, almost all the clan would see the next spring. He had been through too many years where dearth and death displayed themselves long months in advance.

Then satisfaction leaked from him as if he were a cracked pot. There at the edge of a hayfield walked Skjaldvor and Kveldulf, not arm in arm but side by side, their heads close together. Kveldulf explained something with extravagant gestures he must have learned from the Videssians; no man of Halogaland would have been so unconstrained. Skjaldvor laughed, clapped her hands, nodded eagerly. Whatever point he'd made, she approved of it.

Or more likely, she just approves of Kveldulf, Skatval thought with bleak mirth. The chief wondered if she drew a distinction between the blue-robe's doctrines and himself. He had his doubts. But what could he do? What could anyone do with a girl, once she turned into a woman?

He'd answered that question for himself back inside the temple. He did not like the conclusion he'd reached there, but found none better now.

"Tell me, Kveldulf," Skjaldvor said, "how came you to reverence the Videssian god?" She stopped walking, cocked her head, and waited for his reply.

The light that filtered through the forest canopy overhead was clear, pale, almost colorless, like the gray-white trunks of the birch trees all around. The air tasted of moss and dew. When he paused, too, Kveldulf felt quiet fold round him like a cloak. Somewhere far in the distance, he heard the low, purring trill of a crested tit. Otherwise, all was still. He could hear his own breath move in and out, and after a moment Skjaldvor's as well.

As she looked at him, so he studied her. She was tall for a woman, the crown of her head reaching higher than his chin. Flowing gilt hair framed her face, a strong-chinned, proud-cheekboned visage, which along with the unshrinking gaze of her wide-set blue eyes, spoke volumes about the legendary stubbornness of the Halogai. She had, in fact, a close copy of her father's features, though in her his harshness somehow grew fresh and lovely. But Kveldulf, unpracticed with either families or women, could not quite catch that.

He did know she made him nervous, and also knew he spent more time with her than he should. All of Skatval's clansfolk had souls that wanted saving. Still, Kveldulf told himself, winning the chief's daughter to the worship of the good god would greatly strengthen Phaos here. And she could have chosen nothing apter to ask him.

The years blew away as he looked back inside himself. "I was a lad yet, my beard not sprouted, sold as a house slave: Videssian spoil of war. I learned the Empire's tongue fast enough to suit my master. He was far from the worst of men; he worked me hard, but he fed me well, and beat me no worse than I deserved." The hairs of his mustache tickled his lips as they quirked into a wry smile. Remembering some of his pranks, he reckoned Zoïlos merciful now, though he hadn't thought so at the time.

"How could you live—a slave?" Skjaldvor shuddered. "You come of free folk. Would you not liefer have lost your life than live in chains?"

"I wore no chains," Kveldulf said.

"That may be worse," she told him, scorn in her voice. "You stayed in slavery when you could have—should have—fled?" She turned her back on him. Her long wool skirt swirled around her, showing him for a moment her slim white ankles.

"How was I to flee?" he asked, doing his best to inform his voice with reason rather than wrath. "Skopentzana is far from Halogaland, and I was but a boy. And before long, I came to see my capture as a blessing, not the sorrow I had held it to be."

Skjaldvor looked at him again, but with hands on her hips. "A blessing? Are you witstruck? To have to walk at the whim of another man's will—I would die before I endured it."

"As may be," Kveldulf said soberly. A slave as lovely as Skjaldvor was all too likely to have to lie down at the whim of another man's will. Zoïlos, fortunately, had not bought Kveldulf for that. He shook his head to dislodge the distracting carnal thought, went on, "But you asked of me how I found Phaos. Had I not been Zoïlos' slave, I doubt I should have. He often went out of a morning, and one day I asked where. He told me he prayed at the chief temple in Skopentzana, and asked in turn if I cared to go there with him."

"And you said aye?"

"I said aye." Kveldulf laughed at his younger self. "It seemed easier than my usual morning drudgery. So he let me bathe, and gave me a shirt less shabby than most, and I walked behind him to the temple. We went inside. I had never smelt incense before. Then I looked up into the dome . . ."

His voice trailed away. Across a quarter of a century, he could still call up the awe he'd known, looking up into the golden dome and seeing Phaos stern in judgment, staring down at him—seemingly at him alone, though the temple was crowded—and weighing his worth. Then the priestly choir behind the altar lifted up its many-voiced voice in exaltation and praise of the lord with the great and good mind, and then—

Kveldulf remembered to speak: "I knew not whether I was still on earth or up in the heavens. I saw the holy men in the blue robes who lived with the good god every moment of every day of every year of their lives, and I knew I had to be of their number. Next morning, I asked Zoïlos if I might go with him, not he me, and the morning after that, and the one after that. At first, when I was but shirking, he'd hoped me pious. Now, when I truly touched piety, he reckoned me a shirker. But I kept on; I was drunk with the good god. Once I found Phaos, I wished for nothing else. Well, not nothing; I wished for but one thing more."

"What is that?" Skjaldvor leaned toward him. The silver chains that linked the two larger brooches she wore on her breast clinked softly (the shape of those brooches reminded

Kveldulf of nothing so much as twin tortoise shells). All at once he was conscious of how close she stood.

Nonetheless, he answered as he had intended: "I wished the good god might grant me the boon of leading my birthfolk out of Skotos' darkness and into the light of Phaos. For those who die without knowing the lord with the great and good mind shall surely spend all eternity in the icepits of Skotos, a fate I wish on no man or woman, Videssian or Haloga, slave or free."

"Oh." Skjaldvor straightened. Where before her voice had been low and breathy, now it went oddly flat. She studied him again, as if wondering whether to go on. At last she did: "I thought perhaps you meant you wished you might enjoy all the pleasures of other men."

Kveldulf felt himself grow hot, and knew his fair skin only made embarrassment more obvious. He looked to see if Skjaldvor also blushed. Though fairer even than he, she did not. She knew herself free to say what she would, act as she would. He stammered a little as he answered, "I may not, not without turning oathbreaker, and that I shall never do."

"The more fool you, and the worse waste, for you are no mean man," she said. "The other blue-robes are less stupid."

"What do you mean?" he demanded.

"Do you not know? *Can* you not know, without being deaf and blind? Your fellows are far from passing all their nights alone and lonely in their tents."

"Is it so?" Kveldulf said, but by her malicious satisfaction he knew it surely was. Sorrow pressed upon him but left him unsurprised. He bent his head, sketched the sun-circle over his heart. "All men may sin. I shall pray for them."

She stared at him. "Is that all?"

"What else would you have me do?" he asked, honestly curious.

"Were it not for your beard, I should guess the southrons made you a eunuch when they set the blue robe upon you." Skjaldvor took a deep breath, let it hiss out through flaring nostrils. "What else would I have you do? This, to start." As she stepped into his arms, her expression might have been that of a warrior measuring a foe over sword and shield.

The gold of her brooches pressed against him through his robe, then the softer, yielding firmness that was herself. His arms still hung by his sides, but that mattered little, for she held him to her. From the sweat that prickled on his forehead and shaven pate, the cool wood might suddenly have become a tropic swamp. Then she kissed him. Not even a man of stone, a statue like one of those in Skopentzana's central square, could have remained unroused.

She stepped back and eyed not his red face but his groin to gauge her effect on him. That effect was all too visible, which only made his face grow redder. But when she reached out to open his robe, he slapped her hand aside. "No, by the good god," he said harshly.

Now she reddened, too, with anger. "Why ever not? The Videssians do not stint themselves; why should you, when you are not of their kindred nor born to their faith?"

"That they do wrong is no reason for me to follow them. Were they murdering instead of fornicating, would you bid me do likewise?"

"How can anything so full of joy be wrong?" Skjaldvor tossed her shining hair in scorn at the very idea.

"It is forbidden to Phaos' priests, thus wrong for them," Kveldulf declared. "And though I was not born to faith in Phaos, in it I am a son fostered to a fine father. Whatever I was by birth, Phaos' is the house wherein I would dwell evermore."

All he said was true, yet he knew it was incomplete. As a foster son in Phaos' household, he was held to closer scrutiny than the Videssians who entered it by right of birth: they might be forgiven sins that would condemn him, the outsider who presumed to ape their ways. Another man might have grown resentful, struggling against that double standard. But it spurred Kveldulf. If extra devotion was required of him, extra devotion he would give.

"You will not?" Skjaldvor said.

"I will not," Kveldulf answered firmly. Never since donning the blue robe had he known such temptation; the memory of her body printed against him, he knew, would remain with him till his last breath. He still throbbed from wanting her. But priests were taught to rule their flesh. Over and over he repeated Phaos' creed to himself, focusing on the good god rather than his fleshly lust, and at length that lust began to lessen.

Skjaldvor drew near him again. This time, he thought, he would be proof against her embraces. But she did not embrace him. Serpent-swift, she slapped his left cheek, then, on the backhand, his right. He cherished the sudden pain, which seared the last of his desire from him.

"May the lord with the great and good mind keep you in his heart until you place him in yours," he said. "I shall pray that that time be soon, as you have seemed better disposed than most of your fellows to learning of his faith."

She tossed her head again and laughed, an ugly sound despite the sweetness of her voice. Then she spat full in his face. "This for your Phaos and his faith." She spat again. "And this for you!" She spun on her heel and stormed away.

Kveldulf stood and watched her go while her warm spittle slid down into his beard. Very deliberately, he bent his head and spat himself, down between his feet in the age-old Videssian gesture that rejected Skotos. He recited Phaos' creed once more. When he was through, he walked slowly back toward the tents by the shore.

Skatval watched the small crowd of crofters and herders raise hands to the heavens. The sound of their prayers to Phaos reached him faintly. Save for the name of the Videssian god, the words were in the Haloga tongue. Skatval had heard worse poetry from bards who lived by traveling from chief to chief with their songs. *Kveldulf's work, no doubt,* he thought; the blond-bearded priest was proving a man of more parts than he had looked for.

Absent from the converts' conclave was Skjaldvor. For that, Skatval sent up his own prayers of thanks to his gods. He had not asked what passed between her and Kveldulf, but where before she had gone to his services, looked on him with mooncalf eyes, now all at once the sight of him made her face go hard and hateful, hearing his name brought curses from her lips. She was in no danger of coming to follow Phaos, not any more.

But the priests from the Empire had won more folk to their faith than Skatval expected (truth to tell, he'd thought his people would laugh Kveldulf and the rest away in disgrace, else he would have slain them as soon as they set foot on his soil). That worried him. Followers of Videssos' faith would mean Videssian priests on his land henceforward, and that would mean . . . Skatval growled wordlessly. He stalked toward the prayer meeting. He would show his people what that meant.

Kveldulf bowed courteously as he drew nigh. "The good god grant you peace, Skatval the Brisk. May I hope you have come to join us?"

"No," he said, biting off the word. "I would ask a couple of questions of you."

Kveldulf bowed again. "Ask what you will. Knowledge is a road to faith."

"Knowledge is a road around the snare you have set for my people," Skatval retorted. "Suppose some of us take on your faith and then fall out over how to follow it. Who decides which of us is in the right?"

"Priests are brought up from boyhood in Phaos' way," Kveldulf said. "Can newcomers to that way hope to match them in knowledge?"

Skatval grimaced. The Haloga priest—no, the blond Videssian, that was the better way to think of him—was not making matters easy. But the chief bulled ahead regardless: "Suppose the blue-robes disagree, as they may, men being what they are? Who then says which walks the proper path?"

"The prelates set over them," Kveldulf said, cautious now. Skatval had probed at him before, but in private, not in front of the people.

"And the priest against whom judgment falls?" the chief said. "If he will not yield, is he then an outlaw?"

"A heretic, we name one who chooses his own false doctrine over that ordained by his elders." Kveldulf considered the question, then added, "But no, he is not to be outlawed—excommunicated is the word the temples use—yet, for he has right of appeal to the patriarch, the most holy and chiefest priest, the head of all the faith."

"Ah, the patriarch!" Skatval exclaimed, as if hearing of the existence of a supreme prelate for the first time. "And where dwells this prince of piety?"

"In Videssos the city, by the High Temple there," Kveldulf answered.

"In Videssos the city? Under the Avtokrator's thumb, you mean." Skatval showed teeth in something more akin to a lynx's hunting snarl than to a smile. "So you would have us put to Stavrakios' judgment aught upon which we may disagree, is that what you say?" He turned to the converts, lashed them with wounding words: "I reckoned you freemen, not slaves to Videssos through the Empire's god. Your holy Kveldulf here is but the thin end of the wedge, I warn you."

"The patriarch rules the church, not the Avtokrator," Kveldulf insisted. Behind him, his Videssian colleagues nodded vigorously.

Skatval ignored them; without Kveldulf, they were nothing here. At Kveldulf, he snapped, "And if your precious patriarch dies, what then?"

"Then the prelates come together in conclave to choose his successor," Kveldulf answered.

Skatval quite admired him; without lying, he had twisted truth to his purposes. Against many Halogai, even chiefs, his words would have wrought what he intended. But Skatval, mistrusting the Empire more than most, had learned more of it than most. "By the truth you hold in your god, Kveldulf, who names the three men from whom the prelates pick the patriarch?"

Just for a moment, he saw hatred in those blue eyes so like his own. Just for a moment—and when it cleared, it cleared completely. Skatval also saw the Videssian priests visibly willing Kveldulf to lie. But when he answered at last, his voice was firm, if low: "The Avtokrator names those candidates."

"There, you see?" Skatval turned to the converts who had heard him argue with Kveldulf. "You see? Aye, follow Phaos, if you fancy the Avtokrator telling you how to go about it. Videssos has not the strength to vanquish us by the sword, so she seeks to strangle us with the spider's silk spun by her god. And you—you seek to aid the Empire!"

He had hoped forcing Kveldulf to concede that Phaos' faith was dominated by the Emperor would of itself make his people turn away from the Videssian god. And indeed, a couple of men and women left the gathering, shaking their heads at their own foolishness. To the Halogai, Videssos' autocracy seemed like a whole great land living in chains.

But more folk than he expected stayed where they were, waiting to hear how Kveldulf would answer him. The priest, too canny by half to suit Skatval, saw that as well, and grew stronger for it. He said boldly, "No matter whence the faith comes, friends, its truth remains. You have heard that truth in Phaos' holy scriptures, heard it in my own poor words, and accepted it of your free will. Apart from the cost to your souls in the life to come, turning aside from it now at your chief's urging is surely as slavish as his imagined claim that you somehow serve the Empire by accepting the good god."

Skatval ground his teeth when he saw several men soberly nodding. People stopped leaving the field in which the returned Haloga was holding his service. Kveldulf did not display the triumph he must have felt. A Videssian would have done so, and lost the people whose respect he'd regained. Kveldulf merely continued the service as if nothing had happened: he was a Haloga at heart, and knew the quiet gesture was the quicker killer.

Skatval stormed away. Forcing the fight further now would but cost him face. As he tramped into the woods, he almost ran over Grimke Grankel's son. "Are you coming to cast your lot with Phaos, too?" he snarled.

"A man may watch a foe without wishing to join him," the servant of the Haloga gods replied.

"At least you see he is a foe: more than those cheeseheads back there care to notice," Skatval said. "A deadly dangerous foe." His eyes narrowed as he looked back toward Kveldulf, who was leading his converts in yet another translated hymn. "Why, then, does he not deserve some deadly danger?"

Grimke glanced at the sword he wore on his belt. "You could have given it to him."

"I wanted to, but feared it would set his followers forever in his path. If you, however, were to slay the southrons—and Kveldulf, their stalking horse—by sorcery, all would see our gods are stronger than the one for whom he prates."

Grimke Grankel's son stared, then slowly smiled. "This could be done, my chief."

"Then do it. Too long I tolerated the traitor among us, long enough for his treachery to take root. Now, as I say, simply to slay Kveldulf and his Videssian cronies would stir more strife than it stopped. But you would not *simply* slay him, eh?"

"No, not simply." Grimke's face mirrored anticipation and calculation. "Hmm . . . 'twere best to wait till midnight, when the power of his god is at its lowest ebb."

"As you reckon best. In matters magical, you know—" Skatval broke off, stared at his sorcerer. "Do you say that even you acknowledge Phaos a true god?"

"This for Phaos." Grimke spat between his feet, as a Videssian would in rejecting Skotos. "But any god is true to one who truly believes, and may ward against wizardry. Given a choice between sorceries, I would choose the simpler when I may. Thus, midnight serves me best."

"Let it be as you wish, then," Skatval said. "But let it be tonight."

Even at midnight, the sky was not wholly dark. Sullen red marked the northern sky, tracing the track of the sun not far below the ground. Seeing that glow, Skatval thought of blood. Only a few of the brightest stars pierced the endless summer twilight.

A small fire crackled. Bit by bit, Grimke Grankel's son fed it with chips of wood and other, less readily identifiable, substances. The fickle breeze flicked smoke into Skatval's face. He coughed and nearly choked; it had not the savor of honest flames. Almost, he told Grimke to stamp it out and set sorcery aside.

Grimke set a silver *laut*-bowl in the fire, which licked around it until the gods and savage beasts worked in relief on its outside seemed to writhe with a life of their own. Skatval rubbed his eyes. Heat-shimmers he knew, but none like these. The bowl held a thick jelly. When it began to bubble and seethe, Grimke nodded as if satisfied.

Above the bowl he held two cups of similar work, one filled with blood (some was his own, some Skatval's), the other with bitter ale. Slowly, slowly, he poured the twin thin streams down into the *laut*-bowl. "Drive the intruders from our land, drive them to fear, drive them to death," he intoned. "As our blood is burnt, find for them fates bitter as this beer. May they know sorrow, may they know shame, may they forget their god and gain only graves."

Filled with assonance and alliteration, the chant rolled on. Hair rose on Skatval's forearms and at the back of his neck; though the magic was not aimed at him, he felt its force, felt it and was filled with fear. The gods of the Halogai were grim and cold, like the land they ruled. As Grimke prodded them to put forth their power, Skatval wondered for a moment if Phaos would not make a better, safer master for his folk. He fought the thought down, hoping his gods had not seen it.

Too late for second thoughts, anyhow. Grimke's voice rose, almost to a scream. And other screams, more distant, rose in answer from the tents in which the priests dwelt. Hearing the horror in them, Skatval wondered again if he should have chosen Phaos. He shook his head. Phaos might make his folk a fine master, but the Avtokrator Stavrakios would not, and he could not have the one without the other.

Grimke Grankel's son set down the silver cups. The flickering flames showed sweat slithering down his face, harsh lines carved from nose to mouth corners. Voice slow and rough with weariness, he said, "What magic may wreak, magic has wrought."

*   *   *

Kveldulf woke from dreams filled with dread. The sun shining through the side of his tent made him sigh with relief, as if he had no right to see it. He shook his head, feeling foolish. Dreams were but dreams, no matter how frightening: when the sun rose, they were gone. But these refused to go.

He had slept in his robe. Now he belted it on again, went outside to offer morning prayers to the sun, the symbol of his god. Tzoumas, Nephon, and Antilas remained in their tents. *Slugabeds,* he thought, and lifted hands to the heavens. "We bless thee, Phaos, lord with the great and good mind—" Out of the corner of his eye, he saw Skatval bearing down on him, but took no true notice of the chief until he had finished the creed.

"You live!" Skatval shouted, as if it were a crime past forgiving.

"Well, aye," Kveldulf said, smiling. "The good god brought me safe through another night. Am I such an ancient, though, that the thought fills you with surprise?"

"Look to your fellows," Skatval said, staring at him still.

"I would not disturb them at their rest," Kveldulf said. Tzoumas in particular could be a bear with a sore paw unless he got in a full night.

"Look to them!" Skatval said, so fiercely Kveldulf had to obey. He went over to Nephon's tent, pulled back the flaps that closed it, stuck his head inside. A moment later, he drew back, face pale, stomach heaving. Of themselves, his fingers shaped Phaos' sun-circle. He went to Antilas' tent, and Tzoumas', hoping for something better, but in each he found only twisted death, with terror carved irremovably onto all the priests' features.

He turned back to Skatval. "Why did you spare me? I would sooner have died with my fellows." He knew the chief did not favor his faith, but had not imagined he held such hatred as to do—what he had done to the Videssians. By his own standards, Skatval seemed a reasonable man. But where was the reason in this?

Skatval supplied it: "The gods know I hoped Grimke's wizardry would overfall you, too, you more than any of the others. They without you were nothing; you without them remain a deadly foe to all I hold dear: deadlier now, for having survived.

Your god I could perhaps live with, or suffer my folk to do so. But with Phaos you bring Stavrakios, and that I will not have. Flee now, Kveldulf, while life remains in you, if you would save yourself."

Slowly, Kveldulf shook his head. He knew Skatval spoke some truth; half-overheard whispers from Videssian hierarchs said as much. In one of its aspects, the faith of Phaos was the glove within which moved the hand of imperial statecraft. If the Halogai served Phaos, they might one day come to serve Stavrakios or his successors as well.

But that was not the portion of the faith to which Kveldulf had been drawn. He believed with all his soul in the lord with the great and good mind, believed others needed to believe for the sake of their souls, believed most of all his native people had been blind in spirit far too long, that too many of them suffered forever in Skotos' ice because they knew not Phaos. That the good god might have singled him out to lead the Halogai to the light filled him with holy joy he had not known since the day when he first set eyes on Phaos, stern in judgment in the temple in Skopentzana.

And so he shook his head once more, and said, "I shall not flee, Skatval. I told you as much when first I came here. You may slay me, but while I draw breath I shall go on glorifying Phaos to your folk. The good god demands no less of me. He is my shield, my protector, against all evil; if I die here, he shall receive my soul."

To his amazement, Skatval bellowed laughter. "You may follow the southrons' god, but you have a Haloga's soul. We are stubborn, not slippery or subtle like the Videssians. Those three priests dead in their tents, they would have given me all manner of lies, then tried to squirm around them. That way has served Videssos for centuries."

"It is not mine," Kveldulf said simply.

"So I have seen." Skatval's eyes narrowed, sharpened, until they pierced Kveldulf like blued blades. "And so, likely, you still live. Oh, I'll not deny those Videssians served their god—"

"My god," Kveldulf broke in.

"However you would have it. They served him, in their fashion, but they served Stavrakios as well. You, though, you're so cursed full of Phaos, you have no room in you for anything else. Thus your faith warded you, where theirs, thinner, went for naught."

"It may well be so." Kveldulf remembered how Skjaldvor had jeered, saying the three Videssian priests ignored their vows of celibacy. Remembering Skjaldvor, he remembered also her body pressed against his, remembered his manhood rising in desire. He said, "Yet I am no great holy man, to be revered by the generations yet to come. I am as full of sin as anyone, fight it though I may."

"To what man is it given to know in his lifetime how the generations yet to come will look on him?" Skatval said. "We do what we will and what we may with the time we have. Among men, that must be enough; the gods alone see how our purposes intertwine."

"There, for once, but for your choice of words, we agree." To his surprise, Kveldulf found himself bowing to Skatval, as he might have before an ecclesiastical superior. More clearly than ever before, he saw the Haloga chief was also fighting for a way of life he reckoned right. That saddened Kveldulf, for he had always believed those who failed to follow Phaos were without any sort of honor. Yet he remained convinced his own way was best, was true. He said, "But for our choice of creeds, we might have been friends, you and I."

"So we might, though your unbending honesty makes you a dangerous man to keep by one's side: you are a sharp sword without sheath." Skatval stroked his chin, considering. "It might still come to pass. How's this? Instead of bidding us throw down our gods, give over your Phaos, grow out your hair, and live the rest of your days as a Haloga—as you were born to live."

Kveldulf shook his head, though startled at the sadness that surged in him. "Tell my heart to give over beating before you bid me abandon the lord with the great and good mind."

"If you do not, your heart will give over beating." Skatval touched his swordhilt.

Kveldulf bowed again. "If it be so, it shall be so. I will not flee, I will not cease. Do what you will with me on that account. My fate lies in Phaos' hands."

"I would not slay a man I admire, but if I must, I will." Skatval sighed. "As I say, by blood you belong to us. Many are the bold warriors sung of in our lays who chose death over yielding."

"I remember the songs from my boyhood," Kveldulf said, nodding. "But Phaos' faith has its martyrs, too, Videssians who gave all for the good god, and gladly would I be reckoned among their number. Will you give me a shovel, Skatval, that I may bury my friends?"

"I will," Skatval said. "And Kveldulf—"

"Aye?"

"Dig a fourth grave, as well."

Wearing helm and hauberk, ash-hafted spear at the ready, Skatval stalked toward the meeting in the field. Half a dozen chosen men, likewise armed and armored, tramped behind him. One also carried a length of rope. Kveldulf must have seen them, but preached on. By his demeanor, he might have thought they were coming to join his converts.

Before long, perhaps warned by clanking byrnies, some of the converts turned away from Kveldulf. None of them wore mail, nor were they armed for war. Nonetheless, they moved to ring the priest with their bodies; those who bore belt knives drew them. Skatval's jaw tightened. Slaughtering the priest was one thing, fighting his own folk quite another.

"Stand aside," he said. Neither men nor women moved. "Are you so many sparrows, serving to save the cuckoo's spawn Stavrakios has set among you?"

"He is a holy man, a good man," said Kalmar Sverre's son, a fine crofter and not the worst of men himself.

"I do not deny it," Skatval said, which caused more than one of Kveldulf's guards to stare at him in surprise. He went on, "That makes him the greater danger to all that is ours. Ask him yourself, if you believe it not of me." His voice roughened. "Go on, ask him."

Though none of the converts gave way, they did look back to Kveldulf. The blue-robe stared past them to Skatval. Unafraid, he sketched the sun-sign, then set right fist over heart in formal

Videssian military salute. He said, "Skatval speaks the truth. Having taken the lord with the great and good mind into your hearts, you cannot remain what you once were. His truth will melt the falsehoods in your spirit as the summer sun slays the snows of Halogaland."

"By his own words he brands himself our foe," Skatval said. "Would you let him make you into milksop southrons?"

"Kveldulf is no milksop," Kalmar said stoutly. He held his knife low, ready to stab up in the way of those who know how to fight with short blades. But a few people left the converts' circle and stood apart from it, watching to see what would happen next.

Kveldulf said, "I would not see brother spill brother's blood. Stand aside; I told Skatval I would not flee him. Phaos will receive me into his palace; the world to come is finer than the one in which we live now. If your chief would send me to it, I will go."

"But, holy sir—" Kalmar protested. Kveldulf shook his head. The son of Sverre muttered a word that ran round the ring of converts. Skatval heard it, too: "Fey. He is fey." Kalmar looked back to Kveldulf once more. Again Kveldulf shook his head. Tears brightening his eyes, Kalmar lowered the knife to his side and stepped away. One by one, the other converts moved to right or left, until no one stood between Kveldulf and Skatval.

The chief spoke to the men behind him: "We'll take him to the trees over there and tie him."

"No need for that," Kveldulf said. He had gone pale, but his voice stayed steady. "I said I would not flee, and meant it. Do as you deem you must, and have done."

" 'Twere easier the other way, priest," Skatval said doubtfully.

"No. I need not be bound to show I would gladly lay down my life for the lord with the great and good mind; I act by my own will." Kveldulf paused for one long breath. "A favor once I am dead, though, if you would."

"If I may, without hurt to my own," Skatval said.

"Pack my head in salt, as if it were a mackerel set by for the winter, and give it into the hands of the next Videssian shipmaster who enters Lygra Fjord. Tell him the tale and bid him take it—and me—back to the temples, that the prelates there might learn of my labors for the good god's sake."

Skatval stroked his beard as he pondered. Stavrakios might shape the return of such a relic into a pretext for war, but then Stavrakios was a man who seldom needed pretext if he aimed to fight. The chief nodded. "It shall be as you say—my word on it."

"Strike, then." Kveldulf raised hands and eyes to the sky. "We bless thee, Phaos, lord with the great and good mind, watchful beforehand that—"

Skatval struck with all the strength that was in him, to give Kveldulf as quick an end as he might. The spearhead tore out through the back of the blue robe. The priest prayed on as he crumpled. Skatval's followers shoved spears into him as he lay on the green grass. Blood dribbled from the corner of his mouth. He writhed, jerked, was still.

Wearily, Skatval turned to the converts who had watched the killing. "It is over," he said. "Go to your homes; go to your work. You see whose gods are stronger. Would you worship one who lets those who love him die like a slaughtered sow? This Phaos is all very well for Videssians, who serve nobles and Avtokrator like slaves. Give me a god who girds his own to go down fighting, as a Haloga should." He locked eyes with Kalmar Sverre's son. "Or say you otherwise?"

Kalmar met his gaze without flinching, as Kveldulf had before him. In his own good time, he looked away to Kveldulf's corpse. He sighed. "No, Skatval; it is so."

Skatval sighed, too, somber still but satisfied. A low murmur rose from the rest of the converts when they heard Kalmar acknowledge the might of the old Haloga gods. They, too, took a long look at Kveldulf, lying in a pool of his own blood. A couple of women hesitantly signed themselves with the sun-circle. Most, though, began to drift out of the field where they had worshiped. Skatval did not smile, not outside where it showed. By this time next year, his folk's brief fling with Phaos would be as forgotten as a new song sung for a summer but afterwards set aside.

Pleased with the way the event had turned, he said to a couple of his followers, "Vasa, Hoel, take him by the heels and haul him to the hole he dug. But hack off his head before you throw him in; a promise is a promise."

"Aye, Skatval," they said together, as respectfully as they had ever spoken to him: almost as respectfully as if he were Stavrakios of Videssos, sole Avtokrator of a mighty empire, not Skatval the Brisk of Halogaland, one among threescore squabbling chiefs. The feeling of power, strong and sweet as wine from the south, puffed out his chest and put pride in his step as he strode up the path to his longhouse.

But when Skjaldvor spied the bright blood that reddened his spearshaft, she ran weeping through the garden and into the woods. He stared after her, scratching his head. Then he plunged the iron point of the spear into the ground several times to clean it, wiping it dry with a scrap of cloth so it would not rust.

"Try and understand women," he grumbled. He leaned the spear against the turf wall of the longhouse, opened the door, nodded to Ulvhild his wife. "Well, I'm back," he said.

The Seventh Chapter

This tale is also set in the Videssos universe. Like a lot of tales set in that universe, this one is historical based. Its model actually took place in medieval England, but the milieus—or at least this aspect of them—are similar enough to make transposition easy . . . and hair-splitting is much more a Videssian preoccupation than one from the England of long ago.

The snow was falling harder now. Kassianos' mule, a good stubborn beast, kept slogging forward until it came to a drift that reached its belly. Then it stopped, looking reproachfully back over its shoulder at the priest.

"Oh, very well," he said, as if it could understand. "This must be as Phos wills. That town the herder spoke of can't be far ahead. We'll lay over in—what did he call it?—Develtos till the weather gets better. Are you satisfied, beast?"

The mule snorted and pressed ahead. Maybe it *did* understand, Kassianos thought. He had done enough talking at it, this past month on the road. He loved to talk, and had not had many people to talk to. Back in Videssos the city, his clerical colleagues told him he was mad to set out for Opsikion so late in the year. He hadn't listened; that wasn't nearly so much fun as talking.

"Unfortunately, they were right," he said. This time, the mule paid him no attention. It had reached the same conclusion a long time ago.

The wind howled out of the north. Kassianos drew his blue

robe more tightly about himself, not that that did much good. Because the road from the capital of the Empire of Opsikion ran south of the Paristrian mountains, he had assumed they would shield him from the worst of the weather. Maybe they did. If so, though, the provinces on the other side of the mountains had winters straight from the ice of Skotos' hell.

Where was he? For that matter, where was the road? When it ran between leaf-bare trees, it had been easy enough to follow. Now, in more open country, the pesky thing had disappeared. In better weather, that would only have been a nuisance (in better weather, Kassianos reminded himself, it wouldn't have happened). In this blizzard, it was becoming serious. If he went by Develtos, he might freeze before he could find shelter.

He tugged on the reins. The mule positively scowled at him: what was he doing, halting in the cold middle of nowhere? "I need to find the town," he explained. The mule did not look convinced.

He paused a moment in thought. He had never been to Develtos, had nothing from it with him. That made worthless most of the simpler spells of finding he knew. He thought of one that might serve, then promptly rejected it: it involved keeping a candle lit for half an hour straight. "Not bloody likely, I'm afraid," he said.

He thought some more, then laughed out loud. "As inelegant an application of the law of similarity as ever there was," he declared, "but it will serve. Like *does* call to like."

He dismounted, tied the mule's reins to a bush so it would not wander off while he was incanting. Then, after suitable prayers and passes, he undid his robe and pissed—quickly, because it was very cold.

His urine did not just form a puddle between his feet. Instead, impelled by his magic, it drew a streaming line in the snow toward more like itself, and thus, indirectly, toward the people who made it.

"That way, eh?" Kassianos said, eyeing the direction of the line. "I might have known the wind would make me drift south of where I should be." He climbed back onto his mule, urged it forward. It went eagerly, as if it sensed he knew where he was going again.

Sure enough, not a quarter of an hour later the priest saw the walls of Develtos looming tall and dark through the driving snow. He had to ride around a fair part of the circuit before he came to a gate. It was closed and barred. He shouted. Nothing happened. He shouted again, louder.

After a couple of minutes, a peephole opened. "Who ye be?" the man inside called, his accent rustic. "Show yerself to me and give me your name."

"I am Kassianos, eastbound from Videssos the city," the priest answered. He rode a couple of steps closer, lowered his hood so the guard could see not only his blue robe but also his shaven head. "May I have shelter before I am too far gone to need it?"

He did not hear anyone moving to unlatch the gate. Instead, the sentry asked sharply, "Just the one of you there?"

"Only myself. In Phos' holy name I swear it." Kassianos understood the gate guard's caution. Winter could easily make a bandit band desperate enough to try to take a walled town, and falling snow gave them the chance to approach unobserved. A quick rush once the gate was open, and who could say what horrors would follow?

But Kassianos must have convinced the guardsman. "We'll have you inside in a minute, holy sir." The fellow's voice grew muffled as he turned his face away from the peephole. "Come on, Phostis, Evagrios, give me a hand with this bloody bar." Kassianos heard it scrape against the iron-faced timbers of the gate.

One of the valves swung inward. The priest dug his heels into the mule's flanks. It trotted into Develtos. The sentries closed the gate after it, shoved the bar back into place. "Thank you, gentlemen," Kassianos said sincerely.

"Aye, you're about this far from being a snowman, aren't you, holy sir?" said the guard who had been at the peephole. Now Kassianos could see more of him than a suspicious eyeball: he was short and lean, with a knitted wool cap on his head and a sheepskin jacket closed tight over a chainmail shirt. His bow was a hunter's weapon, not a soldier's. He was, in other words, a typical small-town guardsman.

"Want I should take you to Branes' tavern, holy sir, let you warm yourself up outside and in?" asked one of the other guards. But for a back-and-breast of boiled leather and a light spear in place of a bow, he was as like the first as two peas in a pod. He glanced toward the man, who was evidently his superior. "Is it all right, Tzitas?"

"Aye, go on, Phostis, we'll manage here." Tzitas showed his teeth in a knowing grin. "Just don't spend too much time warming yourself up in there."

"Wouldn't think of it," Phostis said righteously.

"No, you wouldn't; you'd do it," said Evagrios, who'd been quiet till then. Tzitas snorted.

Phostis sent them both a rude gesture. He turned back to the priest. "You come with me, holy sir. Pay these scoffers no mind." He started off down the street. His boots left pockmarks in the snow. Still on muleback, Kassianos followed.

The tavern was less than a hundred yards away. (Nothing in Develtos, come to that, looked to be more than a quarter mile from anything else. The town barely rated a wall.) In that short journey, though, Phostis asked Kassianos about Videssos the city four different times, and told him twice of some distant cousin who had gone there to seek his fortune. "He must have found it, too," Phostis said wistfully, "for he never came back no more."

He might have starved trying, Kassianos thought, but the priest was too kind to say that out loud. Videssos' capital drew the restless and ambitious from all over the Empire, and in such fast company not all could flourish.

Even without Phostis', "Here we are, holy sir," Kassianos could have guessed which building was Branes' from the number of horses and donkeys tied up in front of it. He found space at the rail for his mule, then went in after the sentry.

He shut the door behind him so none of the blessed heat inside would escape. A few quick steps brought him to the fireplace.

He sighed in pure animal pleasure as the warmth began driving the ice from his bones. When he put a hand to his face, he discovered he could feel the tip of his nose again. He'd almost forgotten he still owned it.

After roasting a bit longer in front of the flames, Kassianos felt restored enough to find a stool at a table close by. A barmaid came over, looked him up and down. "What'll it be?" she asked, matter-of-fact as if he were carpenter rather than priest.

"Hot red wine, spiced with cinnamon."

She nodded, saucily ran her hand over his shaved pate. "That'll do it for you, right enough." Her hips worked as she walked back to the tapman with his order; she looked over her shoulder at the priest, as if to make sure he was watching her.

His blood heated with a warmth that had nothing to do with the blaze crackling in the fireplace. He willed himself to take no notice of that new heat. Celibacy went with Phos' blue robe. He frowned a little. Even the most shameless tavern wenches knew that. Clerics were men, too, and might forget their vows, but he still found an overture as blatant as this girl's startling. Even in the jaded capital, a lady of easy virtue would have been more discreet. The same should have gone double for this back-country town.

The barmaid returned with his steaming mug. As he fumbled in his beltpouch for coppers to pay the score, she told him, "You want to warm up the parts fire and wine don't reach, you let me know." Before he could answer, someone called to her from a table halfway across the room. She hurried off, but again smiled back at Kassianos as she went.

Before he lifted the cup to his lips, he raised his hands to heaven and intoned the usual Videssian prayer before food or drink: "We bless thee, Phos, lord with the great and good mind, by thy grace our protector, watchful beforehand that the great test of life may be decided in our favor." Then he spat in the rushes to show his rejection of Skotos. At last he drank. The cinnamon nipped his tongue like a playful lover. The figure of speech would not have occurred to him a moment before. Now it seemed only too appropriate.

When his mug was empty, he raised a finger. The girl hurried over. "Another, please," he said, setting more coppers on the table.

She scooped them up. "For some silver . . ." She paused expectantly.

"My vows do not allow me carnal union. What makes you think I take them lightly?" he asked. He kept his voice mild, but his eyes seized and held hers. He had overawed unrepentant clerics in the ecclesiastical courts of the capital; focusing his forensic talents on a chit of a barmaid reminded him of smashing some small crawling insect with an anvil. But she had roused his curiosity, if not his manhood.

"The monks hereabouts like me plenty well," she sniffed; she sounded offended he did not find her attractive. "And since you're a man from Videssos the city itself" (news traveled fast, Kassianos thought, unsurprised), "I reckoned you'd surely be freer yet."

Along with its famed riches, the capital also had a reputation in the provinces as a den of iniquity. Sometimes, Kassianos knew, it was deserved. But not in this . . . "You are mistaken," the priest replied. "The monks like you well, you say?"

The girl's eyes showed she suddenly realized the hole she had dug for herself. "I'm not the only one," she said hastily. "There's a good many women they favor here in town, most of 'em a lot more than me."

She contradicted herself, Kassianos noted, but never mind that now. "Are there indeed?" he said, letting some iron come into his voice. "Perhaps you will be so good as to give me their names?"

"No. Why should I?" She had spirit; she could still defy him.

He dropped the anvil. "Because I am Kassianos, *nomophylax*—chief counsel, you might say—to the most holy ecumenical Patriarch Tarasios, prelate of Videssos the city and Videssos the Empire. I was summoned to Opsikion to deal with a troublesome case of false doctrine there, but I begin to think the good god Phos directed me here instead. Now speak to me further of these monks."

The barmaid fled instead. Eyes followed her from all over the taproom, then turned to Kassianos. The big man whose place was behind the bar slowly ambled over to his table. As if by chance, he held a stout club in his right fist. "Don't know what you said to little Laskara, blue-robe," he said casually, "but she didn't much like it."

"And I, friend, did not much like her seeking to lead me astray from my vows, and liked even less her telling me the monks hereabouts are accustomed to ignoring theirs," Kassianos answered. "I do not think the most holy Tarasios, Phos bless him, would like that, either. Perhaps if I root out the evil, it will never have to come to his attention."

At the mention of that name, the tapman sat down heavily beside Kassianos, as if his legs no longer wanted to support him. The priest heard him drop the bludgeon among the dried rushes on the floor. "The—Patriarch?" the fellow said hoarsely.

"The very same." Kassianos' eyes twinkled. Most of the time, being *nomophylax* was nothing but drudgery. Sometimes, as now, it was fun. "Suppose you tell me about the lecherous monks you have here. Your Laskara thought I was of the same stripe as they, and tried to sell herself to me."

"Aye, we have a monastery here, dedicated to the holy Tralitzes, Phos bless his memory." The tapman drew the good god's sun-circle over his heart. Kassianos had never heard of the local saint, but that hardly signified: every little town had some patron to commemorate. The tapman went on, "But the monks, lecherous? No, holy sir—they're good men, pious men, every one."

He sounded sincere, and too shaken to be lying so well. "Do they then conform to the rules set down by the holy Pakhomios, in whose memory all monks serve?" Kassianos asked.

"Holy sir, I'm no monk. Far as I know, they do, but I dunno what all these rules and things is." The fellow was sweating, and not from the fireplace's being near.

"Very well, then, hear the seventh chapter of Pakhomios' *Rule*, the chapter entitled 'On Women': 'To ensure the preservation of the contemplative life, no brother shall be permitted to entertain women.' "

"I dunno about any of that," the tapman insisted. With a sudden access of boldness, he went on, "And it's not me you should ought to be going after if you've got somewhat against our monks. You take that up with the abbot—Menas, his name is."

"I shall," Kassianos promised. "Believe me, I shall."

The holy Tralitzes' monastery lay a couple of miles outside Develtos. Monks working in the snowy fields and gardens looked up from their labors as Kassianos rode toward Phos' temple, the largest building of the monastery complex. It was further distinguished from the others by a spire topped with a gilded globe.

An elderly monk came out of the temple, bowed courteously to Kassianos. "Phos with you, holy sir," he said. "I am Pleuses, porter of the monastery. How may I serve you?"

Kassianos dismounted, returned the bow. "And with you, brother Pleuses. I have come to see your abbot—Menas is his name, is it not? I am Kassianos, *nomophylax* to Tarasios. Would you announce me to the holy abbot?"

Pleuses' eyes widened. He bowed once more. "Certainly, holy sir. Menas will surely be honored to entertain such a distinguished guest." He shouted for a younger brother to take charge of Kassianos' mule, then, bowing a third time, said, "Will you come with me?"

The abbot's residence lay beyond the dormitory that housed the rest of the monks. "Wait here a moment, will you?" Pleuses said at the doorway. He went in and, as promised, quickly returned. "He will see you now."

Kassianos was expecting a leering voluptuary. The sight of Menas came as something of a shock. He was a thin, pleasant-faced man of about forty-five, with laugh lines crinkling the corners of his eyes. Among the codices and scrolls on bookshelves behind him were many, both religious and secular, that Kassianos also esteemed.

The abbot rose, bowed, hurried up to clasp Kassianos' hand. "Phos bless you, holy sir, and welcome, welcome. Will you take wine?"

"Thank you, Father Abbot."

Menas poured with his own hands. While he was doing so, he asked, "May I be permitted to wonder why such an illustrious cleric has chosen to honor our humble monastery with his presence?"

Kassianos' eyes flicked to Pleuses. Menas followed his glance, and dismissed the porter with a few murmured words. The abbot was no fool, Kassianos thought. Well, abbots were not chosen to be fools. The two men performed the usual Videssian ritual over wine, then Menas returned to his own seat and waved Kassianos to the other, more comfortable, chair in the room. The abbot's question still hung in the air.

"Father Abbot," Kassianos began, more carefully than he had intended before meeting Menas, "I came to Develtos by chance a few days ago, compelled by the blizzard to take shelter here. In Branes' tavern, a chance remark led me to believe the monks practiced illegal, immoral cohabitation with women, contrary to the strictures of the seventh chapter of the holy Pakhomios' *Rule*."

"That is not so," Menas said quietly. "We follow the *Rule* in all its particulars."

"I am glad to hear you say that," Kassianos nodded. "But I must tell you that my enquiries since I came here made me think otherwise. And, Father Abbot, they make me believe this not only of your flock but of yourself."

"Having once said that I adhere to Pakhomios' *Rule*, I do not suppose that mere repetition will persuade you I speak truly," Menas said after a moment's thought. He grinned wryly; shaven head and gray-streaked beard or no, it made him look very young. "And, having now once said something you do not believe, I cannot hope you will accept my oath." He spread his hands. "You see my difficulty."

"I do." Kassianos nodded again. He thought better of Menas for not gabbling oaths that, as the abbot pointed out, had to be thought untrustworthy. He had not expected or wanted to think better of Menas. He had wanted to get on with the business of reforming the monastery. Things did not seem as simple as he'd thought. Well, as *nomophylax* he'd had that happen to him often enough.

"I will follow any suggestion you may have on resolving this difficulty," Menas said, as if reading his thoughts.

"Very well, then: I know a decoction under whose influence you *will* speak truth. Are you willing to drink it down and then answer my questions?"

"So long as you are asking about these alleged misdeeds, certainly."

Menas showed no hesitation. If he was an actor, he was a good one, Kassianos thought. But no one could dissemble under the influence of this potion, no matter how he schooled himself beforehand.

"I shall compound the drug this evening and return to administer it tomorrow morning," the *nomophylax* said. Menas nodded agreement. Kassianos wondered how brash he would be once his lascivious secrets were laid bare.

The abbot peered curiously at the small glass flask. He held it to his nose, sniffed. "Not a prize vintage," he observed with a chuckle. He tossed the drug down, screwed up his face at the taste.

Kassianos admired his effrontery, if nothing else. He waited for a few minutes, watched the abbot's expression go from its usual amused alertness to a fixed, vacant stare. The *nomophylax* rose, passed a hand in front of Menas' face. Menas' eyes did not follow the motion. Kassianos nodded to himself. Sure enough, the decoction had taken hold.

"Can you hear me?" he asked.

"Aye." Menas' voice was distant, abstracted.

"Tell me, then, of all the violations of the holy Pakhomios' *Rule* that have occurred among the monks of this monastery over the past half a year."

Menas immediately began to obey: the drug robbed him of his own will and left him perfectly receptive to Kassianos' question. The *nomophylax* settled back in his chair and listened as Menas spoke of this monk's quarrel with that one, of the time when three brothers got drunk together, of the monk who missed evening prayers four days running, of the one who had refused to pull weeds until he was disciplined, of the one who had sworn at an old man in Develtos, of the monk who had stolen a book but tried to put the blame on another, and on and on, all the petty squabbles to which monasteries, being made up of men, were prone.

Kassianos kept pen poised over parchment, ready to note down every transgression of chapter seven of the *Rule*. Menas talked and talked and talked. The pen stayed poised. Kassianos wrote nothing, for the abbot gave him nothing to write.

Menas, at length, ran dry. Kassianos scowled, ran a hand over his smooth pate. "Do you recall nothing more?" he demanded harshly.

"Nothing, holy sir." Menas' voice was calm; it would not have changed had Kassianos held his hand to the flame flickering in the lamp on the table beside him. The *nomophylax* knew he was deeply under the influence of the potion. He also knew the monks of the monastery of the holy Tralitzes had illicit congress with a great many women of Develtos. His inquiries in the town had left him as certain of that as he was of Phos' eventual victory over Skotos.

Kassianos hesitated before asking his next question. But, having failed with a general inquiry, he saw no choice but to probe specifically at the rot he knew existed: "Tell me of every occasion when the monks of this monastery have transgressed against the seventh chapter of the holy Pakhomios' *Rule*, the chapter which forbids the brethren to entertain women."

Menas was silent. Kassianos wondered if the abbot could somehow be struggling against the decoction. He shook his head—he knew perfectly well it was irresistible. "Why do you not speak?" the *nomophylax* snapped.

"Because I know of no occasion when the monks of this monastery have transgressed against the seventh chapter of the holy Pakhomios' *Rule*, the chapter which forbids the brethren to entertain women."

The rotelike repetition of his words and the tone of the abbot's voice convinced Kassianos that Menas was still drugged. So did the reason he gave for staying quiet before. If someone under this potion had nothing to say in response to a question, he would keep right on saying nothing until jogged by a new one. Which, depressingly, was just what Menas had done.

Kassianos sighed. He neither liked nor approved of paradoxes. Knowing that because of the decoction he was only being redundant, he nevertheless asked, "Do you swear by Phos you have told me the truth?"

"I swear by Phos I have told you the truth," Menas replied.

The *nomophylax* ground his teeth. If Menas swore under the drug that the monks of the monastery of the holy Tralitzes were obeying Pakhomios' *Rule*, then they were, and that was all there was to it. So act as though you believe it, Kassianos told himself. He could not.

He was tempted to walk out of Menas' study and let the abbot try to deal with the monastery's affairs while still in the grip of the potion. He had played that sort of practical joke while a student at the Sorcerers' Collegium. Regretfully, he decided it was beneath the dignity of the Patriarch's *nomophylax*. He sat and waited until he was sure Menas had come around.

"Remarkable," the abbot said when he was himself again. "I felt quite beside myself. Had we been guilty of any transgressions of the sort you were seeking, I would not have been able to keep them from you."

"That, Father Abbot, was the idea," Kassianos said tightly. He knew he should have been more courteous, but could not manage it, not with the feeling something was wrong still gnawing at him. But, not having anything on which to focus his suspicions, he could only rise abruptly and go out into the cold for the ride to Develtos.

He kept asking questions when he got back into town. The answers he got set him stewing all over again. They were not given under the influence of his decoction, but they were detailed and consistent from one person to the next. They all painted the monks of the monastery of the holy Tralitzes as the lechers he had already been led to believe them.

How, then, had Menas truthfully asserted that he and his flock followed Pakhomios' *Rule*?

The question nagged at Kassianos like the beginnings of a toothache for the rest of the day. By this time, the snowstorm had long since blown itself out; he could have gone on to Opsikion. It never occurred to him. After taking his evening meal in Branes' taproom, he went up to the cubicle he had rented over it.

There he sat and thought and fumed. Maybe Menas had found an antidote to his potion. But if he had, it was one that had eluded all the savants at the Sorcerers' Collegium for all the centuries of Videssos' history. That was possible, but not likely. Was it likelier than a deliberate campaign of slander against the abbot's monks? The *nomophylax* could not be sure, but he thought both ideas most improbable. And they were the best ones he had.

He pounded a fist against his knee. "What can Menas be up to, anyway?" he said out loud. Then he blinked, surprised at himself. "Why don't I find out?"

Normally, he would have dismissed the thought with the same automatic discipline he used to suppress the longing of his flesh for women. Spying sorcerously on a man who had proved himself innocent under drugged interrogation went against every instinct Kassianos had. On the other hand, so did believing Menas.

If the abbot is blameless, Kassianos told himself, I'll perform an act of penance to make up for the sin I commit in spying on him like this. Having salved his conscience, the *nomophylax* set about preparing the spell he would need.

The law of similarity was useless to him here, but the law of contagion applied: once in contact, always in contact. Kassianos scraped a bit of skin from the palm of his right hand with a small sharp knife—because that hand had clasped Menas', it still held an affinity for the abbot.

As Kassianos' incantation built, a cloud of smoke grew in his cubicle. It was no ordinary cloud, though, for it formed a rectangle with edges so precise they might have been defined by an invisible picture frame. The analogy pleased Kassianos, for when he spoke a final word of command, the smoke would indeed yield a picture of what Menas was about.

He spoke the word. The trapped smoke before him roiled, grew still. Colors began seeping into it, here and there. The first thing the *nomophylax* clearly made out was the roaring fire in one corner of his magical image. He frowned; the blaze was bigger than any the hearth in the abbot's dwelling could contain.

Of itself, of course, that meant nothing. Menas could have any number of legitimate reasons for not being in his own quarters. Kassianos waited for more of the picture to emerge.

Blue ... Surely that was the abbot's robe. But it lay on the floor, crumpled and forgotten. Where was Menas, and why had he thrown aside his vestments?

Within moments, Kassianos had his answer. He felt a hot flush rise, not just to his cheeks, but to the very crown of his shaven head. He turned away from the image he had conjured up, yet still he saw body conjoined with body, saw that the man straining atop his eager partner was the abbot Menas.

Kassianos spoke another word, felt his sorcery dissolve. His face remained hot, now with fury rather than embarrassment. So Menas thought he could play him for a fool, eh? He imagined the abbot telling his paramour how he had fooled the fellow from the capital, and both of them laughing as they coupled. That thought only made the *nomophylax*'s rage burn hotter.

Then he caught himself wishing he had not turned his back quite so soon. He had not thought be could be any angrier, but found he was wrong. Before, his anger's flame had extended only to Menas and his still unknown lover. Now it reached out and burned him, too.

Kassianos stamped grimly through the snow toward the monastery of the holy Tralitzes. He had left his mule behind on purpose, accepting the walk as the beginning of the penance he would pay for failing to root out the corruption in the monastery at the first try. His footprints left an emphatic trail behind him.

The pale, fitful sun gleamed off the gilded dome topping Phos' temple ahead. Kassianos turned aside before he was halfway there. Scanning the landscape ahead with a hunter's alertness, he spotted a blue-robe strolling toward a small

wooden house several hundred yards to one side of the
monastery. He was not sure whether hunter's instinct or sorcerer's told him it was Menas, but he knew.

The *nomophylax*'s breath burst from him in an outraged
steaming cloud. "Phos grant us mercy! Not content with making
a mockery of his vows, the sinner goes to show off his stamina,"
Kassianos exclaimed, though there was no one to hear him.

The abbot disappeared into the little house. Some men might
have hesitated before disturbing the occupants of a trysting-
place, but not Kassianos. He strode resolutely up to pound on
the door, crying, "Menas, you are a disgrace to the robes you
wear! Open at once!"

"Oh, dear," Menas said as Kassianos withered him with a
glare. "You do take this seriously, don't you?" Now the abbot
did not look amused, as he had so often back in his study. He
looked frightened. So did the woman around whose shoulder he
flung a protective arm.

The night before, her features slack with pleasure, she had
seemed only a symbol of Menas' depravity. Now Kassianos had
to confront her as a person. She was, he realized slowly, not a
whore after all. Perhaps ten years younger than the abbot, she
had an open, pretty face, and wore an embroidered linen blouse
over a heavy wool skirt: peasant garb, not a courtesan's jewels
and clinging silks.

Even without what his magic had let him witness, the way her
hand reached up and clutched for Menas' would have told Kassianos everything he needed to know. It told him other things as
well, things he had not thought to learn. It had never occurred to
him that the cleric's illicit lover might feel all the same things
for her man as another woman would for a proper partner.

Because the woman confused him, Kassianos swung his attention back to Menas. "Should I not take your perjury seriously?"
he said heavily. "It only adds to the burden of your other sins."

"Perjury? I gave you my oath on Phos, holy sir, under the influence of your own drug, that I truly obey my vows. I do; I am
not forsworn."

Kassianos' eyes narrowed. "No? You dare say that, in the company you keep? Hear once again, then, wretch, the seventh chapter of the holy Pakhomios' *Rule*. As you know, it is entitled 'On Women.' I hope you will trust my memory as I quote it: 'To ensure the preservation of the contemplative life, no brother shall be permitted to entertain women.' Standing where you are, with the person whose house this must be, how can you tell me you are no oathbreaker?"

To the amazement of the *nomophylax*, Menas'—companion—burst into laughter. Kassianos stared, thunderstruck. The woman said, "As you guessed, holy sir, this house was my husband's till he died six years ago, and belongs to me now. And so my dear Menas cannot entertain me here. *I* entertain *him*, or at least I hope I shall." She smiled smokily up at the worried abbot, stroked his bearded cheek.

Kassianos felt his jaw drop. He became aware that he had not blinked for some time, either. In fact, he realized his expression had to resemble nothing so much as a fresh-caught perch's. Pulling himself together with a distinct effort of will, he said slowly, "That is the most outlandish piece of casuistry I've heard in a lifetime of theological study."

He waited for his pompous wrath to burst forth in a great, furious shout. What came out instead was laughter. And once free, it would not let itself be restrained. Kassianos laughed until tears ran down his face into his beard, laughed until he doubled over. Now Menas and the woman were staring at him rather than the other way around.

Slowly, the fit passed. Kassianos straightened, felt the sudden pain of a stitch in his side, ignored it. He wiped his eyes with his sleeve, then, more or less in control of himself, asked Menas, "Your monks are all, hmm, entertained themselves, and do no entertaining?"

"Of course, holy sir." The abbot sounded genuinely shocked. "Did we act otherwise, we would violate our vows."

"Hmm," Kassianos said again. "How long has this, ah, custom existed at the monastery of the holy Tralitzes?"

"Truly, holy sir, I do not know. Since before I entered as a novice, certainly, and before the novitiate of the oldest brothers there at that time, for they knew no different way."

"I see." And, curiously enough, Kassianos did. Develtos was just the sort of back-country town where a spurious practice like this could quietly come into being and then flourish for Phos only knew how long before anyone from the outside world noticed it was there.

Menas must have been thinking along with him, for he asked, "Holy sir, is it not the same everywhere?"

"Hardly." Kassianos' voice was dry. "In fact, I daresay you've found a loophole to appall the holy Pakhomios—and one untold generations of monks have prayed for in vain. I suppose I should congratulate you. Oh, my." He wiped his eyes again.

"Perhaps you should, but I doubt you will," Menas' ladylove observed. "What *will* you do?"

The *nomophylax* eyed her with respect: no fool here. "Well, an inquisitor's court might fight its way through your logic," he said. Both the woman and Menas looked alarmed. Kassianos went on, "I doubt that will happen, though."

"What then?" Menas asked.

"First, I'd guess, a synod will convene in Videssos the city to revise the holy Pakhomios' *Rule* so no further, ah, misunderstandings of the seventh chapter will occur. That being accomplished, word of the corrected *Rule* will be sent to all monasteries in the Empire—including, I am comfortably certain, this one."

"And what will they do to us for having contravened their interpretation of the *Rule*?" Menas asked; Kassianos noted the slight emphasis the abbot put on "interpretation." He smiled to himself. In Menas' sandals, he would have tried to appear as virtuous as possible, too.

He answered, "While I cannot speak for the synod, I would expect it to decree no punishments for what is here a long-established, even if erroneous, custom. I would also expect, however, that an *epoptes*—a supervising monk—will come out from the capital to make certain the monastery of the holy Tralitzes diligently adheres to the seventh chapter as redefined."

Neither Menas nor his companion looked very happy at that. The *nomophylax* had not thought they would. He went on, "I mean what I say. If you continue to flout the *Rule* after it is changed to mean in letter what it does in spirit, you will not enjoy the consequences."

He had intended to impress them further with the seriousness of the situation. But the woman said, "Then we will just have to make the most of the time we have left." She shut the door in Kassianos' face.

He knew he should be angry. Instead, to his own discomfiture, he found himself admiring her. He realized with sudden regret that he had never learned her name. He raised his hand to knock on that closed door and ask. After a moment, he thought better of it.

Shaking his head, he turned and slowly started walking back to Develtos.

Twenty-one, Counting Up

Some of you will have come straight here after reading "Forty, Counting Down." Others—more, I hope—will have looked at some of the stories in between. Not much to say about this one that I didn't say about the other, except to note that only my wife and I know which of these two pieces I wrote first; I submitted them simultaneously. I hope the answer isn't obvious in the text. I know I've done my best to keep it from being so.

Justin Kloster looked from his blue book to his watch and back again. He muttered under his breath. Around him, a hundred more people in the American history class were looking at their watches, too. Fifteen minutes left. After that, another breadth requirement behind him. His junior year behind him, too. Three down, one to go.

At precisely four o'clock, the professor said, "Time! Bring your blue books up to the front of the lecture hall."

Like everybody else, Justin squeezed out another couple of sentences before doing as he was told. He wrung his hand to show writer's cramp, then stuck the pen in the pocket of his jeans and headed for the door.

"How do you think you did?" somebody asked him.

"I'm pretty sure I got a B, anyhow," he answered. "That's all I really need. It's not like it's my major or anything." The prof could hear him, but he didn't much care. This wasn't a course for history majors, not that Cal State Northridge had many of

362

those. It was a school for training computer people like him, business types, and teachers. After a moment, he thought to ask, "How about you?"

"Probably about the same," the other fellow said. "Well, have a good summer."

"Yeah, you, too." Justin opened the door and stepped from air conditioning and pale fluorescent light into the brassy sun and heat of the San Fernando Valley. He blinked a couple of times as his eyes adapted. Sweat started pouring off him. He hurried across campus to the parking lot where his Toyota waited. He was very blond and very fair, and sunburned if you looked at him sideways. He was also a little—only a little—on the round side, which made him sweat even more.

When he unlocked the car, he fanned the door back and forth a couple of times to get rid of the furnacelike air inside. He cranked the AC as soon as he started the motor. After he'd gone a couple of blocks, it started doing some good. He'd just got comfortable when he pulled into the gated driveway of his apartment building.

The Acapulco was like a million others in Los Angeles, with a below-ground parking lot and two stories of apartments built above it around a courtyard that held a swimming pool, a rec room, and a couple of flower beds whose plants kept dying.

The key that opened the security gate also opened the door between the lot and the lobby. Justin checked his snailmail and found, as he'd hoped, a check from his father and another from his mother. His lip curled as he scooped the envelopes from his little mailbox. His folks had gone through a messy divorce his senior year in high school. These days, his father was living with a redheaded woman only a couple of years older than he was— and his mother was living with a dark-haired woman only a couple of years older than he was. They both sent money to help keep him in his apartment . . . and so they wouldn't have to have anything more to do with him. That suited him fine. He didn't want to have anything to do with them these days, either.

He used the security key again to get from the lobby to the courtyard behind it, then walked back to his apartment, which wasn't far from the rec room. That had worried him when he first rented the place, but hardly anybody played table tennis or shot pool or lifted weights, so noise wasn't a problem.

His apartment was no neater than it had to be. His history text and lecture notes covered the kitchen table. He chuckled as he shoved them aside. "No more pencils, no more books, no more teachers' dirty looks," he chanted—and how long had people escaping from school been singing that song? He grabbed a Coke from the refrigerator and started to sit down in front of the space he'd cleared. Then he shook his head and carried the soda back into the bedroom instead.

He really lived there. His iMac sat on a desk in a corner by the closet. Justin grinned when he booted it up. It didn't look like all the boring beige boxes other companies made. As soon as the desktop came up, he logged on to Earthlink to check his e-mail and see what was going on in some of the newsgroups he read.

None of the e-mail was urgent, or even very interesting. The newsgroups . . . "How about that?" he said a couple of minutes later. Dave and Tabitha, who'd both been posting in the Trash Can Sinatras newsgroup for as long as he'd been reading it, announced they were getting married. Justin sent congratulations. He hoped they'd get on better than his own folks had. His girlfriend's parents were still together, and still seemed to like each other pretty well.

Thinking of Megan made him want to talk to her. He logged off Earthlink—having only one line in the apartment was a pain—and went over to the phone on the nightstand. He dialed and listened to it ring, once, twice . . . "Hello?" she said.

"What's the story, morning glory?" Justin said—Megan was wild for Oasis. He liked British pop, too, though he preferred Pulp, as someone of his parents' generation might have liked the Stones more than the Beatles.

"Oh. Hiya, Justin." He heard the smile in her voice once he recognized his. He smiled, too. With exams over for another semester, with his girlfriend glad to hear from him, the world looked like a pretty good place. Megan asked, "How'd your final go?"

"Whatever," he answered. "I don't think it's an A, but I'm pretty sure it's a B, and that's good enough. Want to go out tonight and party?"

"I can't," Megan told him. "I've got my English lit final tomorrow, remember?"

"Oh, yeah. That's right." Justin hadn't remembered till she reminded him. "I bet you're glad to get through with most of that lower-division stuff." She was a year behind him.

"This wasn't so bad." Megan spoke as if telling a dark, shameful secret: "I kind of like Shakespeare."

"Whatever," Justin said again. All he remembered from his literature course was that he'd been damn lucky to escape with a B-minus. "I'll take you to Sierra's. We can get margaritas. How's that?"

"The bomb," Megan said solemnly. "What time?"

"How about six-thirty? I start at CompUSA tomorrow, and I'll get off a little past five."

"Okay, see you then," Megan said. "I've got to get back to *Macbeth*. 'Bye." She hung up.

Justin put *This Is Hardcore*, his favorite Pulp album, in the CD player and pulled dinner out of the freezer at random. When he saw what he had, he put it back and got another one: if he was going to Sierra's tomorrow night, he didn't want Mexican food tonight, too. Plain old fried chicken would do the job well enough. He nuked it, washed it down with another Coke, then threw the tray and the can in the trash and the silverware into the dishwasher. When he started running out of forks, he'd get everything clean at once.

He went back into the bedroom, surfed the Net without much aim for a while, and then went over to bungie.net and got into a multiplayer game of Myth II. His side took gas; one of the guys didn't want to follow their captain's orders, even though his own ideas were a long way from brilliant. Justin logged off in disgust. He fired up his Carmageddon CD-ROM and happily ran down little old ladies in walkers till he noticed in some surprise that it was after eleven. "Work tomorrow," he sighed, and shut down and went to bed.

Freshly showered, freshly shaved, a gold stud in his left ear, he drove over to Megan's parents' house to pick her up. Her mother let him in. "How are you, Justin?" she said. "How do you like your new job?"

"I'm fine, Mrs. Tricoupis," he answered. "The job's—okay, I guess." One day had been plenty to convince him his supervisor was a doofus. The guy didn't know much about computers, and, because he was pushing thirty, he thought he could lord it over Justin and the other younger people at the store.

Megan's mom caught Justin's tone. Laughing, she said, "Welcome to the real world." She turned and called toward the back of the house: "Sweetie! Justin's here!"

"I'm *coming*," Megan said. She hurried into the living room. She was a slim, almost skinny brunette with more energy than she sometimes knew what to do with. "Hiya," she told Justin. The way she looked at him, she might have invented him.

"Hi." Justin felt the same way about her. He wanted to grab her right then and there. If her mother hadn't been standing three feet away, he would have done it.

Mrs. Tricoupis laughed again, on a different note. It didn't occur to Justin that she could see through Megan and him. She said, "Go on, kids. Have fun. Drive carefully, Justin."

"Whatever," Justin said, which made Megan's mom roll her eyes up to the heavens. But he'd been in only one wreck since getting his license, and that one hadn't quite been his fault, so he couldn't see why she was ragging on him.

He didn't grab Megan when they got into the car, either. At the first red light, though, they leaned toward each other and into a long, wet kiss that lasted till the light turned green and even longer—till, in fact, the old fart in the SUV behind them leaned on his horn and made them both jump.

Sierra's had stood at the corner of Vanowen and Canoga for more than forty years, which made it a Valley institution. They both ordered margaritas as they were seated, Megan's strawberry, Justin's plain. The waiter nodded to her but told Justin, "I'm sorry, *señor,* but I'll need some ID."

"Okay." Justin displayed his driver's license, which showed he'd been born in April 1978, and so had been legal for a couple of months.

"Gracias, señor," the waiter said. "I'll get you both your drinks." Justin and Megan didn't start quietly giggling till he was gone. Megan was only twenty, but people always carded Justin.

The margaritas were good. After a couple of sips of hers, Megan said, "You didn't even ask me how I did on my final."

"Duh!" Justin hit himself in the forehead with the heel of his hand. "How *did* you do?"

"Great," she said happily. "I think I might even have gotten an A."

"That rocks." Justin made silent clapping motions. Megan took a seated bow. He went on, "How do you feel like celebrating?"

"Well, we probably ought to save club-hopping for the weekend, since you've got to go to work in the morning." Megan stuck out her tongue at him. "See? *I* think about what's going on with *you.*" Justin started to get chuffed, but didn't let it show. A couple of seconds later, he was glad he didn't, because Megan went on, "So why don't we just go back to your place after dinner?"

"Okay," he said, and hoped he didn't sound slaveringly eager. Maybe he did; Megan started laughing at him. But it wasn't mean laughter, and she didn't change what she'd said. He raised his margarita to his lips. At twenty-one, it's easy to think you've got the world by the tail.

He hardly noticed what he ordered. When the waiter brought it, he ate it. It was good; the food at Sierra's always was. Afterwards, he had to remember to stay somewhere close to the speed limit as he drove up Canoga toward the Acapulco. Getting a ticket would interrupt everything else he had in mind.

When he opened the door to let Megan into his apartment, she said, "You're so lucky to have a place of your own."

"I guess so," Justin answered. He thought she was pretty lucky to have parents who cared enough about her to want her to stay at home while she went through college. As far as he was concerned, the checks his father and mother sent counted for a lot less than some real affection would have. He'd tried explaining that, but he'd seen it made no sense to her.

She bent down and went pawing through his CDs and put on *I've Seen Everything*, the Trash Can Sinatras' second album. As "Easy Road" started coming out of the stereo, she sighed. "They were *such* a good band. I wish they'd made more than three records before they broke up."

"Yeah," Justin said. However much he liked the Sinatras, though, he didn't pay that much attention to the music. Instead, he watched her straighten and get to her feet. He stepped forward to slip an arm around her waist.

She turned and smiled at him from a range of about six inches, as if she'd forgotten he was there and was glad to be reminded. "Hiya," she said brightly, and put her arms around him. Who kissed whom first was a matter of opinion. They went back into the bedroom together.

They'd been lovers for only a couple of months. Justin was still learning what Megan liked. He didn't quite get her where she was going before he rather suddenly arrived himself. "Sorry," he said as his heartrate slowed toward normal. "Wait a few minutes and we'll try it again." It was only a few minutes, too. At his age, he could—and did—take that for granted. After the second time, he asked, "Better?"

"Yeah," Megan answered in a breathy voice that meant it was quite a bit better. Or maybe that breathy voice meant something else altogether, for she was still using it as she went on, "Get up, will you? You're squashing me."

"Oh." Justin slid his weight—*too much weight,* he thought, not for the first time—off her. "I didn't mean to."

"A gentleman," she said darkly, "takes his weight on his elbows." But she laughed as she said it, so she couldn't have been really mad.

Justin scratched his stomach, which gave him an excuse to feel how too much of it there was. He wasn't really tubby. He'd never been really tubby. But he would never have six-pack abs, either. Twelve-pack or maybe a whole case, yeah. Six-pack? Real live muscles? Fuhgeddaboutit. Unlike some other girls he'd known, Megan had never given him a hard time about it.

"Shall we go down to the Probe Friday night?" he said. "They don't have me working Saturday, so we can close the place and see what kind of after-hours stuff we can dig up."

"All *right*," Megan said. She slid off the bed and went into the bathroom. When she came back, she started dressing. Justin had half hoped for a third round, but it wasn't urgent. He put his clothes on again, too.

The drive back to Megan's house passed in happy silence. Justin kept glancing over at her every so often. *I'm a pretty lucky fellow,* he thought, *finding a girl I can . . .* Then he clicked his tongue between his teeth. He didn't even want to think the word *love*. After he'd watched his parents' messy breakup, that word scared the hell out of him. But it kept coming back whether he wanted it to or not. He told himself that was a good sign, and came close to believing it.

The Probe lay a couple of blocks off Melrose, the heart of the L.A. scene. Justin snagged a parking space in front of a house not far away. Megan gave him a hand. "I thought we'd have to hike for, like, miles," she said.

"Well, we've got the shoes for it," Justin said, which made her grin. They both wore knockoffs of Army boots, big and black and massive, with soles that looked as if they'd been cut from tractor tire treads. Justin made sure he put the Club on the steering wheel before he got out of the car. Things in this neighborhood had a way of walking with Jesus if you weren't careful.

He and Megan had no trouble snagging a table when they got inside the Probe. "Guard it with your life," he told her, and went over to the bar to buy a beer. He got carded again, and had to haul out his license. He brought the brew back to Megan, who couldn't pass the ID test, then got another one for himself.

They both eyed the deejay's booth, which was as yet uninhabited. "Who's it supposed to be tonight?" Megan asked. Before

Justin could answer, she went on, "I hope it's Helen. She plays the best mix of anybody, and she's not afraid to spin things you don't hear every day."

"I dunno," Justin said. "I like Douglas better, I think. He won't scramble tempos the way Helen does sometimes. You can really dance when he's playing things."

Megan snorted. "Give me a break. I have to drag you out there half the time."

"Proves my point," Justin said. "I need all the help I can get."

"Well, maybe," Megan said: no small concession. She and Justin analyzed and second-guessed deejays the way football fans played Monday-morning quarterback. Their arguments got just as abstruse and sometimes just as heated, too. Megan didn't drop it cold here: she said, "As long as it's not Michael."

Justin crossed his forefingers, as if warding off a vampire. "Anybody but Michael," he agreed. "I don't know how they can keep using him. His list is so lame—my *father* would like most of it." He could find no stronger condemnation.

A couple of minutes later, a skinny redheaded guy with a buzz cut even shorter than Justin's, little tiny sunglasses, and a silver lip ring that glittered under the blazing spots sauntered across the stage to the booth. "It's Douglas," Megan said. She didn't sound too disappointed; she liked him next best after Helen.

"Yeah!" Justin let out a whoop and clapped till his hands hurt. A lot of people in the club were doing the same; Douglas had a considerable following. But there were also scattered boos, and even one raucous shout of, "We want Michael!" Justin and Megan looked at each other and both mouthed the same word: *losers*.

Douglas didn't waste time with chatter. That was another reason Justin liked him—he didn't come to the Probe for foreplay. As soon as the music started blaring out, an enormous grin spread over his face. He didn't even grumble when Megan sprang up, grabbed him, and hauled him out onto the floor. He gave it his best shot. With the bass thudding through him like the start of an earthquake, how could he do anything else?

Tomorrow, he knew, his ears would ring and buzz. His hearing wouldn't be quite right for a couple of days. But he'd worry about that later, if he worried at all. He was having a good time, and nothing else mattered.

Somewhere a little past midnight, a guy with a pierced tongue drifted through the crowd passing out flyers xeroxed on poison-ously pink paper. RAVE! was the headline in screamer type—and in a fancy font that was barely legible; Justin, who'd just taken a desktop-publishing course, would never have chosen it. Below, it gave an address a few blocks from the Probe and a smudgy map.

"Wanna go?" Justin asked when the thundering music stopped for a moment.

Megan tossed her head to flip back her hair, then wiped her sweaty forehead with the sleeve of her tunic. "Sure!" she said.

After the Probe closed at two, people streamed out to their cars. The not quite legal after-hours action—at which Justin saw a lot of the same faces—was in an empty warehouse. He'd never been to this one before, but he'd been to others like it. Dancing till whenever was even more fun than dancing till two, and there was always the chance the cops would show up and run every-body out.

There were other ways to have fun at raves, too. A pretty blond girl carried an enormous purse full of plastic vials half full of orange fluid. "Liquid Happiness?" she asked when she came up to Justin and Megan.

They looked at each other. Justin pulled out ten bucks. The girl gave him two vials. She went on her way. He handed Megan a vial. They both pulled out the stoppers and drank. They both made faces, too. The stuff tasted foul. The drugs you got at raves usually did. Justin and Megan started dancing again, waiting for the Liquid Happiness to kick in.

As far as Justin was concerned, it might as well have been Liquid Wooziness. He felt as if his head were only loosely at-tached to the rest of him. It was fun. It would have been even more fun if he'd been more alert to what was going on.

Things broke up about a quarter to five. Justin's head and the rest of him seemed a little more connected. He didn't have too much trouble driving back to the Valley. "Take you home or go back to my place?" he asked Megan as he got off the Ventura Freeway and onto surface streets.

"Yours," Megan said at once. "We're so late now, another half hour, forty-five minutes won't matter at all."

He reached out and set his hand on her thigh. "I like the way you think."

His boss knew even less about Macs than he did about other computers. Since said boss was convinced he knew everything about everything, persuading him of that took all the tact Justin had, and maybe a little more besides. He got home from CompUSA feeling as if he'd gone through a car wash with his doors open.

As usual, he sorted through his snailmail walking from the lobby to his apartment. As usual, the first thing he did when he got to the apartment was toss most of it in the trash. And, as usual, the first worthwhile thing he did was turn on his computer and check e-mail. That was more likely to be interesting than what he got from the post office.

At first, though, he didn't think it would be, not today. All he had were a couple of pieces of obvious spam and something from somebody he'd never heard of who used AOL. His lip curled. As far as he was concerned, AOL was for people who couldn't ride a bicycle without training wheels.

But, with nothing more interesting showing on the monitor, he opened the message. He didn't know what he'd been expecting. Whatever it was, it wasn't what he got. *Who but you,* the e-mail read, *would know that the first time you jacked off, you were looking at Miss March 1993, a little before your fifteenth birthday? Nobody, right? Gorgeous blonde, wasn't she? The only way I know is that I am you, more or less. Let me hear from you.*

The signature line read, *Justin Kloster, age 40.*

Justin Kloster, age twenty-one, stared at that: stared and stared and stared. He remembered Miss March 1993 very, very well. He remembered sneaking her into the bathroom at his parents' house, back in the days before they'd decided to find themselves and lose him. He remembered not quite being sure what would happen as he fumbled with himself, and how much better reality had been than anything he'd imagined.

What he didn't remember was ever telling anybody about it. It wasn't the sort of thing you advertised, that was for damn sure. Could he have mentioned it when he was shooting the bull with his buds, maybe after they'd all had a few beers, or more than a few? He shook his head. No way.

He looked at the signature line again. *Justin Kloster, age 40?* "Bullshit," he muttered. He wasn't forty, thank God. Forty was the other side of the moon, the side old men lived on. Not really old, ancient, but old like his father. Old enough. The only thing that made the idea of getting to forty even halfway appealing was that he might do it with Megan. After all, she'd only be thirty-nine then.

What to do about the message? He was tempted to delete it, forget it. But he couldn't, not quite. He chose the REPLY function and typed, *What kind of stupid joke is this? Whatever it is, it's not funny.* He thought about adding *Justin Kloster, age 21* to it, but he didn't want to acknowledge it even enough to parody. He sent the bald e-mail just the way it was.

He walked out to the kitchen and threw a Hungry Man dinner in the microwave. As soon as it started, he opened the refrigerator and dithered between Coke and a beer. He seldom drank alcohol when he was by himself. Today, he made an exception. He popped open a can of Coors Light and took a long pull. The beer slid down his throat, cold and welcome.

As if drawn by a magnet, he went back to the computer. He had no way of knowing when the smartass on AOL who signed himself with his own name would send more e-mail soon, or even if he'd send any more at all. But the fellow might—and Justin spent a lot of time online just about every evening, anyhow.

Sure as hell, new e-mail from that same address came in before the microwave buzzed to tell him his dinner was done. He took another big swig of beer, then opened the mail.

No joke, it read. *Who else but you would know you lost your first baby tooth in a pear at school when you were in the first grade? Who else would know your dad fed you Rollos when he*

*took you to work with him that day when you were eight or nine?
Who else would know you spent most of the time while you were
losing your cherry staring at the mole on the side of Lindsey
Fletcher's neck? Me, that's who: you at 40. Justin Kloster.*

"Jesus!" Justin said hoarsely. His hands were shaking so
much, the beer slopped and splashed inside the can. He had to
put the can down on the desk, or he would have spilled beer on
his pants.

Out in the kitchen, the microwave did let him know his dinner
was ready. He heard it, but he hardly noticed. He couldn't take
his eyes off the iMac's monitor. Nobody knew that stuff about
him. *Nobody.* He would have bet money neither his mother nor
his father could have told how he lost his first tooth, or when. He
would have bet more money his dad couldn't have remembered
those Rollos to save himself from a firing squad.

As for Lindsey Fletcher . . . "No way," he told the words, the
impossible words, on the screen. Telling them that didn't make
them go away. Lindsey was a cute little blonde he'd known in
high school. They'd never even broken up, not in the sense of a
fight or anything, but she'd moved out to Simi Valley with her
folks the summer his parents' marriage struck a mine, and
they'd stopped dating. A damn cute little blonde—but she did
have that mole.

Justin went to the kitchen, opened up his dinner, and carried it
and a couple of dish towels and (almost as an afterthought) a
knife and fork back into the bedroom. He put the towels in his
lap so the dinner tray wouldn't burn his legs and started to eat.
He hardly noticed what he was shoveling into his face. *What do
I say?* he kept wondering. *What the hell do I say?*

That depended on what he believed. He didn't know what the
hell to believe. "Time travel?" he said, and then shook his head.
"Bullshit." But if it was bullshit, how did this guy sending him e-
mail know so goddamn much? The truth, no doubt, was out
there, but how could anybody go about getting his hands on it?

The line made him decide how to answer. *I don't watch*
X-Files *much,* he typed, *but maybe I ought to. How could you*

know all that about me? I never told anybody *about Lindsey Fletcher's neck.*

Whoever the other guy was, he answered in a hurry. Justin imagined him leaning toward his computer, waiting for AOL's stupid electronic voice to tell him, "You've got mail!" and then writing like a bastard. *How do I know?* he said. *I've told you twice now—I know because I am you, you in 2018. It's not X-Files stuff—it's good programming. Believe me, I'm back here for a good reason.*

"Believe you?" Justin yelped, as if the fellow sending him e-mail were there in the bedroom with him. "How am I supposed to believe you when you keep telling me shit like this?" His fingers said the same thing, only a little more politely. *But that's impossible,* he wrote, and sent the message.

Okay. The reply came back almost instantly. *But if it is impossible, how do I know all this stuff about you?*

That was a good question, what his grandfather called the sixty-four-dollar question. Justin would have been a lot happier had he had a sixty-four-dollar answer for it. Since he didn't, being flip would have to do. *I don't know,* he wrote. *How* do *you know all this stuff about me?*

Because it's stuff about me, too, said the fellow on the other end of the computer hookup. *You don't seem to be taking that seriously yet.*

Justin snorted. "Yeah, right," he said. "Like I'm supposed to take any of this crap seriously. Like anybody would." He snapped his fingers and laughed out loud. "I'll fix you, you son of a bitch. Hassle me, will you?" His fingers flew over the keyboard. *If you're supposed to be me, then you'll look like me, right?*

He laughed again. That'd shut Mr. Mindgames up, by God. Except it didn't. Again, the reply came back very fast. *Right,* wrote the stranger who claimed to be his older self. *Meet me in front of the B. Dalton's in the Northridge mall tomorrow night at 6:30 and I'll buy you dinner. You'll see for yourself.*

"Huh," Justin said. He hadn't expected to have his bluff

called. He hadn't thought it was a bluff. He typed three defiant words—*See you there*—sent them off, and shut down his iMac. It was still early, but he'd had enough electronic weirdness for one night.

Like Topanga Plaza, the Northridge mall was one of Justin's favorite places. He'd spent a lot of time at both of them, shopping and killing things at the arcade (though Topanga, for some reason, didn't have one) and hanging out with his buds and just being by himself. He'd been especially glad of places to be by himself when his parents' marriage went south. Northridge had just reopened then, after staying shut for a year and a half after the big quake in '94. If they'd let him, he would have visited it while it was in ruins. Even that would have beat the warfare going on at his house.

He parked in the open lot on the south side of the mall, near the Sears. Everyone swore up and down that the new parking structures they'd built since the earthquake wouldn't come crashing down the way the old ones had. Maybe it was even true. Justin didn't care to find out by experiment.

His apartment was air-conditioned. His Toyota was air-conditioned. He worked up a good sweat walking a hundred feet from the car to the entrance under the Sears façade that was also new since the quake. Summer was here early this year, and felt ready to stay for a long time. *Global warming,* he thought. He opened the door. The mall, thank God, was also air-conditioned. He sighed with pleasure at escaping the Valley heat again.

He walked through the Sears toward the entryway into the rest of the mall. None of the men's clothing he passed looked interesting. Some of it was for businessmen—not particularly successful businessmen, or they wouldn't shop at Sears. The rest of the clothes were casual, but just as unexciting.

An escalator took Justin up to the second level. The B. Dalton's was on the right-hand side as he went north, not too far past the food court in the middle of the mall. He paused a couple of times to eye pretty girls sauntering past—yeah, he was seeing Megan all the time and happy about that, but it didn't mean he

was blind. One of the girls smiled at him. He wasn't foolish
enough to let himself get distracted. Not quite.

Past the food court, on toward the bookstore. A guy was leaning against the brushed-aluminum rail—a blond, slightly
chunky guy in a black T-shirt, baggy jeans, and Army boots.
He'd been looking the other way. Now he swung his head back
toward Justin—and he had Justin's face.

Justin stopped in his tracks. He felt woozy, almost ready to
pass out, as if he'd stood up too suddenly from a chair. He had to
grab the rail himself, to keep from falling down. He didn't know
what he'd expected. That the other guy's e-mail might be simple
truth had never crossed his mind.

He wanted to get the hell out of there. His older self also
looked a little green around the gills. And why not? He was
meeting himself for the first time, too. Justin made himself keep
going.

When he got up to himself-at-forty, his older self stuck out a
hand and said, "Hi. Thanks for coming." His voice didn't sound
the way Justin's did in his own ears, but it did sound the way he
sounded when he got captured on videotape.

Both Justins looked down at the hands that matched so well.
"Maybe I'm not crazy," Justin said slowly. "Maybe you're not
crazy, either. You look just like me." He studied his older self.
Despite the buzz cut that matched his own, despite the Cow Pi T-
shirt, he thought himself-at-forty did look older. But he didn't
look a lot older. He didn't look anywhere close to the age he was
claiming.

"Funny how that works," his older self said with a tight smile.

He was sharper, more abrupt, than Justin. He acted like a goddamn adult, in other words. And, acting like an adult, as if he
knew everything there was to know just because he had some
years under his belt, he automatically ticked Justin off. Justin
put his hands on his hips and said, "Prove you're from the future." Maybe this guy was a twin separated at birth. Maybe he
was no relation, but a double anyhow. Maybe . . . Justin didn't
know what.

His older self reached into the pocket of his jeans and pulled out a little blue plastic coin purse, the kind only a grownup would use. Squeezing it open, he took out a quarter. "Here—this is for you." He gave it to Justin.

It lay in Justin's hand, eagle side up. Justin turned it over. It still looked like any other quarter . . . till he saw the date. He thought his eyes would bug out of his head. "It's from 2012," he whispered. "Jesus. You weren't kidding." Four little numbers stamped onto a coin, and the reality of what he'd just walked into hit him over the head like a club.

"I told you I wasn't." His older self sounded like an adult talking down to a kid. That helped convince him, too. Himself-at-forty continued, "Come on. What's the name of that Korean barbecue place over on Reseda?"

"The Pine Tree?" Justin said. He liked the restaurant. He'd taken Megan there once, and she'd liked it, too.

"Yeah." Himself-at-forty sounded as if he'd needed reminding. Did that mean he didn't go there in 2018? Before the question could do anything more than cross Justin's mind, his older self went on, "Let's go over there. I'll buy you dinner, like I said in the e-mail, and we can talk about things."

Justin was hungry—he usually ate dinner earlier—but that wasn't tops on his list. He came out with what was: "Like what you're doing here."

His older self nodded. "Yeah. Like what I'm doing here."

As often as not, Justin and whomever he was with turned out to be the only Caucasians in the Pine Tree. He and Megan had been. He and his older self were, too. The waitresses were all Korean; none of them spoke a whole lot of English. Himself-at-forty ordered marinated beef and pork they could cook themselves at the gas grill set into the tabletop. He ordered a couple of tall OB beers, too. Justin nodded at that. God knew he could use a beer right now.

As their waitress wrote down the order, she kept looking from his older self to Justin and back again. "Twins," she said at last.

"Yeah," himself-at-forty said. Justin wondered if he was lying or telling the truth. *Damned if I know,* he thought as the waitress headed back to the kitchen. He wanted to giggle. This whole business was too bizarre for words.

Instead of giggling, he pointed at his older self. "Tell me one thing," he said in deep and portentous tones.

"What?" Himself-at-forty looked alarmed. Heaven only knew what he thought would come out of Justin's mouth.

Justin leered at him. "That the Rolling Stones aren't still touring by the time you're—I'm—forty."

"Well, no." Now his older self looked irked, as if he couldn't believe Justin would come out with anything as off-the-wall as that. *Don't have much fun at forty, do you?* Justin thought.

Here came the waitress with the beer. She hadn't asked either of the Justins for his driver's license. *A good thing, too.* Justin wondered what kind of license his older self had, or if himself-at-forty had one at all. But he had more important things to worry about. After the waitress went off to deal with a party of Koreans at another table, Justin said, "Okay, I believe you. I didn't think I would, but I do. You know too much—and you couldn't have pulled that quarter out of your ear from nowhere." He took a big sip of his OB.

"That's right," himself-at-forty said. Again, he sounded as if he knew everything there was to know. That rubbed Justin the wrong way. But, goddamn it, his older self did know more than Justin. *How much more?* Justin didn't know. *Too much more.* He was sure of that.

He drank his glass empty, and filled it from the big bottle the waitress had set in front of him. Pretty soon, that second glass was empty, too. Justin killed the bottle pouring it for a third time. He waved to the waitress for another beer. Why not? His older self was buying. Himself-at-forty hadn't even refilled his glass once yet. *Terrific,* Justin thought. *I turn into a wet blanket.*

Not only did the waitress bring his new beer, but also dinner: plates of strange vegetables (many of them potently flavored with garlic and chilies) for Justin and his older self to share and the marinated beef and pork. She started the gas fire under the grill and used a pair of tongs to put some meat on to cook for them. As the thinly sliced strips started sizzling, Justin pointed at them and said, "Oh my God! They killed Kenny!"

"Huh?" His older self clearly didn't remember *South Park*. *Wet blanket,* Justin thought again. Then a light came on in his older self's eyes. "Oh." Himself-at-forty laughed—a little.

Justin said, "If you'd said that to me, I'd have laughed a lot harder." He decided to cut his older self some slack: "But the show's not hot for you any more, is it? No, it wouldn't be. 2018. Jesus." He made a good start on the new OB.

His older self grabbed the tongs and took some meat. So did Justin. They both ate with chopsticks. Justin wasn't real smooth with them, but he looked down his nose at people who came to Asian restaurants and reached for the knife and fork. They could do that at home. Himself-at-forty handled the chopsticks almost as well as the Koreans a couple of tables over. *More practice,* Justin thought.

After they'd made a fair dent in dinner, Justin said, "Well, *will* you tell me what this is all about?"

His older self answered the question with another question: "What's the most important thing in your life right now?"

Justin grinned. "You mean, besides trying to figure out why I'd travel back in time to see me?" Himself-at-forty nodded, his face blank like a poker player's. Justin went on, "What else could it be but Megan?"

"Okay, we're on the same page," himself-at-forty said. "That's why I'm here, to set things right with Megan."

"Things with Megan don't need setting right." Justin could feel the beer he'd drunk. It made him sound even surer than he would have otherwise. "Things with Megan are great. I mean, I'm taking my time and all, but they're great. And they'll stay great, too. How many kids do we have now?" That was the beer talking, too. Without it, he'd never have spoken so freely.

"None." Himself-at-forty touched the corner of his jaw, where a muscle was twitching.

"None?" That didn't sound good. The way his older self said the word didn't sound good, either. Justin noticed something he should have seen sooner: "You're not wearing a wedding ring."

His older self nodded. He asked, "Does that mean we don't get married?"

"We get married, all right," his older self answered grimly. "And then we get divorced."

Ice ran through Justin. "That can't happen," he blurted.

He knew too goddamn much about divorce, more than he'd ever wanted to. He knew about the shouts and the screams and the slammed doors. He knew about the silences that were even deadlier. He knew about the lies his parents had told each other. He knew about the lies they'd told him about each other, and the lies they'd told him about themselves. He had a pretty fair notion of the lies they'd told themselves about themselves.

One of the biggest lies each of them had told him was, *Of course I'll still care for you just as much afterwards as I did before.* Megan wasn't the only one who envied him his apartment—a lot of people his age did. What the apartment meant to him was that his folks would sooner give him money to look out for himself than bother looking out for him. He envied Megan her parents who cared.

And now his older self was saying he and Megan would go through that? He sure was. His voice hard as stone, he squashed Justin's protest: "It can. It did. It will." That muscle at the corner of his jaw started jumping again.

"But—how?" Justin asked, sounding even in his own ears like a little boy asking how his puppy could have died. He tried to rally. "We aren't like Mom and Dad—we don't fight all the time, and we don't look for something on the side wherever we can find it." He took a long pull at his beer, trying to wash the taste of his parents out of his mouth. And he hadn't smiled back at that girl in the mall. He really hadn't.

With weary patience, his older self answered, "You can fight about sex, you can fight about money, you can fight about in-laws. We ended up doing all three, and so . . ." Himself-at-forty leaned his chopsticks on the edge of his plate and spread his hands. "We broke up—will break up—if we don't change things. That's why I figured out how to come back: to change things, I mean."

Justin poured the last of the second OB into his glass and gulped it down. After a bit, he said, "You must have wanted to do that a lot."

"You might say so." His older self drank some more beer, too. He still sounded scratchy as he went on, "Yeah, you just might say so. Since we fell apart, I've never come close to finding anybody who makes me feel the way Megan did. If it's not her, it's nobody. That's how it looks from here, anyhow. I want to make things right for the two of us."

"Things *were* going to be right." But Justin couldn't make himself sound as if he believed it. Divorce? He shuddered. From everything he'd seen, anything was better than that. In a small voice, he asked, "What will you do?"

"I'm going to take over your life for the next couple of months." His older self sounded absolutely sure, as if he'd thought it all through and this was the only possible answer. Was that how doctors sounded, recommending major surgery? Justin didn't get a chance to wonder for long; himself-at-forty plowed ahead, relentless as a landslide: "I'm going to be you. I'm going to take Megan out. I'm going to make sure things are solid—and then the superstring I've ridden to get me here will break down. You'll live happily ever after. I'll brief you to make sure you don't screw up what I've built. And when I get back to 2018, I *will have lived* happily ever after. How does that sound?"

"I don't know." Now Justin regretted pouring down two tall beers, one right after the other. He needed to think clearly, and he couldn't quite. "You'll be taking Megan out?"

"That's right." Himself-at-forty nodded.

"You'll be . . . taking Megan back to the apartment?"

"Yeah," his older self said. "But she'll think it's you, remember, and pretty soon it'll be you, and it'll keep right on being you till you turn into me, if you know what I mean."

"I know what you mean. Still . . ." Justin grimaced. "I don't know. I don't like it." When you imagined your girlfriend being unfaithful to you, you pictured her making love with somebody else. Justin tried to imagine Megan being unfaithful to him by picturing her making love with somebody who looked just like him. It made his mental eyes cross.

His older self folded his arms across his chest and sat there in the booth. "You have a better idea?" he asked. He must have known damn well that Justin had no ideas at all.

"It's not fair," Justin protested. "You *know* all this shit, and I've gotta guess."

With a cold shrug, himself-at-forty said, "If you think I did all this to come back and tell you lies, go ahead. That's fine. You'll see what happens. And we'll both be sorry."

"I don't know. I just don't know." Justin shook his head. He felt trapped, caught in a spider's web. "Everything sounds like it hangs together, but you could be bullshitting, too, just as easy."

"Yeah, right." Amazing how much scorn his older self could pack into two words.

Justin got to his feet so fast it made him lightheaded for a couple of seconds—or maybe that was the beer, too. "I won't say yes and I won't say no, not now I won't. I've got your e-mail address. I'll use it." Out he went, planting his feet with exaggerated care at every stride.

Night had fallen while he and himself-at-forty were eating. He drove back to his apartment building as carefully as he'd walked. Picking up a 502 for driving under the influence was the last thing he wanted. One thought pounded in his head the whole way back. *What do I do? What the hell do I do?*

He'd just come out of the bathroom—the revenge of those two tall OBs—when the telephone rang. He wondered if it was his older self, calling to give him another dose of lecture. If it was, he intended to tell himself-at-forty where he could stick that lecture. "Hello?" he said suspiciously.

But it wasn't his older self. "Hiya," Megan said.

"Oh!" Justin shifted gears in a hurry. "Hi!"

"I just called up to say I think you're the bomb," she told him, and hung up before he could answer.

He stared at the telephone handset, then slowly set it back in its cradle. "God damn you," he whispered, cursing not Megan but his older self. "Oh, God damn you." He had a girl like this, and himself-at-forty was saying he'd lose her? *I can't do that,* he thought. *Whatever it takes, I can't do that.*

Even if it means bowing out of your own life for a while? Even if it means letting him stick his nose in? But his older self sticking his nose in didn't worry Justin. His older self sticking something else in . . .

I don't have to make up my mind right away. I'm not going to make up my mind right away. This is too important. And if my older self can't figure that out, tough shit, that's all.

Justin checked his e-mail even before he brushed his teeth the next morning. Himself-at-forty hadn't started nagging, anyhow. There was e-mail from Megan, though. Everything else could wait, but he opened that. It said, *The bomb.*

He grinned and shook his head. But the grin slipped a moment later. *I can't let her get away from me. Knowing she might . . .* He ground his teeth. He didn't just know she might. He knew she would. He'd never thought of being blind to the future as a blessing, but knowing some of it sure felt like a curse.

At work, his boss chewed him out for not paying attention to anything going on around him. He couldn't even blame the guy; he *wasn't* paying attention to anything going on around him. Too many important things spun through his mind.

He gulped lunch at the Burger King four doors down from the CompUSA, then went to the pay phones around the side of the building. He fed in a quarter—*not* the one from 2012; he was saving that—and a dime and called Megan. "Hello?" she said.

"Hi. I think you're the bomb, too." It wasn't *I love you*—it wasn't even close to *I love you*—but it was the best he could do.

Megan giggled, as if she'd been waiting by the telephone for him to call. "I bet you say that whenever you phone a girl who isn't wearing any clothes," she answered—and hung up on him again.

He spluttered, which did him no good. He reached into his pants pocket for more change to call her back and find out why she wasn't wearing any clothes—or if she really wasn't wearing any clothes. But that didn't matter. He had the image of her naked stuck in his head—which had to be just what she'd had in mind.

As he walked back, he realized he'd made up his mind. *I can't lose her. No matter what, I can't lose her.* If that meant letting his older self fix things up—whatever there was that needed fixing—then it did, and that was all there was to it.

Despite deciding, he took another day and a half to write the e-mail that admitted he'd decided. *All write, dammit,* he typed. *I still don't know about this, but I don't think I have any choice. If me and Megan are going to break up, that* can't *happen. You better make sure it doesn't.*

After he'd sent the e-mail, he looked at it again. It wasn't exactly gracious. He shrugged. He didn't feel exactly gracious, either.

An answer came back almost at once. Himself-at-forty must have been hanging around the computer waiting for him to say something. *You won't be sorry,* the e-mail told him.

Whatever, Justin wrote. His hands balled into fists. He made them unclench. *How do you want to make the switch?*

Meet me in front of the B. Dalton's again, himself-at-forty replied. *Park by the Sears. I will, too. Bring whatever you want in your car. You can move it to the one I'm driving. I'll do the same here. See you in two hours?*

Justin sighed. *Whatever,* he wrote again. Packing didn't take anything like two hours. He thought about bringing the iMac along, but ended up leaving it behind and taking his PowerBook instead. It was old, but it would do for games and for the Net. He scribbled a note and set it by the iMac's keyboard: *In case you don't remember, here's Megan's phone number and e-mail. Don't screw it up, that's all I've got to tell you.*

Once he'd stuffed everything he thought he needed into a pair of suitcases, he put them in the trunk of his Toyota and headed for the mall. He'd gone only a couple of blocks when he snapped his fingers and swung down to the Home Depot on Roscoe first.

Even with the stop, he still took his place in front of the bookstore before his older self got there. This time, seeing himself-at-forty made him grim, not boggled. "Let's get this over with," he said.

"Come on. It's not a root canal," his older self said. Justin shrugged. He'd never had one. Himself-at-forty went on, "Let's go do it. We'll need to swap keys, you know."

"Yeah," Justin said. "I had spares made. How about you?"

"Me, too." His older self grinned a lopsided grin. "We think alike. Amazing, huh?"

"Amazing. Right." Justin abruptly turned away and started walking toward Sears and the lot beyond it. "This better work."

"It will." Himself-at-forty sounded disgustingly confident.

The two Toyotas sat only a couple of rows apart. They were almost as much alike as Justin and his older self. Justin moved his things into the other car, while himself-at-forty put stuff in his. They traded keys. "You know where I live," Justin said. "What's my new address?"

"Oh." His older self gave it to him. He knew where it was—not as good a neighborhood as the one the Acapulco was in. Himself-at-forty went on, "The car's insured, and you'll find plenty of money in the underwear drawer." His older self patted him on the shoulder, the only time they'd touched other than shaking hands. "It'll be fine. Honest. You're on vacation for a couple of months, that's all."

"On vacation from my *life*," Justin exclaimed. He glared at his older self. "Don't fuck up, that's all."

"It's my life, too, remember." Himself-at-forty got into the car Justin had driven to the mall. Justin went to his older self's Toyota. Still half wondering if this were some elaborate scam, he tried the key. The car started right up. Justin drove off to see where the hell he'd have to wait this out.

Sure enough, the Yachtsman and the apartment buildings on the block with it were older and tireder-looking than the Acapulco and its surroundings. It wasn't a neighborhood where guys sold crack from parked cars, but it might be heading that way in a few years. The one bright spot Justin saw was the Denny's on the corner. If he got sick of frozen dinners and his own bad cooking, he could always eat there.

He found his parking space under the apartment building. When he went out to the lobby, a mailbox had KLOSTER Dymo-taped onto it. He checked. His older self hadn't got any mail. Justin went inside and found his apartment. The door key and dead-bolt key both worked. "Well, what have we got?" he wondered.

When he discovered what he had, his first impulse was to walk right out again. The TV just plugged into the wall: no cable, not even a VCR hooked up. The stereo had to have come out of an antique store. It played cassettes and vinyl, but not CDs. He could play CDs on the PowerBook, but even so . . .

He opened the underwear drawer, more than half expecting BVDs and nothing else. But under the briefs lay . . . "Christ!" he exclaimed. How much was there? He picked up wad after wad of cash, threw them all down on the bed, and started counting. By the time he was through, he'd had almost as much fun as he'd ever had in his life.

Close to seventy grand, he thought dazedly. *Jesus.* All at once, he stopped doubting his older self's story. Nobody—but nobody—would spend, or let him spend, that kind of money on a scam. The bills weren't even crisp and new, as they might have been if they were counterfeits. They'd all been circulating a good long while, and couldn't be anything but genuine.

"Okay," he said, fighting the impulse to count them again. "I'm on vacation. Let the good times roll." He *did* recount a couple of thousand dollars' worth, just for the hell of it.

He'd never been in a spot where he could spend all the money he wanted, do whatever he felt like doing. If he wanted to go out and get a VCR, he could—and he intended to. He could charge right down to Circuit City or Best Buy or Fry's and . . .

"Uh-oh," he muttered. If he went to any of those places, there was some chance he'd run into Megan. His older self didn't want him running into Megan for a while, and his older self had left him all this money to play around with so he wouldn't. He shrugged. He could go over to Burbank or out to Simi Valley or wherever and get a VCR. Then he could charge right down to Blockbuster and rent enough tapes to keep him from getting too . . .

Uh-oh. He didn't say it this time, but he thought it. Megan was liable to show up at either of the local Blockbusters; she liked watching movies on video as much as everybody else did.

"Okay," Justin said, as if somebody were arguing with him. "I'll find some video place out in the boonies, too."

That made him happier. He had time to kill—nothing but time to kill—and movies were a great way to kill it. But he couldn't watch movies and play computer games all the damn time. *I can go down to . . .* But that thought stopped before it was even half formed. He couldn't go to the mall, not to Northridge, not to Topanga Plaza, not even to the half-dead Promenade farther down Topanga or to tacky Fallbrook. Megan visited all of them.

"Shit," he said in a low voice. And he really couldn't go to any of his favorite restaurants, because where would himself-at-forty be taking Megan? To one of them or another, sure as hell. What would she think if she were with his older self and then saw him come in by himself in different clothes? Nothing good, that was for damn sure.

Great, Justin thought. *I can do whatever I want, as long as I don't do it in any of the places I usually go to. Or I can just sit here in this miserable apartment and jack off.* He suspected he'd end up doing a lot of that. Thinking about Megan immediately made him want to do more than think about Megan: he was, after all, twenty-one.

Down, boy, he told himself. Himself didn't want to listen. While he was holed up here by his lonesome, himself-at-forty would be taking Megan out, taking Megan home, taking Megan to bed. No, he didn't like that worth a rat's ass. He tried again to imagine Megan being unfaithful to him with somebody with his own face. He came a lot closer to succeeding this time.

He paced out to the kitchen. Even looking at the bed turned him on and pissed him off, regardless of whether it had cash strewn all over it. When he opened the refrigerator, he found a couple of six-packs of microbrews along with fresh vegetables and other things he was unlikely to eat. He tried to unscrew the cap from one of the beers, only to discover it didn't unscrew. That meant he had to rummage in the drawer till he came up with an opener. Once he got the cap off, he threw it at the waste-basket—and missed. He had to bend down and drop it in—and even then he almost missed again.

Sighing, Justin sipped the hard-won Anchor Porter . . . and made a horrible face. "People pay a buck a bottle for *this*?" he said. "Jesus! Gimme Coors Light any day."

When he opened the freezer, he found steaks and chops and chicken in there. He supposed he could do up the steaks in a pan on the stove, but chicken was out of his culinary league. Fortunately, there were also several frozen dinners. He didn't know what he would have done if his older self had turned into a total foodie.

Like hell I don't know, he thought, and grinned. *I'd just eat out all the time. With that Denny's right at the end of the block, I might anyway.*

After watching network TV that night, he realized he would have to get a VCR ASAP if he wanted to stay anywhere close to sane. He ate bacon and eggs and hash browns at the Denny's the next morning, then drove over to an electronics place he knew on Ventura Boulevard in Encino—only twenty minutes' drive from the Yachtsman, but not a place where he was at all likely to run into Megan. He bought the VCR, put the box in his trunk, and headed to a Blockbuster a few doors away to get some tapes.

His address came up on their computer system. "You do know we have locations closer to your home, sir?" the clerk said.

"Yeah." Justin nodded. "This is near where I work."

He'd never been a great liar. He was, at the moment, wearing a Dilbert T-shirt and a pair of baggy shorts. The clerk raised an eyebrow. But Justin's credit checked out okay, so that was all she did.

Having lugged the VCR into his apartment, he discovered, not for the first time, that being a computer-science major didn't make the damn thing easy to set up. He fumed and mumbled and cussed and finally got the gadget acting the way it was supposed to. With *Deep Impact* on the TV and a Coke in his hand, life looked better.

He put his feet on the coffee table and belched enormously. Nothing to do but kick back and watch movies for a couple of months? *Okay, I can handle it,* he thought. Then he snapped his fingers. "Potato chips!" he said out loud. "Doritos. Whatever."

That day went fine. The next day went all right. By the middle of the afternoon on the third day, he was sick of movies and computer games and hoped he'd never see another nacho-cheese Dorito as long as he lived. He went into the bedroom and picked up the phone. He'd dialed four digits of Megan's number before he remembered he wasn't supposed to call her.

"God damn it," he muttered. "This is so lame. What am I going to do, stay cooped up here till I get all dusty?"

His older self wanted him to do exactly that. His older self had left him plenty of money so he would do exactly that. But what good was the money if he had trouble finding places to blow it? After staring at the walls—and the TV screen, and his laptop's monitor—for two days straight, his affection for his older self, which had never been high, sank like the Dow on an especially scary day. He'd never understood people saying money couldn't buy happiness. Now maybe he did.

He wanted to talk with his girlfriend. Hell, he wanted to lay his girlfriend. Himself-at-forty was telling him he couldn't do either. Himself-at-forty, the son of a bitch, was probably doing both. Justin was no better at handling frustration than anyone else his age. The hornier he got, the worse he got, too.

If he couldn't talk to Megan, he damn well could talk to his older self. He dialed the number at his apartment, which felt funny. He never called there. Why would he? If he wasn't home, who would answer? A burglar?

But somebody was home to answer now. And, after three rings, somebody did. "Hello?" Himself-at-forty sounded as if he were talking from deep underwater.

"Hi," Justin said cheerfully; he had all he could do not to say hiya, the way Megan did. "How are things?"

"Things are fine," his older self answered after a longish pause. He still sounded like hell; if he hadn't been ridden hard and put away wet, Justin had never heard anybody who had. Another pause. Then himself-at-forty tried again: "Or they were till you called. I was asleep."

"Now?" Justin exclaimed in disbelief. He looked at his watch: half past two. He didn't think he'd been asleep at half past two since he was three years old and quit taking naps. "I called now 'cause I figured you wouldn't be."

"Never mind." His older self yawned, but seemed a little less fuzzy when he went on, "Yeah, things are okay. We went to the Probe last night, and—"

"Did you?" Justin broke in. He didn't like the way that sounded: him stuck here in this miserable place, himself-at-forty having a good time at his favorite club. No, he didn't like that at all. "What else did you do?"

"That after-hours place," his older self answered. "Some guy came through with flyers, so I knew how to get there."

Yeah, you'd have forgotten, wouldn't you, you sorry bastard? Aloud, Justin said, "Lucky you. And what *else* did you do?" He could imagine Megan in his older self's arms, all right. Now he could. He'd had plenty of time to try. Practice made perfect, dammit. He could hate what he imagined, too.

"About what you'd expect," himself-at-forty said. Christ, he sounded arrogant. "I'm you, remember. What would you have done?" Justin sighed. He knew what he would have done, by God. But no. He'd stayed here by his lonesome—by his very lonesome—so his older self could do it instead. He sucked in a long, angry breath preparatory to telling himself-at-forty where to head in. Before he could, his older self went on, "And when I took her home, I told her I loved her."

"Jesus!" Justin yelped, forgetting whatever else he might have said. "What did you go and do that for?"

"It's true, isn't it?" his older self asked.

"That doesn't mean you've got to *say* it, for Christ's sake,"

Justin answered. He shook his head in disbelief, though his older self wasn't there to see it. His parents must have said they loved each other once upon a time, too, and how had that turned out? "What am I supposed to do when you go away?"

"Marry her, doofus," himself-at-forty said, as if it were just that simple. "Live happily ever after, so I get to live happily ever after, too. Why the hell do you think I came back here?"

"For your good time, man, not mine," Justin snarled. "I'm sure not having a good time, I'll tell you." He belched again. No surprise—how many Cokes had he poured down since he got to this place? Too many. With the carbonation, he tasted stale nacho cheese.

His older self took a deep breath, too, and said, "Look, chill for a while, okay? I'm doing fine."

That only made Justin angrier. "Sure you are. You're doing fucking great. What about me?"

"You're fine. Chill. You're on vacation," himself-at-forty answered. If he didn't know everything, he didn't know he didn't know everything. "Go ahead. Relax. Spend my money. That's what it's there for."

When his older self mentioned the money, Justin forgot how chuffed he was, at least for a little while. "Where'd you get so much?" he asked. "What did you do, rob a bank?"

"It's worth a lot more now than it will be then," his older self told him. "Inflation. Have some fun. Just be discreet, okay?"

Which brought Justin back to square one. His older self kept trying to blow him off, and he didn't want to put up with it. "You mean, keep out of your hair."

"In a word, yes." Himself-at-forty sounded as if he was having trouble putting up with Justin, too.

"While you're in Megan's hair." No, Justin had no trouble at all seeing pictures in his mind, pictures nastier than any he could have pulled off the Net. He sighed, trying to make them go away. "I don't know, dude."

"It's for you," himself-at-forty said. "It's for her and you."

That, goddammit, was the trump card. If Justin-now was fated to break up with Megan, he didn't see that he had any choice other than letting his older self set things right. He hated the idea. Every minute he spent in this miserable apartment made him hate it more. But he couldn't find any way around it. Get married and get divorced? That was worse. "Yeah," he said, and hung up.

Every minute he spent in that miserable apartment . . . from then on, he spent as little time as he could there. That worked better than staring at the TV and the PowerBook's monitor and, most of all, the four walls. When he was out and doing things, he didn't think about himself-at-forty and Megan . . . so much.

Getting out would have worked better still if he'd been able to go to the places he really liked, the local malls and the movie theaters and coffeehouses and restaurants where he'd gone with Megan. But he didn't dare. He couldn't imagine what he'd do if he saw her and his older self together. And what would himself-at-forty do? And Megan? Those were all terrific questions, and he didn't want to find out the answers to any of them.

So he went to places where he could be sure he wouldn't run into Megan or anybody else he knew. He killed an afternoon at the Glendale Galleria. He killed a whole day at the enormous Del Amo mall down in Torrance, which was supposed to be the biggest shopping center this side of the Mall of America. By the time he'd trekked from one end of it to the other, he believed all the hype. He hadn't come close to hitting all the stores that looked interesting.

He grabbed some pizza down there, and stayed for a movie after the shops closed. That turned out to be a mistake. Sitting in a theater by himself was the loneliest thing he'd ever done, much worse than watching a movie on the VCR without any company. All the other people there seemed to have somebody else to have a good time with, and he didn't.

And he was sure Megan would have loved this flick. She'd have gone all slobbery over the male star, and he could have had a good time teasing her about it. And she would have told him he only went to movies for the special effects—and they were pretty damn special. And then they would have gone back to his place and screwed themselves silly.

He went back to the place that wasn't his: a long haul up the San Diego Freeway, which had plenty of traffic even after eleven at night. When he got there, he masturbated twice in quick succession. It wasn't the same—it wasn't close to the same—but it let him fall asleep.

The next morning, he drove out Topanga Canyon Boulevard to the ocean and spent the day at Zuma Beach. That would have been better with Megan along, too, but it wasn't so bad by itself, either: nothing to do but lie there and watch girls and keep himself well greased with sunscreen. It let him get through another day without being too unhappy.

But, in spite of all the sunscreen, he came home with a burn. He was so fair, he could sunburn in the moonlight. Hot and uncomfortable, he couldn't fall asleep. Finally, he quit trying. He put on some shorts and a T-shirt and went out front to watch TV. That experiment didn't last long: nothing there but crap of the purest ray serene. After about twenty minutes, he turned it off in disgust.

"Now what?" he muttered. He still wasn't sleepy. He walked back into the bedroom and got his car keys. He was an L.A. kid, all right: when in doubt, climb behind the wheel.

Driving around with a Pulp cassette in the stereo and the volume cranked made Justin feel better for a while. But he wasn't just driving around. His hands and feet figured that out a little before his head did. The conscious part of his mind was surprised to discover they'd sent him down his own street toward his own apartment building.

If he parked between the Acapulco and the building next to it, he could look between them and see his bedroom window, a foreshortened rectangle of light. The curtain was drawn, so light was all he could see, light and, briefly, a moving shadow. Was that his older self? Megan? Were they both there? If they were, what were they doing? *Like I don't know,* Justin thought.

"I've got spare keys," he told himself in conversational tones. "I could walk in there and . . ."

Instead, he started up the car and drove away, fast. What

would he do if he did walk in on himself-at-forty and Megan? He didn't want to find out.

The sunburn bothered him enough the next day that staying in the apartment and being a lump suited him fine. The day after, though, he felt better, which meant he also started feeling stir-crazy. He went out and drove some more: west on the 118 into Ventura County. Simi Valley and Moorpark were bedroom communities for the Valley, the way the Valley had been a bedroom community for downtown L.A. when his parents were his age.

I could be going to Paris or Prague or Tokyo, he thought as he put the pedal to the metal to get on the freeway, *and I'm going to Simi Valley?* But, in fact, he couldn't go to Paris or Prague or Tokyo, not without a passport, which he didn't have. And he didn't really want to. He just wanted to go on living the way he had been living. He'd spent his whole life in the Valley, and was in some ways as much a small-town kid as somebody from Kokomo or Oshkosh.

Justin didn't think of himself like that, of course. As far as he was concerned, he stood at the top of the cool food chain. And so, when he'd pulled off the freeway and driven the couple of blocks to what his Thomas Brothers guide showed as the biggest shopping center in Simi Valley, he made gagging noises. "It's not even a mall!" he exclaimed. And it wasn't, not by his standards: no single, enormous, air-conditioned building in which to roam free. If he wanted to go from store to store, he had to expose his tender hide to the sun for two, sometimes three, minutes at a time.

He almost turned around and drove back to his apartment. In the end, with a martyred sigh, he parked the car and headed toward a little mom-and-pop software store. It turned out to be all PC stuff. He had Virtual PC, so he could run Windows programs on his Macs, but he left in a hurry anyway. They'd go okay on the iMac, which was a pretty fast machine, but they'd be glacial on the old PowerBook he had with him.

The Wherehouse a couple of doors down was just as depressing. Grunge, metal, rap, bands his parents had listened to—yeah, they had plenty of that stuff. British pop? He found one, count it, one Oasis CD, filed under THE REST OF O. Past that? Nada.

"Boy, this is fun," he said as he stomped out in moderately high dudgeon. He spotted a Borders halfway across the shopping center and headed toward it. Even as he did, he wondered why he bothered. The way his luck was running, it would stock a fine assortment of computer magazines from 1988.

Behind him, somebody called, "Justin!" He kept walking. Half the guys in his generation—all the ones who weren't Jasons—were Justins. But the call came again, louder, more insistent: "Hey, Justin!"

Maybe it is me, he thought, and turned around. A startled smile spread over his face. "Lindsey!" he said. Sure as hell, Lindsey Fletcher came running up to him, rubber-soled sandals scuffing on the sidewalk. He opened his arms. They gave each other a big hug.

"I can't believe it," Lindsey said. "What are you doing up here? You never come up here. I've never seen you up here, anyway." She spoke as if one proved the other.

She'd always liked to talk, Justin remembered. He remembered the mole on the side of her neck, too. It was still there, a couple of inches above the top of her T-shirt. "How are you?" he said. "How've you been?"

"I'm fine." She looked him up and down. "God, you haven't changed a bit."

"Yeah, well," Justin said, a little uncomfortably. He knew how little he would change, too, which she didn't.

"What *are* you doing up here?" Lindsey asked again.

"Whatever," Justin answered. "A little shopping. Hanging out. You know."

"Here? It's a lot better in the Valley." She looked astonished and sounded wistful.

"Yeah, well," he said again: he'd already discovered that. "Something new."

"Slumming," Lindsey told him. "But as long as you're here, that donut place over there isn't too bad." She pointed. "I mean, if you want to get something and, you know, talk for a little while."

"Sure," Justin said. Like a lot of the little donut shops in Southern California, this one was run by Cambodians: a middle-aged couple who spoke with accents and a teenage boy who talked just like Justin and Lindsey. Lindsey tried to buy; Justin wouldn't let her, not with his older self's money burning a hole in his wallet. They got jelly donuts and big fizzy Cokes, sat down at one of the half-dozen or so little tables in the shop, and proceeded to get powdered sugar all over their faces.

"What have you been up to?" Lindsey asked, dabbing at herself with a paper napkin.

"Finished my junior year at CSUN," Justin answered, pronouncing it *C-sun*, the way anybody who went there would.

"What's your major?"

"Computer science. It's pretty interesting, and it'll pay off, too—I've got a summer job at the Northridge CompUSA." *Which my older self is welcome to.* Half a beat slower than he should have, Justin asked, "How about you?"

"I've been going to Moorpark Community College kind of on and off," Lindsey said. "I've got a part-time job, too—pet grooming."

"Ah, cool," Justin said. "You always did love animals. I remember."

She nodded. "Maybe I'll end up doing that full-time. If I can save some money, maybe I'll try and get into breeding one of these days." She sipped at her Coke, then asked, "Do I want to know about your parents?"

"No!" Justin exclaimed. "God no! Let's see . . . I think you'd already moved here when my mom came out of the closet."

"Oh, Lord." Lindsey's eyes got big. "That must have been fun."

"Yeah, right," Justin said. "Somebody shoot me quick if I ever set out to discover myself." He turned his mother's favorite phrase into a curse.

Lindsey didn't ask about his father. The bad news there had been obvious while she still lived in the Valley. After some hesitation, she did ask, "What about you? Are you . . . seeing anybody?"

Justin had just taken a big bite of jelly donut, so he didn't have to answer right away. When he did, he did his best to make it sound casual: "Uh-huh."

"Oh." Lindsey looked disappointed, which was flattering. And Justin couldn't have sounded too casual, because she asked, "Are you serious?"

"Well, it kinda looks that way," he admitted. And then, not so much out of politeness as because he didn't want to think about how he *wasn't* seeing Megan right this minute and his older self *was*, he said, "What about you?"

Lindsey shook her head. A strand of her short blond hair—she'd worn it longer in high school—fell down onto her nose. She brushed it away with her hand. "Not right now. Not so it matters, anyhow, I mean. I've gone with a few guys since I got up here, but nobody I'd want to settle down with. You're lucky."

She sounded wistful again. She also sounded as if she really meant it. She'd never begrudged happiness to anybody else. Justin would have had trouble saying the same thing—he was mad as hell thinking about himself-at-forty having a good time with Megan. And how lucky was he if his older self had to come back from 2018 to try to straighten things out? But Lindsey didn't—couldn't—know about that, of course.

He finished the donut in a couple of big bites. "I better get going. I have to be at work before too long." He could almost feel his nose getting longer, but the lie gave him an excuse to get away.

"Okay." Lindsey stood up, too. "It was great to see you. I'm glad you're doing so well." She sounded as if she really meant that, too. Nope, not a mean bone in her body. She gave him another hug, this one a little more constrained than the one when they first ran into each other. "Listen, if you ever want to just talk or anything, I'm in the book." She made a face. "I sorta wish I wasn't, but I am. I get more damn telemarketers than you can shake a stick at."

"Always at dinnertime, too," Justin said, and she nodded. "They ought to do something about 'em." He didn't know who *they* were or what they could do, but that didn't stop him from complaining. He headed for the door. "So long."

"So long, Justin." Lindsey followed, but more slowly, making it plain she wasn't going to come with him once they got outside. He headed for his car. Lindsey walked in the direction of the Wherehouse he'd already found wanting. He looked back toward her once. She was looking toward him. They both smiled and waved. Justin pulled out his keys, unlocked the Toyota, and slid inside. Lindsey went into the Wherehouse. Justin drove back to the Valley. For some reason he couldn't quite fathom, he didn't feel so bad once he got there.

He kept feeling halfway decent, or even a little better than halfway decent, for a while afterwards. The driving need to call up either his older self or Megan and find out how things were going went away. What that amounted to, of course, was finding out whether anybody in the whole wide world cared if he was alive—and a good-sized fear the answer was no. Lindsey Fletcher cared. Justin didn't think of it in those terms—on a conscious level, he hardly thought of it at all—but that was what it added up to.

And so, over about the next ten days, he found things to do and places to go that let him kill time without seeming to be doing nothing but killing time. He drove over to the Sherman Oaks Galleria, which had gone from the coolest place in the world to semi–ghost town in one fell swoop after the '94 quake. He beat the parking hassles at the new Getty Museum looming over the San Diego Freeway by taking a cab there—*spending my older self's money,* he thought, feeling half virtuous and half *so there!* He found a pretty good Japanese restaurant, Omino's, on Devonshire near Canoga. It'd be a good place to take Megan once himself-at-forty got the hell back to 2018, where he belonged.

"Superstrings," Justin muttered in the apartment that wasn't his. He'd fought his way through his physics classes; he couldn't say much more than that. He wished he knew more. His older self did, dammit. That was definitely something to think about when he planned his schedule for his senior year.

Before so very long, though, he started muttering other, more incendiary, things. His decent mood didn't last, not least because he didn't fully understand what had caused it in the first place. The apartment in the Yachtsman started feeling like a prison cell again. Going out stopped being fun. Minutes crawled past on hands and knees.

Justin thought about calling his older self to complain: he thought about it for a good second and a half, as a matter of fact. Then he laughed a bitter laugh that lasted a lot longer. He knew just what his older self would say. *Live with it.* He could tell himself that and save the price of a phone call. It wasn't quite *fuck off and die*, but close enough for government work.

Besides, he didn't really want to talk to himself-at-forty. He wanted to talk to Megan. His older self had given him all sorts of reasons why that wasn't a good idea. Justin had only one reason why it was: he was going out of his tree because he couldn't. Eventually, that swamped everything his older self had said.

He felt as if he'd just pulled off a jailbreak when he dialed her number. Her father answered the phone. "Hi, Mr. Tricoupis," he said happily. "Can I talk to Megan, please?"

Instead of saying *Sure* or *Hang on a second* or anything like that, Megan's father answered, "Well, I don't know, Justin. I'll see if she wants to talk to you."

I'll see if she wants to talk to you? Justin thought. *What the hell's going on here?* But he couldn't even ask, because a clunking noise meant Mr. Tricoupis had put the phone down. He could only wait.

After what seemed like forever but couldn't have been more than half a minute, Megan said, "Hello?" He needed no more than the one word to hear that she didn't sound happy.

But he felt something close to delirious joy at hearing her voice. "Hi!" he burbled. "How you doing?"

Another pause. Then, very carefully, Megan said, "Justin, didn't I tell you last night not to call here for a while? Didn't I say that?"

He knew what that meant. It meant his older self wasn't as goddamn smart as he thought he was. By the look of things, it also meant he'd have to bail himself-at-forty out instead of the other way round. He wondered if he could. He and Megan hadn't had any great big fights, which meant he had no sure feel for how to fix one.

Silly seemed a good idea. "Duh," he said, the standard idiot-noise of the late '90s, and then, "My big mouth." That wasn't just an apology; it was also the title of an Oasis song Megan liked.

"Your big mouth is right," she said, but a little of the hard edge left her voice—either that or wishful thinking was running away with Justin. She wasn't going to let him down easy, though; she went on, "Do you have any idea how far over the line you were? Any idea at all?"

"Definitely maybe," he answered: an Oasis album title that had the added virtue of keeping him off the hook.

He wasn't sure Megan had noticed the first title he used, but she definitely noticed the second; he heard her snort. "You're funny now," she said, as if fighting to stay mad. "You weren't funny last night after the movie, believe me you weren't."

Which movie? Justin wondered. He could hardly ask; he was supposed to know. He couldn't even waste any more time cursing his older self, not when he was trying to jolly Megan back into a good mood. "Charmless man, that's me," he said. It wasn't just him—it was also a track on a recent Blur CD.

"Justin . . ." But Megan was fighting back laughter now. "What am I supposed to do about you?"

"Roll with it, my legendary girlfriend," Justin said: one Oasis song, one from Pulp. "I'm just a killer for your love. Advert." Two from Blur. He didn't know how long he could keep it up, but he was having fun while it lasted.

With that, Megan gave up the fight and giggled. "Okay," she said. "Okay. I didn't think you could do anything to make me forget last night, but you did. How did you manage?"

"Only tongue will tell," he answered gravely. "Worked a miracle." That set Megan off again. She recognized Trash Can Sinatras titles, sure enough, and there probably weren't three other people in the San Fernando Valley who would have.

"I'll see you soon, Justin," she said, and hung up.

But she wouldn't be seeing him, dammit. She'd be seeing his older self. Justin started to call his old apartment to tell himself-at-forty what he thought of him, but held off. He didn't see what good it would do. He wasn't quite ready to throw his older self out of his place on his ear, and nothing short of that would make a nickel's worth of difference. *I'll wait,* he thought. *For a little while.*

He didn't have to wait long. Twenty minutes later, the phone rang. He hurried into the bedroom from the kitchen, hoping it was Megan. He'd just picked up the phone when he remembered she didn't have the number here. By then, he was already saying, "Hello?"

"Oh, good. You're home." His older self sounded half disappointed Justin hadn't walked in front of a truck.

"Oh, it's you," Justin answered, still wishing it were Megan. Throwing himself-at-forty out on his ear suddenly looked more attractive. He went on, "No, *you're* home. I'm stuck here." He looked around the little bedroom, feeling like a trapped animal again.

His older self had gone into dictator mode: "Didn't I tell you to lay low till I was done here? God damn it, you'd better listen to me. I just had to pretend I knew what Megan was talking about when she said I'd been on the phone with her."

"She's my girl, too," Justin said. "She was my girl first, you know. I've got a *right* to talk with her." As talking to Lindsey Fletcher out in the wilds of Simi Valley had, it reminded him he was alive.

But himself-at-forty didn't want to hear any of that. Maybe he wasn't a dictator; maybe he was just a grownup talking down to a kid. Whatever he was, he sure sounded like somebody convinced he knew it all: "Not if you want her to keep being your girl, you don't. You're the one who's going to screw it up, remember?"

"That's what you keep telling me." Justin was getting sick of hearing it, too. "But you know what? I'm not so sure I believe you any more. When I called her, Megan sounded like she was really torqued at me—at you, I mean. So it doesn't sound like you've got all the answers."

"*Nobody* has *all* the answers." His older self sounded as if he believed that. Justin didn't; like *The X-Files*, he was convinced the truth was out there, provided he could find it. And then, throwing gasoline on the fire, his older self added, "If you think you've got more of them than I do, you're full of shit."

That did it. Justin wanted to turn his head real fast to see if he had smoke coming out of his ears. "You want to be careful how you talk to me," he ground out, biting off each word. "Half the time, I still think your whole setup is bogus. If I decide to, I can wreck it. You know damn well I can."

If that didn't scare the crap out of himself-at-forty, Justin didn't know what would. But if it did, his older self didn't show it, damn him. Instead, he kicked back with both feet, like a mule: "Yeah, go ahead. Screw up your life for good. Keep going like this and you will."

And that scared the crap out of Justin. Himself-at-forty had to know it would. It was the only weapon he had, but it was a nuke. Justin tried not to let on that he knew it, saying, "You sound pretty screwed up now. What have I got to lose?"

Maybe, for once, he got through to himself-at-forty, because his older self, also for once, stopped trying to browbeat him and started trying to explain: "I had something good, and I let it slip through my fingers. You wreck what I'm doing now, you'll go through life without knowing what a good thing was." And then he trotted out the ICBMs again. "You want that? Just keep sticking your nose in where it doesn't belong. You want to end up with Megan or not?"

There it was. Justin did want that. He wanted it more than anything else in the world, and he couldn't let on that he didn't. If himself-at-forty was bluffing, he'd just got away with it. "All right," Justin said, though it was anything but all right, and he didn't think he sounded as if it were. "I'll back off—for now."

He got the last word by hanging up. Then he masturbated again. It made him feel good, but it didn't come close to making him feel better.

He rented *Titanic* and watched it several times over the next few days, which certainly went a long way toward keeping him out of circulation. He wasn't watching it for the romance.

Christ, no. Jack died. He wanted his life with Megan to go on and on, even if he couldn't stand Celine Dion.

What he watched obsessively was the way the enormous liner took on water and sank after it hit the iceberg. Here in this apartment that wasn't his, as far out of the loop as he could be, he felt he was taking on water, too.

Running into Lindsey Fletcher, sitting down with her and eating messy jelly donuts and talking, had let him believe for quite a while that he wasn't alone in the world. He cared about Megan a lot more, but talking with her on the phone didn't satisfy his people jones nearly as long. For one thing, talking on the phone was like looking at a picture of a great dinner—pretty, yeah, but not the real thing.

And, for another, he'd had the row with himself-at-forty just afterwards. He might have stayed happier longer if he hadn't. The main reason—the only reason—he'd gone along with his older self and this whole craziness was that he couldn't stand the idea of losing Megan, of having to go through a divorce. If his older self could smooth things out now, make sure that never happened, great.

But if his older self was fighting with Megan, was making her angry at him . . . Where the hell did that leave Justin? He'd already saved the day once, which made him want to gallop back into the scene like a knight in shining armor coming to rescue the fair maiden. Would he rescue her, though? Or would he gallop in and screw things up, the way his older self said?

He didn't hop into his car—which was actually his older self's car—and drive over and throw himself-at-forty out of his rightful apartment. But he couldn't stand staying here and doing nothing, either, not for very long he couldn't.

After a bit more sitting on his hands, he hit on a compromise—or, to look at it another way, he found an excuse for doing what he wanted to do anyhow. *I'll call Megan,* Justin thought. *I did some good the last time. Maybe I can do some more now. And then I'll brief my older self on what we talked about, so he doesn't get caught short.*

Man is the rationalizing animal.

Justin felt good, felt alive, felt part of things again, as he dialed the phone. It rang a couple of times, then somebody picked it up. "Hello?" Hearing Megan's voice made him smile big and wide. It also made him horny as hell.

"Hiya!" He gave her back her own favorite greeting.

Silence, about fifteen seconds' worth, on the other end of the line. Then Megan said, "Justin, this is way over, I mean *way* over, the top. Didn't I tell you not two hours ago that I didn't want to see you any more, I didn't want to talk to you any more, I didn't want to have anything to do with you any more? Didn't I?"

"But—" Justin heard the words, but he had a hard time making them mean anything.

Megan didn't give him much of a chance, either. She went on, "Didn't I tell you that if I ever changed my mind, *I'd* call *you*? Didn't I? I don't want to be on the phone with you any more, Justin, I mean I really don't." She sounded furious, big-time furious.

"Wait a minute," Justin said frantically. "What—?"

He was trying to say, *What are you talking about?* but he never got the chance. Megan filled in the blank for him: "What about the sex? I already told you, I don't care how good it was. I don't care that it got better the last couple weeks, either. I don't want you treating me like I was twelve years old, and I *do* care about that. Now get out of my life, goddammit. Goodbye!" The phone crashed down.

Slowly, like a man in shock—which he was—Justin hung up, too. *I don't care that it got better the last couple weeks, either?* One day, when he had time to think about it, that would be a separate torment of its own. Right now, it was just part of the general disaster.

"What do I do?" he asked, as if the bedroom could tell him. What he wanted to do was call Megan back and explain, really explain, but that wasn't gonna fly. If he got in even two words before she hung up on him, it'd be a miracle.

"E-mail!" he exclaimed, and ran for his PowerBook. He wrote

the message. He sent it. Less than a minute later, it came back, with PERMANENT FATAL ERROR at the top and an explanatory paragraph underneath saying that she was refusing all mail from his address. "Jesus!" he cried in real anguish. "I've been bozo-filtered!" That added insult to injury, and none of this, not one single thing, was his fault.

He knew whose fault it was, though. Anguish didn't last. Rage replaced it.

The phone rang four times before his older self answered. "Hello?" He sounded groggy.

Justin didn't much care how he sounded. "You son of a bitch," he snarled. "You goddamn stupid, stinking, know-it-all son of a bitch."

"I'm sorry," himself-at-forty said. Of all the useless words in the world right now, those were the big two. "I tried to—"

"I just tried calling Megan," Justin said, interrupting his older self the way Megan had interrupted him. "She said she didn't want to talk to me. She said she never wanted to talk to me again. She said she'd told me she never wanted to talk to me again, so what was I doing on the phone right after she told me that? Then she hung up on me." He didn't say anything about the refused e-mail. Somehow, that hurt even worse, too much to talk about.

"I'm sorry," his older self said again. "I—"

"Sorry?" Justin yelled. If he hadn't had a buzz cut, he might have pulled his hair. "You think you're sorry now? You don't know what sorry is, but you will. I'm gonna beat the living shit out of you, dude. Fuck up my life, will you? You think you can get away with that, you're full of—" He hung up on himself-at-forty even harder than Megan had hung up on him.

He hadn't been in a fight since middle school, and he'd lost that one. It didn't matter. He stormed out of the apartment, slamming the door behind him. He ran down to his car—no, to his older self's car—and headed to his old apartment, his proper apartment, as fast as he could go.

That meant somewhere between ten and fifteen minutes. He was still incandescent when he got there. He turned the key in the lock to the security gate and drove into the Acapulco's parking lot. His own car, the one himself-at-forty had been driving, was still in its space.

"You thought I was kidding, did you, you bastard?" Justin's lips skinned back from his teeth in a savage smile. "I'll show you who was kidding, asshole."

Finding a parking space out on the street took another minute (a well-trained Southern Californian, he never thought to use one of the empty ones in the parking garage; those weren't *his*). Then he stormed up the steps into the lobby, opened the security door, and charged toward his apartment.

Click! One key in the dead bolt. *Click!* The other in the lock. The door opened. Justin slammed it shut behind him. "All right, you fucker, now you're gonna get it," he growled.

No one answered. Justin strode into the bedroom. It was as empty of life—except his own—as the front room and kitchen had been. He checked the bathroom. He checked the closets. He checked under the bed. He didn't take long to decide he was the only one in the place.

But his older self hadn't taken his car. "He can't have gone far," Justin muttered: again, the Southern California assumption that nobody without wheels could do much. Justin scratched his head. Was himself-at-forty running for his life? Hopping a cab? Waiting for a bus? None of those made much sense.

But the chair in the bedroom was pulled a long way out from the desk. You couldn't use the iMac with the chair out there. You could sure as hell use a laptop, though. What would a laptop from 2018 be able to do? Justin didn't know, but the mere thought was plenty to make him salivate.

His older self had said coming back from then to now was a matter of good programming. If he had a machine like that, if he had the program on the hard drive, could he go back the way he'd come?

"How should I know?" Justin asked nobody in particular. But the apartment felt very, very empty. Maybe his older self had fled where he couldn't hope to follow for nineteen years.

Or could he? He knew some things he wouldn't have if his older self hadn't come back and . . . *And screwed up my life,* Justin thought. He knew going back in time involved superstrings and programming. The combination wouldn't have crossed his mind in a million years—no, in something close to nineteen years—if himself-at-forty hadn't returned to 1999 to meddle.

And he knew the thing could be done in the first place. Knowing that was half the battle, maybe more than half. He'd never let himself get discouraged. No matter how bleak things looked, he wouldn't give up and decide he was chasing something impossible.

And . . . A slow smile stole over his face. He had a nest egg now that he hadn't had before, thanks to the cash his older self had left behind. He hadn't blown very much of it. If he made some investments and they worked out, he could be sitting pretty by the time he got to the frontiers of middle age.

"Inflation," he said, reminding himself. "Gotta watch out for inflation." Himself-at-forty had said his stash of cash wouldn't be worth nearly so much in 2018 as it was now. Whatever he put the money into, he'd have to make sure rising prices didn't erode it into chump change.

What he had to do right now was get his hands on the cash, which was still sitting back at the other apartment. Then he'd have to figure out how to put it into his bank account without getting busted as a drug runner or money launderer. You could put only so much cash in at a time, or else the bank had to report you to the Feds. He knew that. But what was the upper limit? He had no idea. *I'll find out on the Net,* he thought, and put it out of his mind for the time being.

As he drove over to the other apartment, something else struck him: *I can get rid of this car. That'll bring in some more money to help set me up.*

All that assumed his older self wasn't hanging around in 1999. Justin didn't *know* himself-at-forty wasn't, not for a fact. If his older self *did* remain here in the twentieth century, Justin still intended to punch his lights out the first chance he got.

He was loading twenties and fifties and hundreds into shopping bags, feeling a lot like a gangster, when he thought, *I can move out of this apartment, too, and get back whatever security deposits my older self paid—part of them, anyway.* In spite of the handfuls of greenbacks he was taking out of the drawer, every dollar felt important.

He wondered what his quarter from 2012 would be worth, and whether it would be worth anything at all. But then he shook his head. "I'll keep it," he declared, as if someone had told him not to. "It'll remind me what I'm shooting for."

More than a little nervously, he took the cash down to the car. He managed it without getting mugged. He didn't think he'd ever driven so carefully in his life as on the trip back to the Acapulco. He'd never watched the rear-view mirror so much, either. *Don't want to get rear-ended now. Oh, Jesus, no.*

As he parked in front of the apartment building, a nasty thought hit him. *What'll I do if he just walked away for a few minutes and now he's back in my place?* Punching his older self's lights out still seemed like a good plan.

But the apartment was empty. With a sigh of relief, Justin stashed the bags of cash in the little closet in the hallway that led from the living room back to the bedroom. Then he put a couple of pans by the door. He'd have to get the locks changed, but in the meantime at least he'd have some warning if his older self was still around and tried to come in.

"Have to get the rest of my stuff out of that other place, too," he said. But, for the time being, that could wait.

He quickly went through the apartment, looking for whatever his older self had left behind. Finding a laptop from 2018—if himself-at-forty had had one with him—would have been the grand prize. He didn't. But he did find a statement from a bank he wouldn't have patronized if a stagecoach had run over him. When he saw how much it was for, his eyes bugged out of his head: about as much as he had in those bags in the closet.

And it's mine, too, he thought dazedly. *If he's gone, it's mine. I can prove I'm Justin Kloster just as well as he could. I know my mother's maiden name just as well as he did.*

For a moment, thinking of only one thing at a time, he actually felt grateful toward his older self. A twenty-one-year-old guy with six figures' worth of money in the bank and with a plan to get ahead . . . What couldn't he do?

I can't have Megan. His joy blew out. Cash was great, but without his girl? Whatever his older self had done there, he'd screwed it up big-time. And he'd said he'd never found anybody else who came close to her.

Maybe I can get her back, Justin thought. *Maybe in a couple weeks, or when school starts again and I see her. Or something.*

He shoved the thought aside. He couldn't do anything about it now. Himself-at-forty had seen to that. Justin started getting angry all over again.

And he didn't get any happier when he looked at what was in the refrigerator. It was all stuff he'd have to cook if he wanted to eat it: even worse stuff than had been in his older self's other place when he first got there. What were you supposed to do with ginger root or hoisin sauce? He didn't know, and he wasn't interested in learning. But then he started to laugh. He could afford to eat out, by God.

Eat out he did. Yang Chow was odds-on the best Chinese place in this end of the Valley. He devoured kung-pao chicken and chili shrimp, with a Tsingtao beer to put out the fire from the peppers. No sign of his older self when he got back.

Justin called the other place. The phone rang and rang. After it had gone on ringing for more than a minute, he hung up again, nodding. His older self wasn't there, either. The more he wasn't there, the more convinced Justin was that he'd gone back to 2018.

"He should have stayed there, the son of a bitch," Justin said. "Maybe Megan and me would have made it. Shit—even if we didn't, I'd still have the good memories he did. What have I got now? Not one damn thing."

Before he went to bed, he changed the sheets and bedspread. He didn't even want to think about what had happened on the ones he threw in the clothes basket.

*   *   *

He slept late the next morning, which annoyed him. He had a lot of stuff he wanted to do that day: formally leave the other apartment, close his older self's banking account and move the money to his own, sell that other Toyota and put the proceeds from the deal in the bank, too. He was just heading out the door when the phone rang.

"Jesus!" he said, and hurried back to the bedroom. Maybe it was his older self. That would screw things up. Or maybe it was Megan. That would do anything but. "Hello?"

It wasn't himself-at-forty. It wasn't Megan, either, dammit. It was his boss at CompUSA, and he sounded pissed to the max. "Where the hell are you, Kloster?" he shouted. "That graphic-design outfit is coming in this morning to order their new Macs, and they don't want to deal with anybody but you." He said something under his breath about "Macintosh prima donnas," then went back to bellowing: "What are you doing there when you're supposed to be here?"

Justin had forgotten all about his CompUSA job. Evidently, his older self had been holding it down pretty well. With all the money he had, he was tempted to tell his boss to stuff it, but he didn't. That would look bad on a résumé. He gave the best excuse he could think of: "I must have forgotten to set my alarm last night. I'll be right there."

His boss promptly tempted him to regret his choice, roaring, "If they show up before you do, you're toast!" and hanging up hard.

He did get there first, and had enough time to review things before the graphic designers trooped in. Before they trooped out again, they'd bought about fifty grand worth of computers and peripherals, and his boss was acting amazingly human. Said boss even took him to lunch at a Mexican place not nearly so good as Sierra's—though he wouldn't have wanted to go there now—and didn't say boo when he ordered a margarita to go with his enchilada and rice and refried beans.

After lunch, he was upgrading system software on one of the iMac demos when he heard footsteps behind him. He turned around to see who it was; the Macintosh ministore inside the

CompUSA didn't get nearly the foot traffic he thought it deserved. "Lindsey!" he exclaimed. "What are you doing here?"

"Well, you told me where you worked." She looked nervous. "I just thought I'd come over and say hi. Hi!" She fluttered her fingers at him in an arch little wave, then quickly went on, "I don't want to make trouble or anything. I know you said you were seeing somebody." By the way she stood on the balls of her feet, she was poised to flee if Justin barked at her.

But that, right this second, was the last thing he wanted to do. "I was, yeah," he answered, and watched her eyes widen at the past tense, "but we just broke up. Somebody came between us, I guess you'd say."

"Oh, my God!" Lindsey exclaimed, and then frowned anxiously. "I hope you don't mean me. She wasn't, like, jealous 'cause you went up to Simi Valley and ran into me or anything? That'd be awful."

"No, no, no," Justin assured her. "Had nothing to do with you. It was another guy. An older guy." The first and last parts of that were true, anyway. The middle? He wasn't so sure.

"That's terrible!" Lindsey said. "You must be all torn up inside." She reached out and put a sympathetic hand on his arm.

"I was bummed," he admitted—about as much as a male his age was likely to say. "It's really nice, that you came all the way from Simi to see me." They both laughed, even though Justin hadn't quite made the joke on purpose. Lindsey smiled at him. He wasn't always fast on the uptake, but something got through. He set his hand on hers. "Who knows?" he said. "Maybe it won't work out too bad after all."

HOMEWARD BOUND
By Harry Turtledove

The amazing conclusion to the saga that began with the Lizard invasion in WORLDWAR: IN THE BALANCE and continued in the explosive COLONIZATION series. Now, the first human vessel makes its way to the alien homeworld in an attempt to end the interplanetary conflict once and for all.

Fleetlord Atvar pressed his fingerclaw into the opening for a control. *There is a last time for everything,* he thought with dignity as a holographic image sprang into being above his desk. He'd studied the image of that armed and armored Big Ugly a great many times indeed in the sixty years—thirty of this planet's slow revolutions around its star—since coming to Tosev 3.

The Tosevite rode a beast with a mane and a long, flowing tail. He wore chainmail that needed a good scouring to get rid of the rust. His chief weapon was an iron-tipped spear. The spearhead also showed tiny flecks of rust, and some not so tiny. To protect himself against similarly armed enemies, the Tosevite carried a shield with a red cross painted on it.

Another poke of the fingerclaw made the hologram disappear. Atvar's mouth fell open in an ironic laugh. The Race had expected to face that kind of opposition when it sent its conquest fleet from Home to Tosev 3. Why not? It had all seemed so reasonable. The probe had shown no high technology anywhere on the planet, and the conquest fleet was only sixteen hundred years behind—eight hundred years here. How much could technology change in eight hundred years?

Back on Home, not much. Here . . . Here, when the conquest fleet arrived, the Big Uglies had been fighting an immense war among themselves, fighting not with spears and beasts and chainmail but with machine guns, with cannon-carrying landcruisers, with killercraft that spat death from the air, with radio and telephones. They'd been working on guided missiles and on nuclear weapons.

And so, despite battles bigger and fiercer than anyone back on Home could have imagined, the conquest fleet hadn't quite conquered. More than half the land area of Tosev 3 had come under its control, but several not-empires—a notion of government that still seemed strange to Atvar—full of Big Uglies (and, not coincidentally, full of nuclear weapons) remained independent. Atvar couldn't afford to wreck the planet to beat the Tosevites into submission, not with the colonization fleet on the way and only twenty local years behind the fleet he commanded. The colonists had to have somewhere to settle.

He'd never expected to need to learn to be a diplomat. Being diplomatic with the obstreperous Big Uglies wasn't easy. Being diplomatic with the males and females of the conquest fleet had often proved even harder. They'd expected everything to be waiting for them and in good order when they arrived. They'd expected a conquered planet full of submissive primitives. They'd been loudly and unhappily surprised when they didn't get one. Here ten local years after their arrival, a lot of them still were.

Atvar's unhappy musings—and had he had any other kind since coming to Tosev 3?—cut off when his adjutant walked into the room. Pshing's body paint, like that of any adjutant, was highly distinctive. On one side, it showed his own not particularly high rank. On the other, it matched the body paint of his principal—and Atvar's pattern, as befit his rank, was the most ornate and elaborate on Tosev 3.

Pshing bent into the posture of respect. Even his tailstump twitched to one side. "I greet you, Exalted Fleetlord," he said in the hissing, popping language of the Race.

"And I greet you," Atvar replied.

Straightening, Pshing said, "They are waiting for you."

"Of course they are," Atvar said bitterly. "Eaters of carrion always gather to feast at a juicy corpse." His tailstump quivered in anger.

"I am sorry, Exalted Fleetlord." Pshing had the courtesy to sound as if he meant it. "But when the recall order came from Home, what could you do?"

"I could obey, or I could rebel," Atvar answered. His adjutant hissed in horror at the very idea. Among the Race, even saying such things was shocking. There had been mutinies and rebellions here on Tosev 3. Perhaps more than anything else, that told what sort of place this was. Atvar held up a placating hand. "I obey. I will go into cold sleep. I will return to Home. Maybe by the time I get there, those who will sit in judgment on me will have learned more. Our signals, after all, travel twice as fast as our starships."

"Truth, Exalted Fleetlord," Pshing said. "Meanwhile, though, as I told you, those who wish to say farewell await you."

"I know they do." Atvar waggled his lower jaw back and forth as he laughed, to show he was not altogether amused. "Some few, perhaps, will be glad to see me. The rest will be glad to see me—go." He got to his feet and sardonically made as if to assume the posture of respect before Pshing. "Lead on. I follow. Why not? It is a pleasant day."

The fleetlord even meant that. Few places on Tosev 3 fully suited the Race; most of this world was cold and damp compared to Home. But the city called Cairo was perfectly temperate, especially in summertime. Pshing held the door open for Atvar. Only the great size of that door, like the height of the ceiling, reminded Atvar that Big Uglies had built the place once called Shepheard's Hotel. As the heart of the Race's rule on Tosev 3, it had been extensively modified year after year. It would not have made a first-class establishment back on Home, perhaps, but it would have been a decent enough second-class place.

When Atvar strode into the meeting hall, the males and females gathered there all assumed the posture of respect—all save Fleetlord Reffet, the commander of the colonization fleet, the only male in the room whose body paint matched Atvar's in complexity. Reffet confined himself to a civil nod. Civility was as much as Atvar had ever got from him. He'd usually had worse, for Reffet had never stopped blaming him for not presenting Tosev 3 to the colonists neatly wrapped up and decorated.

To Atvar's surprise, a handful of tall, erect Tosevites towered over the males and females of the Race. Because they did not slope forward from the hips and because they had no tailstumps, their version of the posture of respect was a clumsy makeshift. Their pale, soft skins and the cloth wrappings they wore stood out against the clean simplicity of green-brown scales and body paint.

"Did we have to have Big Uglies here?" Atvar asked. "If it were not for the trouble the Big Uglies caused us, I would not be going Home now." *I would be Atvar the Conqueror, remembered in history forever. I will be remembered in history, all right, but not the way I had in mind before I set out with the conquest fleet.*

"When some of them asked to attend, Exalted Fleetlord, it was difficult to say no," Pshing replied. "That one there, for instance—the one with the khaki wrappings and the white fur on his head—is Sam Yeager."

"Ah." Atvar used the affirmative hand gesture. "Well, you are right. If he wanted to be here, you could not very well have excluded him. Despite his looks, he might as well be a member of the Race himself. He has done more for us than most of the males and females in this room. Without him, we probably would have fought the war that annihilated the planet."

He strode through the crowd toward the Big Ugly, ignoring his own kind. No doubt they would talk about his bad manners later. Since this was his last appearance on Tosev 3, he didn't care. He would do as he pleased, not as convention dictated. "I greet you, Sam Yeager," he said.

"And I greet you, Exalted Fleetlord," Yeager replied in the language of the Race. His accent was mushy, as a Big Ugly's had to be. But the rhythms of his speech could almost have come from Home. More than any other Tosevite, he thought like a male of the Race. "I wish you good fortune in your return. And I also want you to know how jealous I am of you."

"Of me? By the Emperor, why?" When Atvar spoke of his sovereign, he swung his eye turrets so he looked down to the ground as a token of respect and reverence. He hardly even knew he did it; such habits had been ingrained in him since hatchlinghood.

"Why? Because you are going Home, and I wish I could see your world."

Atvar laughed. "Believe me, Sam Yeager, some things are better wished for than actually obtained." Would he have said that to one of his own species? Probably not. It somehow seemed less a betrayal and more a simple truth when told to a Tosevite.

Yeager made the affirmative gesture, though it was not one Big Uglies used among themselves. "That is often true. I am jealous even so," he said. "Exalted Fleetlord, may I present to you my hatchling, Jonathan Yeager, and his mate, Karen Yeager?"

"I am pleased to meet you," Atvar said politely.

Both of the other Big Uglies assumed the posture of respect. "We greet you, Exalted Fleetlord," they said together in the Race's language. The female's voice was higher and shriller than the male's. Her head fur was a coppery color. Jonathan Yeager cut off all the fur on his head except for the two strips above his small, immobile eyes; Big Uglies used those as signaling devices. Many younger Tosevites removed their head fur in an effort to seem more like members of the Race. Little by little, assimilation progressed.

On Tosev 3, though, assimilation was a two-way street. In colder parts of the planet, males and females of the Race wore Tosevite-style cloth wrappings to protect themselves from the ghastly weather. And, thanks to the unfortunate effects of the herb called ginger, the Race's patterns of sexuality here had to some degree begun to resemble the Big Uglies' constant and revolting randiness. Atvar sighed. Without ginger, his life would have been simpler. *Without Tosev 3, my life would have been simpler,* he thought glumly.

"Please excuse me," he told the Yeagers, and went off to greet another Tosevite, the foreign minister—foreign commissar was the term the not-empire preferred—of the SSSR. The male called Gromyko had features almost as immobile as if he belonged to the Race.

He spoke in his own language. A Tosevite interpreter said, "He wishes you good fortune on your return to your native world."

"I thank you," Atvar said, directly to the Tosevite diplomat. Gromyko understood the language of the Race, even if he seldom chose to use it. His head bobbed up and down, his equivalent of the affirmative gesture.

Shiplord Kirel came up to Atvar. Kirel had commanded the *127th Emperor Hetto,* the bannership of the conquest fleet. "I am glad you are able to go Home, Exalted Fleetlord," he said, "but this recall is undeserved. You have done everything in your power to bring this world into the Empire."

"We both know that," Atvar replied. "Back on Home, what do they know? Signals take eleven local years to get there, and another eleven to get back. And yet they think they can manage events here from there. Absurd!"

"They do it on the other two conquered planets," Kirel said.

"Of course they do." Atvar scornfully wiggled an eye turret. "With the Rabotevs and the Hallessi, nothing ever happens."

Seeing that Ttomalss, the Race's leading expert on Big Uglies, was at the reception, Atvar went over to him. "I greet you, Exalted Fleetlord," the senior psychologist said. "It is a pleasure to find Sam Yeager at your reception."

"He is your corresponding fingerclaw on the other hand, is he not?" Atvar said, and Ttomalss made the affirmative gesture. The fleetlord asked, "And how is Kassquit these days?"

"She is well. Thank you for inquiring," Ttomalss answered. "She still presents a fascinating study on the interaction of genetic and cultural inheritances."

"Indeed," Atvar said. "I wonder what she would make of Home. A pity no one has yet developed cold-sleep techniques for the Tosevite metabolism. As for me, I almost welcome the oblivion cold sleep will bring. The only pity is that I will have to awaken to face the uncomprehending fools I am bound to meet on my return."

Sam Yeager looked at the doctor across the desk from him. Jerry Kleinfeldt, who couldn't have been above half his age, looked back with the cocksure certainty medical men all seemed to wear these days. *It wasn't like that when I was a kid,* Yeager thought. It wasn't just that he'd almost died as an eleven-year-old in the influenza epidemic of 1918. Back then, you could die of any number of things that were casually treatable now. Doctors had known it, too, and shown a little humility. Humility, though, had gone out of style with the shingle bob and the Charleston.

Kleinfeldt condescended to glance down at the papers on his desk. "Well, Colonel Yeager, I have to tell you, you're in damn good shape for a man of seventy. Your blood pressure's no higher than mine, no sign of malignancy, nothing that would obviously keep you from trying this, if you're bound and determined to do it."

"Oh, I am, all right," Sam Yeager said. "Being who you are, being what you are, you'll understand why, too, won't you?"

"Who, me?" When Dr. Kleinfeldt grinned, it made him look even more like a kid than he did already—which, to Yeager's jaundiced eye, was quite a bit. The fluorescent lights overhead gleamed off his shaven scalp. Given what he specialized in, was it surprising he'd ape the Lizards as much as a mere human being could?

But suddenly, Sam had no patience for joking questions or grins. "Cut the crap," he said, his voice harsh. "We both know that if the government gave a good goddamn about me, they wouldn't let me be a guinea pig. But they're glad to let me give it a try, and they halfway hope it doesn't work. More than halfway, or I miss my guess."

Kleinfeldt steepled his fingers. Now he looked steadily back at Sam. The older man realized that, despite his youth, despite the foolishness he affected, the doctor was highly capable. He wouldn't have been involved with this project if he weren't. Picking his words with care, he said, "You exaggerate."

"Do I?" Yeager said. "How much?"

"Some," Kleinfeldt answered judiciously. "You're the man who knows as much about the Race as any human living. And you're the man who can think like a Lizard, which isn't the same thing at all. Having you along when this mission eventually gets off the ground—and *eventually* is the operative word here—would be an asset."

"And there are a lot of people in high places who think having me dead would be an asset, too," Sam said.

"Not to the point of doing anything drastic—or that's my reading of it, anyhow," Dr. Kleinfeldt said. "Besides, even if everything works just the way it's supposed to, you'd be, ah, effectively dead, you might say."

"On ice, I'd call it," Yeager said, and Dr. Kleinfeldt nodded. With a wry chuckle, Sam added, "Four or five years ago, at Fleetlord Atvar's farewell reception, I told him I was jealous that he was going back to Home and I couldn't. I didn't realize we'd come as far as we have on cold sleep."

"If you see him there, maybe you can tell him so." Kleinfeldt looked down at the papers on his desk again, then back to Sam. "You mean we own a secret or two you haven't managed to dig up?"

"Fuck you, Doc," Sam said evenly. Kleinfeldt blinked. How many years had it been since somebody came right out and said that to him? Too many, by all the signs. Yeager went on, "See, this is the kind of stuff I get from just about everybody."

After another pause for thought, Dr. Kleinfeldt said, "I'm going to level with you, Colonel: a lot of people think you've earned it."

Sam nodded. He knew that. He couldn't help knowing it. Because of what he'd done, Indianapolis had gone up in radioactive fire and a president of the United States had killed himself. The hardest part was, he couldn't make himself feel guilty about it. Bad, yes. Guilty? No. There was a difference. He wondered if he could make Kleinfeldt understand. Worth a try, maybe: "What we did to the colonization fleet was as bad as what the Japs did to us at Pearl Harbor. Worse, I'd say, because we blew up innocent civilians, not soldiers and sailors. If I'd found out the Nazis or the Reds did it and told the Lizards that, I'd be a goddamn hero. Instead, I might as well be Typhoid Mary."

"All things considered, you can't expect it would have turned out any different," the doctor said. "As far as most people are concerned, the Lizards aren't quite—people, I mean. And it's only natural we think of America first and everybody else afterwards."

"Truth—it is only natural," Sam said in the language of the Race. He wasn't surprised Kleinfeldt understood. Anyone who worked on cold sleep for humans would have to know about what the Lizards did so they could fly between the stars without getting old on the way. He went on, "It is only natural, yes. But is it right?"

"That is an argument for another time," Kleinfeldt answered, also in the Lizards' tongue. He returned to English: "Right or wrong, though, it's the attitude people have. I don't know what you can do about it."

"Not much, I'm afraid." Yeager knew that too well. He also knew the main reason he remained alive after what he'd done was that the Race had bluntly warned the United States nothing had better happen to him—or else. He asked, "What are the odds of something going wrong with this procedure?"

"Well, we think they're pretty slim, or we wouldn't be trying it on people," the doctor said. "I'll tell you something else, though: if you ever want to have even a chance of seeing Home, Colonel, this is your only way to get it."

"Yeah," Sam said tightly. "I already figured that out for myself, thanks." One of these days, people—with luck, people from the USA—would have a spaceship that could fly from the Sun to Tau Ceti, Home's star. By the time people did, though, one Sam Yeager, ex–minor league ballplayer and science-fiction reader, current expert on the Race, would be pushing up a lily unless he went in for cold sleep pretty damn quick. "All right, Doc. I'm game—and the powers that be won't worry about me so much if I'm either on ice or light-years from Earth. Call me Rip van Winkle."

Dr. Kleinfeldt wrote a note on the chart. "This is what I thought you'd decide. When do you want to undergo the procedure?"

"Let me have a couple of weeks," Yeager answered; he'd been thinking about the same thing. "I've got to finish putting my affairs in order. It's like dying, after all. It's just like dying, except with a little luck it isn't permanent."

"Yes, with a little luck," Kleinfeldt said; he might almost have been Montresor in "The Cask of Amontillado" intoning, *Yes, for the love of God.* He looked at the calendar. "Then I'll see you here on . . . the twenty-seventh, at eight in the morning. Nothing by mouth for twelve hours before that. I'll prescribe a purgative to clean out your intestinal tract, too. It won't be much fun, but it's necessary. Any questions?"

"Just one." Sam tapped his top front teeth. "I've got full upper and lower plates—I've had 'em since my teeth rotted out after the Spanish flu. What shall I do about those? If this does work, I don't want to go to Home without my choppers. That wouldn't do me or the country much good."

"Take them out before the procedure," Dr. Kleinfeldt told him. "We'll put them in your storage receptacle. You won't go anywhere they don't."

"Okay." Yeager nodded. "Fair enough. I wanted to make sure." He did his best not to dwell on what Kleinfeldt called a storage receptacle. If that wasn't a fancy name for a coffin, he'd never heard one. His wife had always insisted on looking for the meaning behind what people said. He muttered to himself as he got up to leave. He and Barbara had had more than thirty good years together. If he hadn't lost her, he wondered if he would have been willing to face cold sleep. He doubted it. He doubted it like anything, as a matter of fact.

After reclaiming his car from the parking lot, he drove south on the freeway from downtown Los Angeles to his home in Gardena, one of the endless suburbs ringing the city on all sides but the sea. The sky was clearer and the air cleaner than he remembered them being when he first moved to Southern California. Most cars on the road these days, like his, used clean-burning hydrogen, a technology borrowed—well, stolen—from the Lizards. Only a few gasoline-burners still spewed hydrocarbons into the air.

He would have rattled around his house if he'd lived there alone. But Mickey and Donald were plenty to keep him hopping instead of rattling. He'd raised the two Lizards from eggs obtained God only knew how, raised them to be as human as they could. They weren't humans, of course, but they came closer to it than any other Lizards on this or any other world.

The Race had done the same thing with a human baby, and had had a twenty-year start on the project. He'd met Kassquit, the result of their experiment. She was very bright and very strange. He was sure the Lizards would have said exactly the same thing about Mickey and Donald.

"Hey, Pop!" Donald shouted when Sam came in the door. He'd always been the more boisterous of the pair. He spoke English as well as his mouth could shape it. Why not? It was as much his native tongue as Sam's. "What's up?"

"Well, you know how I told you I might be going away for a while?" Yeager said. Both Lizards nodded. They were physically full grown, which meant their heads came up to past the pit of Sam's stomach, but they weren't grownups, or anything close to it. He went on, "Looks like that's going to happen. You'll be living with Jonathan and Karen when it does."

Mickey and Donald got excited enough to skitter around the front room, their tailstumps quivering. They didn't realize they wouldn't be seeing him again. He didn't intend to explain, either. His son and daughter-in-law could do that a little bit at a time. The Lizards had taken Barbara's death harder than he had; for all practical purposes, she'd been their mother. Among their own kind, Lizards didn't have families the way people did. That didn't mean they couldn't get attached to those near and dear to them, though. These two had proved as much.

One of these days before too long, the Race would find out

what the United States and the Yeagers had done with the hatchlings. *Or to them,* Sam thought: they were as unnatural as Kassquit. But, since they'd meddled in her clay, how could they complain if humanity returned the compliment? They couldn't, or not too loudly. So Sam—so everybody—hoped, anyhow.

He did put his affairs in order. That had a certain grim finality to it. *At least I get to do it, and not Jonathan,* he thought. He took the Lizards over to Jonathan and Karen's house. He said his goodbyes. Everybody kissed him, even if Donald and Mickey didn't have proper lips. *I may be the only guy ever kissed by a Lizard,* was what went through his mind as he walked out to the car.

Next morning, bright and early—why *didn't* doctors keep more civilized hours?—he went back to Dr. Kleinfeldt's. "Nothing by mouth the past twelve hours?" Kleinfeldt asked. Sam shook his head. "You used the purgative?" the doctor inquired.

"Oh, yeah. After I got home yesterday." Sam grimaced. That hadn't been any fun.

"All right. Take off your clothes and lie down here."

Sam obeyed. Kleinfeldt hooked him up to an IV and started giving him shots. He wondered if he would simply blank out, the way he had during a hernia-repair operation. It didn't work out like that. He felt himself slowing down. Dr. Kleinfeldt seemed to talk faster and faster, though his speech rhythm probably wasn't changing. Sam's thoughts stretched out and out and out. The last thing that occurred to him before he stopped thinking altogether was, *Funny, I don't feel cold.*